SOFT TARGET

A CYBERTECH THRILLER

JOHN D. TRUDEL

Soft Target is a work of fiction. Names, characters, places, and incidents either are products of the author's imagination or are used fictitiously. Any resemblance to actual events or locales or persons, living or dead, is entirely coincidental.

Author: John D. Trudel
Cover Design and Art: Bruce DeRoos

Soft Target is available on Amazon.com, through major book distributors (e.g. Ingram, Amazon, etc.), and in all major eBook formats. Please ask your local bookstore and library to stock it.

ISBN: 0983588619
ISBN 13: 9780983588610

TESTIMONIALS FOR SOFT TARGET

"*Soft Target* looks like a prize winner to me. So good luck, keep writing, and stay well...."

Tony Hillerman, outstanding novelist, gentleman, mentor, and friend, 1925-2008. Tony was one of the great ones.

"*Soft Target* opens strong and continues to grip. I often wondered if I were reading a conspiracy satire or a future history. And I kept reading."

Jerry Pournelle, Best Selling Author, Chaos Manor

"*Soft Target* stands head-and-shoulders above any contemporary SpecOps novel of my recent experience. I am standing by for sequels! As a career-long SEAL, I find it encouraging that you went to such lengths to make Soft Target so true-to-life."

Captain Larry W. Bailey, USN (Retired)

"It's a gripping tale and a dramatic depiction of what 'civil rights as usual' does in the face of islamofascism."

Roger G. Smith, MD, Naval Aviator and author of *Guppy Pilot*

"Marine General Mike Mickelson reports to one person only, but if caught he cannot tell. With the help of the beautiful daughter of an old friend, who is missing, Mike is after Arab bioterrorists inside the US, but can he escape the clutches of their unwitting and willing accomplices in our own government? A military techno-thriller set in the modern day Global War on Terrorism, which is a must-read for anybody who likes suspense, intrigue, romance, and lots of action. I highly recommend SOFT TARGET, but be warned, you will be rubbing your red-rimmed eyes at 3AM, because you will not be able to set the book down."

Don Bendell, Vietnam Vet, Green Beret officer and top-selling author of 26 books, including his 2009 novel *Detachment Delta*.

"John Trudel's latest thriller, *Soft Target,* is his best yet. The dialogue is punchy and gives the reader wonderful insight into his characters. This is a must-read for thriller lovers."

Joseph Badal, author of *The Lone Wolf Agenda*

"A superb governmental thriller in the flavor of Mr. Trudel's *Privacy Wars*. This time a virus called ECP is introduced to the world and there are issues with the vaccine. Trudel has again created a novel with one thrill ride after another. This is an enjoyable read, with a fantastic winding plot and well defined characters. I give it a five-star rating only because there is not six. Trudel has done it again!

Award winning author G. R. Holton

DEDICATION

This novel is dedicated to Pat. Without her, **Soft Target** would not exist. As an Author's wife, she is patient with public demands, book signings, endless details, and my need to sometimes sit alone, uninterrupted, communing with imaginary friends.

Her kids gave me a T-Shirt: *"Careful, or you'll wind up in my novel."*

ACKNOWLEDGEMENTS

E rnest Hemingway once said, "There is no such thing as writing, only rewriting." Novels are that way. I would never have made it without my small band of critical readers and editors who assiduously scanned years of drafts with eagle eyes and brutally honest criticism. Each time they touched my words, my novels got better. Kay Jewett deserves special credit.

Two departed friends deserve thanks: Captain Langford C. Metzger, a Vietnam hero who gave me early encouragement, and Tony Hillerman, who gave me advice and moral support back when I was trying to break into novels. I spoke at Tony's memorial service. His daughter, Anne, has written the next installment in the Jim Chee/Joe Leaphorn series. Her novel, *Spider Woman's Daughter*, will be released in the fall.

I've been blessed to live the American Dream, and to have a rewarding life that has touched interesting science, events and people. It was freedom, innovation, and a career in technology at the peak of "the American Century" that helps give context for my writings, and it is freedom, innovation, and technology that let me break through and get my novels published.

Over my years in High-Tech, I worked with ELINT (ELectronic INTelligence) systems and the early Spectre (AC-130) gunships. Later, as a consultant with my own company, I had assignments for technology firms dealing with computer and network architecture, including trusted/managed networks and the Internet.

The West is in crisis. Too much of what we see in Thriller novels is real, and too few know history's lessons. God bless our Vets, founders, and builders, and may God Bless America.

> *"In this snug over-safe corner of the world ... we may realize that our comfortable routine is no eternal necessity of things, but merely a little space of calm in the temptious untamed streaming of the world, and in order that we may be ready for danger. Out of heroism grows faith in the worth of heroism."*
>
> Oliver Wendell Holmes, Memorial Day 1895. (A veteran of Antietam and other Civil War battles.)

Many have contributed to the publication and success of this book. Thank you all for your inspiration, friendship, and support. Finally, you, my readers, are most important of all. Thank you for reading my novels. I appreciate your support, suggestions, and kind words.

If you like *Soft Target*, please post reviews on Amazon and tell your friends. There are links on my web page, www.johntrudel.com that will lead you to my author's pages and allow you to get on my (private) lists for information about my novels. Next year, expect *Raven's Run.*

CHAPTER ONE
NEVER SAY ANYTHING

Washington, DC

Mike studied the serious young woman in his office. She was taller than he was, maybe six feet in her short heels, and perhaps ten years younger. Contrary to the scantily clad starlets in Hollywood spy movies, most of the female spooks he'd met were unattractive, Valerie Plame being the exception.

She was good looking, but dressed conservatively in a dark blue skirt, white blouse, and matching jacket. No jewelry, except for a gold watch on her left wrist. She looked fit, but not athletic. Short hair, but still feminine, just touching her shoulders and almost matching the color of his, light brown.

He glanced down at his desk where he'd placed her card. "Gerry Patton, Special Programs, National Security Agency," with a holographic image of the NSA seal – an eagle holding a large key in its talons – embossed in its upper right corner. All of which told Mike exactly nothing he didn't already know.

He was mildly amused that she felt no need to speak. She was sitting there politely, watching him watch her. The silence lengthened.

She was revealing nothing, making it subtly obvious she was waiting for him.

Typical, he thought. *They never tell you anything.*

Mike occasionally liked to drink a beer with people from Langley, but NSA didn't socialize much. The intelligence community was compulsively paranoid, but even by those standards NSA was over the top. They'd made "deep black" into an art form. Not a hint of light leaked out.

NSA never asks for help, Mike thought. *They run their own programs and avoid the Pentagon like it was a leper colony. But this woman bulls her way in here unannounced, demands to see me, then hands me a note from the President, marked "personal," and to hell with protocols and the chain of command.*

He felt a twinge of discomfort as he read the note for the third time. It said, "Problems at home. I need a favor, Mike. Talk to Ms. Patton. Then burn this yourself." It was signed with the initials he recognized, a scrawled "CH," and "yourself" was underlined.

We're wasting time sitting here looking at each other, he thought. *How the hell can I "talk to Ms. Patton" when she won't say anything? I don't have a clue what's going on, I can't read her mind, and I don't have anything to say. I need to get rid of her diplomatically so I can get back to work.*

"I'm sorry." Mike spread his hands in a placating gesture. "Obviously there's been a misunderstanding. I'm hardly an expert on satellites or codes."

"That doesn't matter," she said.

Her eyes were a vivid blue, and her gaze was appraising. It triggered a vague memory. Those eyes were familiar, but he couldn't place why. It bothered him.

"I don't know much about NSA. I'm just a mud marine they cleaned up and put behind a desk."

"The sign on the door says Director of Intelligence."

"For Marine Headquarters. I push papers around and give briefings. I go to embassy parties and try not to hurt anyone with the salad forks. I can't help you."

"Why not?" Her voice was a perfect contralto: Crystal clear, powerful, and vivid. She enunciated her words carefully. An opera singer or actress would be envious.

Mike shrugged. "I'm not a spook. I'm not involved in agency matters." After the fall from grace of Petraeus, senior officers were more careful about boundaries.

"It's not that simple, General." Emotion ghosted across her face. It might have been a smile, but it was hard to tell. "May I speak frankly?"

Mike nodded carefully, doubting she would. The notion of someone from NSA speaking frankly was out of character.

"I need your help in Oregon."

Mike frowned. "Oregon was in the United States the last I checked."

"It still is. Barely."

"That's within the jurisdiction of the FBI, or perhaps the Office of Homeland Security, not mine."

"Your expertise is in the Middle East. Indonesia. Asia."

He raised an eyebrow.

"The President said to call you 'Twenty Mike.' Why?"

"It was my radio call sign in Yemen."

"Why'd you pick that?"

"I didn't. My commander said at the time it was to remind me I was a pain in the ass."

She looked surprised. "You were reprimanded?"

"No, cautioned. When he promoted me later, he gave me his stars to wear and said they'd brought him luck."

"So why 'Twenty Mike'? The caliber of a small cannon? I don't get it."

"I preferred gunships and tactical air with rapid-fire 20 millimeter guns – twenty-mike-mike – and antipersonnel lasers to conventional fire support."

"Why?"

He looked at her.

"Humor me," she said. "I want to know your reasoning."

He shrugged. "Flexibility, security, mobility, resource conservation, and intensity. Why lug the bloody artillery and its supply train around hostile territory? It's a lot of work, and then you have to tie troops up to keep your own equipment from being overrun."

"But you did. Get overrun."

Mike winced. "That was later. The call sign wasn't a censure. It was a cautionary reminder." *My command post got overrun, lady, but our TAC Air was still coming in hot and on target. They were there when I needed them.*

She blinked and shook her head. "I don't understand."

"Close is dangerous, like a knife fight in a telephone booth. The Air Force's AC-130 Spectres haven't used guns that light since Vietnam, because they are not considered to be expendable. They prefer to stand off, stay out of range, and lay down surgically precise fire with long range guns. Mostly 40 MM and up these days. Way up. 105 MM."

"He was telling you to be careful? That the range of a gun that small is working too close?"

"Pretty much. Indirectly." Mike shrugged. "It was a metaphor, not an order."

"But you got close anyway?"

"Sometimes you have to. That's what we do. The Marines are big on tradition."

She sighed. "The Agency **never** gets close. Not to anyone. We'd rather crawl on our bellies over broken glass than ask for outside help."

"Washington is like that," he said. It wasn't a value judgment, just a statement of fact.

"Yes."

He looked at her directly. "Why are you here?"

She met his eyes. "Your unconventional methods work, General, and you have a reputation for taking good care of your people."

She's talking about combat. I'm not ready for this, Mike thought. His body was coming back, but it had been too close. He'd been too close. *Senior officers do not belong in foxholes. Remember the lesson.*

Her eyes were like laser beams.

Mike shook his head. "You need to do more research. I lost eighty-three out of six hundred in Yemen. Over sixty percent of my force was wounded. That was my last combat command."

"I've **done** the research," she said. "I remember when your picture and story was the lead on the nightly news, and on front pages all over the world."

Mike sighed. Some reporter had even won a Pulitzer. The media frenzy had mostly passed by the time he got out of intensive care. By then, the media was on to the next story.

She was still staring at him, her eyes demanding a response.

Silence lengthened. Finally he said, "You should know better than most not to trust the media."

"I also reviewed the classified action reports from Yemen and your medical records. The Marines said you'd never walk again."

"They were mistaken."

"The Army teaches your Yemen action at the War College. They say it's the best example of a small force defeating hopeless odds since the Chosin Reservoir."

"War stories are often exaggerated, Ms. Patton. I had good people. They prevailed after I went down." He didn't like talking about Yemen. "You've dug up a hell of a lot about me."

She nodded. "You were at Bethesda Naval Hospital in rehab for quite some time after Yemen. You passed the time getting a Ph.D. from Georgetown in Mideast studies."

"Do you know where you're going with this?" *It had actually been a doctorate in government, with a focus on security and the Middle East, but he got the point: He wasn't the usual Marine. So what?*

"I do my homework, General. You know the Mideast academically, militarily, and diplomatically. You were President Hale's Mideast interpreter. You speak the Egyptian dialect of Arabic like a native."

"I'm adequate."

"You're proficient, and you speak Farsi too. You know the culture. Your most impressive accomplishments are classified and you have Arab friends in high places who trust you."

"Not really." He shook his head. "There's not a lot of trust in the Mideast."

"No, there isn't," she agreed. "That makes you rather special, don't you think?"

He didn't reply. He waited to see where she was headed.

"Your job goes beyond being a soldier. The Marines are the best force we have for low intensity operations. You've got brains, and you use them. You're not afraid to innovate, to embrace new technology. That's why I'm here. I need your help."

Interesting, he thought. "Did the agency send you?"

She shrugged. "I have a certain latitude of action in my current assignment."

That wasn't an answer. She means, *"No,"* he thought. *That's curious.*

"Are you here on personal business?" Mike said.

She nodded. "Yes."

He didn't believe it. "What else?"

"Let's just say the President, our mutual Commander in Chief, suggested I should talk to you."

"And your current assignment is exactly what?"

She shook her head. "That's restricted information, General. Let's just say we're doing a special project for the President. If I can persuade you to help, he said you'd have a 'need to know' and he'd brief you personally."

"This somewhat limits our conversation." Mike frowned and thought for a moment. "When the agency straps you to a lie detector, which I presume they do regularly, you'll be able to say you didn't talk to me about your work."

"That's right." She smiled wryly. "Do you know why we call it NSA?"

He shook his head, wondering what she'd say.

"For the policy, of course – 'Never Say Anything.' We *never* talk about our work to *anyone* without specific authorization from our direct superior, and we never request such permission. I'm here to pay you a social visit because of a personal request from the President."

In a pig's eye, Mike thought. *Translation: her boss would have her ass on a platter if she talked shop with me, much less asked for help. I'm ordered to talk to a woman who can't say anything, and she's risking her job to be here.*

Mike considered her. It was obviously his move.

I suppose I can live with the facade. I'm just having a personal chat with an attractive woman. He smiled to himself. *Just like real people. It has nothing to do with the twilight zone these spooks live in.*

"Okay, Ms. Patton, if we can't talk about business, let's discuss personal things," he said tentatively. "Perhaps I should try to get to know you better...."

She nodded, watching him carefully. He decided to take it as approval.

"Just who the hell are you, lady?"

Surprisingly, she smiled. "My father is Colonel John Giles. He and President Hale are personal friends."

"Iron John?" he asked, surprised.

She nodded.

He glanced at her left hand, but saw no wedding ring. He looked at her more closely. She had John's ice blue eyes. "You're John's daughter?"

"I'm afraid so," she said. "Dad's a little controversial at the agency, and I wanted to make it on my own. My marriage failed. Afterwards, I had my name legally changed. Patton is my mother's maiden name."

"Your father's controversial at NSA?"

She nodded. "He is. Definitely."

"Changing your name is a pretty thin cover."

"It's not a cover; it's a symbol," she said. "I'm not my father."

"Your dad retired and went into business," Mike said musingly. "They say he makes crypto gear even NSA can't break."

"Actually, my brother Will is the mad scientist who invents things. Dad runs the company. It's called Cybertech."

"I'd expect having competition from a private firm might drive some of your bosses to distraction. I'd guess they'd be annoyed."

"It's a matter of public record that there was litigation between Cybertech and the government over technical matters relating to COMSEC," she said. "It was some time ago."

"Meaning NSA backed down." Mike was watching her carefully. "Interesting. I'll change my speculation to 'highly pissed.' Is that more accurate?"

She shrugged.

"Someone high up didn't want communications security discussed in an open court. I'll bet there are people at the agency who'd like to string John up for treason."

"If you say so."

"Are you telling me President Hale has a project running that somehow involves Cybertech as a contractor to NSA?" he asked, pointedly. "Why would he be involved in operational matters?"

"No comment." She shook her head. "I'm not telling you anything, General."

Meaning, "Yes," he thought. For a lady who says nothing, she's telling me a lot. Iron John must have access to some killer technology, and the President must have banged some heads to get John and the agency to play nice and work together.

"Your dad saved my ass once."

"I know. I hope you might want to return the favor."

"What exactly do you want me to do, Ms. Patton?"

"My friends call me Gerry. If you talked with the President about my visit, I'd be very grateful."

"Don't expect much," he said. "NSA doesn't take orders from the military."

She smiled demurely. "They do from the President."

He looked at her speculatively, nodding slowly. "As do I."

"Well, there you are," she said. "I knew we'd find something in common if we chatted long enough."

He took a deep breath, letting it out slowly, and making a decision. *I need to find out what the hell is going on.*

"You intrigue me, Gerry. I'll look into it and do what I can," he said. "How should I contact you socially?"

"When is more important than how. Soon would be good. It's best if you called me at home. My number is unlisted, so I took the liberty of writing it on the back of my card." Her smile increased by just a notch. Her face was pretty when she smiled.

"I didn't think you'd want to get involved," she said. "Was it the note from the President?"

"It got my attention," Mike admitted. "Let's just say I'm curious, and, like you said, I owe your dad."

"Thank you, General."

"Please call me Mike. I'll be in touch, but I can't say when. I have access to the President, but it usually takes several weeks to get on his calendar. Sometimes longer. Maybe we could get together for dinner afterwards and continue our social chat?"

"I'd like that." She stood and extended her hand. "I think you'll find he has an open slot for you tomorrow at 4 pm."

Mike took it, peering carefully to see if she was serious. Apparently she was. He escorted her to the door and stood watching as she walked away. *Nice legs*, he thought.

CHAPTER TWO
THE BEST STRATEGY

Portland, Oregon

Ahmed Mahmoud Muhammad peered out the aircraft window, trying to see though the mist and the rain-streaked Plexiglas. For a time, he watched the driving rain in the powerful beams of the landing lights, but then they dropped into denser clouds and all he saw was a diffused glow through the fog.

What a horrible place, Ahmed thought, remembering his briefing. *Oregon. Why would people choose to live in a land of constant rain?* He shook his head in disbelief.

The plane lurched uncomfortably as the landing gear thumped into place. Flying was always a miserable experience for him, and this mission made it worse.

He'd been traveling for more than thirty hours. His mind was sluggish. *When you get tired, you make mistakes*, he thought. He couldn't afford any mistakes.

The cabin lights came on, and the attendants started their litany about seats and tray tables. Ahmed shoved the tray into place, keeping his face turned to the window.

It seemed like a very long time passed before the fog thinned and he saw lights on the ground, but his watch said it was only a few minutes. They hit the runway hard, the engines roared in reverse, and the aircraft slowed.

Ahmed suppressed a sigh of relief. *Stay with your cover*, he thought. *Don't attract attention.* He wiped his sweaty palms on his pants.

Ahmed took a deep breath and turned his thoughts to the operation at hand. He needed to come to Portland himself. He didn't *want* to come, but he needed to come. The planned operation was basic, but there would be serious repercussions if anything went wrong. That was how things worked in his world.

The point was driven home the day his predecessor, Colonel Quamar, was replaced. It happened in what was now Ahmed's office, two years ago. He'd never forget that day.

"*It's not my fault.*" *Quamar fell to his knees and looked up at Supreme President Nassid. "I'm loyal to you. I follow the teachings of Allah."*

"*It is not attributable to Allah that he should lead you astray. He brings to life, and he causes to die." Nassid quoted the Koran coldly.*

Nassid reached down and grabbed Quamar by the hair. He lifted Quamar to his feet and walked him over to the window.

"*Come here, Ahmed." Nassid spoke in a casual tone and without turning to look at him.*

"*Yes, President Nassid," Ahmed said. He was shaking.*

"*What do you see?" asked Nassid, pointing out over the city. Towering black plumes darkened the horizon.*

"*I see smoke, Sir," Ahmed said.*

Quamar was sobbing. Nassid cuffed the back of his head brutally, slamming his face against the window. "You see five years of work and half a billion petro dollars burning, Ahmed. You see the end of our ballistic missile program. That's what you see."

"*Yes, President Nassid," Ahmed said. Streaks of Quamar's blood ran down the glass.*

"*I'm going to replace it with something better. I want you responsible for security." Nassid cuffed Quamar again, and he groaned in pain. "This fool was responsible for counter intelligence, and yet our enemies knew exactly where to strike."*

"*Yes, President Nassid," Ahmed said.*

"*You will make sure this never happens again."*

"*Yes, Your Eminence," Ahmed said.*

Quamar collapsed to the floor, pleading for his life. Nassid approached, took his time, and kicked him squarely in the ribcage. Ahmed heard something snap. Quamar rolled onto his back, silent, blinking, his arms and legs splayed.

"Take him away. Ayatollah Fouhad will handle his punishment."

"Yes, President Nassid."

Quamar was moaning quietly as Ahmed pulled him to his feet and led him away. He started struggling when he saw who was waiting in the hall.

Ahmed looked out at the rain and fog as they approached the gate. The tarmac was slick and shiny with water, and the workers on the ramp were wearing yellow raincoats with the hoods up. The plane stopped with a jerk, and the engines spooled down into silence.

He kept telling himself the mission was safe. His cover was first-rate, the risk of detection was low and it was absolutely necessary he supervise his local help to prevent mistakes. Whatever dangers he might face here, the ones at home were certain.

Portland was barely an international airport, mostly due to local flights from its friendly neighbor to the North. Security was loose. The bored workers almost went out of their way to avoid paying any special attention to Ahmed when he stepped off the half-empty Air Canada flight.

The twilight war that bin Laden started had been going on for years, and, through it all, the Americans had remained predictable and legalistic, with their leaky, open borders. Their notion of political correctness still forbade the profiling of Muslims. Not that the big airports like Washington, LA, New York, and San Francisco were safe penetration points.

They were not. *The Americans may be clumsy, divided, and tangled in their own bureaucracy, but they're not all stupid,* Ahmed reminded himself. Mistakes were to be avoided.

TSA consisted of drones in a mindless bureaucracy following procedure, but somewhere critical eyes could be watching him and it was best to not attract attention.

The big airports were hard targets, best avoided if possible. Six months ago one of his agents was blown when TSA found a harmless plastic bottle of shampoo in his luggage. He panicked, tried to run, and was arrested.

But this was Oregon, a distant, sleepy, sleepy province. Even illegal aliens with federal deportation orders against them were usually safe from scrutiny. He should be safe.

Ahmed didn't commit crimes himself. It wasn't his job. He was an executive with a limitless supply of young men eager to die carrying out his orders.

He didn't like fieldwork at this phase of his career, preferring to work indirectly and at a distance, but his tradecraft was still good. He'd chosen the legend of a Saudi named Nassar Fuad, an actual banker connected to the Saudi royal family who was known to visit Portland periodically. Ahmed had all the proper papers, and the photos and descriptions matched his appearance. He even had biosculpted fingerprints and credit cards that matched Faud's.

Those shouldn't be needed.

The automatic alarms remained silent as he walked through the checkpoint. The four TSA agents seemed preoccupied with a white haired old woman, a senior citizen whose driver's license had apparently expired while she was traveling. One was waving the license and lecturing her in a loud voice about having proper photo identification.

They'd opened her bag and had her belongings spread out on a table. A young man in a National Guard uniform was standing back, looking embarrassed, uninvolved. He had an M-16 slung over his shoulder, unloaded – the clip was missing – and therefore useless.

Ahmed would never understand the Americans.

The woman was sobbing. Ahmed pretended not to notice. He muttered excuses in heavily accented English, and they waved him through after a cursory glance at his ticket and Saudi passport.

No one checked Ahmed's papers or looked in his hand luggage. They wouldn't have found anything incriminating if they had. There were no bio-scans, and no questions. It went just as they'd said at his briefings and practice sessions.

Ahmed wandered nonchalantly down to baggage claim. He took his time, stopping in a shop to purchase a local paper and some mints. His baggage would be late. American airports were notorious for that, and it was best not to linger in any one public location.

The people here should be paying me, he thought. In a strange sense, the reason he was here personally was to help keep their state safe. Oregon was a useful sanctuary, and Ahmed intended to make sure they kept it that way.

I'm safer here than at home. But instead of comforting him, that thought reminded him that Oregon's safe haven status was part of his current dilemma.

"Make sure nothing happens that might cause Oregon to change its policies. Their tolerance for foreigners is useful," Ayatollah Fouhad had warned.

Ahmed feared the Ayatollah and dared not offend him. Unfortunately, his orders from Nassid were quite clear. They required violence.

My mujahedeen are eager to kill and die, and President Nassid wants an incidental problem cleaned up quickly. A simple bomb would do what's needed, but the mullahs insist we avoid drawing attention. I dare not anger them if I want to live.

Ahmed forced his mind to tranquil thoughts. He relaxed into the simple knowledge that he was safe as long as he appeared normal and stayed in character. He kept his mind on his cover persona, ignoring the watchers that he knew would be observing him.

When Ahmed arrived at baggage claim, the first wave of passengers had already moved on, but there were still enough around for him to easily blend in. He'd timed it perfectly. As per basic tradecraft, he'd purchased a round trip ticket and checked one small bag containing TSA approved, innocuous items.

He took his bag off the carousel and walked casually out of the terminal. He didn't look around, but acted as if he visited Portland routinely and was bored. He kept his face averted and avoided eye contact. It was important not to look directly at the security cameras he knew were scanning the baggage claim area.

Ahmed approached the first cab in line, putting a little more determination in his step, and opened the door. "Downtown Portland, please. Naito Parkway," he ordered assertively. His English had suddenly lost all traces of an accent.

"Okay," grunted the cabby in a bored tone, punching the button on his meter.

Ahmed tossed his small bag into the back seat. He slid in with his hand luggage, and closed the door. It was a nasty night, and the weather seemed to be getting worse.

He'd made it through the perimeter defenses, but this taxi was still a danger zone. Americans still had enough money to plant informants, bugs, and hidden cameras everywhere, and enough decadence, crime, and drugs so that they often did.

Ahmed had lost an agent that way. His man had stopped for tea at a coffee shop and was accidentally caught in a drug raid. In the end, his cover was blown. He was convicted as a terrorist just because he was in the wrong place at the right time.

Ahmed remembered the lesson. Accidental or not, attracting attention could be fatal. For all its talk of freedom, the Great Satan kept a close watch on its citizens. His cover was designed to divert attention, not withstand scrutiny.

Ahmed buried his face in his newspaper to discourage conversation, not that the driver showed any interest in talking. He waited until they were passing large trucks throwing sheets of spray. The driver, struggling to keep the cab in its lane because of the ruts and puddles of standing water, now had both hands on the wheel and was squinting through his thick glasses at the nearly opaque windshield. The wipers clacked frantically back and forth, leaving streaks on the glass.

Ahmed casually opened his bag, pulling out a shoulder strap and a rain jacket. He put on the jacket, slung the strap, stuffed his hand luggage into the bag, resealed it, and went back to his newspaper. The cabbie, fully occupied with his driving, paid no attention.

They entered downtown Portland and approached the riverfront district near the hotels. "Pull over," Ahmed ordered. "Let me out here. I want to walk." He pulled up the hood on his jacket and paid in cash, well-worn small bills. "Keep the change."

Ahmed shouldered his bag and waited as the cab pulled away. Then he sauntered off into the fog and vanished into the city.

Jackson's Knoll, rural Virginia

The woman looked like an aging news anchor, older than the usual crowd, a thin brunette with hazel eyes. "I want to watch the sun set over your little millpond," she said assertively.

The waitress looked puzzled.

"Seat me over there in the far corner of the lounge, by the window."

"Yes, ma'am."

The woman ordered brusquely and slipped the girl a twenty.

"I can run a tab for you, ma'am."

"Do that, young lady. The money is to ensure some peace and quiet. I don't want anyone seated near my table. I'm expecting a friend and we'll want to talk in private."

"Yes, ma'am."

The girl pocketed the money and rushed off to fill the order.

The woman scanned the dimly lit room as the waitress spoke with the bartender and returned with her order. The girl carefully poured the wine, leaving the cork as she'd been trained to do.

The older woman ignored it, and took a sip. "Just put the bottle on the table. My friend won't want a wine glass, just the whisky. I'll signal you if I need anything else."

"Thank you, ma'am." The girl retreated, taking the stand and ice bucket she'd brought to keep the expensive wine chilled.

Senator Harriet Stiles sipped the white wine, outwardly relaxed. *This place was a good choice*, she thought. She glanced out at the stream. The sign at the entrance claimed there had been a working grain mill there once, back in the 1700s. The little millwheel was a nice touch.

Harriet liked this type of restaurant. Its dark wood and discreet demeanor reflected the best of the old Virginia elegance, and it was far enough from the Capitol that she wasn't likely to be seen by her colleagues or their staffers.

It's quite private, she thought, *an excellent place for an assignation.*

That wasn't her main intent, of course, but it was a delightful fantasy. Burt was cute, and she knew he was discreet. *Maybe I can screw him while I'm screwing him*, she mused, smiling to herself.

Things were going well. As an incumbent with a deep war chest, her Senate seat was secure. At this point no one would dare campaign against her.

Success felt good. *I'd have to be caught groping an alter boy on video to blow a popularity rating as high as mine*, she thought. Her power was growing, her wildest dreams were coming true and the man she was meeting tonight would help her move to the next level.

Burt paused at the door to let his eyes become accustomed to the light. She waved to get his attention, their eyes met, and he smiled. He walked over to the table, took her hand, and sat down.

She'd worn pink accented by smart pearls, portraying vulnerability and understated success. There was nothing understated about Burt. He wore his usual dark gray business suit and power tie. His shirt was a soft pastel. Just the right amount of cuff showed, along with a heavy Rolex and monogrammed cufflinks. His gold jewelry glinted in the subdued lighting.

"You chose a good place." He glanced around. "I've always preferred the low key sophistication of old money to the hustle of Washington."

"Except maybe when you're doing the hustling?" She smiled and gave him a calculating look. The smile never touched her eyes.

He grinned back at her. "Maybe." Burt glanced down at the glass in front of him. "You ordered for me?"

"Scotch. Highland Park 18 year old. Straight."

From the Orkney Islands, it was the most expensive whisky on the menu. *Does Burt prefer it because it is distinctive or does it actually please his palate?* She didn't bother to ask. Harriet thought men's chauvinist banter about whisky and cigars was trivial. The topic was boring, and the discussion was better suited for Victorian England than modern Washington.

He took a sip, smiled appreciation, and raised his glass in a toast. "I understand congratulations are in order. You did it."

"Yes." She gave him a knowing look.

They clinked glasses. She took a deep swallow, then another. The wine was excellent. *Two hundred dollars a bottle, and worth every penny*, she thought.

He dutifully refilled her glass. "Few expected it."

"Senator Crenshaw's support was crucial." She was watching Burt keenly. "I lacked seniority, but since he'd named me as his co-chair, that's how it went down."

"Crenshaw's untimely death was tragic." There wasn't a flicker of emotion in Burt's face.

She reached over the table, grabbed him by the face with her sharply manicured nails, and whispered, "My father left my mother when I was seven years old, Burt. That old man was the only father I ever had. Forget that at your peril."

She watched the fear in his eyes. Long moments passed. Slowly his face turned pale and beads of sweat appeared.

"You're hurting me," he said softly.

She couldn't detect any deceit, just fear. Slowly she relaxed the pressure and removed her hands, watching the white marks on his face turning red. "I want you to think about how sorry you'll be if you ever cross me, Burt."

"I did exactly what you wanted. Nothing more. I swear it on my mother's grave. It cost us a lot of money."

"All right; the main thing now is that it's handled. Crenshaw was in the way. I disagreed with many of his stands but he was, actually, a kind, decent old man."

"I'm told it was a heart attack. He and his young wife were into…."

She silenced him with a gesture. "Never mind," she said. "I believe you." *Buying Crenshaw's support must have cost you a bundle. He'd wanted to retire from politics and buy a plantation in Louisiana.*

Burt pulled out a handkerchief, mopped his face and then looked at it. There was no blood, just sweat. He seemed relieved. "Did you leave any marks on my face?"

She shook her head. "Of course not. You'll be fine. I was just upset."

"I didn't realize you were that close to the Senator."

"Next time ask."

"I'm asking now," Burt said. "Is there anything I can do?"

"I want you to give a generous donation to his estate."

"Of course. Money isn't a problem."

"Good." It wasn't, she realized. Burt was cheap, but his backers wouldn't cut corners. Far too much was at stake, and they knew it.

Burt was recovering his composure. He took a sip of whisky and smiled innocently. "Would you like to toast his memory?"

She considered his words for a long moment before she lifted her glass. "To Senator Crenshaw."

"To Senator Crenshaw." Burt raised his glass and clinked hers. "And to the future, of course. A lot of power comes with that chairmanship, Harriet."

Oh, yes. She was silent for a long moment, thinking. "You know, Hillary Clinton was a fucking genius."

"She sure was, up until Benghazi, but how do you mean?"

"Way back then, she realized health care was the perfect women's issue."

"Un huh." Burt nodded. "You've got control of education too."

"Control education and you control the future," she said. "Control health care and you control the voters. I couldn't have done it without your help, Burt. You were most generous."

"My friends are pleased, Harriet. I brought the new Chair of Health, Education, Labor and Public Welfare a present." He handed her a check.

She glanced at it and, despite herself, felt her eyes widen.

"There's a lot more where that came from. We know you have a good shot at the White House. President Hale can't run again, and his Vice President is, ah, tarnished…"

She shrugged. "My advisors think it's too soon."

"Hale's party won't win the next election," he said flatly.

"No, they won't." Her smile turned sharp, and there was a glint in her eyes.

Burt didn't say anything. He took a sip of scotch and waited for her to continue.

"The current administration has squandered its political capital," she said. "While President Hale pisses away the nation's resources chasing ghosts and terrorists, I'm out there in the public eye protecting the common man, safeguarding public health."

"That's why my friends support you, Harriet," he agreed. "They know you're very shrewd and have great timing. You plan so well it all seems to fall in place naturally, but only because you're always two or three moves ahead of everyone else."

She smiled, accepting the compliment and looking at him intently over her wine glass. "I think we should be alone. They have some very private cabins here, down on the river. I took the liberty of booking one for the night."

He nodded slowly, running his eyes over her body.

"Not under my name, of course. I have the key here." She patted her purse.

"You know our talks are always in strict confidence," he said. "I still belong to the bar association. If you wish, you could pay me a dollar. Then our discussions will be attorney-client privileged. Not even a federal court order can intrude."

She nodded, reached into her purse, and handed him a dollar bill. He put it in his pocket, pulled out a business card, jotted a receipt on the back, and handed it to her.

She glanced down and laughed. "Retainer for services rendered? Legal services, I presume."

He lowered his voice. "I thought a celebration might be in order. I brought us some primo powder."

Her eyes were sparkling. She smiled and carefully put the check in her purse, along with his card.

"We need to talk business first." A serious look crossed her face and they both glanced around. The room was empty, except for a young couple by the door who seemed totally engrossed with each other. They were much too far away to eavesdrop.

"All right," Burt said. "What's bothering you?"

"Timing and probabilities." She pinned him with a look. "We can't depend on an election."

"We've discussed that." He spread his hands in acquiescence. "It's your call."

"Are you certain?" She was watching his eyes.

"Yes," he said without hesitation. "Absolutely."

"Then what the fuck is going on with your Arab friends, Burt? Is there a problem?"

He shook his head. "Not a problem, just a delay."

"I don't like delays. To make plans, I need to know what my options are."

"It's just a delay." Burt shrugged. "I told you the vaccine was taking longer to produce than expected. That's all. It's a technical matter of some sort. What else is on your mind?"

"Hale's people are still talking about a virtual Congress. What has them blocked is a lack of technology for secure electronic voting and conferencing. Rumor has it that the problems of validation and verification have been solved."

"No." He shook his head again. "NSA hasn't blessed their encryption. They finally have a little company willing to work on their problems, but they don't have solutions."

"It still sounds dangerous. You don't have a vaccine, and you can't tell me when you'll get one. If they disperse Congress all over the fucking country and vote electronically, it gets a lot harder...." She left the rest unsaid.

"My friends are on it, Harriet. It won't be a problem."

"You're certain?"

"We'll do what's needed." He shrugged. "Whatever's needed. You can take that to the bank, along with our check. My backers know a virtual Congress means our project is dead."

She looked at him for a long moment, speculatively, and then nodded. It wasn't worth pursuing further. *It's best I don't know the details. I don't want any dirt on my hands*, she thought.

Even if Burt and his friends screwed up, they were expendable. There wouldn't be a link back to her. She had a solid base of power in the Senate. *The best strategy is one where all outcomes lead to success.*

"You **will** keep me apprised of that situation, won't you, Burt?"

"Absolutely. Have I ever let you down?"

"Not yet." She smiled, finishing her wine. "I don't expect you will tonight either."

CHAPTER THREE
NONE DARE CALL IT TREASON

The White House

Twenty Mike was smiling as they escorted him into the Oval Office. He looked at the man behind the desk, and his smile faded. President Hale's craggy face was wizened and haggard. There were dark rings under his eyes, and his thick thatch of hair was showing lots of gray. Even seated, there was the hint of a stoop in his shoulders.

He's aged a lot, Mike thought.

The President looked up from his paperwork. "Mike, good to see you again." He glanced at his aides. "The general and I are going to talk in the bubble. Please get it ready."

"That's been attended to, Mr. President."

"Thank you. We'll be along directly." He waved them away, and they left, closing the door behind them.

"You look tired, Sir," Mike said.

"It comes with the job." The President smiled, but without his old energy. "That, plus becoming an old fart."

"I can relate, Mr. President."

"Thank you for coming," the President said, getting up from his chair. "I need someone I can talk with, someone I can trust. I need someone with your special talents."

"Yes, Sir."

The two men walked down the hall to the bubble, entered, and sat across from each other at the small table. They didn't speak until the door closed with a solid thunk.

"This room is, as you know, totally secure." The President glanced to his right, assuring himself the green light over the door was on. "We can speak freely."

"Yes, Sir." Mike nodded and shot the President a perplexed look. "Your note said something about trouble at home, Sir?"

"You destroyed it?"

"Yes, Sir. I shredded and burned it personally."

"Good." The President's look was grim. "Be very careful about security. We seem to have a leak in my administration, and I'm not sure how far it goes. I also suspect one of my key programs is being sabotaged, but, if so, it's being done subtly."

"Sir?"

"Why is it that treason never prospers, Mike?"

"It's from an old poem, Mr. President. 'Treason doth never prosper: What's the reason? For, if it prosper, none dare call it treason.' "

"Very old," the President said. "It predates the United States."

"Do you suspect a traitor in your administration? Or in Congress?"

"I'm damned if I know. There are more registered lobbyists in Washington than the Capitol Hill workforce, and half the bastards represent foreign interests. The lines between trade, politics, and aiding and abetting our enemies can get pretty blurred in this age of globalization, media cartels, and the endless alphabet soup of Non Governmental Organizations...."

The President's voice trailed off. He rubbed his eyes. "You're right," he finally said. "I can't call it treason."

"Can't or won't, Sir?"

The President's voice was soft. "Any accusations would be counterproductive."

"Politics?"

"It goes deeper, Mike. Patriotism and nation-states are unfashionable. Non -Government Organizations are ascendant these days.

"The NGOs have more power than most governments. They're bureaucracies with their own agendas, infiltrated by our enemies and accountable to no one."

Like the UN and the World Trade Organization, Mike thought. **"We laugh at honor and are shocked to find traitors in our midst."**

The President shot him a sharp look. "Did you come up with that on your own?"

"C.S. Lewis said that back when most wanted to appease Hitler."

"At least then the propaganda came from the enemy, not from within, not from groups claiming high purpose. From Goebbels, Axis Sally, Tokyo Rose, and Lord Haw-Haw."

"Treason is still a high crime, Sir."

The President shook his head. "I'm advised the word 'traitor' loses any useful legal meaning without a formal declaration of war."

"What does counterintelligence say?"

"That's not your concern."

Mike waited. He couldn't help without information.

The President sighed, relenting. "They're divided."

"Yes, Sir," Mike said. It was hardly a surprise.

"Very few know about my suspicions," the President said. "Far as I can go, Mike."

Mike frowned. "Yes, Sir, I understand." He didn't understand at all.

"I do know we have a serious problem." The President took a deep breath. "We're leaking sensitive, highly classified information to our enemies. I think a few key people near the top of our government, or perhaps in our security agencies, are the sources. I think they're working to serve the interests of groups with terrorist agendas."

"Sir?" Mike said.

"I have no proof, but I believe it to be true. Does that make me sound paranoid?"

Interesting question, Mike thought. "Not to me, Sir," he said carefully.

The President rubbed his eyes and let his breath out slowly. His face was a study in frustration. "I need you to do something for me. I'll give you what support I can, but I can't jeopardize the Office of the President because of my personal suspicions."

Politics, Mike thought grimly. He had a fleeting mental image of a mongoose being dispatched into a den of cobras. He suppressed the thought. "And if I'm successful, Sir?"

"No one will ever know. It will be a blank spot in your personnel file."

"I'm sworn to protect our nation from all enemies, foreign and domestic," Mike said, wondering what he was getting into.

The President sensed his hesitancy. "I need a firm commitment, Mike."

"I'm not sure I'm qualified, Sir," Mike said. "My background...."

"I'll make that decision." The President was watching him closely. "I know your qualifications, perhaps better than you do yourself. I saw you fight your way back when everyone wanted to retire you as a burned out cripple."

"Not everyone, Sir." Mike took a deep breath. He owed this man a lot. He thought for a long moment, then said, "I'm in, Mr. President."

"You're certain?"

"Yes, Sir," Mike said, meeting the President's eyes. "Whatever it is, I'll do my best."

"That's all I can ask." The President smiled grimly. "Thank you. You will report directly to me."

"Yes, Sir," Mike said. "I'd need you to ask General Myers to put me on temporary duty to assist the White House. He's my commanding officer."

"I had the Secretary of Defense give Toby a heads up. It's taken care of. Your transfer orders will be on his desk by the time you get back to your office."

Mike nodded. At least the protocols were attended to.

"Your official duty assignment will be 'special assistance with security matters.' I gave SECDEF the impression I want you to give me an independent look at some black programs. That's true, so far as it goes."

"I understand, Sir." *What kind of 'special assistance' does he have in mind? That could cover almost anything.*

The President was quiet for a long moment. When he spoke, his tone was somber. "What I'm going to tell you would be political suicide if it became public. The last thing I need to end my term is yet another controversy about yet another conspiracy theory."

"Yes, Sir."

"Also, public discussion or a Congressional witch hunt would surely drive any enemy agents in our government underground. We'd never be able to prove anything. You're not to discuss this, not even with those in your former chain of command."

"Not even with General Myers, Sir?"

"No." The President scowled. "Not with *anyone* unless I give you specific approval. That's a direct order, Mike. I want a very close hold on this. I will deal brutally with anyone who compromises anything about what I'm going to tell you. Do you understand me?"

"Yes, Sir," Mike said. "Tight security, with only the people you specifically authorize privy."

"Exactly," the President said. "Do you know the woman who brought you my note?"

"No, Sir, I'd not met her before. She said she was Iron John's daughter."

"That's right. I'm her godfather." The President smiled. "I remember her with curls, sitting on my knee. Now she's at NSA running a deep black program. I have a strong personal interest in that program."

"Yes, Sir."

"I trust Gerry completely," the President said. "You have my authorization to share information with her as you deem appropriate."

"Yes, Sir," Mike said.

"Unfortunately, I don't know who else you can trust at the agency. I suspect Gerry's boss may be part of our problem. She does too."

NSA's spooks are deeply vetted for loyalty, Mike thought. *Still, we've had moles before.*

"I'm certain of nothing, Mike, but I see disturbing patterns." The President shrugged. "Things keep going wrong, and I have a bad feeling about it. Gerry's boss is a deputy director named Kendrick Tibbs. He's an ambitious, evasive, backstabbing little guttersnipe. I don't trust him any further than I can throw him, but he's Mitchell's chosen man for this project."

Mike had only met Jack Mitchell, the director of NSA, a few times. He didn't know much about him except he'd been a spook for decades, came up from the technical side, and tended to pontificate about how science could displace the messy human element of intelligence.

"Have you met Tibbs?" the President asked.

Mike frowned, trying to remember his meetings with NSA. Most of his discussions had been with people on the OPS side.

"Little guy. Balding. Affected Boston accent. Wire rimmed glasses."

Mike shook his head. "I don't think so, Sir."

Everyone's worst fear was that a trusted executive would turn. *A mole at a high level in NSA would be very bad*, Mike thought. *As Deputy Director for Science and Technology, Tibbs could be Mitchell's heir apparent.*

Mike waited for the President to say more, but he'd apparently finished. "Can you get me Tibbs' personnel file?" Mike finally asked.

"Certainly," the President said. "But the main thing troubling me won't be in it. Gerry's program has top-level security. It's tight."

"How tight, Sir?"

"It's as totally black as we're capable of making it. Unfortunately, CIA has a foreign source that reported on its status. The report was accurate in every detail."

"Ouch," Mike said. "How many people had access to program information, Sir?"

"Very damned few, Mike." The President sighed in frustration. "That's an especially relevant question, and one I'm going to depend on you to answer. The DCI knew I wanted Gerry's program protected. He set a tripwire and it was sprung three days ago."

The Director of Central Intelligence is personally involved in this too, Mike thought, *and he just caught NSA with its fly unzipped.* "You said a foreign source?"

The President nodded grimly.

"Someone here in one of the embassies?"

"No. Oddly enough, the information came in from the Mideast, from a single source in Bukhari. We have no diplomatic relations there."

We sure don't, Mike thought. "How did it leak? Do we have any suspects?"

"No suspects and no leads. Nothing," the President said.

"How many at CIA know about this?"

"Until now, very few. The report was 'eyes only' for the DCI." The President shrugged. "He says he shared it only with me. It came in from the field three days ago encrypted in a personal code to which only he and the Heads of Stations have the key. I don't know about security at the other end...."

"You said, 'until now,' Sir?"

"You can't search for a leak unless the searchers know what they're looking for. It's a fine balance," the President said glumly. "Both CIA and FBI now have their counter intelligence people on a watch alert. I'll arrange a briefing."

"How many inside NSA have program access?"

"That's where I want you involved. Perhaps a dozen people, plus a few contractors, all cleared above Top Secret and for Special Intelligence. Gerry has the access list. I want you to find the leak and deal with it."

" 'Deal with it.' That's an interesting phrase," Mike said slowly. "Marines don't know much about arresting people, Sir."

"Irrelevant," the President said. "I want direct action." His demeanor and tone were grim.

It's not just concern, Mike realized, *it's command responsibility. The buck stops here.*

A look of comprehension passed between the two men, and Mike nodded slowly. *I'm his cutout if this blows up in our faces. He can disavow me if he must for the sake of the Office. The mongoose is expendable.*

"What are your orders, Sir?"

"Gerry's program could change how we run our government," the President said. "I want you to take over and give her some cover."

Mike blinked. "When?"

"Tomorrow. You have a need-to-know by my personal authorization. The necessary papers will be on your desk, and on Jack Mitchell's, by the time you get back to your office. I'm meeting with Jack tonight to order NSA's full cooperation and ensure there won't be any misunderstandings."

"Yes, Sir," Mike said. The President might be a bit weary, but he could still chew ass.

"I'm taking over program control in the interests of national security. Gerry will report directly to you, and you will report directly to me. Do you have any problem with that?"

"NSA protects its turf, Sir." Mike took a deep breath, letting it out in a deep sigh. "Still, if you'll be, ah, very specific with Director Mitchell, I'm yours to command."

"I assure you that will **not** be a problem. You don't work for Jack; you work for me."

"I'm not to talk with him?" Mike asked. It was a NSA program, after all.

"Talk with him all you like. Just don't reveal anything about what you're doing. He's out of the loop," the President said. "If pressed, tell him I gave you a direct order to that effect."

"Yes, Sir."

"I'll keep the director informed as I deem necessary, after he satisfies me he's put Tibbs under a microscope." The President gave Mike a hard look. "And after **you** come up with a credible explanation of how the CIA, the Israelis, the Bukharis, and God knows who else, possess the intimate details about what is supposed to be his blackest program."

"Yes, Sir," Mike said, thinking NSA might just be getting a new director in the not too distant future and wondering how the Israelis were involved. "I'll need some Marine assets, Sir."

"That's been anticipated. If you need anything else, anything at all, let me know. Judy keeps my calendar. I'll give you her special phone number. Keep me informed. I don't want any more surprises on this."

"Yes, Sir," Mike said. "Anything else?"

"I'll get to that, but Gerry's project is your current priority. I want to know if it's being sabotaged. I want any blockages removed."

"Yes, Sir."

"I'll get you a copy of the CIA report. It's highly sensitive material. They're worried about exposing their source."

"I'd expect so, Sir. CIA's track record isn't too good in the Mideast," Mike said.

"Don't get me started," the President said. "The Arab Spring turned into the Islamic Winter and the greatest foreign policy debacle in American history. Mostly, it was the State Department to blame, but CIA turned a blind eye to what was going on."

"Roger that, Sir. But we're recovering. Your programs are working. The Saudis and the Israelis are starting to trust us again. Even the Turks."

"They don't have much choice, do they?"

"No, Sir."

"We're still too dependent on third party sources. CIA got its information from Israeli intelligence, from a deep cover agent Mossad's running in the Bukhari Republic. I'm damned disturbed Bukhari has a line into NSA."

"Does NSA know about the report?"

"Not yet. I'll inform Jack tonight," the President said. "There's a second link to Bukhari that concerns me even more."

"Sir?" Mike said, listening intently.

"Bioweapons," the President said. "Something new. The threat is *exactly* the type of attack Gerry's program is intended to protect against. Strange, isn't it?"

"I hope so, Sir," Mike said dubiously. No intelligence officer would accept such a coincidence.

"There may be inside help."

"I would think any conspiracy to aid such an attack would have to go far beyond NSA if it were to have any hope of success."

"I think so too." The President glanced down at his watch. "Paranoia be damned. Even paranoids have real enemies."

"Yes, Sir." Mike was watching the President's hands. There was a slight tremor, but you had to look closely to see it.

The President saw the look. "I've been going through a bit of a rough patch."

"I'll do whatever I can to help, Sir."

The President took a deep breath, and his shoulders straightened. He'd made a decision.

"I'm grateful," the President said. "I'm going to give you a quick briefing on a few more things I deem relevant. Bear with me."

"Yes, Sir."

"The world changed forever when the towers went down. Fanatics who commit such acts fundamentally reject any rules of war, any compassion for innocents. Their goal is to destroy our civilization, to move humanity back a thousand years. To that end, they embrace suicide and killing their own." The President looked directly into Mike's eyes. "What I've only realized recently is just how much Armageddon appeals to them."

"No one in America can ever forget the first nine eleven," Mike said slowly. "But the *second* 9-11, in 2012 under Obama, did us far more long term damage. It was the biggest attack on our military since the Tet

Offensive. It wasn't just Benghazi; it was the whole region. Marine Air suffered its biggest losses since Wake Island, 1941. We had an entire attack squadron taken out in Afghanistan and its CO killed. Lt. Col. Raible was a friend of mine…."

"I don't want to talk about Benghazi, Mike, not even the attack on Camp Bastion. That debacle was self-inflicted, caused by bad policy at high levels, and aided by foreign agents inside State and the White House. Those issues are now addressed. It was a campaign promise of mine to fix that mess, and I did. Let's stick with the signal event, the first one, the beginning, 9-11-2001. That's when the world changed."

"Yes, Sir."

"You may recall that Congress was shut down for a time by a bioweapons attack. That was the wake up call for me, not the towers. That attack convinced me the greatest future threats would be in the shadows, not on the battlefield. I decided to phase out of my military career and go into politics."

Mike nodded. They'd discussed this before.

It was never voiced publicly, but in private discussions many officers considered Rumsfeld to have been even worse than McNamara: heavy handed, political, and notoriously intolerant of contrary opinions or professional military advice. A number of senior officers had chosen retirement in the months and years after Baghdad fell, and Carson Hale was one.

Hale then served three terms in Congress, declining a fourth because he believed in term limits. He moved back to his beloved rocky coast of Maine, but soon got bored and headed a foundation for government ethics that actually accomplished some of what it preached.

The eventual result was Hale being drafted as a dark horse candidate for President by a party that was strongly favored to lose. The pundits were astonished when he won his first term by a surprisingly good margin on a moderate platform.

President Hale was sometimes compared to Eisenhower. A military leader versed in statesmanship and tolerant of the intrinsic messiness and compromises of democracy, a statesman who both deplored the horrors of war and understood why it was sometimes necessary. Neither party was comfortable with him, but it seemed the public – tired of corruption, cronyism, blunders and scandals – deemed him honest and able to keep us safe and get back to the old prosperous America. In any case, they'd voted for him.

"The world is more dangerous now than when I first took office," the President said solemnly, "and time's running out for me. One of my biggest concerns has been that a single point failure could take down our entire government. One of the commitments I made when I took office was to fix that."

"I remember," Mike said.

The notion wasn't popular inside the beltway, and the President had made no progress at all during his first term. Experts were dubious. The common wisdom was that any computer system could be broken, given enough time, effort, and expertise.

"Gerry's program at NSA is to develop and deploy totally secure, distributed, verifiable communications and computer links so we can operate a virtual Congress. The world situation demands the option of having our government officials being able to work effectively from wherever they choose." The President smiled thinly. "Anywhere in their districts."

Mike noted the smile and the qualifier. *Anywhere in their **districts**: Close to their constituents and accountable to them. Just like when America was founded.*

"Is that technically possible, Sir?"

"Gerry says it is, and I'm giving her a chance to prove it."

"Yes, Sir."

"There are major technical challenges, to be sure," the President said. "Unfortunately, the political problems are larger. I have enemies, especially in the Senate, who see any plan to disperse Congress as a nefarious scheme on my part to destroy representative democracy in the United States."

Mike was trying to recall the Senator who was so vocal about that. He couldn't quite pull up her name.

"An independent, functional Congress is a vital part of our political system." The President sighed. "Checks and balances. Separation of powers. Constitutional limits. I need to keep America safe, but also to leave a robust Republic when I term out. A few years back, we came too close to tyranny and a dictatorial, unaccountable Executive Branch. I don't want a repeat on my watch, no matter what the justification. We never want to go there again."

Mike nodded without speaking. He'd sworn an oath to defend the Constitution no matter who got elected, but he was thinking, *Thank God this man took over before the world repeated the horrors of the 1930s. He brought us back from the brink.*

"Without a Declaration of War, Congress has every right to question, criticize, and publicly hold me accountable. What bothers me is that, despite my administration's full support, Gerry's program has gone nowhere."

"Why?"

"I have my opinions, but I don't want to bias you. I'd rather you got the information first hand. What I do know is my term is running out, and I want to leave that option for my successor. Kennedy had the space program, Reagan had ending the Cold War and this is what I want to contribute. It's the legacy I want to leave, Mike."

"The ability to operate a geographically dispersed government?"

"Precisely. No matter who wins the next election, I want that option on the table for the next President. Weapons technology has outstripped any reasonable ability to defend, and there are fanatics willing to use these weapons without warning. I see a real possibility we could be attacked, have our government destroyed and not even know who struck the blow."

"Sir?" Mike found it hard to believe. If a swallow fell, one of the agencies would have someone there to write it down and a satellite or drone overhead to photograph it.

"Not by direct military action." The President waved his hands dismissingly. "We're too strong for that. A direct attack on Washington would leave a return address. I'm worried about a more subtle attack."

"Mailing contaminated letters?" Mike suppressed a smile.

The President shook his head. "That was crude and ineffective as a weapon. It wouldn't work again."

Why are we discussing old history? Mike wondered. *Why is he fixated on this?*

A desolate look crossed the President's face. "I've had several teams developing scenarios of how an enemy could take out Congress without our being able to block the attack or identify the attackers so we could retaliate, attacks that left us with no defense options."

Mike nodded, paying close attention.

"For the most dangerous threats we had 'red' teams plan out detailed attacks and 'black' teams design counters. We took it to the full war-games level, with computer simulations and fieldwork. I had the agencies compete against each other, kept it highly compartmentalized. Only four people know what conclusions came out of the games. You'll be the fifth."

Mike watched the President, waiting. There are times when it's best to listen.

"There are three attack scenarios we know might succeed, plus at least five more that'll be possible in a few years," the President said. "All these methods and weapons are within the capability of minor nations, NGOs, and perhaps even private organizations."

"You said, 'No defense options,' Sir. How do you mean that?" asked Mike.

"None hopeful to prevent an attack," the President said. "Not if we want to preserve a free, democratic society, and maybe not in any case. We've been lucky so far, but I keep thinking we're living on borrowed time."

"What do you mean, Sir?" Mike asked. *There are always options.*

"What if bin Laden's first bombing of the Towers had used a small, dirty, nuclear device? We'd have lost the whole city and most of Northern New Jersey."

"We ran that scenario years ago, Sir." Mike felt a surge of relief, "and planned for it. Radiation monitors can detect such devices."

"That's hopeful theory," the President said. "Washington has the tightest detector wall of any of our cities, but, two months ago, we found a small nuke here. We got it in time, but it was a near thing."

Mike felt stunned. That shouldn't have been possible. "A military suitcase nuke?"

"No." The President shook his head. "It was crude, the size of a large refrigerator, with a yield of about fifty kilotons. It had a kill zone of 98% casualties within a one-mile radius, and 50% at three or four miles. And it was also loaded with cesium 137."

"I'm sorry, Sir. I'm not very knowledgeable about the technical details of nuclear weapons."

"Nor was I," the President said wryly. "Since that bomb was found, I've become morbidly interested in the details of unthinkable weapons."

"Yes, Sir," Mike said.

"Cesium 137 is commonly available. It leads an innocuous existence, for example, in industrial instruments like moisture sensors. But it's very nasty, if mishandled. Direct contact produces severe radiation burns and genetic defects, as it did at Chernobyl. The bomb would have rendered downtown Washington uninhabitable for months, maybe years, even with a maximum effort cleanup."

"Who did it?" Mike asked. "Where was the bomb made? How'd they get it in?"

"I asked the same questions," the President said. "We don't know. The weapon used Russian technology from the Cold War. I'm told it could have been constructed almost anywhere."

"Yes, Sir," Mike said. *How could we not know?*

The President gave him a bleak look. "The FBI has a team working on it, of course."

No wonder he looks tired, Mike thought.

"For obvious reasons I have a close hold on this, but I'll get you cleared. Seven different sets of checks and balances were circumvented to get that weapon into Washington. Someone is trying to take down our government, and I think they have inside help."

"There's no link to Bukhari about the bomb, Sir?"

"Not yet," the President said, "but we're still looking. It's not the first time we've had problems. We had to take out their delivery systems a few years back."

Mike nodded. He remembered that well. "Is there a scenario for response?"

The President sighed. "Not a good one. We don't need another Iraq. Saddam was a sadistic tyrant, but he kept a lid on things, contained Iran, and blocked Hezbollah. We should have left the blood-soaked, psychotic bastard in power, but made sure he wasn't any threat to us or our strategic interests."

"I agree, Sir. Mubarak too, a despot who kept the Muslim Brotherhood in check. There are worse alternatives than tyrants. Globalization enables some hellish blowback. The Muslims, at the core, are Theocratic Socialists. They prefer heavy-handed central governments, be it Kings, dictators, or

Ayatollahs. It was lunacy to think that Iraq would embrace Jeffersonian Democracy, and worse for us to provide weapons for radical Islamists who hate us. Obama's 'Responsibility to Protect' was foolish at best. So was Bush's invading Iraq."

"I can't say such things publicly."

"Fourth generation warfare is tricky, Sir. If we pound an enemy too hard, their state fails, and the *jihadists* and fanatics move in. If we have to occupy, it's an endless commitment. So what's left? We kill the bad guys, but get demonized and politically trashed by the leftists, the UN and the media."

"That's the current reality." The President sighed. "When I took office I thought the Barbary Pirates were ancient history, a problem that Thomas Jefferson and the Marines had solved centuries ago on the shores of Tripoli. Did you know it's worse now?"

"Really?"

"Pirates add over $20 **Billion** a year to the cost of world trade. The insurance companies pay tribute. World opinion won't let us hang them summarily, and I dare not level their ports. Tyrants would be better than allowing situations like Lebanon, Palestine, or Somalia, failed states populated by kids with hatred in their hearts and weapons in their hands. Do you know the average age in Palestine is fifteen?"

"I do, Sir. 15.2 years and dropping in Palestine. Less than that now in Iraq. *Jihidists* put the young crazies up front and have them throw rocks. It gives them useful TV footage of soldiers shooting down innocent children."

"My options are constrained. If we get sucked into nation building, it's endless."

Mike said, "History says nation building takes decades, if it works at all, which is very seldom, and never in the Mideast. It's a hard slog. Meanwhile our enemies ridicule us, play the media like a cheap fiddle, and put video clips of endless carnage up on *Al Jazeera* to recruit suicide bombers. Remember Gore? He built a U.S. network, sold it *Al Jazeera,* and became a multimillionaire in the process?"

The President smiled thinly. "It could have been worse. He almost made President."

"That too, and it *did* get worse, Sir."

The President nodded, and his smile vanished. "The new reality is sound bites, third world shit holes with limitless supplies of barbarians closely intermingled with piteously suffering noncombatants, Western educated propagandists and sponsors, and fanatical Muslim populations with a predilection for violent suicide and killing infidels. It's the same problem Rome faced, except physical borders don't work anymore and we have self-imposed rules and Political Correctness. The new barbarians have cell phones, tax-exempt foundations, Internet access, and credit cards to buy airline tickets. The whole world gets to watch the slaughter nightly, second-guess decisions, and blame the West.

"Bush should have talked to his father instead of Cheney before Iraq. Sometimes it's better to leave it as the tyrant's problem...."

"Yes, Sir, I think so. You know my views. Tyrants are better than failed states, and much better than radical Islamists, like the Muslim Brotherhood. Egypt and Benghazi were blunders. "

"*Jets and nets.* I remember your lectures. I miss your inputs on strategy."

Mike blinked. The President was watching him closely. He chose his words carefully. "I blathered a lot when I was going though rehab and getting my doctorate, but I've done my time at staff. Professor Bernstein has an excellent grasp of geopolitics and is respected by the Intelligence Committees. You have better military strategists as well."

"I do?"

"Certainly. Neumann and Vorkosigan...."

"Ah, but you can't name a third, though," murmured the President.

"That's not the point, Sir. You don't need a special ops maverick in this political climate. I'm controversial enough at the staff colleges."

"Don't squirm so much, Mike." The President actually smiled faintly. "There is an unfortunate lack of good strategic options, and it turns out I have something more urgent I need you for."

"What we're discussing...."

"Is background, and a key part of it. But only a part."

"Sir?"

"Gerry needs some temporary help and administrative cover, but this is bigger. Your talents are better suited for the field."

He's talking about combat. Mike frowned and chose his words carefully. "Conventional military force hasn't worked well lately, Sir."

"I agree...."

Mike waited.

"I'm not looking for conventional approaches, and your transfer to NSA moves you entirely out of the military chain of command."

"I don't understand, Mr. President."

"The priority so far is to quietly contain Bukhari. We've tightened up security to where another nuke is unlikely, but I'm afraid the method of attack will shift."

"To bioweapons...."

"Perhaps. This is why the bioweapons link to Bukhari worries me, though CIA has discounted it."

"CIA doesn't deem it to be a threat?" They usually saw everything as a threat.

"No." The President shrugged. "For technical reasons, they say it's a program that doesn't make any sense. They're rather pleased that Nassid's wasting a significant fraction of his money and resources."

"And you disagree, Sir?"

"Let's just say I want to you to look into it."

"And if the trail ties into a planned bioweapons attack by Bukhari?"

"Then you must preempt it. If your investigations lead there, that becomes a part of your job. However unlikely my conspiracy theory may seem, I will not put politics and caution ahead of defending the homeland. Nor will I wait for Congress."

"Or the U.N."

"You've got that one right." The President drummed his fingers on the table for a moment, thinking. "What do you know about smallpox, Mike?"

"I know we worry about it. I had a vaccination."

"We must vaccinate to prevent a disease that no longer exists in nature." The President sighed deeply. "There are times when I think the world has gone mad. Do you know the history of smallpox?"

Mike shook his head.

"It was the most devastating and feared pestilence in human history. The plagues were a recurrent problem for centuries." The President paused and gave him a searching look. "Today most scholars think they started in the Mideast."

Mike was paying intense attention. "That's very interesting, Sir."

The President paused for a moment, and then spoke slowly. "Bukhari has developed a new virus derived from camelpox. The experts are calling it ECP, Encapsulated Camel Pox."

"Camelpox?" Mike frowned. "I've never heard of it, Sir."

"That's not surprising," the President said. "There is a lot of camelpox around, but not in the West. It's endemic among the world's 20 million camels. Smallpox and camelpox are both members of the orthopox family, and Iraq admitted having an active program to develop the camelpox virus as a bioweapon back in the 90s...."

"With what results?"

The President started explaining.

An Upscale Condo in Laurel, Maryland

The phone on his nightstand kept ringing insistently. Burt Cassidy struggled to wakefulness and glanced at the time, 3:47 A.M. He picked up the phone. "This better be pretty fucking important, whoever you are."

"They just pulled me off the project. Is that important enough?"

"Kendrick?"

"Who the hell do you think it is, the Tooth Fairy? Yes, it's me. I'm off the project. They have some damned Marine General taking over. It's unprecedented. What should I do...?"

"Hold on. Let me think." Burt's mind was fuzzy from the mix of sex and drugs. He'd just gotten to sleep. "Wait a minute. I'll be right back."

He put the phone down, stumbled into the bathroom and splashed cold water on his face. He took a few deep breaths, then walked back and picked up the phone. "Calm down. You're not making any sense. How can a Marine take over your project?"

"Damn good question," Tibbs said. "It beats the shit out of me."

"Does the Patton woman know anything about this?"

"I doubt it. Mitchell would have told me first."

"That's not what I mean. Has she been meeting with anyone to suggest management changes?"

"Not at the agency."

"What about outside the fucking agency?"

"No."

"Are you sure?"

"Christ, yes, I'm sure. I've got her on the box every month. The standard question is, 'Have you discussed your project with anyone outside NSA besides your authorized contractor's representatives?' The polygraph says she hasn't."

"All right," Burt said. "Tell me what you do know."

"I got reamed out and yanked. Mitchell suspended my project clearances and cancelled my access."

"This just happened? In the middle of the night?"

"Yes."

"Why?"

"The director has been tracking the Palestine situation." Tibbs sounded puzzled. "He stays late to watch the morning satellite feeds and does his administrative work at night."

"No, not that. Why'd he pull your clearances?"

"We're not real big on explanations around here. He gave me the usual management bullshit. 'A personal lack of confidence in my ability to direct the program,' that sort of thing."

"What precisely did he say?" Burt asked.

"He wasn't in a real good mood. I believe his exact words of summation were, 'Piss poor performance.' Is that precise enough for you?"

"I want to know his specific reasons for replacing you."

"Jesus Christ, Burt, it doesn't work that way. He said he was making some changes, and I was going to be reassigned."

"Slow down." Burt thought for a long moment. "Can you get into your office?"

"Without a program clearance, I can't even get back on the floor. What should I do?"

"You said you got reamed out. Why? About what?"

"That's not how it works. Mitchell asked questions. He got pissed when I couldn't answer them to his satisfaction."

"What kind of questions?"

"About the project. He said he wanted to review the reasons for its 'chronic lack of progress.' I blamed the woman, of course, but he didn't buy it."

"He'll get over it," Burt said. "He needs you."

"I don't think so. He's having the combination to my safe changed and the classified documents inventoried. He took my card keys and removed me from the access lists. I don't know what's going on."

This is bad, Burt thought. "What's with the Cybertech people in Oregon? What's their status?"

"They're coming in tomorrow to give us a proposal."

"Do you know their flight number?"

"They don't have one. They have a private plane. The Patton bitch has them cleared into Andrews Air Force Base. You can't stop them at an airport, if that's what you're thinking."

The hell I can't, Burt thought. "Do you know the tail number of their airplane? Do you know what kind of a plane it is?"

"Jesus, Burt. It's just an airplane. A corporate jet. They're coming tomorrow. That's all I know."

"Tomorrow? Then we have some time."

There was a muttered curse at the other end of the line. "No. That's wrong. It's already tomorrow. They're coming today. Tonight."

"Okay. Okay, calm down. I'll handle it. Just stay loose."

Tibbs was babbling questions frantically, but Burt cut him off. "I need to make some calls. I'll get back to you."

Burt slowly put the phone down. His hand was shaking.

Burt slapped his face twice to clear his head, trying to think. *Harriet will know what to do*, he thought.

He took several deep breaths to calm himself. Then he dialed the Senator's number.

CHAPTER FOUR
NEIGHBORHOOD FRIENDLY

River Glen, MD

Gerry studied herself critically in the mirror and frowned. She glanced at her watch. *If I leave now, I can be at work half an hour early. I'll just get coffee on the way and eat breakfast at my desk again.*

She was surprised by a knock at the door. "Just a minute," she called, running a comb thorough her hair one last time. *I look awful*, she thought. *Well, it'll just have to do.*

"I'm coming," she called out. She looked through the peephole and felt a surge of surprise.

She pulled the door open. "General Mickelson. I thought you'd phone...."

He was grinning and shaking his head. "You promised to call me Mike, remember?"

"I didn't expect to see you so soon. This is a bad time. I have to get to work."

"Actually, you don't." He was holding a paper bag. "I need to talk with you. I took the liberty of bringing you a latte, and what might serve as breakfast. Do you like bagels and lox?"

She frowned, studying him carefully. He wore MARPAT woodland digital camouflage fatigues, the post 9-11 pixilated, bit-mapped, digital camo that suggested shapes and colors without actually *being* shapes and colors—like visual white noise. They were open at the neck, with heavy military boots that made him almost her height. He had a mischievous twinkle in his brown eyes, like a little boy with a secret.

When they'd met in his office, he'd been all business. *Damn,* she thought. *I wish I had the time....*

"I love bagels and lox, Mike, but I've got a problem," she said. "My boss and I don't get along. He's been keeping a log of when I'm late to work as part of his latest crusade to get me fired. He's watching me like a bug under a microscope. I'd better...."

Mike's grin broadened. "I thought you said, **soon**? You seemed insistent, as I recall. So here I am. Can't women ever make up their minds?"

"Well, yes, I did say that." She was getting flustered, and it annoyed her. "Mike, I'm really glad to see you. I was hoping you'd call. It's just a bad time."

He shook his head again. "Nope. Best time possible."

"Mike, bless you. But I'm afraid you don't know Kendrick Tibbs. The man's a vicious little bureaucrat with political connections. He's ruined more than one career."

"I know the type," Mike agreed. "They're dangerous and Washington seems to attract the breed. But I don't think you need to worry about Tibbs...."

Gerry felt a flash of irritation. "It's not going to do either of us any good if I get kicked off the project. Tibbs has been trying to do that for some time, and I don't want to give him any...." She trailed off. Mike was shaking his head.

"I don't know Tibbs, except by reputation. However, I do know he's no longer your boss."

"The agency doesn't...." Gerry's voice trailed off again, as his words sunk in. "Did you just say Tibbs is no longer my boss?"

"That's right. Tibbs is now on special assignment. Elsewhere."

"Really?" She frowned. "Where exactly is elsewhere, if I might ask?"

"Beats me." Mike shrugged. "Somewhere that doesn't overlap your project. The main thing is you no longer work for Tibbs."

How does he know that? She looked at him sharply. "What are you doing here, Mike?

"You said you needed my help?"

"Yes." Gerry nodded. *I sure do.*

"Be careful what you ask for," he said wryly. "I'm your new boss, at least temporarily."

"What?" She blinked and shook her head. "Are you serious?"

"I'm afraid so. President Hale intervened, and I've just been assigned to run your project. Problem is, I don't have a clue what that entails. This time I need *your* help. I need to talk to you privately before I go blundering into Fort Meade offending your Agency insiders."

Gerry felt her surprise shifting to elation. "Thank God," she said softly. "The past several months have been a bit of a strain. How did...?"

He held up the bag. "Can we talk over breakfast?"

"Yes. Yes, of course we can. Come in." She smiled, holding the door open. He followed her in, closed the door, and clicked the lock.

"Do you have this place swept for bugs?"

That made her smile. "You're out of your element, Mike...."

"I assume that means, Yes?"

She nodded, as they sat down at her small breakfast table. "Of course. It's standard practice. We had some embarrassments a few years ago, and now the agency sends teams out regularly to check. They've never found anything. Last year they put piezoelectric oscillators on the windows to defeat laser taps. My house is EMI screened and the security system is first rate."

"Just a minute." She unplugged the telephone from the wall. "It's not a bubble, but we're reasonably secure."

"Good." Mike nodded approvingly. "I had my conversation with President Hale. He shared some things with me that were, ah.... Well, let's just say, 'disquieting.'"

"Disquieting?"

Mike flashed his quick grin again. "I'd say *scary as hell*, but Marines aren't supposed to notice fear." The grin faded. "So I won't say that. Disquieting will do."

"The President put you in charge of a NSA program? That's going to make some waves. Congress isn't going to stand for having the military in charge of codes and COMSEC."

"Actually, the military is not in the loop. I report to the White House directly on this. My boss, General Myers, the Marine Commandant, has put me on temporary duty."

"So?" *Where's he going with this?*

"I report *only* to the White House. I'm now totally outside the military chain of command. That means so are you, and so is your project."

"What about the NSA chain of command?" she asked.

"That's ambiguous." Mike shrugged. "Apparently some issues need to be resolved. I have a written authorization clearing me for unrestricted program access and directing you to report to me." He handed her a note. It was on NSA letterhead, signed, with a thumbprint she assumed was Director Mitchell's. The signature looked like his, and it was dated today.

Gerry examined it carefully. "It seems to be in order." She looked at Mike questioningly. "What is the director's position on this, ah, organizational adjustment?"

"I have no idea." Mike shrugged. "I haven't discussed it with him. If anyone asks about your chain-of-command, just say you report to me. Tell them the director assigned you to me. If the director asks anything, send him to me."

"You'll fit right in," she said.

Mike looked puzzled.

"NSA. Never Say Anything."

"Loose lips sink ships," Mike agreed. "The President said he'd keep your director informed after some issues he deems troublesome are adequately addressed. I hope all this doesn't put you in an impossible position."

She gave a wry smile. "No more impossible than it has been. What are your orders?"

"To remove blockages. He suspects NSA has a leak and wants me to find it. He wants information closely held. He wants your project completed, and on an urgent basis. He's not happy about the delays."

No, he's not. "What do you want of me?" she asked.

"Information and discretion," he said without hesitation. "Nobody outside the program has a need-to-know except the President. If anyone asks who you work for, give them my name. If anyone asks who I work for, you document it and find out why they are asking. If pressed, you tell them I'm on temporary duty to support the funding agency, which in this case happens to be the White House. We do **not** mention the President. Okay?"

"Yes, and gratefully. Thank you. What about my dad, at Cybertech?"

"He's in. Cybertech is our prime contractor, and I'd trust Iron John with my life. Tell him on a secure line that we have a leak. Get him to give you a list of everyone at the firm who absolutely must have access, and get me a copy. I also want a list of everyone at NSA who's had program access to date."

"I can do that," she said.

"By the way, does your program have a name?"

She gave a faint smile. "Yes. GIRL TALK. "

"I'm going to cancel that, redo the background checks, and get new clearances issued. We'll need a new cover name."

She thought for a long moment. "How about VINEYARD?"

"Why?"

"Three reasons. First, we are building a virtual grapevine, where insiders can communicate privately. Secondly, vineyard has an old, archaic meaning that's also relevant, 'sphere of endeavor.' We're redesigning how government can interact. We're building a new sphere...."

"I like that. And I can guess the third reason." He grinned. "Hopefully, no one will have a clue as to what the hell the name means."

She nodded. "You catch on fast. Did the President say anything else?"

The grin reappeared. "He said you used to have cute curls...."

Gerry stopped for a moment, lost in thought. "Those were happier days. Actually, I was a rather gangly child...." She gave him a serious look. "I'm not a child anymore. Don't worry about my career. You have my full support. Just do what you need to do, okay?"

He nodded.

"Did the President give you specific directions?"

"Not really. I'm afraid he's expecting us to do something clever."

"I hate it when they do that," she said.

"Me too." Mike sighed deeply. "One more thing. If anything goes wrong, it's my fault. You were just following orders. Understand? I'm going to generate a paper trail to cover your ass, including my order directing you to communicate program information to your dad."

How strange. What's going on here? She looked at him intently. "What are you trying to say? Please spell it out for me."

Mike gave her an enigmatic look. "The Office of the President is not to be put at risk. The President is not directing this program. I am. I'm just a dumb-assed Marine who's been asked to dabble in matters he doesn't understand. GIRL TALK, a mismanaged program in deep trouble, has been shut down. You need to understand that clearly."

She felt an odd sensation. It took her a moment to recognize it as fear.

Whatever's wrong, it must go beyond the agency, she realized. *This isn't just about my program. It's bigger. I've seen that look before, when Dad used to leave on a mission where he knew people would die. Something bad is going to happen, and Mike's already trying to protect President Hale from fallout.*

She nodded slowly. "I understand."

"The problem is I really don't know much about COMSEC, codes, encryption, and that sort of thing," Mike said. "I don't know what I've gotten myself into.

"I'm going to have to follow your lead on technical things. I've only had time to scan the highlights, but there doesn't seem to be much depth on this project. If anything happens to you, it appears we won't have much of a program."

"I suppose not." She shook her head and frowned. "We're just in the research phase. Budget wasn't assigned for...."

He waved her to a stop, reached into his paper bag and held out a latte. "Might need to warm it up," he said.

She took a sip. "It's fine. Thank you."

"No time for what wasn't," Mike said. "I want to know what's needed to get the job done. For starters, I'm going to assign some security to cover you. We need you safe."

She raised an eyebrow. "If you think that's necessary."

"I do," he said. "And I want to get you some help, so you don't work sixteen hour days without any breaks."

He's been reading the access logs, Gerry realized. She looked at him, studying his face carefully. *He hides it well, but his eyes look tired. He must have been up all night studying the project files.* "Thank you," she said, taking a deep breath. "Where do you want me to start?"

"Wherever you want."

"You sure?"

He nodded. "I need to hear it. Everything."

"Okay." She started talking. When she next looked at her watch, it was early afternoon.

Mike jotted a few more details in a small notebook and glanced at the time. "That's enough for now. I think it's time we went out to Fort Meade. They'll have me on the access lists by now. I'd like you to show me around the project."

"My pleasure," she said. "Just give me a moment to freshen up."

He was waiting by the door when she came out. "Do you want me to follow you?"

"I'd prefer it if we rode together, Gerry. That way we can talk. I'll arrange transportation back for you."

She nodded, and they stepped out on to the small porch. He waited for her to lock the door and set the security system, and they walked together toward his vehicle. It was tall, bulky, and painted in military camouflage, brown and tan, desert colors. She was turning to ask him about it when a shrill whistle sounded. "What...?"

She never had a chance to finish. Mike wrapped his arms around her and threw her to the ground. A volley of fire ripped past them, bullets slamming into and ricocheting off the General's armored vehicle.

Several guns were firing, from at least two separate locations. Full auto. Long bursts.

Gerry gasped as she hit the ground. Bullets tore through the space they'd just vacated and she heard voices yelling in the distance.

"Go. Crawl. Get behind that low wall on your patio and stay there." Mike pushed her in that direction. "I'll try to draw them off. Move, move, move..."

I am moving, damn it. Gerry was crawling across the wet lawn on her belly. She heard people running. The sounds were getting closer.

Dear God, they're shifting to get a better shot at us, she thought. She looked back in time to see Mike dash zigzag for the big oak tree in front of her bedroom.

Gerry rose to her hands and knees, moving as fast as she could, staying low. Dead leaves had piled up around the patio. They felt cold and slimy and smelled of mold. Then she was behind the wall, pressed against the ground, thankful for the shelter, face down in a puddle of water.

Gerry could taste blood. She'd bitten her lip when Mike pushed her down. She groped in her purse for the gun the agency issued her. Designed for concealment and last ditch self-defense, it only held two shots.

There was another long burst of fire. She heard bullets whistling over her and thunking into the house. It seemed hopeless. *Why aren't we running? We're sitting ducks here.*

She peeked over the wall and saw him: a big man with wild eyes and a bushy black beard, holding an assault rifle. The man stopped, aimed, and fired two short bursts.

Kak kak, kak kak.

Bullets slammed into Mike's tree. Gerry could hear solid impacts over the gunfire as 7.62 full-jacketed slugs thunked into the big oak. The man fired again. He clamped the trigger down and hosed bullets, gouging chunks of wood and bark from Mike's refuge.

Mike was turned sideways behind the tree, pinned down, trying to present as small a target as possible. His shelter was being shot to pieces. That tree might help against pipsqueak American .223 rounds, but the heavier bullets were ripping it apart.

He doesn't have a chance, Gerry thought.

Her fingers touched the gun in her purse. The weapon was designed for concealment, not accuracy or stopping power. She rolled to her knees, pointed it carefully at the man's center of mass, and squeezed the trigger. The tiny gun made a muffled pop pop.

The man laughed and swung his assault rifle toward her. Gerry flattened, pressing her face into wet leaves as bullets whizzed overhead and ricocheted off the top of the wall.

I'm going to die in a puddle of water on my own patio, she thought. Then the man's weapon clicked empty and she heard Mike yell.

She peeked over the wall. Mike was a blur of motion, running hard, grunting with effort, arms and legs pumping, charging straight at the man.

"Drop the weapon," Gerry screamed, standing up. Her training kicked in, and her front sight centered on the man's head.

It was a bluff. She had no reloads.

The rifle swung left, toward her, away from Mike. The man fumbled a fresh clip into his weapon, but Mike was close. Then he was there, knocking the gun aside.

Mike stepped inside the arc of the barrel and hit the man in the throat with the edge of his hand. The man made a choking sound and staggered back. He was six inches taller and must have outweighed Mike by fifty pounds.

The man dropped his weapon when Mike's second blow, upward, palm open, smashed his nose and snapped his head back. Mike grabbed the man's beard, braced, pivoted, and slammed him airborne against the vehicle. He hit with a dull thud, making the big machine rock slightly on its suspension.

Incredibly, the man landed on his feet, turning to face his antagonist with bright blood gushing down his face.

Gerry saw a glint of metal. "He's got a knife," she screamed.

"Don't shoot! I want to…"

The sniper's bullet made a sound like an ax hitting a side of beef, and the man fell without a sound.

In the distance, there were three short bursts of heavier fire, a more authoritative, throaty *braap braap braap* that echoed off the trees. Two quick pairs of shots followed: a lighter, sharper *bam-bam, bam-bam*. Followed by silence.

Then the whistle she'd heard before sounded twice. Mike was looking down at the body, sucking in deep breaths of air. He picked up the man's weapon, checked it, and clicked the safety on.

Mike glanced over at Gerry. "Are you all right?" he asked.

She nodded, not trusting herself to speak. *The whistle was a signal*, she realized. *Two blasts must be an all clear.*

In the sudden stillness, she could hear the voices more clearly. "The Tangos are down. So is Ensign Mallory. We need a medic. Check the General and the girl."

"Yes, Sir."

Two men ran around the vehicle holding nasty looking automatic weapons at the ready. They wore camouflage uniforms and body armor. Gerry was surprised to see the barely visible black emblems on their collars indicated Navy ranks, a Senior Chief Petty Officer and a Petty Officer

Second Class. The junior man checked the body while his Chief covered him, eyes constantly scanning, his weapon ready.

"No pulse," the junior man said. They both relaxed.

"Are you all right, Sir?" asked the Senior Chief.

"I'm fine. Good work," Mike said. He handed him the weapon and walked over to Gerry. "Can you stand up?"

She nodded, and he helped her to her feet. Her clothes were muddy and her lip hurt. Mike took a handkerchief from his pocket and handed it to her. "You've got blood on your face."

Gerry dabbed at it. Her hands were shaking.

A man with double bars on his collar, also in dark black, came walking slowly around the vehicle, looking grim. "The area is secure, Sir."

"Did you get any prisoners?" Mike asked.

"No, Sir. My Ensign's down, and the Tangos are dead. It kind of turned to shit, General." He glanced at Gerry. "Excuse me, ma'am."

"What happened, Lieutenant?" Mike asked.

"A panel van with three Tangos in it arrived nine minutes after you did, Sir. It has the name of a local cable TV outfit on the side. They parked just off the road and sat there watching the house. We stayed out of sight and observed."

"One of them made a call on a cell phone, but otherwise there was no activity. When you went to leave, they came charging out with assault rifles. We interdicted them using minimum force. The rules of engagement specify we should challenge, Sir."

Mike nodded.

"Ensign Mallory did so. He ordered the Tangos to drop their weapons. They apparently didn't want to do that. They cut him down and started shooting at you. Their weapons were AK variants and handguns. They displayed standard *jihad* weapons handling and had good fire discipline, Sir."

"Explain," Mike said.

"It was a two-man *jihad* assault team, plus the leader. No security element, no support, just the shooters. They carry and fire their long guns rotated ninety degrees, with the ejection port up. That's a signature move, as you know, Sir."

Mike nodded. It made no sense, but that was what the jihadists typically did.

"They were aggressive. They got the initiative, and our suppression fire was ineffective. The big one got past us. They were on their second clips when we went full offensive and took them down, Sir."

"Quite right, Lieutenant." Mike's look was still questioning.

"Their tactics were unusual, Sir. Usually if it's a residential assassination, they dress innocuously, go to the door, knock, stand in front of the peephole, and wait for the door to open."

"Right," Mike said. "Then they draw and empty their weapons into the victim."

The Lieutenant looked embarrassed. "There was no attempt to do that, Sir. They were acting like surveillance, not a kill team. When they suddenly broke and started shooting, it caught us off guard. We didn't expect so much firepower."

"I heard the double taps," Mike said, frowning. "Head shots?"

"Yes, Sir. I issued the kill order. My orders were to protect you. That objective was at risk, and I didn't want to chance any more casualties, Sir." A dark look crossed the Lieutenant's face. "Ensign Mallory is a good officer, General."

Mike nodded. "What went wrong?"

"The Tangos were wearing sophisticated body armor, Sir. German stuff. Some advanced Kevlar with ceramic chest plates. It's better than what we have. It stopped Mallory's nine millimeter at point blank range, and it stood up to our suppressing fire with .223s."

Mike winced. "I want our weapons people to know about that armor."

"Yes, Sir. I'll see to it." The Lieutenant gave a grim smile. "Whatever it is, it didn't do much good against Kowalski's .50 caliber or our sniper team."

"How's your Ensign?"

"Mallory was hit several times. Left leg, both arms, and throat. His body armor stopped the rest, but he's got broken ribs and possible internal injuries. They could have finished him, but didn't try. We'd have taken more casualties, but they kept firing at you instead. Right up to when we dropped them. The shooters were pretty determined, Sir."

"Please keep me advised about your officer's medical condition. I know some good doctors," Mike said. "One nice thing about having rank is sometimes you're in a position to do some good for your men. Remember that, Lieutenant, and call me if you need anything."

"Thank you, Sir. A medevac copter's five out, and we got the bleeding stopped. My corpsman says Mallory might make it if we can get him to a hospital quickly."

"Thank *you*, Lieutenant. Good work." Mike scowled darkly. "I made a mistake. No more neighborhood friendly."

"Sir?"

"I'm authorizing lethal force as needed to protect me and this woman. If anyone reaches for a weapon, kill them. Issue full combat loads. Give Captain Roberts my compliments, and tell him I said he was right."

"Yes, Sir!" the Lieutenant said, enthusiastically. "I'll pass the word. Thank you, Sir."

"One more thing, Lieutenant. I'm going back inside. I'm going to call on the landline and see if I can get the FBI out here. I'll ask for a crime scene unit, so tell your men not to touch anything. Keep a tight perimeter until the FBI gets here. When they arrive, turn it over to them."

"Yes, Sir."

Gerry could hear sirens in the distance as they walked back into the house. A large helicopter with military markings was just settling down in the driveway as she closed the door.

The Agency wanted me to keep a low profile, she thought ruefully. *I don't think this is quite what they had in mind.*

There was a soft tap at the door. Gerry glanced at Mike, and he nodded. "I'm sure it's safe, but perhaps it would be best if you let me get it."

"Go right ahead," she said. *If it's so damned safe, why'd you get a pump shotgun out of your vehicle?*

Mike peered through the peephole and opened the door. A large black man entered, holding a badge and keeping his hands in plain sight. Mike studied the badge and looked the man up and down carefully. "Obadiah?" he asked, slowly lowering his weapon.

The man nodded. "My mother wanted me to be a minister. I can give you a verification code if you want to call the FBI and check me out."

"Not necessary." Mike smiled faintly. He clicked the safety and set the shotgun by the door. "I don't think the *mujahedeen* shooting at us are creative enough to use a Hebrew name like Obadiah for a cover. If they are, we're in deep trouble."

He passed the badge back and turned to Gerry. "The FBI has arrived, Ms. Patton. This is special agent Obadiah B. Simpson."

Gerry nodded, but didn't speak. The man's blue flak jacket clearly had "FBI" emblazoned in large white letters on the front, and, she presumed, also on the back. He was staring at the Glock 20 on the table next to her hand.

"That's a ten millimeter," Simpson said.

"Uh huh...."

"It's a lot of gun for a woman."

She smiled sweetly. "I don't lug it around in my purse. My father gave it to me for home defense. He taught me to shoot it and assured me when I hit someone, they'd fall down."

"The Bureau has stopped using 10s. Our female agents said they didn't fit their hands, and that it hurt to fire them."

"You use Sigs?"

Simpson nodded. "Mostly."

"Perhaps you should have your armorer reconsider. I find the recoil-dampening of the Glock's hi-tech polymer frame to be excellent. Dad once finished a large Grizzly with a head shot from this gun.

"It's a useful weapon. The ammo I'm using would punch through your vest like paper."

Simpson frowned.

"It's good to feel safe in your own home, don't you think?"

Mike smiled. She'd been shot at, her clothes were ruined, she looked like she'd been mud wrestling and she obviously didn't much give a damn what the FBI thought.

"Would you put it away, please?" Simpson asked.

Gerry glanced at Mike, who nodded. Her tone was acerbic. "If you wish. I'm sure we're all much safer now that the Bureau's here to protect us."

It earned her a sharp look from Simpson. There was a certain tension between the agency and the FBI. It wasn't so much rivalry as a difference in viewpoints and missions.

"Ms. Patton's a little nervous, Agent Simpson."

Simpson's attention shifted to Mike, but not until she'd slid her Glock into a drawer.

"So?"

Gerry started to speak, but stopped at a gesture from Mike.

"I am too, Agent Simpson. Nervous. The last time we walked outside, we got hosed with automatic weapons fire."

"Do you have any ID, General?" asked Simpson brusquely, looking at the stars on Mike's fatigue uniform.

Mike pulled a card from his pocket, passing it to the man. Simpson examined it closely. Without waiting, Mike gestured to Gerry, and she handed the agent her photo badge. He glanced at it and did a double take.

"You're with the National Security Agency, Ms. Patton?"

She nodded. "I'm a project manager."

Simpson frowned and looked like he wanted to say something. He reconsidered, sighed, and simply handed the cards back. "Ms. Patton, General Mickelson, thank you."

He looks like he's had a rough day too. "May I offer you a cup of tea, Agent Simpson? I've just made a fresh pot." She smiled ruefully. "It helped settle my nerves."

"Thank you, ma'am, I'd appreciate that, if it comes with an explanation."

"We'll do our best," Mike said, pulling out a chair at the kitchen table.

The agent sat down and Gerry poured his tea. He sipped it and gave the General a bemused look. "Our director got a call from the White House to get someone out here immediately with a crime scene team."

Mike nodded. "I requested your help. We were attacked. I'm not totally clear about law enforcement protocols, but I believe the FBI has jurisdiction."

"Do the Marines report to the White House now?" Simpson asked, obliquely.

"The President is our Commander-in-Chief," Mike said. "Always has been."

Simpson was staring at Mike, his dark eyes intense. His demeanor radiated skepticism. "I'm talking chain-of-command, not political philosophy. Can I get a straight answer, please?"

"I'm on temporary duty to the White House, a detached assignment helping out NSA. Ms. Patton and I are working together."

Simpson seemed to think about that for a time. He didn't reply directly. "I didn't expect to find a war zone out here. Your guards are intimidating, General."

"You shouldn't call Lieutenant Clover's detachment 'guards.' They'd feel insulted."

Simpson looked at him, taking another sip of his tea. "They seem to have a lot of firepower deployed for what I expected was a peaceful residential neighborhood."

"It's a nice neighborhood," Mike agreed.

"If they're not guards, who are they?"

"Lieutenant Clover is assigned temporarily to Marine Headquarters, who loaned him to me. He commands SEAL Detachment Bravo. One component of his responsibility is security."

Simpson frowned. He didn't look happy.

"SEALs aren't much inclined toward colorful names," Mike said with a half smile and a shrug. "Detachment Bravo consists of three six-man combat units, each usually under the command of a Lieutenant Junior Grade. Their expertise is Counter Terrorism, and one of those units is outside."

"SEALs are Navy," Simpson said. "They're your security force?"

"Among other things...."

"Why not Marine assets?"

"I was told our MSOR forces are otherwise occupied. They report to SOCOM, not Marine Headquarters."

Simpson shook his head.

"U.S. Special Operations Command, down at MacDill, in Florida. I was assigned SEALs because they have some unique capabilities in special recon and direct action."

Simpson's frown was more of a scowl. "What kind of capabilities?"

"I can't discuss that." Mike shrugged. "SEALs get a lot of special training. There are also support elements assigned to Team Bravo."

"What kind of support elements? I want my investigators to interview everyone involved."

"None were involved in this operation." Mike waved his hands in an ambiguous gesture. "Air and logistics support, interpreters, that sort of thing. It varies, depending on the mission."

"Like maybe a carrier battle group?"

"Not needed," Mike said. "It's a nice neighborhood."

"The FBI wasn't informed the military was running a C-T exercise, General."

"We're not. I just stopped by to talk with Ms. Patton and give her a ride to work."

"A SEAL combat team is here to help you take Ms. Patton to work?"

"Yes. That's right," Mike said.

Simpson raised an eyebrow, glanced at his watch, and looked at Gerry skeptically. "Do you have a lot of trouble getting to work on time, Ms. Patton?"

"My last supervisor thought so," Gerry said glumly. "It's in my personnel file."

"Do you know it's 2:30 pm? You don't seem to be making much progress."

"I can see that," she said, poker faced.

"We're working on the problem," Mike said.

Simpson glanced at him sharply and then back at Gerry. He frowned. "General Mickelson and a SEAL detachment stopped by to talk to you and help you get to work? Are you shitting me, Ms. Patton?"

"Actually, I'm not, Agent Simpson." She smiled sweetly. "I'm answering your questions."

There was a flicker of irritation in Simpson's eyes. "Go on," he said.

"The General stopped by unexpectedly to talk with me. He offered to take me to work. We stepped outside and people started shooting. The General knocked me down to get me out of the line of fire. I heard the bullets going past."

"Do you have any idea who was shooting at you?"

"Not a clue."

"There was no warning? They just started shooting?"

"Yes. That's correct."

"Had the General ever been here before?"

"No."

"May I ask what your involvement is with the General, and how it relates to NSA?"

Gerry looked at Mike, who shook his head, and then back at Simpson. "That's a very relevant question," she said. "Perhaps the best way I can answer it is to ask if you are familiar with the terms 'black operation' or 'black project'?"

Agent Simpson nodded slowly.

"Then if I were to explain that we are working on a White House-authorized black project...?"

Simpson sighed in exasperation. "The manager of a black project is fully and completely authorized to take whatever means are necessary to maintain the security and confidential nature of the project ... up to and specifically including the use of any and all necessary lethal force." Simpson recited the words as if by rote, his eyes fixed on Mike. "Is that what's going on here?"

"Ms. Patton didn't say that," Mike said.

"No, she didn't. That's why I'm asking you, General."

"I came here to talk with Ms. Patton and take her to work. We stepped outside and people started shooting at us. Lieutenant Clover's men dealt with the situation. Then I called the White House and requested FBI help. That's what we've been telling you."

"Yes, you have." Simpson's look was quizzical.

"The White House said you're the experts at crime scene investigations. We're urgently looking forward to the results of such an investigation. Ms. Patton did not make any statements about black projects. If you'll recall, she merely asked if you were familiar with black projects...."

"I recall just fine," Simpson said. "What's your point?"

"I'm not going to tell you how to do your job, Agent Simpson. Still, it shouldn't be necessary to overreact and start speculating about black projects to investigate what appears to be a simple case of self-defense."

"Self-defense," Simpson said musingly. "Mentioning 'overreact,' your SEALs have antitank weapons and heavy machine guns out there. Were you expecting serious resistance?"

Mike shook his head. "We didn't expect any trouble."

Simpson frowned. "You didn't expect any trouble?" he asked, watching them closely.

"No," they said in unison.

"All you were doing here was talking and driving someone to work?"

"That's right," Mike said. "Ms. Patton."

"There are two corpses in the driveway, spent shell casings all over the place, and the front of the house looks like it's been used for target practice."

"Three bodies, actually. There's another one over by my vehicle. It's a mess. We're more than happy to turn the crime scene over to the FBI. I asked Lieutenant Clover to keep the area secure until you got here."

"That's what he said." Simpson scowled. "Problem is, he refused to stand down his men and unload their weapons. I gave your officer a direct order. His response was unprintable."

Mike spread his hands in a placating gesture. "We're all on the same side here. What were your specific orders?"

"Like I said: to get out here with a CSI team. To introduce myself to you and offer the Bureau's assistance."

"Then I suggest perhaps you should do that. We could use some help. We screwed up. We lacked aggressiveness and didn't deploy sufficient firepower."

Simpson blinked. He looked startled, then incredulous. His mouth opened. "I saw two bodies out there with double taps to the head, and you're...."

"I expect Lieutenant Clover is feeling distressed, Agent Simpson. The bad guys got past his unit. His second-in-command – an exceptional young Ensign who's due to become the youngest Lieutenant JG in the Navy next month – just got the shit shot out of him."

Mike's expression was grim. Simpson's was impatient. Their gazes locked.

"Clover feels responsible."

"We all have problems..." Simpson said.

"You might want to cut him some slack," Mike interrupted. He had the snap of command in his voice. "He's doing his job. I *ordered* Lieutenant Clover to use deadly force if there's a second attack. I can identify with his feelings, because I share them."

"Yes, Sir," the agent said, giving up. He spread his hands in acquiescence. "I'm sorry to hear about your officer. Will he be all right?"

"Thank you," Mike said. "We don't know yet."

"I've got two CSI teams on their way out here, under the supervision of a Senior Forensic Scientist. What exactly are we supposed to be looking for, General?"

"I'm not sure." Mike shrugged. "Anything and everything. We want to know who the Tangos were. We want to know their nationalities, who they worked for, where their weapons came from, and why they were sent. Soon would be good. National security issues are involved."

"Yes, Sir."

"When you get some answers, please classify them Top Secret and expedite one copy to the White House and one to me. I want those reports serial numbered, logged, delivered by safe hand, and marked 'eyes only.'"

"Where do we find you, General?" asked Simpson.

"Call this number on a secure phone." Mike handed him a card. "Identify yourself, and they'll tell you where to find me."

"Eyes only," Simpson said. He didn't look happy. "To whom should the White House copy be addressed?"

"Ask your director." Mike shrugged. "He may want to deliver it himself."

"Upward delegation doesn't work too well at the Bureau, but I'll tell him what you said. I'll also suggest this appears to be a case of self-defense." Simpson rolled his eyes helplessly. "The director knows as well as I do if we get tangled up in black projects and spooks, we'll never get this sorted out."

"What black projects?" Mike asked, innocently.

"Yeah, right…. By the way, whoever your assailants were and whatever their mission, I don't think they were after you."

"Why do you say that?" Mike asked.

"We found a picture of Ms. Patton in their van. They came to her house."

"That's not conclusive."

"There's more. You've never been here before, have you?"

"No," Mike said. "I haven't."

"No one could have known you'd drop in to see Ms. Patton unless they had exceptional intelligence. I assume you didn't publicize the fact you were planning to visit her?"

"I did not. Except to Lieutenant Clover and his team, of course."

"Who are, we can assume, trained to be quite professional and discrete with sensitive information. And even if the assailants somehow did acquire such prescient information, they never would have tried to take on a SEAL team."

Mike nodded.

"From where they parked their van, they had a clear field of fire when she backed out of her garage. When you unexpectedly stepped out the front door, you were partially shielded by your vehicle.... Do you want me to go on?"

"That's not necessary," Mike said slowly, giving the agent a respectful look. "You're good at your job, Agent Simpson."

"Thank you," Simpson said. "Based on preliminary evidence, I think Ms. Patton was the target, not you. That's not an official report or an FBI position. We're just talking off the record."

"I understand." Mike pondered for a moment. Finally he nodded. "Did Lieutenant Clover discuss the Tangos' tactics with you?"

"They didn't do a knock and pop; they waited. I can't explain that either. I still think they were after her."

Mike turned to Gerry. "That's one more reason we need to get going. You'll be safe at the Agency. Can you get an overnight kit together quickly?"

"I keep a bag packed in case I need to stay over. Just give me a moment to clean up and change clothes."

"Agent Simpson, we appreciate your help. I'll make sure our gratitude is conveyed to your director."

Simpson nodded.

"The card I gave you also has the number of a voicemail message box written on the back," Mike said. "Keep it to yourself, please. If you need me urgently, just leave your name and a phone number, nothing else. I'll call you back as soon as I can."

"I'll keep in touch." The black man smiled for the first time. "I do have a small request for you, Sir. I've got reinforcements coming, but I'd appreciate it if you and your SEALs would stick around until they get here."

"Not a problem," Mike said. "Is there anything else we can do to make your job easier?"

"Just wish me luck, General." Simpson sighed deeply. "If this gets screwed up, I have a feeling I'm going to be filling out forms for the rest of my life."

CHAPTER FIVE
A TRICKY SITUATION

Cybertech Plant

Colonel John Giles stretched and ran his fingers through his hair. He was tired. He sighed, gazing at the photos on his office wall. He wondered if he should have stuck with the military or just retired and written his memoirs. *Old soldiers never die…*

Some days, the frenetic uncertainty of high tech got him down. Innovation was such a messy process. You crossed your fingers, trusted your experts, did the best you could to make the right calls, and never knew for sure until it was over. He felt like an aging woolly mammoth, a creature from a different era caught in a time warp.

John brushed the negative thoughts aside. *No, running Cybertech for Will was the right thing to do. He's a genius, but that boy is totally lost outside of his lab, where people would waste no time taking advantage of him. Now we're leading an industry and about to implement something that might return our Republic to where it started, back with the citizens, not the lobbyists.*

He smiled to himself about that, looking down at his large rosewood desk. *What the hell, the Army was going to stick me behind a desk too. It's been quite a while since anyone shot at me, and I get a more comfortable office this way. Could be worse…*

He pressed the buzzer twice and his assistant Kate Chambers immediately popped into his office, closing the door behind her. They'd been working together long enough that she almost knew his thoughts.

She looked at John critically. He was still fit and trim, even at 66. His gray military-style crew cut was turning to white.

The old man was tough as nails. "Iron John" worked out every day for an hour. He loved teaching judo and sparring with the young guards they'd been hiring recently. The only one who could ever beat him in hand-to-hand combat was his old Top Sergeant, Harry Conners.

Kate looked closer, noting the bags under his eyes. She glanced past him to the photo on the wall behind his desk. President Hale was pinning a medal on John's chest during his retirement ceremony. The past few years had aged him, slowly, inexorably, like water wearing away hard granite.

She studied her boss appraisingly. "You should get some rest."

He growled like a friendly tiger and shook his head. "No can do. I can sleep on the airplane. That's one of the reasons we spend money on it."

"You want to go tonight?" she asked, somewhat surprised. "Why don't you get a good night's sleep and leave in the morning?"

"It's a three hour time difference to DC. I'd waste the whole damned day. This way I'll be in bed before midnight and, with luck, home for a late dinner tomorrow."

He glanced at his watch. "They'll have our proposal ready in another hour or so. Please have Ed get the plane fueled and a flight plan on file."

"Yes, Sir. Where to, Dulles?"

"Not this time. I pulled some strings. We'll be cleared direct into Andrews Air Force base. Saves me over an hour, door to door."

"I promised your wife I'd take care of you," she said, frowning.

"Deb worries too much."

Her frown deepened. "You really need to get some rest, John. Couldn't you have someone else deliver the proposal?"

He shook his head. "No, I have to do this one myself. It's special. Just have Ed ask for Andrews when he files the plan. Tell him to assume a departure at 1800 hours. Say we'll want extra pillows and blankets so I can nap."

"Yes, Sir," she said, giving up. "You're the boss. Now may I ask you to please do something for me, John?"

He nodded wearily, rubbing his eyes.

"I insist you take a shower and get some sleep until then. **Please.** That's why we added those facilities for you. You are not going to do Cybertech or yourself any good if you are so tired you can't think straight. You've been up for over 72 hours now."

He looked up at her, but said nothing.

"The engineers can finish the proposal without your help. I'll have Olivia in Sales proof it. You know no one is pickier. I'll call Deborah and explain, and I'll get ten copies of the proposal run, collated, and bound."

He waved his hand in acquiescence. He really *was* exhausted. "Okay, Kate, whatever you say. Make it a dozen copies. Have them stamped 'Top Secret, Special Intelligence,' numbered, and boxed."

"Yes, Sir."

He paused, trying to think. He didn't want to forget anything. "And tell everyone who worked on the proposal to take tomorrow off. Thank them for me. Tell Deb I love her and that I'll be home tomorrow in time to take her out for a nice dinner."

"I promise. Now get some rest. Please. I'll wake you when it's time."

He grinned, but it was a tired grin. "Thank you, Katherine. I do appreciate your help."

"It's my job," she said. "You were there when Deborah made me promise to help take care of you. She was very specific about that, and you agreed."

"You women are tough," he said with a sigh. John nodded and made a gesture of resignation. Then he went into the small bedroom and closed the door.

Kate waited until she heard the shower running before she left to carry out his instructions.

Fort Meade, Md.

Gerry straightened up her desk, shoving the classified documents back into the safe and spinning the combination lock. She glanced up at the soft rap on her door. "Come in."

General Mickelson entered slowly and eased himself into the lone chair. She studied him carefully. "You look like you've been rode hard and put away wet."

He sighed deeply, venting volumes of frustration. "You have a quaint way of expressing yourself, but, yes, that's a pretty accurate assessment.

Let's see now – for starters I didn't get much sleep last night. Then we got shot at. And I've just spent three hours with some of the most anal-retentive, compulsively paranoid security bureaucrats I've ever encountered in my life. You have some sick people working here, Gerry."

"Ah, we may be paranoid, but are we paranoid enough?" she asked with a twinkle in her eyes.

"They wanted me to fill out freaking forms about where I went to grammar school and who my teachers were, Gerry. I've had every body fluid drained and every orifice probed. I've been strip-searched, retina scanned, palm scanned, finger printed, X-rayed, and DNA sampled. They took imprints of my feet to verify – God knows how – that they matched the images on my birth certificate. Then they ran me though an MRI, probably to check out if any of the little green aliens had implanted devices in my brain."

Gerry suppressed a chortle, pressing her lips together firmly. *"Ve mussed haf or-dah, hair kenn-er-al,"* she said deadpan.

He gave her a thoroughly disgusted look, and they both broke out laughing. She tried to speak, failed, and dissolved into laughter again. Finally she wiped her eyes, took a deep breath, and looked at him sympathetically.

"I assume, because you are here, you've received your project clearances?"

He nodded. "Provisionally. Only if I get all their forms filled out in the next 48 hours. Only because the Commandant of the Marine Corps and the Chairman of the Joint Chiefs of Staff vouched for me and sent over signed statements by courier."

"Not the President?"

Mike wasn't smiling. "I didn't want to get him involved."

She nodded.

"I suspect your director may not be entirely pleased with my posting. Your security chief wanted me to submit to a psych exam – something about suppressed anger and violent tendencies. I told him it was my job to be violent, at least occasionally, and he'd just have to accept the word of my Marine shrink that I'd not pop off randomly and kill the wrong people."

She raised an eyebrow. "Suppressed anger?"

"NSA and I had a little disagreement in Yemen. The only secure COMM was in the embassy, my troops were at risk, and your local OPS guy wouldn't let us use 'his' satellite link. So I used my diplomatic skills to convince him that interagency cooperation was needed to ensure harmony and accomplish our mutual objectives."

"That sounds quite reasonable. I can't see why we'd get...."

"I shoved an MP-20 in his mouth, chambered a round, and offered to blow his fucking head off," Mike said. "It apparently caused him to put unkind words into your agency's records about me. I should have shot the son-of-a-bitch."

"Oh...."

"I told security to take you off Tibb's monthly polygraph cycle. I've suspended all his standing orders. We're going to start with a clean slate."

They looked into each other's eyes for a long moment. Finally she reached out and took his hand. His grip was gentle. "Thank you for taking this job," she said. "Thank you for helping. I'm glad you're here, Mike."

He nodded without speaking. It had been a hell of a day.

She glanced at her watch. "It's late, past seven, and we're both beat. I can finish briefing you tomorrow."

"Fine by me," he said. "Let me take you to dinner, Gerry. I don't want you to go home until we've made better security arrangements. You can stay at my place. I have an extra bedroom."

She smiled. "I'd like that. Thank you."

Sandy Junction, Oregon

Ahmed peered though the fence, trying to ignore the water dripping down his neck. The fog was now so thick he could barely see the first row of hangar buildings. *This miserable weather will help us*, he thought.

He'd wanted a few days to practice with the weapons, but there wasn't time. *I haven't run a field operation in years, and these men probably haven't fired weapons since they were in training camp.*

He pushed the concerns away. His agent in Washington had never been wrong. Fortunately, this was a soft target. Except for perhaps a bodyguard with a handgun, the Americans would be unarmed. *The killing will be easy.*

"Do you see anything?" Mohammad Habib asked. Ahmed had appointed him as his second in command, mostly because he was older than the others.

"Not with this fog. Everyone's left, except for the pilot. He's waiting in the aircraft out of the rain. There are no guards. Did the woman at the gas pumps leave?"

"Yes, Sir. She locked up the building and left. The far side of the airport is deserted. There are no guards there either. Praise Allah."

"Allah is great," Ahmed agreed. *We should praise the agent who called to warn me we had to intercept them tonight. That makes it easy,* Ahmed thought. *Cybertech's president will come like a lamb to the slaughter. Then I can go home, having completed my mission.*

"The passengers should be here in the next fifteen minutes. Their flight plan requires they leave soon." He looked at Mohammad sharply. "Tell me again what we'll do when they arrive."

"There will be only one car, and it will stop to activate the electronic gate. Fuad will wait for it to pass. Then he'll run out and jam a rock in the rollers for the gate so it can't close."

"Yes. And then?"

"I'll start timing, bring the van, and guard the gate. You'll lead everyone to the hangar and kill the infidels. After two minutes, I'll bring the van to you. We must leave with the bodies within five minutes. You'll drive, and drop Fuad and me at the gate. We'll remove the stone, and make sure the gate closes behind you. You will take the van back."

"What else?"

"I'll take a separate route and we'll meet you back at the farm."

"Drive carefully," Ahmed said. "Don't get into an accident. Don't do anything to attract attention. Has everyone been warned to pick up his spent shells? We don't want to leave any evidence."

"Yes, Sir."

"Go around once more and remind them again. Check that all the men have suppressors on their weapons. We don't want any noise."

The man slipped away, vanishing into the thick fog. Ahmed strained his ears, but could hear nothing except the constant patter of the rain. He jumped when his phone beeped softly. "This is Aaron," he answered, using his new cover identity.

"Aaron, it's Burt. Your package will be one hour late. We just got the new schedule."

"I understand. One hour late. We'll be ready for it." Ahmed ended the call, put the phone back in his pocket, and hunched his shoulders against the cold rain. *It's been raining ever since I got here. Why do people live in a wretched place like this?*

Georgetown, Md.

Mike watched approvingly as Gerry pushed away the remains of her bluefish. "You were hungry."

"I was *starving*. I'm not accustomed to eating this late." She smiled. "I love seafood, and I think the East Coast has more interesting fish...." She was interrupted by a musical tone from her purse. "That's odd. I don't give my phone number to many people. Excuse me."

She extracted the phone, looking puzzled. "This is Gerry. *What?* I thought they were coming tomorrow. I didn't get any messages. Actually, Tibbs isn't my boss anymore. It's a long story. No, I haven't heard from Dad. I'll check and call you right back, Kate."

She frowned. "I need to check something, Mike."

He nodded, taking a sip of his wine.

She pushed buttons on the phone. "This is Geraldine Patton, with NSA. Yes, that's right. I want to check on the status of an aircraft coming in from Oregon. No, it's not military. It's a corporate aircraft. I want to know when 7133 XRAY is scheduled to land and where it is at present. Can you check? Yes, I'll hang on."

Mike gave her a puzzled look, but she didn't notice. She had her eyes closed and was listening intently to whoever was on the other end of the phone. Two minutes passed. Then one more.

"I don't know," she said. "I was told they should be in the air by now." She listened again, frowning and shaking her head. "That doesn't make any sense at all. Can you please check with the FAA and find out what's going on? I'll call you back. Thank you."

Something just went wrong, big time, Mike thought. *That's an "Oh Shit" look if I ever saw one.* He waved the waiter away with a gesture, being careful not to distract Gerry from her conversation.

She pushed recall. "Kate, it's Gerry. Andrews says they never got an arrival time. They don't know anything." She listened for a long moment. "Yes, they said a flight plan should have been filed. Call the local police and ask them to check the airport. Yes, immediately, and please call me back. Thank you."

Again, she hit a recall. "I need the duty officer. Yes, this is Geraldine Patton again. Nothing? They should have been airborne some time ago." She listened for a moment. "We're having the local police in Oregon go out to the airport now. What about their flight plan? That's very odd. No, of course you can't. Thank you for the information...."

She put the phone back in her purse slowly and took several breaths, obviously trying to compose herself. When she looked up, Mike studied her face carefully. *She didn't look that upset after we were shot at.* He waited for her to say something.

"We have a problem, General." Her hands were shaking, and she looked down at them, placing them on the table until the tremors subsided. Then she carefully took a sip of water and set the glass down, fighting for control. "Something may have happened to Dad."

He watched her carefully.

"It may be my fault...."

"Talk to me, Gerry." His tone was soft and patient.

"That was Kate Chambers, Dad's assistant. Dad was coming out from Oregon with a proposal for our system. The meeting is tomorrow, but he decided to come tonight. Kate called my office, but I wasn't there. She left a message with Tibbs, but I didn't get it."

Mike nodded slowly, accepting the data without comment.

"Kate says Dad left for the local airport hours ago with one security guard. Andrews Air Force Base hasn't heard anything. They're missing."

She was silent for a long moment, organizing her thoughts. "They should have taken off over two hours ago. They'd put a flight plan on file. They were scheduled to leave Oregon at five, local time. They were delayed, so Dad's pilot called and amended it to set the departure back an hour. But their flight plan was never activated, so the FAA dropped it out of the system."

"Dropped it out of the system?"

"Apparently it's standard procedure. If a flight plan isn't activated within an hour of the departure time on file, it's canceled. They don't worry about planes that haven't taken off. That's not their responsibility."

"Where's the plane now?"

"I don't know. Kate is having the local police check. It's a small airport, and is unattended at night. There's no control tower."

"It's possible they just had a minor mechanical problem, Gerry. Your father is probably fine. There is no reason to suspect an accident, is there?"

She took several deep breaths, and shook her head. "No, but...."

"But you're fearful, and you're assuming the worst may have happened?"

She nodded. "I should have called and warned Dad, told him about those men at my house who ambushed us...."

"Don't." Mike held up a hand. "Second guessing doesn't help. Worrying about things you can't control will make you crazy, Gerry. Trust me, that's one thing I've learned."

She looked at him and her eyes filled with tears. "Mike, I'm not physically brave. I majored in physics and math. I'm an analyst, a computer geek turned project manager...."

Mike took her hand in his and held it until she stopped talking. He leaned across the table and kissed her on the forehead. "Bravery isn't a lack of fear; it's doing what's needed even when you're terrified. That assassin at your house had me cold until you stood up, yelled, and waved an empty gun to distract him. That was one of the most courageous things I've ever seen."

"Somehow I doubt that." She was sobbing quietly.

"Don't. You're a gutsy lady, and you probably saved my life." Mike took out a handkerchief and gently wiped the streaks from her face. He looked down at her. Her hair was disheveled, her makeup was a mess and she was beautiful. They sat like that for what seemed a long time, until he could feel her growing calm.

"Are you okay?" he asked.

"I'm working on it." She forced a weak smile. "Until today the only things I've shot in my life are paper targets. I saw you charging down the barrel of that man's weapon to save me, and I had to do something. I'm not used to putting people in harm's way...."

Especially your dad, Mike thought. He paused for a moment and when he spoke his voice was very calm. "Even if something has happened to your father, it's not your fault."

She looked carefully around the room, checking that no one was within earshot. "I'm not going to discuss anything classified here."

He nodded slowly.

"It's a tricky situation between Cybertech and the agency. Neither side trusts the other."

"Yes," he said. *That's hardly surprising. Iron John was always tough as nails, and NSA doesn't trust anyone.*

"It's why I have this job. Dad trusts me, as does the agency. I'm in the middle."

"That's a very odd arrangement," he said.

She sighed, glancing around the room. "There's an uneasy truce between the agency and Cybertech, and a lot of pressure to get this program in place and running. You know where the pressure is coming from."

"I sure do," Mike said wryly, not wanting to speak the President's name. He suppressed a smile, trying to imagine how NSA's director felt about having a maverick Marine put in charge, and his deputy pulled off the project.

He's got to be pissed. He apparently didn't trust Gerry enough to let her run the program without supervision, he thought. *Hence Tibbs, whom neither you nor President Hale trusted. Bad move, especially for a spook, and that's why I'm involved.* Mike waited for Gerry to continue.

"As you probably know, my employer has a mix of developmental and operational responsibility. We sometimes use technology that others develop. Do you know what a skunkworks is?"

"Of course," he said. "I sometimes teach military history. It's an antiquated term, meaning 'a department or laboratory involved in secret, cutting-edge research.' Right?"

Gerry nodded. "The agency generally purchases equipment to its specifications. Generally, but not always. Sometimes when we're working at the edges of technology and we trust the contractor, we give them a lot of room to write the specs. That's the case here. Dad is coming with a proposal that defines our project."

Mike thought for a long moment. "That document would be highly classified."

"Very much so," she said. "Cybertech has the appropriate facility clearances." Just then her phone rang. She quickly snatched it off the table.

"Yes?" She listened for a long time, then put her hand over the phone and turned to Mike. "Cybertech's aircraft is still on the ground, abandoned. Dad and his people are missing. Kate has the local police chief on the line. Do you want to talk to him?"

"I sure do." Mike slid closer, took the phone and held it out so she could listen. "This is General Mickelson, USMC. I request your cooperation. The missing people were working on a classified project for me. I need to know the local situation."

"General, I'm Chief Ward, Sandy Junction police." There was a short laugh. "The local situation is dark, wet, and foggy as hell. I just got here. Black as the inside of a goat, and spooky. Creeps me out."

"What do you mean?" asked Mike.

"Like something out of a bad movie, where the monsters get 'em. Fog eats up sound like a blanket, and you can't see shit. Makes the hair on the back of my neck stand up.

"There's not a soul around, far as I can tell. The airport perimeter gate was closed and we had to use the code to get in."

"How does that make it spooky?" persisted Mike.

"Well, it damn sure ain't normal. There's a vehicle sitting with the front doors open, lights on, and engine running. Cybertech's hangar door is wide open. All the hangar lights are on and their aircraft is pulled out. Fancy jet sitting there with the door open in the rain and its lights on. Like I said, maybe the monsters got 'em. It ain't natural."

"Can you secure the area?"

"Can and did. Figured this would be evidence. Buddy Johnson was the first man here, and I told him on the radio not to let nobody touch nothing."

"Good work, Chief. Please give me your phone number." Mike listened, wrote it in a small notebook, and then read it back for confirmation.

"I'm sending you help. They'll mention my name, but check their ID anyway."

"Thank you, General."

"This is a national security matter. I need you to keep everyone away, especially the press. I'm coming myself, tomorrow, soon as I can get there. Keep a secure perimeter. I'll inform the FBI, ask them to send the best CSI unit they have out there and tell 'em to call you."

"No problem." A faint laugh came over the phone. "I'll be right here, waiting for the little green guys to come back, or whatever."

Mike thanked the Chief and hung up. "I need to make one more call." Gerry nodded, and he punched in a sequence of numbers on her phone.

"This is General Mickelson. I need to speak with Judy immediately."

"I'm Judy, and I know who you are, General. Is this line secure?"

"No, it's not. I need two things urgently. When can I see the boss for 15 minutes?"

"Will 0600 do? I don't want to wake him unless it's absolutely necessary."

"That'll work. I need one more thing. I'm going to call the Homeland Security Director and ask for a 48-hour situation-red lockdown on the Portland, Oregon area."

"Now?" she asked, sounding surprised.

"Yes, now. I'll make the call as soon as I get off with you. I'd appreciate a backup call from your office confirming my authority. I'll be leaving for Oregon tomorrow morning."

There was a long pause on the line. "That's within your authority, General. I confirm a lockdown on Portland, Oregon. We'll back you up. Is there anything else?"

"Not now. I'll see you in the morning, I expect. Thank you, Judy."

He punched the phone off, and looked across the table. "Let's get out of here, Gerry. It's going to be a long day tomorrow…."

"May I come with you? To Oregon, I mean."

"Sure, if you'll promise me something." He threw some money down and got ready to leave.

"What?"

"Don't start blaming yourself. I know there's nothing harder than waiting and sweating it out, but blaming yourself for doing your job doesn't help."

"I'll try." She sounded stronger. "Thank you."

"I'm glad to have you along." Mike smiled gently. "For one thing, John's your father, and I doubt I could stop you. For another, you're not expendable. I don't want to let you get too far away until we can assess the threats and ensure your safety. There's one more thing you need to understand."

She looked at him questioningly.

"Gerry, since last night I've had command responsibility for this project and its security. If you want to blame anyone, blame me. This has been a rolling screw up from the beginning, and I'm still trying to get out ahead of events."

She shook her head. "Don't you start blaming yourself either, okay?"

"I'm not, but I *am* taking responsibility," he said, passing her his car keys. "Will you drive? I have to get a couple of things started before I update the President."

"Sure, why not?" She flashed a quick grin. "I've always wanted to drive a tank, but Dad wouldn't let me."

At least she still has her sense of humor, Mike thought. *This is one ballsy lady I've got here.* He calmly got up, helped pull her chair back, and followed her to the door.

What the hell do I tell the President? he wondered. *I've been on this for less than a day. I almost lost my program manager, and now our prime contractor is missing in action – along with the master plan for whatever the hell it is that we are supposed to be doing to accomplish what the President wants us to do. We've been attacked twice and the FBI doesn't have a clue as to what's going on or who's behind it. This is becoming a monumental cluster fuck.*

CHAPTER SIX
CRAZY AS IT SOUNDS

52,000 Feet above the Rockies

Gerry walked into the small lounge and pulled the curtain closed behind her. She smiled at Mike reading a thick folder of papers, eased herself into a chair, and glanced out the window.

There was no sense of motion. Except for the drone of the engines, it was if they were suspended in space. At this altitude, the cloudless sky was a penetrating violet so intense that its shimmering clarity hurt her eyes. Far below, she could see a blanket of white. Up here, it was oddly peaceful and the outside world seemed far away.

"You look rested," she said

"I'm doing better. I caught a power nap, and it helped quite a bit. It was nice of the President to provide us with such comfortable transport."

"Yes," she agreed, easing the shade down. "It's certainly well equipped. What is this, Air Force Three?"

"Not quite." Mike grinned. "The military calls it a C-20. It's a modified Gulfstream XII, and the President's entourage wouldn't fit, I'm afraid. He borrowed this from the State Department. It has an intercontinental range and carries twelve plus the crew comfortably."

She nodded.

"Lieutenant Clover said his men thought they'd died and gone to heaven." His grin broadened. "Military transport is rather more basic. Would you like some coffee?"

"Please," she said. He poured her a cup, then one for himself from a small carafe.

She took a sip. It was excellent.

"You've been working," she said. "Is there any news?"

"We're starting to make some progress." He was avoiding her eyes.

"They haven't found Dad, have they?"

"Not yet."

"I need to know about my father, Mike. We need to find him."

"Yes." He nodded somberly. "The President said the same."

"I appreciate it," she said, watching him closely.

Mike tried to look encouraging. He didn't succeed very well.

"You're not hopeful of finding Dad alive, are you?" She searched his face, wondering if he knew more than he was telling her.

"I'm not sure," he admitted, "but there is always hope."

She closed her eyes and put her face in her hands. A long moment passed; then she slowly raised her head and looked at him. "How well did you know my father?"

"I was a junior officer when I served under him. I was a Marine, and he was regular Army, but we got along well." Mike paused and seemed to think for a moment. "We all respected him. He had integrity and honor."

We're talking about Dad in the past tense. "I want to know about the investigation."

"Remember the big black guy? The FBI agent?"

"Yes, of course. He has a biblical name," she said. "Sampson, wasn't it?"

"Simpson, spelled with an 'I.' Obadiah Simpson," Mike said, nodding. "I've checked him out thoroughly, and I like what I learned. Simpson's got an excellent reputation for results. He thinks you were the target in Maryland."

"How is that relevant?"

"He thinks your father's disappearance in Oregon is linked to the Maryland attack and apparently the Bureau is deploying resources to back his hunch. Simpson has a crime scene team out at the airport in Oregon now."

That's hopeful, she thought. "Have they learned anything?"

"Not yet. Simpson says it's very odd."

"How so?" she asked. "What's odd?"

"The total absence of evidence baffles the CSI team. Whatever happened out there, the people involved tidied up fastidiously." He tapped the yellow folder. "That country police chief was right. He said it was spooky, not like anything he'd seen. The crime scene evidence has the FBI scratching their heads."

"Tell me why," she said.

"It doesn't fit an assassination, theft, or abduction. It doesn't fit espionage. It doesn't fit anything they've run across, and that's their expertise."

She searched his eyes, but didn't say anything.

"The shooters in Maryland were using standard *jihad* tactics. Those are very predictable and usually messy. Fanatics sent on a mission to kill and die. The Oregon incident was nothing like that."

"I don't understand," she said. "What does that mean?"

"I'm damned if I know," Mike admitted. "Until we find out, we should assume your father is still alive. If someone wanted to kill him, there should be a body, but there's not."

"I'll hold that thought," she said, "and pray he's safe." She thought for a long moment. "There's more, isn't there?"

He nodded.

"What else?"

"Whatever happened in Oregon, it was tightly managed. Your father just vanished into thin air. *Poof.*"

"What's your point?"

"There is purpose at work here. Simpson thinks some mastermind is managing these events, and I think he's right. There's a pro behind this. We just don't know who."

"And the main evidence for his saying so is the total lack of evidence?"

"Pretty much," Mike agreed. "Crazy as it sounds...."

"You're right. That doesn't make any sense at all."

Mike shrugged. "It's like how the astronomers discover planets and moons they can't see. They study unusual patterns and motions in other celestial bodies that can be observed. That leads them to find and even describe invisible objects. Likewise, some powerful outside force is at work here. It creates patterns of anomalous behavior in the things that we can observe."

It's not as exact as celestial mechanics, but I do respect professional intuition, Gerry thought. *I'd still like some hard evidence though.*

"Didn't the FBI find anything?" "They're still looking," Mike said softly, "and we'll be there ourselves soon. Where is Sandy Junction, anyway? The pilot says the airport there is adequate."

And you're changing the subject, she thought. "Is there any good news?"

"I was getting to that. The FBI thinks our project plans are safe."

She frowned. "How can they be sure?"

"Your dad's secretary told the FBI he'd put them in some type of a portable vault protected with a Thermite self-destruct. The vault was found locked to housings in his car. NSA has identified the vault. They say it's tamperproof and say they can't open it. They're assuming the plans are still safely secured in the vault. Do you know anything about this?"

Gerry nodded.

"Can you open it?"

She nodded.

Mike looked at her, but didn't speak. He waited and let the silence build.

Finally he said, "You need to make a decision. For this arrangement to work, you are going to have to talk with me freely, to trust me."

"You're right," she finally said. "It's experimental. We call it a Q9 box. I gave one to Dad and showed him how to use it. We put docking stations in his office and the aircraft too. If anyone tries to open it improperly, or it's away from its docking station for more than ten minutes, it self-destructs."

"Thank you. Could your father have opened it under duress?"

"He could not have opened it under any circumstances. Once it's sealed, it takes two key codes to open it. Dad had only one, the slave code. Only I had the master."

"You didn't share the codes with anyone, did you?"

"Of course not," she said with a tinge of anger. "Nor did I leave them written on my desk pad or in the ladies' restroom, if that's what you're going to ask next."

"I wasn't implying anything, Gerry," he said softly. "I just wondered if your former boss might have the access code."

"*Tibbs?*"

Mike's eyes widened, and she forced herself to take several breaths and speak calmly. She hadn't meant to scream. "No, absolutely not. I certainly did not give the codes to Tibbs."

"Okay," he said, with a placating gesture.

"The Q9 is a denial device, not a safe. It's designed to destroy, not preserve, to keep sensitive materials out of the wrong hands."

He nodded.

"I programmed it myself, and I didn't share my codes with anyone. I wrote the slave code on a piece of paper and showed it to my father. We didn't even speak it aloud. I told Dad to memorize it and not write it down. He did so in my presence. When he'd done that, I burned the paper myself."

Mike nodded and flashed a grin. "That's what I bet Agent Simpson."

"What are you talking about?"

"Twenty bucks." Mike's grin broadened. "He was worried the Cybertech plan might have been compromised. I told him I had more faith in you than that."

"Only twenty dollars?"

"It was a symbolic wager." Mike grinned. "I expected I'd win and didn't want to take advantage of Obie."

"Thank you." She thought for a moment. "Do you think NSA told Simpson about the Q9 devices?"

"He only knew it existed and was some kind of security device. They warned him not to try and open it."

"That's still restricted information. Apparently my director is cooperating."

"NSA is cooperating fully." His look was grim, and he didn't elaborate.

"Sharing is a two way street, Mike. I have to know what happened to Dad."

"I know," he said, looking uncomfortable.

"About the arrangement: Whether my father is alive or dead, I have to know what happened." There was anger in her voice. "I want to know who targeted my father and why."

"Me too," Mike said. "So does the President. He's made the investigation a top priority for the FBI. We'll get to the bottom of this. If there's any way to get your father back, we will. I give you my word."

"Thank you." Gerry felt less alone. It was a relief to trust him.

A Remote Farm House in Jasper County, Oregon

Ahmed looked up in irritation as his man entered.

"Ana Mehtag El Doctor." Mohammad looked worried.

"Speak English," Ahmed ordered.

"We need a doctor for Karim. Fuad got the bleeding stopped, but it's a stomach wound, and the bullet is still in there."

"Explain to me how this could have happened," Ahmed said with no noticeable sympathy in his tone, demeanor, or expression.

"I do not know, Ahmed," Mohammad said, averting his eyes. "Fuad and I heard a muffled shot. It was all over when we got there in the van. Karim was on the ground bleeding."

"Karim was careless. The old man had a weapon, a relic of some type." He opened the drawer in the table, and pulled out a gun. "An M1911A1 Colt .45, to be specific. A small cannon. He got off one shot, through the seam of Karim's body armor."

"Karim said you prevented him from killing the old man."

"I do not want that man killed," Ahmed said, slamming his hand down on the table. "That's what I told Karim, what I told Fuad, and what I am telling you. That is my order."

"I don't understand, Sir," Mohammad said, shaking his head. "You wanted them all killed and disposed of…"

"I changed my mind about this one."

"Yes, Sir."

"We can kill him later. While he lives, he may be useful. The Koran says, 'My mercy encompasses all things, so I will ordain it specially for those who guard me against evil,'" Ahmed said. "I show mercy now because the old man may yet be useful to us."

"Yes, Sir," Mohammad said, averting his eyes.

"Have you disposed of the pilots?" Ahmed asked.

"Yes, Sir. We buried them behind the tree line, about ten meters back into the forest. We covered the graves with brush. No one will notice them." Mohammad paused and looked at Ahmed pleadingly. "What of Karim?"

"Allah will decide," Ahmed said.

Mohammad frowned. "The Koran says, 'We responded to him and took off what harm he had, and We gave him his family...' Karim's last name is Aziz, but he is Yasir Fuad's cousin, the son of his mother's twin sister. They are family and Fuad wants to help him."

"Then let him tend his cousin's wound and don't bother me with this matter," Ahmed said, making a gesture of dismissal.

"Karim needs medical help, Sir." Mohammad looked somber, but determined. "He's served us well. Surely, we can let Fuad take him to a doctor?"

"Not in Oregon," Ahmed said. "What keeps us safe is that no crime has been noticed. Taking someone with a gunshot wound to a doctor would raise questions."

"The men are worried, Sir. Watching the news. There are roadblocks up already. They're looking for us. It's on the television."

"No." Ahmed shook his head and held up the newspaper he'd been reading. "This is the local paper, the *Oregonian*. Have you read it?"

"I don't read English," Mohammad said.

Or anything else, Ahmed thought. "The headlines say federal authorities have declared Portland a 'lock down.' State and local officials are angry. They're protesting that interference, saying there's no explanation, much less any evidence that justifies it. There's only a small mention on a back page about Cybertech's missing people."

Mohammad frowned, looking puzzled.

"Do you know how many people are missing in Oregon right now?" Ahmed demanded.

"No, Sir," Mohammad said.

"Over two hundred," Ahmed said. "They're not really looking for the Cybertech people, though they've added them to the missing persons list. There's no mention of a crime. No one here is looking for us."

"Except for the federal lock down."

"That too shall pass," Ahmed said. "Don't worry about it."

"Tend to Karim. Keep him comfortable. Tell Fuad and Karim to trust in Allah. Oregon's officials will solve the problem for us." *Then I can go home and leave this dank place.*

"How will they solve it?" Mohammad asked.

"They resent federal interference. Soon they'll make them lift this lock down and go on to their next crisis." Ahmed smiled. "All we have to do is wait."

"Do you have a plan, Sir?"

"I always have plans." Ahmed smiled thinly. "Right now, we'll wait and trust Allah. We've accomplished our primary mission. Now we must avoid attracting attention."

"Yes, Ahmed." Mohammad looked hesitant. "One more thing, Sir...."

"What do you want?" Ahmed asked.

"Fuad wants to kill the old man."

Ahmed thought for a moment before he nodded. "He and Karim may do it together when I so order. It will be good for morale."

"*Insh'allah,*" Mohammad said. "I'll tell them."

"Until I give the command, they are to guard our captive's life as if it were their own," Ahmed said. "If anything happens to him, I will hold them both responsible. I will also hold you responsible. Do you understand me?"

"Yes, Ahmed. The man will not be harmed until you give the order." Mohammad bowed his head in acceptance of the order and took his leave.

8,000 Feet over Sandy Junction, Oregon

So much for the smooth comfortable ride, Gerry thought. *This is awful.*

The airplane plummeted, then recovered, its engines howling in protest. It lurched again as they dropped through the clouds. She looked over at Mike. He was trying to cinch his seat belt tighter.

She heard muttered curses from Clover's SEALs in the back of plane. Her own belt bit into her hips painfully, and she groped a sick sack out of the pocket next to her.

"They're having a storm," Mike said mildly, his voice sounding too loud as the engine noise softened again. Then the power came back up, and there were thuds and whirring noises.

"Landing gear, flaps, and speed brakes, sounds like," he said. "Must be getting close."

She didn't dare answer. Her palms were sweaty, and she was struggling to keep from throwing up.

Suddenly they dropped out of the clouds. Trees flashed by, reaching for them, and they slammed down hard on the runway. The plane was jerking rapidly from side to side and the engine noise was now deafening. She couldn't see anything out the window but water and spray.

"Don't worry; this is normal," Mike said over the roar. "Must be a short damned runway though. Anti-skid's working hard. Reverse thrust too."

Then they were slowing rapidly. The engine noise faded to a soft murmur. When they turned, Gerry could see the plane was right at the end of the runway. There was maybe a hundred yards of grass and then a chain link fence topped with barbed wire.

Into the near silence, one of the SEALs in the back said clearly, "I hate fucking airplanes."

"Hold it down." That was Lieutenant Clover's voice.

"Yes, Sir," came the reply.

"That's normal too," Mike said quietly. "SEALs prefer to jump out of perfectly good airplanes, rather than endure landings. It's one of those macho things…."

They have a point, Gerry thought. She pulled out a bottle of water and took a sip, then another. It helped, but her stomach was still unsettled. She took several deep breaths.

"Are you all right?"

"I think so." She nodded and tried to smile. "Did you say that was a normal landing?"

Mike shrugged. Before he could answer, the engines were whining down into silence.

The cockpit door popped open, and a voice called out. "Stay strapped in till they get us chocked. They want us to park out here. We're going to shut down now."

In the rear, she heard Lieutenant Clover echo the command. "Stay put till they get everything shut down." A chorus of acknowledgments followed.

They could hear the pilots going through their checklists. There were clunking noises from outside, and then she heard the door opening at the rear of the airplane. *It's so good to be on the ground*, she thought.

Gerry closed her eyes and took a few deep breaths. When she looked up, one of the pilots was standing over Mike. He was very young and wearing an Air Force uniform with captain's bars on the shoulders.

"We've arrived, Sir." He looked pleased.

Mike looked at him quizzically. "I noticed," he said. "Why are we parking here?"

"We're kind of large for this field, Sir," the pilot said. "Landing weight was about 47,000 pounds, and the locals are worried we might be too heavy for their ramp. They asked us to shut-down out here in the boonies on the run-up pad." He shrugged. "We wouldn't want to break up their asphalt, would we?"

"No," Mike said.

"It's raining pretty hard, so the FBI types are sending a van for you and the lady."

"Very good." Mike nodded. "Thank you."

"It's our pleasure, Sir. Thank you for flying the friendly skies."

Another man came out of the cockpit. He was somewhat older. "Another safe landing," he said.

Mike looked up at him and raised an eyebrow. "What if you'd run off the end of the runway, Major?"

"Then I wouldn't say that, Sir. My orders were get you here quickly, General. It would have added two or three hours if we'd gone into Portland International and you had to take surface transport. The field's a bit tight, and the braking action was only fair with all that standing water, but that's what they pay us for, Sir. No sweat."

"Yes, quite right." Mike popped his seat belt and stood up, studying the pilot's nametag. "Nice landing, Major Collins. Thank you."

"Thank you, Sir," the pilot said. He managed a smile.

The CSI team was wearing yellow rain slickers with large white letters "FBI" on the front and back. Agent Sommers, a tall thin man with freckles and red hair, was in charge. Sommers was damp but polite, and his team seemed to have most of the airport marked out with crime scene tape.

They were standing in front of an open hangar. A small jet with Cybertech's name and logo on the side was sitting on the ramp looking forlorn. Its front hatch was open and the navigation lights were still on. Gerry wondered how that could be. Then she noticed someone had hooked up a ground power unit to save the aircraft's batteries.

A white Lincoln was sitting next to the plane, blocking it. Gerry thought it was an odd place to park. There were two agents working in the car, and she could see several more through the aircraft windows.

"We were taking bets on that landing, General. Interesting to watch," Sommers said pleasantly. "Pretty big airplane for this field, isn't it?"

Mike shrugged. "The pilot said it was perfectly safe."

"They always do, don't they?" Sommers said with a knowing smile. "We're not doing much good standing out here in the rain. We turned off the heat in the hangar with the doors open like that, but there's a warm, dry building on the other side of the field."

"Have your people found anything?" Mike asked, leading the agent and Gerry over into the shelter of the open hangar.

"Off the record, General?" Sommers asked, looking at Gerry questioningly.

"She's with NSA," Mike said, "and one of the missing people is her father. Yes, off the record is fine. Just tell us what you've found."

"Excuse me, ma'am," Sommers said, looking at Gerry. He sounded sincere.

She nodded and tried to smile. There was water running down her neck, and her hair was hanging down in her eyes. She brushed it back absently. She was cold, worried, and she felt vaguely nauseous.

"I've been getting a stream of rockets from Washington." Sommers turned his look to Mike. "People are pretty upset over this. Do you know Agent Simpson?"

Mike nodded. "Obadiah Simpson. I've met him."

"He's the agent in charge," Sommers said. "Wants a prelim report on this in his hands by tomorrow. He told me the Bureau is putting together a task force, but didn't explain what's going on. Can you tell me anything?"

Mike and Gerry exchanged a look. He looked grim. She shrugged and spread her hands in a helpless gesture.

"Unofficially?" asked Mike. "The FBI has the lead on this investigation."

"Yes," Sommers said. "That's fair enough, General."

"There was an incident in Maryland yesterday. Arab assassins with high tech body armor and automatic weapons. Agent Simpson thinks they were after the lady here, Ms. Gerry Patton. Her maiden name is Giles, and her father John Giles runs Cybertech."

"Is there any other connection to Cybertech?" Sommers asked.

Mike sighed. "Cybertech is a contractor to NSA. As part of that work, John Giles was coming to Washington last night. He never got there."

"I see." Sommers was frowning. Clearly he didn't see at all. "Exactly what does Ms. Patton do for NSA?" he asked. "And how are you involved?"

Mike shook his head. "I'm afraid that's classified. And a separate issue. The key thing is John's probable abduction and the attack on Gerry."

"Which are related?"

"Agent Simpson is convinced that the shooters in Maryland were after Gerry. He's calling it a terrorist attack, and he thinks whatever happened out here is a part of it. The FBI has jurisdiction for that investigation, and we need some answers fast."

"Yes, Sir," Sommers said. He didn't look happy.

"I can fill you in a bit more about the Maryland shootings when we're out of the weather." Mike looked at Gerry, then out around the field. "Do you have perimeter security out?"

"The airport is fenced, there are local cops at both gates and my team is armed," Sommers said. "Sandy Junction's a pretty quiet place."

So was my neighborhood, Gerry thought. She didn't speak. She was watching Mike and wondering when they could get into a warm building.

"So what exactly did you find, Agent?" Mike asked.

"What did we find?" Sommers looked embarrassed. He sighed. "So far nothing. Nada. Zero. Zip. Not a thing. I've got my people going through the crime scene for the third time. We checked, we rechecked, and now we're checking again. Nothing."

Mike looked at him questioningly.

"We're taking samples and prints for the lab to check, but I'm not optimistic," Sommers said glumly. "Washington's not going to like that, are they?"

"It seems you have a problem," Gerry said softly.

Mike paused and thought for a few moments. "Where exactly have you looked?"

"At the crime scene, of course," Sommers said in a puzzled tone. "Inside the area we have taped off. We've checked the hangar, the vehicles, and the ground around here. Normal procedure. There's nothing. The people just vanished. *Poof.* It's odd."

"I see," Mike said thoughtfully. He seemed to come to a decision. "I brought a SEAL team with me."

Sommers looked surprised. "I thought SEALs were Navy?"

"They are." Mike shrugged. "I borrowed them. Interagency cooperation."

"Sort of like having the military working with the FBI?"

"Maybe not that extreme." Mike smiled thinly. "If you have no objections, I'd like to put my SEALs out for perimeter security. They have recon and C-T training."

"Of course," Sommers said, looking perplexed. "I'll want a joint team briefing so we don't accidentally start shooting at each other, of course. Do you want to take local command?"

"No," Mike said. "Your crime scene investigation is the main thing. We'll just give you some extra eyes and security support."

"What are you looking for?" Sommers asked.

"I have no idea," Mike said with a sigh. "Maybe we'll get lucky. Let's get out of the weather and go somewhere we can talk."

"Sure. Incidentally, the local police chief wanted to see you when you got here. I'll give him a call."

"Please don't, not yet," Mike said. "I want to see what Lieutenant Clover and his men come up with first. Drop me at our aircraft first. I'll walk over when we get done."

"Certainly," Sommers said, holding the rear door of his car open for Gerry.

Mike and Lieutenant Clover slowly walked around the inside of the airport perimeter fence. Clover carried an assault rifle, and Mike had a pistol holstered on his belt. Clover had a radio earpiece in his right ear, the push-to-talk button dangling from his left sleeve.

Their boots sloshed as they walked. The rain had let up, and the sun started to peek through in places, but the ground was soggy.

"The Bureau boys are baffled?" asked Clover.

"So far there's a lack of evidence," Mike said. "They're working on it."

"Seaman Andrews is part Cherokee, Sir. He's a great tracker and point man. I've got him checking around. He'll find something if it's there."

I hope so, Mike thought. *If not, we've come a long way for nothing.*

They were most of the way around the field when Clover looked surprised and clicked his radio, raising his left hand to his mouth. "Affirmative," he said softly into the microphone. "Where are you?"

He stopped and listened for a moment, then clicked the radio again. "Anyone else see anything?" He listened. "Okay, hold your stations. The general and I are going over to see what Andrews found."

Inevitably, it was on the far side of the field. They slogged across and studied the fence carefully. It was a good six feet high with three strands of barbed wire on top. The fence was intact, with no marks and no footprints anywhere around.

"Want me to cut it, General?" Clover asked.

"I do not," Mike said. "Don't want to climb it either. Tell your man to hang on, Lieutenant. We'll go through the gate."

It took them another fifteen minutes to get there. Rather than follow the fence line though the puddles, they went out to the road and walked back, stopping when they heard a soft whistle from the bushes.

"In here, Sir." Andrews appeared as if by magic, holding the bushes back for them.

"Put your feet where I do, please," he said. "Don't want to mess up any sign."

They complied without comment. Andrews led them back almost to the fence. Mike looked around. They could see both the main gate and the Cybertech hangar. Andrews pointed that out, and they both nodded in acknowledgment.

"So what do you have?" Clover asked.

"It's right here, Sir. See for yourself." Andrews pointed at the ground in a sweeping gesture. Mike looked, but didn't see anything.

"What?" Clover asked. Apparently he didn't see anything either.

"Good place for a shooter, Sir," Andrews said. "There was one man here. See the indentation under that bush? He rested the butt of a weapon there, probably an AK. He was here for a while, I think."

Andrews pointed toward the fence. "There are three cigarette butts over by that tree. Seven matches. Nasty habit, but he must have been determined to light his cancer sticks in the rain. Several footprints too, maybe, but it's hard to tell with all this rain to wash it out."

"Good work, Andrews," Clover said. "I'll get the FBI types to come over. They have all the goodies to take imprints and things like that."

"Saved the best for last, Sir," Andrews said, looking pleased. "Over here."

He pointed under a bush. Mike looked. So did Clover. They frowned at each other and shook their heads.

"I don't see shit," Clover said. "What are we looking for?

"Evidence, Sir." Andrews grinned. He took a pencil from his pocket and lifted the leaves gently. "See that?"

Mike saw a faint glint of metal. Brass.

"Bingo," Andrews said. "NATO 7.62 round. Common for assault weapons, but not much used for hunting. Not fired. Clumsy bastard dropped it."

"Is that what those Arab types were shooting at us in Maryland?" Mike asked.

"Yes, Sir," Clover said.

"It's what everybody shoots at us," Andrews said. "Shoot 'em at each other too. 7.62s are common as Coca-Cola. You just ain't a man 'till you get a weapon and cap off a few rounds. Ain't nothing like the sound of an AK to wake up the neighborhood, Sir."

Clover laughed. "It ought to be every kid's first gun."

"Yes," Mike said, smiling. "Thank you, Seaman. I think you've made Agent Conner's day. Good work."

"Thank you, Sir," Andrews said.

"You've made my day too," Mike said. *We were past due for some good news.*

CHAPTER SEVEN
YOU'VE BOXED ME IN

Sandy Junction Airport

When the police chief entered, Gerry was sipping a warm diet Pepsi. It tasted odd, but helped settle her stomach.

She looked him up and down, a large man with a paunch, clear aviator glasses, a big revolver on his belt, and a badge that said "Chief." She frowned and then realized she knew him.

He and Dad used to go hunting together, she remembered. *He's gained weight.* She struggled for a moment before she could come up with his name. "Chief Ward," she said, finally. "It's been years. How have you been?"

"Call me Bobby, Ms. Giles," he said, nodding. "Been good. Nice to see you again, but wish it was under better circumstances. Damned sorry about your father...."

"Thank you," she said. "I appreciate your help."

"Not a problem. Your dad's a good man. Been hunting together for years. We got us an elk just a month or so back, and split it."

"He liked hunting with you," she said. "I go by Gerry Patton now. Patton's my mother's maiden name. Dad and my employer got crosswise, and I got tired of explaining."

"Happens," the chief said. "Have you seen your mom?"

"Not yet. I just got here."

He looked vaguely uncomfortable for a moment. "I came out to meet the Marine. Is he around?"

"General Mickelson is out doing something with his men, but he's coming. He'll be here in a moment. Do you have any idea what happened?"

"Don't. Wish I did." The chief scowled, pulling out a chair and sitting down across from her. "That's what those fancy assed FBI boys are supposed to be figuring out. Never had a disappearance right here in town. Certainly nothing like this."

"Have you had them elsewhere?" she asked. "Disappearances, I mean."

"A few. Hikers get lost, sometimes." He shrugged. "Rob Parker was out hunting in the hills three years ago and fell in a ravine. Broke his damned fool neck. His wife, Helen, made a big stink about finding him cause of the life insurance. Put up a reward."

"Did you find him?"

"Nope. We combed the hills for weeks. Burned up a lot of hours. State Police put up an airplane too."

He shook his head, remembering. "Some kid and his dog finally found him a few months ago. Not much left after the coyotes and other critters got done, but it was Rob's gun and the dental records matched, so the kid got a $10,000 reward. Helen got the insurance money and Rob's kids are now going to U of O, down in Eugene."

Now there's a happy ending, Gerry thought.

"That kind of thing breaks the monotony." The chief shrugged again. "Mostly we put a few drunks in jail on weekends and try to keep people from beating up on each other. Like everywhere, lots of petty stuff: Vandalism, burglary, traffic stops, neighbors hassling each other. Keeps me busy, but it's a peaceful town, basically."

"No one's ever disappeared from town?" she persisted.

"Not like this, they haven't. A few kids run off, maybe one or two a year. Wives or husbands skip sometimes too. Had a pair of 'em run off together, last year." The chief laughed briefly, almost a snort. "Turned out the abandoned mates got together a few months later to comfort each other. Now they're all friends again. Everybody just sorta swapped partners and houses. Good neighbors, I guess."

Gerry didn't smile. Her look was somber. "If my father had been abducted, wouldn't someone have seen him leaving?"

"You'd think so, but we don't have any witnesses. There's only one road in, and Buddy, my Sergeant, didn't see anyone leaving," the chief said. "But it was a couple of hours before your father was missed, so a kidnapping is possible. I'll leave that to the FBI, Ms. Patton."

He sighed and shook his head. "Nothing like this has ever happened before. Nothing even close. This airport's a secure area. All the gates were shut tight when my people got here. Had to use the code to get in. Doesn't make sense."

"No, it doesn't," she agreed. "Do the gates automatically open to let cars out?"

"Yeah, they do." He nodded. "There is no automatic log. The gates look okay, but there are some scrapes on the tarmac where they roll out. It's hard to tell...."

Just then Mike entered with Agent Sommers.

"Afternoon, Chief," Sommers said. He looked around the room, helped himself to coffee and a doughnut, and finally sat down next to Gerry.

"Chief Ward, I appreciate your help," Mike said. "Thanks for keeping the area secure."

"Not a problem," the chief said. "Do you know what happened yet?"

"We're working on it," Mike said.

"Be nice if you shared," the chief said.

Mike nodded, looking at the FBI man.

Agent Sommers gave Mike an odd look, but didn't protest. He gave the chief a rundown of what his team had done, taking time to detail the procedures used, using many technical terms. His discussion went on for about five minutes.

It's the same as what they told Mike, Gerry thought, *but a longer version. He's talking about what they did, not what they found. Because they didn't find anything.*

The chief apparently had similar thoughts. He was looking at Sommers skeptically, frowning. "Might have been some blood on the grass by the driver's door of the car. We told your team. Put a tarp down over it. Did you check it out?"

"Yes, of course." Sommers sounded irritated. "The ground's too wet to tell much, but there is a faint discoloration. We classified it as 'unknown.' That's one of the samples we're sending to the lab. My team isn't optimistic, but you never know…"

The chief drummed his fingers on the table absently. "Let me see if I got this right," he said. "You got nothing. Not a damned thing. Is that about it?"

Sommers looked annoyed. "Like the general said, we're working on it. Our investigation is just getting started."

Mike didn't comment. Gerry gave him a questioning look. He shrugged noncommittally and shook his head. He was watching the two men carefully. *Mike knows something*, Gerry thought. She could see it in his eyes.

"This is a key point, Agent," the chief said. "Is there evidence of a crime, or not? I need to know."

"I can't say yet," Sommers said.

The chief shook his head. "If you can't say, then you do say. You're saying 'no,' aren't you?"

"That's not what I said at all." Sommers looked exasperated. "This is an active case. We're just getting started."

"Okay for you, maybe. Not so good for the general and me though," the chief said. "Makes problems for him. Makes problems for me."

"Why?" Mike asked.

"We don't have staff like the FBI, General. I got nine officers to cover maybe a third of Jasper County. Five are on duty now, and all but one is tied up working on this."

"So you're spread thin. Life's a bitch," Sommers interrupted. "What's your point?"

"My point is without any proof of a crime, the mayor expects me to be out doing my job. He wants my officers out patrolling. He wants me to keep the town peaceful and out of the news. Anything bad happens, I have to explain," the chief said. "He's already riding my ass."

"We're just asking for professional courtesy," Sommers said.

"You're getting it," the chief said. "Unfortunately, things are getting political. Mayor wants me to stay out of this, but I left officers at the gates. Got another one out on the highway."

"What are you saying?" Mike asked. "People are missing, national security is involved, and…." He stopped. The chief was shaking his head.

"FBI said those secret papers were recovered." The chief gave Sommers an intense look. "Isn't that right?"

"Yes," Sommers said. "They were recovered."

"No national security is involved then. Just some missing people. City attorney says it's the FBI's problem." The chief sighed. "It gets worse. There's a rumor some rag head aliens are involved. That so?"

"The proper term is Arabs," Sommers said.

He's got that odd look again, Gerry thought. *I think Sommers was ready to refuse when Mike asked him to brief the chief. I wonder why.*

"Arabs," Mike said, softly. "Interesting. How did this rumor get started?"

"City attorney said it was on CNN," the chief said. "He saw a file photo of you and some footage of three dead Arabs. Something about a shooting in Maryland. Mayor wants to know if it's connected."

"What did you tell him?" Sommers asked.

"Told him I didn't know," the chief said. "Was it?"

"I can't say. We're still investigating," Sommers said.

"You're going to have to say, and pretty soon." The chief hitched up his gun belt. "Anyone been charged with a crime?"

"We have three dead assassins in Washington," Mike said. "Foiled in the act with weapons in their hands. The FBI is investigating. Yes, they were Arabs. They had Mideastern complexions and were using *jihad* tactics and weapons handling. Does that help?"

"Nope. You didn't answer my question, General." The chief turned his attention to Agent Sommers. "Neither did you. Has anyone been charged with a crime here?"

"Not yet," Sommers admitted.

"And your best suspects are some foreigners, probably, but you don't know who?" the chief asked.

"We haven't identified any suspects," Sommers said, "but, yes, some of my superiors are inclined to suspect foreign involvement."

"Muslims?"

"Possibly."

"Here illegally?"

"Maybe."

"Would have been nice if you'd mentioned that," the chief said.

"I didn't know it myself until the general told me an hour ago," Sommers said. "I was ordered to get a CSI investigation started. That's what I'm doing."

"But you're looking for foreign nationals at the checkpoints?" the chief asked. "Checking ID to see if they're legal to be in the country?"

"I'm not involved in that operation," Sommers said.

Why is he evading the question? Gerry wondered. Apparently so did Mike.

"I ordered the lock down," Mike said. "Federal agencies are looking for the missing people, especially John Giles, and also for those who caused them to be missing. Whoever they are. What the hell's wrong with that?"

The chief shrugged.

"I can assure you national security is involved, papers or not," Mike said. "Colonel Giles was working on a highly classified program. We need to find him. That's why I'm here."

"Fair enough," the chief agreed, nodding, "but I still have a problem." He was looking at Agent Sommers. "You've boxed me in."

"What are you talking about?" Mike asked. "We're on the same side here."

"I'm talking about the fact that we have a big problem. I'd like to help you, but I can't," the chief said.

"Come on, Bobby," Gerry interrupted. "I want to find my father. So does the federal government. So do you."

"God's truth, I do," the chief agreed, "but we've got us a problem. ORS 181.850."

Gerry and Mike exchanged puzzled frowns. They glanced at Sommers, who had the odd look again. Finally, they both stared at the chief.

"Maybe you'd better explain," Mike said.

"Oregon Revised Statute 181.850." He was watching Sommers. "He knows."

The agent sighed deeply. "They have some funny laws out here, General."

"What's that got to do with finding her father?"

"No law enforcement agency of the State of Oregon or of any political subdivision of the state shall use agency monies, equipment or personnel for the purpose of detecting or apprehending persons whose only violation of law is that they are persons of foreign citizenship residing in the United States in violation of federal immigration laws," Sommers quoted.

"That's how it works," the chief said quietly. "Sorry."

Gerry felt her mouth hanging open in astonishment. "Aliens have their rights protected, even if our own citizens are at risk?"

"Un huh," the chief said. "We gotta be politically correct these days…"

Gerry took several deep breaths and closed her mouth firmly, not trusting herself to speak. *If you put it in a movie, no one would believe it. We need to move quickly to find my father and catch the people who took him, but we're wasting time talking about some stupid Oregon law. This is nuts.*

Mike looked like he was about to explode. It was the first time Gerry had seen him angry, even when they were being shot at.

"Are you saying you won't help us?" Mike demanded.

"I'm saying I **can't** help you." The chief shook his head. "It's the law, General. ORS 181.850. If aliens are involved, until you have names of people charged with a crime and warrants for their arrest, I can't help you look. If I do, I'm breaking the law. I could lose my job and my retirement. I could even go to jail."

"You're kidding," Gerry said. "Tell me this is some sick joke."

"No ma'am. Wish it was," the chief said sadly, shaking his head. "It's a bitch, but that's how it is. It's the law."

"How do we get around it?" Mike asked.

"I don't know," the chief said. "I honest to God don't know. But if you can find a way, I'd like to help." His voice was almost pleading. "I really would. John was my friend."

They all looked at Agent Sommers.

"For now, can we just agree we have a possible kidnapping and we don't know who did it?" Sommers asked. "That it's an FBI matter. That we're trying to save lives and we could use some help. Hell, for all we know, U.S. citizens may have committed the crime. Can we just let it float?"

"Can for a while," the chief said. "General's going to catch some shit though. Officials in Portland are all upset about the lock down. The mayor gave me a phone number and said to have him call them when he arrived."

"How long can you give us to sort this out, Bobbie?" Gerry asked softly.

"Couple of days. Maybe a bit longer. I'll tell the mayor I don't know anything about aliens. No little green guys, and no Arabs." The chief grinned. "Maybe I'll check around to make sure Arabs *weren't* involved. Mayor can't object to that, can he?"

"Thank you," she said.

"We appreciate the help, Chief," Mike said.

"I'll call Special Agent Simpson in Washington and ask for guidance as soon as I get my CSI team on its way," Sommers said. He shrugged and spread his hands. "I strongly suggest you don't discuss the lock down without legal counsel, General. Not with anyone."

"That's real good advice," the chief said.

Mike nodded.

Why is this so hard? Gerry wondered. "I just want to find my father. Why do we need to involve lawyers?"

The men exchanged grim looks, but no one answered her.

Lounge at the Sandy Junction Bed And Breakfast

Gerry looked at Mike. "Did we accomplish anything today?"

"It's too soon to say." He shrugged. "Your father didn't just wander off. It had to have been abduction. We'll meet again with Captain Ward and the FBI tomorrow."

"Are the people who did this still in Oregon?"

"Almost certainly." Mike nodded. "I've had the state locked down tight since about 30 minutes after the incident at the airport."

"What are you going to do next?"

"I'm not sure," he admitted. "We're losing the initiative."

She felt a tinge of alarm. "What do you mean?"

"We're getting diverted. This isn't about cops and crime scenes and Oregon laws, it's about national security."

"What about my father?"

"When we find out who did it and find them, we'll find your father."

"Bobby Ward is afraid to help," she said. "He's a family friend, but he's not going to put his job on the line. The locals aren't helping much."

"Kidnapping is a federal offense. So is interfering with a program crucial to the national security. The FBI has jurisdiction," Mike said.

"How does that help find my father?"

"I told you we'd discovered an unfired round at the crime scene. Brass case. American made, nothing fancy, but better than the old Soviet surplus stuff, a 7.62x39mm Federal Power-Shok 123 Grain SP Bullet 2350 fps."

"Did it have fingerprints on it or something?"

"They're still checking. The place where we found it had a clear view and field of fire to both the Cybertech hangar and the airport main gate. It's a good position for a sniper. About a hundred and fifty yards to the main gate, two hundred to your dad's car, and under three to the secondary gate where your father drove in."

"Knowing that doesn't tell us who did it," she said.

"It's a start," Mike said. "This was a military action, run by a trained field commander. There was planning and a recon. Had to have been."

"Does that help?" she asked

"Sure does." Mike smiled grimly. "Think about it. How did the shooter get there?"

She shot him a puzzled look.

"He was in a *preplanned* position. The best place to provide both cover fire and perimeter defense. Someone either came to the airport and did a recon – unlikely, that's too obvious – or they went and got the plans and maps beforehand. Sommers is checking."

She was watching him carefully.

"There's more. Whoever did this was professionally trained, but they were big time screw-ups. They put their sniper in the wrong place."

"You said it was a perfect location."

"Under normal conditions," he said. "But the night your father disappeared, it was dark, raining and foggy. You couldn't see more than a few feet. Even a green second lieutenant would know better than to put his security forces off somewhere where they couldn't see shit. Whoever was running this operation not only did so, but had them out there for a significant period of time."

"How do you know?"

"The sniper had nothing to do. He couldn't see anything, so he was screwing around smoking cigarettes. Rigid planning. No initiative. Bad choice of weapons too. Short case 7.62 is a shitty round for a long-range shooter, even if you put it though a decent weapon. Do you see the pattern?"

"I understand what you're saying, but I don't see how it helps us find my father."

"It's just like Maryland. *Jihad* tactics: violent and lethal, but dumbed-down and inflexible. It's probably the same people. Find who did it and we find your father."

She thought for a long moment. "This is going to take awhile, isn't it?"

"It could," he admitted, "but we will find them. I promise you we'll make every effort to find your dad, no matter how long it takes."

"And those who harmed him will see justice done?"

"The FBI is good at kidnappings. That's what they do."

"There's something else, isn't there?"

"We have to move on, Gerry." Mike looked uncomfortable. "We still have a job to do. The President is counting on us. I need you to get the program restarted."

Gerry was silent for a long time staring out the window into the darkness before she spoke. "I can't."

"Why not? Your father would want us to continue."

She sighed. "That's the way he was."

"I need you to keep things rolling."

"I can't, Mike." She looked directly into his eyes. "We don't have a program. Without Dad, there is no Cybertech."

"Well, certainly it's a setback, but this isn't the time...."

"You're wrong." She interrupted him. "You don't understand. Pardon me if I'm being overly blunt, but I need to tell you some things straight if this is ever going to work. Can you handle unpleasant truth?"

"Yes," he said.

"Here's where it starts. Like most people in Washington, including my employer, you've got a lot to learn about business."

He blinked. "Go on..."

"A few minutes ago, I almost broke into tears. You don't have a clue as to why, do you?"

"Because your dad is missing, and perhaps...."

"No," she said. "Because I'm responsible. I tried to do the right thing for my country and to help my dad, and I wound up doing neither. Our program is dead. You don't even understand why, or what to do. You can't just order me to 'fix it,' General. That's not how it works."

She paused and studied his face, trying to place his expression.

"Keep talking," he said, watching her intently.

"You were planning to send me back to Fort Meade in the aircraft with the Cybertech proposal, weren't you?"

He nodded slowly.

"That won't work. The proposal, whatever its contents, is just scrap paper unless it's implemented. Who exactly do you think is going to implement, now that Dad's missing?"

"Why, Cybertech will...."

"No." She laughed without any joy and shook her head. "At the core Cybertech is – or was – three inexperienced social misfits out of engineering school, my father, a highly neurotic marketing woman, and a secretary. There is also one senior engineer whose day job is at Intel. He provides adult supervision for the techno-geeks. Plus my brother Will, of course, who teaches full time."

Mike looked confused. "There's only a half dozen people?"

She said, "Have you been in the military all your life?"

"Since the academy," Mike said.

"For each engineer or scientist, any given high tech company employs at least ten other people. Sales, order entry, technical support, manufacturing, accounting, payroll, quality control and so forth. Figure over ten to one. Cybertech has over a hundred employees."

"I didn't know there were only a handful of engineers," Mike said. "How can Cybertech be so much more advanced than NSA when it comes to cyber security? The agency has thousands of people."

"Like I said, that's not how it works," she said. "Small can be good when it comes to creativity. It's my genius brother, Will, who invents things.

"Will enjoys computer science, but doesn't want to run a business. He's tenured at the University of Oregon. It doesn't pay much, but he likes the work. He supplements his income, amuses himself, and adds to his professional credentials by having Cybertech produce and market his inventions. Dad runs the firm."

"I see," Mike said, looking puzzled.

"Will's research papers are highly respected by the small group of experts able to understand them. He wins science awards. Some think he may become a Nobel laureate one of these days. The school turns a blind eye to his casual lifestyle and occasional liaisons with graduate students.

"Well, mostly they do," Gerry said. "There are exceptions, like the young lady who was using him as the subject of experiments involving marijuana and group sex. She was a psychology major. Said it was all in the name of science."

Mike smiled. "Did the University agree?"

"Not exactly, but they didn't make an issue of it either. Just told Will to knock it off before someone complained. No harm was done, and the lady got a dissertation out of it. She's a professor now, writing a book."

"You're pretty tolerant in Oregon."

Gerry frowned. "Does my brother's lifestyle bother you?"

"No." He seemed amused. "What I'm wondering, however, is how did the firm get into...?"

"The critical path of a deep black project?"

"Yes."

"Well, God bless America, Mike. It was just serendipity," Gerry said sardonically, shaking her head in exasperation. "For one thing, my brother's crypto technology is years ahead of anyone else's. For another, no one else was willing to bid the work, not when it was common knowledge that Tibbs opposed it and didn't want to pay for it. I was desperate.

"I used my personal connections to put pressure on the Agency to fund the project. Tibbs caved, but then I got resistance from Oregon."

"Cybertech didn't want to take NSA's money?"

"Right. Cybertech didn't come to me. I went to them. I went to Oregon and begged Dad and my brother to take on this job. It caused quite a bit of tension in the family."

"Why?"

"My brother is Cybertech's largest stockholder. He wasn't enthusiastic. He said working for NSA was going to be, as he so quaintly put it, 'a major pain in the ass.' He wanted to stick to commercial work. Will loathes bureaucracy. He told Director Mitchell he didn't want Tibbs or anyone from the agency but me anywhere near Cybertech."

"NSA accepted those terms?"

"Reluctantly. It was the only way my brother would agree to the project."

Mike's was watching her carefully.

"Will doubted Cybertech would ever be paid for its work, at least not enough to compensate for all the hassle and bureaucracy. He and Dad had a big fight about it, and so far my brother's been proven right." She sighed deeply, shaking her head. "Cybertech hasn't been paid a dime, despite my promise and best efforts."

"Why not?" Mike asked.

"NSA is a huge bureaucracy. We have hundreds of people in accounts payable, and when it comes to buying equipment, there are tens of thousands of pages of regulations. The folks in purchasing couldn't care less if the contractors get paid promptly. In fact, they get rewarded for delaying payments and making sure all the details and minutiae are exactly right."

"Surely, NSA pays its bills."

"Eventually, they do," she agreed. "I want to go fast, and I want our contractors paid. Accounts payable wants to pay our suppliers slowly. They see it as doing their job. Tibbs backed the clerks, not me."

"Tibbs is gone," Mike said. "All Cybertech has to do is submit invoices. Surely, that's not unreasonable?"

"Ya think? They've been trying and it's killing them. Cybertech has been submitting invoices and justifications for months. They had the engineers stop work for several weeks to provide additional documentation. The firm is pushing its credit limit, and Will's furious. He wants to charge the government for the costs incurred in billing the government. I pleaded with him not to."

"Why?"

"I'm not allowed to pay such costs."

"It's not allowed?" Mike asked incredulously.

"Not directly." She sighed. "The big defense contractors cover such costs by adding overhead and burden. That's why toilet seats sometimes cost the government five hundred dollars, instead of twenty dollars, because they really do cost that much by the time the suppliers are paid. Large firms like Lockheed and Boeing have rooms full of accountants and lawyers to build things like that into their costs, but Cybertech doesn't."

Mike was shaking his head in disbelief. "Oh."

"Dad and I argued Will into doing this project. My timing was lucky. Will wanted to add technical staff. Dad wanted to hire his old sergeant, who was down on his luck and flat broke, but wouldn't accept charity. The contract requires security guards."

Mike nodded.

"They never got funding to pay for guards. As a result, Cybertech's security force consists of one sixty year old man and some students in Dad's martial arts class.

"It gets worse. No one bothered to tell me that the intimate details of my black project were being leaked directly to our nation's enemies." She was getting angry.

"We didn't know...."

She brushed his words aside with an impatient gesture and continued. "That must be why a kill team was sent to break the weakest link, which, of course, was Cybertech. It was just like painting a target on Dad's chest...."

She sighed, took several deep breaths to calm herself, and then looked at him intently. "How the hell does our nation ever survive, Mike?"

"You know how." He met her gaze. "Because of patriots like your father, innovators like your brother, and people like you who try to make the world a little better or safer. Your father spent his whole life going in harm's way for his country. He wouldn't have stopped even if he'd known he was targeted. Surely you know that?"

"Damn you," she said softly, looking away. A tear ran down her cheek, and she angrily dabbed it with her napkin. The silence lengthened into minutes.

Gerry finally turned her gaze back to him. "Yes," she said softly. "I know."

She took a deep breath and let it out slowly. "Dad wanted to do the project. He thought it was important. That's why Will finally agreed."

"I'm over my head on this, Gerry. What do you want me to do?"

"If I can get a team put together, I want you to sit down and let Cybertech present their proposal to you."

"When?"

"Today. Just as soon as Will gets here and can present it to you. Okay?"

Mike nodded. "I agree."

"You're in charge now. After his presentation, you and I are going to get down on our knees and beg my brother to take a sabbatical from his teaching and run the firm. You may use patriotism or profit for arguments if you wish, but I'm going to ask him to do it so my father won't have died for nothing."

"We don't know your father is dead."

The look she gave him was bleak. "Dad was either killed or abducted. I'm going to have the family post a reward, and I want your help to get it spread all over the news."

"Ouch."

Mike winced, and she finally recognized the look on his face. It was respect.

"What else do you need, Gerry? Just ask."

"If you approve the proposal, I want an advance sent to Cybertech immediately."

"Makes sense to me." Mike spread his arms in acquiescence. "They need to be paid."

"Of course they do," she said. "So they can pay their bills and to hell with the paperwork. I want a first class security system installed. I want Cybertech and my family guarded by enough firepower to make even the most wacko terrorist fanatic re-think his heavenly virgins many times before going after them. I don't want my friends and family to be considered soft targets."

Mike looked embarrassed. "I agree. I'm so sorry this wasn't handled well. Your demands are reasonable."

"They're not demands," she said softly, "just requests. I don't know any other way to make this work."

"I understand," he said. "We're in a difficult spot. I need you to run the program so I can deal with the other issues."

"Oh, yes," she breathed. "I'm counting on you to deal with those issues."

She was quiet for a long moment, and then she looked him in the eyes. "Get Cybertech's work approved and funded and get some adequate security in place. Make sure everything possible is being done to find my father and apprehend the people who took him. Then I'll gladly go back to Fort Meade, and I'll do my best for you. I promise."

"You've got a deal," Mike said. "Thank you. You have my word. Do you want to shake hands on it?"

"Is that how you Marines seal important agreements to trust and communicate openly with each other?" Gerry asked with a twinkle in her eyes.

"Usually we're not so formal." Mike grinned. "We just yell something like 'HOO-AH' or 'SEMPER FI' and pound each other on the arms."

"Sounds painful," she said doubtfully.

"Hmmm. I don't have a lot of experience in working closely with high-level, liberated civilian females." Mike's grin widened. "Maybe a kiss?"

"Definitely not," Gerry said, suppressing a smile.

She feigned incredulity, shook her head emphatically, and spoke in her most precisely correct professional voice. "Such Neanderthal behavior, even by a Marine, would certainly border on sexual harassment. I'd have to report it, and you'd be shot or something. However well justified, it wouldn't advance our program."

"The kiss or having me shot?"

"Either," she said. "Or is it neither? Whatever. Both are bad ideas. Trust me on this one."

"I suppose you're right." Mike wrinkled his brow and paused, as if thinking. "I've got it." He snapped his fingers. "How about an inter-organizational letter of agreement? We could sign it, stamp it classified, and put our thumbprints on it."

"God, no." Gerry laughed. "That's even worse. Much worse. The agency never says anything, and putting it in writing is worse. You'd get us both shot."

She shook her head. *He's incorrigible,* she thought, *and he's trying to get my mind off my losses and fears. I like him.* The more she thought about Mike's suggestion, the funnier it seemed. "Maybe we should just shake hands after all."

"Knew you'd see it my way," he said. His look had turned serious.

She offered her hand, and he took it gently and shook it. She didn't pull it back for a long time.

There was nothing more to say. They both knew something special had just happened.

CHAPTER EIGHT
HARD TO EXPLAIN

Sandy Junction Bed and Breakfast, the next morning

T he breakfast nook was bright and airy, all windows. Gerry felt much better. She looked across the table at Mike. "This is a nice place. Quiet with decent food. And a wonderful view, now that the weather's broken. A day like this makes you glad to be alive."

Mike nodded absently, sipping his coffee. He seemed preoccupied.

Sandy Junction was where the Big Sandy River split and forked down to connect with the Columbia. The far bank was wetlands, a nature preserve. Gerry could see a dozen gray sandhill cranes in the marsh and other birds with long necks she couldn't identify. There was even a pair of rare white whooping cranes. They were distinctive by their large size, and she'd heard their unique trumpeting calls.

The sunlight reflected off the ripples in the river, white and dazzling sharp in the clear air. The rain had cleaned the air, and the world was sparkling and new. It made the events of the past two days seem distant, like a bad dream.

Gerry gasped as a bald eagle swooped down and caught a large fish in its talons. "Wow," she said, pointing. "Look at that."

The elegant bird was barely able to carry the fish. It was flapping powerfully, struggling, its wingtips almost touching the water on each stroke. Unable to gain altitude, it finally landed in a clear spot on the far bank with its catch still flopping around.

Mike glanced up, looked closely, and nodded. A smile flickered across his face briefly. "Chinook salmon," he said, extracting his secure phone from his pocket and putting it on the table. "Birds need to eat too."

Something's on his mind, she thought. "What's wrong? Is there news about my father?"

"Nothing yet." Mike sighed, venting deep frustration. "I'm scheduled to check in with the boss in a few minutes. Don't have much to report, though."

He pulled some notes out of his pocket, spread them out, and looked at them dourly. "Nothing good anyway. They had more demonstrations in Portland last night. Several groups are protesting my lockdown."

"Oh," she said, reality crashing back. She felt a tinge of guilt for enjoying the bright new day when her father could be dead or a hostage. "Do you want me to leave while you report in?"

"No," he shook his head. "This won't take long."

He punched the speed dial and waited for the connection. "Hello, Judy. This is General Mickelson. Can we go secure?"

He punched the button and waited for the green light to come on. "I'm showing a lock. We're scrambled, but this is a wireless phone and I'm in a public area. The FBI checked for bugs, and they say we're clear, but I think we should be careful. All the wireless traffic runs through Echelon and this is just a standard DOD scrambler."

He's afraid of someone at NSA listening in, Gerry realized. *And who else?*

Mike listened for a long moment. "Sorry, I can't. The fancy COM gear on the airplane won't work on the ground unless they run the engines, and the pilots object to that." He paused. "They told me they don't have an APU big enough to run all the radios and encryption gear on for very long. It's a small airport. Our airplane is parked way off in the boonies, and there's no place to plug into local power."

"An Auxiliary Power Unit, some kind of generator to power the aircraft systems." He paused, listening. "Right, we'll make do. Please put him on."

"Yes, Sir. Good morning to you." He frowned. "I know, Sir. They already hit me with it and warned me not to discuss the lockdown until we had legal advice. Something about an Oregon law. I'm meeting with Agent Sommers in an hour. He's going to update me then."

"Sommers. He's the local agent in charge. Yes, Sir. I know about the demonstrations. It's been all over the news out here, and Sommers called me last night to give me a heads up. Absolutely. I'll stay away from interviews."

Gerry found herself wishing she could hear the other end of the conversation. So far they didn't seem to be discussing her father or the project.

"What?" said Mike. "Please repeat that...." His eyebrows went up in astonishment. "In today's *Washington Post*? I understand. Our communications are a bit fragile here, Sir. I'll have someone bring a copy from Portland or get one downloaded when we get power to the plane."

Mike waited, listening. "Soon. Maybe an hour," he finally said.

Mike listened. "There really isn't much to report yet. Are you in the loop with the Bureau?" There was a long pause. "Beats me, Sir."

He listened. "I understand. I agree, and there's some evidence that the tactics here were consistent with such a group. I can head back as soon as we get some loose ends wrapped up. The company and the local investigation."

Mike frowned, nodding. "I understand, Sir. Their immediate problem is funding. These people were never paid."

There was a long pause as Mike listened.

"Cybertech has not been paid," Mike said. "Yes, Sir, I'm sure."

He held the phone away from his ear. The President sounded angry, but Gerry couldn't make out the words.

"Gerry told me, Sir. She's sitting right here," Mike said. "Bureaucracy. Yes, Sir, we need to fix it. I've given it a priority." He paused again, listening. "Yes, certainly. I'll take full responsibility and keep Gerry in the loop."

Make paused again, listening. He looked out across the river. The eagle had finally managed to lift what was left of its catch into a tall tree and was perched there finishing it.

"Right, Sir. We've done about all we can here," Mike said. "Tonight, I think. I'll call Judy and schedule when I know. Thank you, Sir."

Mike punched the phone off and put it down. He took a deep breath, and looked at Gerry. "The President sends his condolences about your father."

"They were friends," she said, simply.

Her joy was gone, and she suddenly felt like a big weight was pressing her down. *I hate using the past tense to discuss my father*, she thought, feeling a flash of anger.

Mike was watching her. "Are you okay?" he asked.

"No," she said. "Did the President have any news about Dad?"

"Not yet, but we're not going to back off on this." Mike gave her an intense look. "Not now, not ever. That's my promise to you, and it's also what President Hale just told me."

"Thank you," she said. "Mom agreed to have the family post a reward."

"Good," he said. "The President wants the FBI to put one up too. Are you agreeable to coordinating with them about the details?"

"I don't have a problem with it," she said. "I'll need to talk with Will and my mother, though. Can I let you know this afternoon?"

"Yes, sure," he said, "that will work."

"Did the President have any other news?"

"Oh, yes." Mike nodded. "Your old boss made today's *Washington Post*."

"Is he going to make trouble for us?" she asked, feeling a tinge of alarm. "Tibbs is a dangerous player. He's destroyed more than one career. The man has powerful political connections."

Mike said, "Tibbs is dead. The FBI found the body at his home. There's a suicide note."

"Does anyone believe that?"

"I doubt it," Mike said, "but it didn't seem a good topic to discuss on an open COM line. I'll ask Simpson when we get back. The President said the Bureau suspects a *jihad* connection to both the Maryland incident and your father's disappearance."

What's going on here? Gerry wondered, recalling that Mike and the President had just considered a fully scrambled link to be non-secure. "Is there proof?" she asked

"Proof of a *jihad* tie-in? No, I don't think so," Mike said. "Call it a reasonable provisional hypothesis. The interesting thing is we're getting some strong push back on our attempts to catch whoever is doing this. There were demonstrations in Portland last night about my lockdown. It made the national news, apparently. Sommers is going to fill me in."

"May I attend?"

"I'm not sure. If not, I'll brief you." Mike shrugged. "We've got a lot to do and not much time. The President wants me back in Washington tonight if possible. When are you meeting with your brother?"

"Will's driving in from Eugene. He'll be here by lunchtime."

"Can you get me a quick briefing on the Cybertech proposal this afternoon? I just told the President that I was going to get you paid. We need to get this going."

"You haven't even seen the proposal yet."

"Don't need to." Mike laughed. "This is war, and we need to take some shortcuts. Someone powerful wants your project shut down. My job is to prevent that, to see it gets done. Getting it done means first keeping you and your brother alive, and then getting the project funded and running. I need to focus on that."

"What do you want me to do?" She felt overwhelmed.

"Read the proposal. Advise me. You know more about the technology than I ever will, so run the damn project and tell me what you need. Tell me when I should release funding and how much. Get paperwork to cover what's required. Tell your brother to have Cybertech hire as many clerks, accountants, and lawyers as they need to process all this bullshit to get things rolling and make sure it's legal."

"You're going to give me free rein?"

"Yes."

"I have an obvious conflict of interests. My family owns Cybertech. What if I can't be trusted, what if I'm wrong?"

"Don't be wrong." Mike smiled grimly. "I have to trust someone. I'm not worried about your family's integrity and neither is the President. The bad guys apparently want you all dead and the project stopped. Let's stop them instead."

"Do we know who they are?" she asked. "The bad guys…"

Mike looked around the room, seeing no one close. He pulled a pad out of his pocket and wrote one word, "Bukhari."

She registered surprise. "Really?"

He slowly tore the paper into small pieces and put it in the ashtray, lighting it with the candle on the table. They watched as it burned, and then Mike stirred the ashes with his fork and moved them around.

"Strong suspicions," he said, "but not acting alone. Probably friends in Washington."

Tibbs, she thought. *The FBI found his body and is probably frustrated they didn't get to question him. They must suspect others. Mike didn't trust a secure phone.*

"May I tell my brother about all this?" she asked.

"Later. Job number one is we keep him alive. I want to get him a bodyguard and a police escort to ensure he gets here safely. I'll take you to my meeting with the law enforcement types, and we'll get that started."

"You sound angry."

"Not at you. I need to stop making mistakes and get out ahead of this."

"Mistakes?"

"Yes," he said. "Mistakes. It's been a rolling screw up since the get-go. Your program is compromised, and the FBI just lost the best suspect they had. I almost let you get shot. The Tangos caught us unprepared, and we took causalities. Your father is MIA, and Clover lost a man. This shit has gotta stop right now."

He really cares. "Thank you," Gerry said, simply.

"Don't thank me; it's my job," Mike said. "And please stop blaming yourself for your father being missing. That responsibility is way over your pay grade, and the President and I are going to do our best to get him back and find out who did this."

"When can I tell Will about this?"

"I'll tell him myself when we can get to a secure room. Can you move up the schedule, and meet with him sooner? I'll come out to the Cybertech plant as soon as I get done with the FBI and the local police."

"Yes," she said. "Sure. I've got Will's cell phone number."

"Good." Mike nodded and gave her an encouraging look. "Give it to me, and I'll pass it along and make sure he gets security protection. I'm also going to send some of Lieutenant Clover's men with you to make sure you're safe. From now on, I want Cybertech fully secured."

"Okay." Gerry looked out the window again at the bright new day, taking a deep breath and feeling the weight coming off her shoulders. *It's good to have friends you can depend on.*

She fished her phone out of her purse and punched her brother's number.

Sandy Junction Airport

Mike looked across the table at Agent Sommers and Chief Ward. He'd just sent Gerry off to Cybertech with Clover's SEALs to guard her. The FBI was attending to getting her brother there safely, and as soon as possible. Sommers had dispatched a team and helicopter.

The chief hitched up his gun belt and scowled. "This is getting worse, General." It was the first he'd spoken, other than to ask for coffee. "Don't like it a bit."

Mike frowned. "We've not made any progress at all. How can it get worse?"

"The politics are getting worse," the chief said. "They had a shit fit over in Portland last night. Demonstrations. A small riot. Seven people hurt, including one police officer. Reporter got hit with a beer bottle."

Mike glanced at Agent Sommers, who had on a poker face, then back at the chief. "I saw the news," he said, nodding.

"Portland's mayor is highly pissed," the chief said. "She called my boss. Then he called me and chewed my ass. Gave me a message to deliver. They want you to come to Portland and meet with the city council. Your lockdown is screwing up traffic. Minority groups are bitching. Say they're being harassed."

"No," Mike said.

The chief blinked and then frowned.

"I'm not going to get into a public argument with Portland's mayor."

"Why not?"

Because the President ordered me not to, Mike thought. "I don't work for your mayor, or Portland's mayor, or the city council, or any Oregon officials. I'm not in the loop about the roadblocks, nor do the personnel involved work for me. I doubt anyone is being harassed, but I have no first hand knowledge and can't comment."

"You're not in charge of this investigation?" the chief asked.

"I'm not in law enforcement at all," Mike said. "My job involves classified national security issues. To do my job, I have to get Cybertech secure and find their missing people, if possible."

"The mayor insisted…."

"I don't have time for this shit, Chief. If you want someone to talk with your local politicians, the FBI is running this investigation."

The chief looked at Agent Sommers. "Will you talk with the mayor?"

"Not a chance."

"So what do I tell her?"

Sommers shrugged. "Homeland Security is sending someone from Washington to coordinate with local officials. I've not been advised yet who's assigned, or when they'll be here. I'd guess tomorrow. I can give you a phone number."

"Do that," the chief said. "He can work it out with Portland."

"Good," Mike said. "I need to find John Giles. Is there any progress on the case?"

"Off the record?" the chief asked.

Here we go again. We sit here talking like a bunch of old women, and meanwhile the Tangos are getting away. Mike sighed and looked at Sommers, who nodded. "Yes."

"The Sandy Junction City Engineer and the Planning Manager had a visit four days ago. Two males. Both dark, mid-twenties, olive complexions, brown eyes, about five foot eight or nine. Got some photos."

The chief slid a folder across the table. Sommers intercepted it and flipped it open. "Any prints?"

The chief shook his head. "Nope, just the security camera photos. Said they were with a group that wanted to maybe buy some land. Looked at the plans and maps for the airport. Asked questions. Took copies. Paid cash and got a receipt."

"Were they foreign nationals?" Sommers asked, showing the photos to Mike. They looked like Arabs.

"Not allowed to ask," the chief said. "They had Oregon driver's licenses, but, as you know, we issue them to aliens. Unfortunately, the planning folks didn't think to make copies. They had Arabic names, but nobody remembers what they were."

"Would your city officials be able to recognize them from a line up?" Sommers asked.

The chief shrugged. "You can always try."

"Do you have a copy of the receipts?"

"Thought you'd ask that," the chief said. "No, I do not."

Mike frowned. "Look, this is a lead. We suspect there's a *jihad* connection. If these people are identified with an organization, we need to know about it."

The chief looked at Agent Sommers, pointedly. "I showed you the photos. Is either of those people wanted for a crime?"

"I can't say." Sommers shrugged. "We'd need to check it out."

"But you think they might be aliens," the chief said. "Foreigners. Not citizens."

"No comment," Sommers said.

"What the hell is going on here?" Mike asked. "We're wasting time. We have missing people. We have a suspected crime. You've found evidence an organized group did a recon on the crime scene, but you didn't bother to bring copies of the receipts to show us?"

"The subjects might be illegal aliens," the chief said. "You don't know they're not, and Sommers here just told me they're not wanted for a crime, far as he knows."

"What difference does it make?" Mike found himself raising his voice. He took a deep breath and forced himself to speak in a reasonable tone. "Chief, what's going on here? Help me with this, please."

"You want to tell him?" the chief asked, looking at Sommers. "Better if he hears it from you Feds than us Oregon boys."

Sommers looked disgusted. "Remember last time the chief was worried about breaking the law, ORS 181.850, that prevents state or local officials from detecting or apprehending aliens unless they're wanted for a crime?"

"Yes," Mike snapped, "you read it to me in detail. Of course I remember. What's it got to do with wanting to see a copy of a receipt?"

"Nothing, directly," Sommers said. "That's not the problem this time, but it's similar. They have another law out here, ORS 181.575. That's what we're bumping into now. That's why the chief didn't copy the receipts."

"**What!**" Mike exclaimed, suppressing the desire to scream obscenities. "Are you telling me Oregon has a law to prevent the police from running a copy machine?"

The chief laughed, a quick snort, which got him a glare from Mike. "It's not my fault, General." He waved an arm at Sommers. "He knows. Tell him to keep talking."

Sommers sighed, deeply. "It's hard to explain, General"

"Try," Mike said. He was not amused.

"The law in question is ORS 181.575. It dates back to the early 1980s," Sommers said.

"And it says...?" Mike demanded, angry at the runaround.

"Specific information not to be collected or maintained," quoted Sommers, from a sheet he'd pulled out of a folder. "This statute is longer, so I don't have it memorized. I'll read it."

"No law enforcement agency, as defined in ORS 181.010, may collect or maintain information about the political, religious or social views, associations or activities of any individual, group, association, organization, corporation, business or partnership unless such information directly relates to an investigation of criminal activities, and there are reasonable grounds to suspect the subject of the information is or may be involved in criminal conduct."

"What are you telling me?" Mike asked.

"Those two laws work together," Sommers said. "Unless people are charged, detecting or apprehending aliens is a no-no. Collecting information on groups is also a no-no. If an Oregon cop does either, he's in trouble. If he does both, he's in big trouble. If the chief made copies of the receipts for those public records, he could be charged with collecting information illegally."

Mike shook his head and blinked, trying to understand. "What if the group in question is terrorist, or connected with a foreign enemy? We're looking for foreign assassins here."

"Makes no difference," the chief said, shaking his head. "Law doesn't care."

"He's right," Sommers agreed. "Those laws were on the books long before the towers went down. Oregon wouldn't change them then, and isn't likely to change them now."

"This is insane," Mike said incredulously.

"No shit, General, but that's how it works." The chief shrugged. "It's the law. Got five to go for retirement, and kids in college. Gotta keep my nose clean."

"We'll need to get our own copies of the receipts," Sommers said. "Or I'll have to first get a judge to sign an arrest warrant for these specific suspects. I'll do both. Suspicion of murder and kidnapping on both the John Does, for starters. Those are crimes. We're making progress."

Mike shook his head in total disbelief. "I sure as hell don't see how."

"The chief's helping us as much as he can, General. Now we know these subjects have Oregon driver's licenses."

"So what?" Mike asked. "They probably used phony names and addresses."

"Probably did," the chief agreed. "Doesn't matter. Illegal aliens usually do, but the department of motor vehicles fingerprints folks and takes photos when it gives them licenses."

"That's right," Sommers agreed. "We've almost certainly got their prints."

"There's more," the chief said. "How'd they know to come to Sandy Junction in the first place?"

"What are you getting at?" Mike asked, puzzled.

"Whoever these people were, they were out scouting around systematically," the chief said. "Casing things out days or weeks ahead of time. If this is some national security thing, I bet the tie in was to John's company, Cybertech."

"So?"

"So the subjects probably went down to Salem," Sommers said. "It's likely the group that did this has been searching the state's corporate records. Maybe the same people, or maybe others in their organization. I'll send agents to check."

"Because the state won't do it for us?" Mike asked.

"Can't," the chief said. "Not till charges are filed. Sorry." Surprisingly, he smiled. "When you get them identified and get warrants out, I can help. Then the state people in Salem will have to help too. We're making progress."

The police can't help us find suspects, until the suspects are identified. That's nuts. Why is this so hard? Mike wondered. He looked at Sommers. To his astonishment, the agent was also smiling.

"I brought some things for today's show and tell myself," Sommers said, smugly. He pulled out a thick folder, extracted some papers, and distributed them to Mike and the chief.

Mike studied the handouts. *More photos of Arabs.* He compared them to the chief's photos. They were different people.

"First one is Basam Mallah. His prints were on the 7.62 round your SEALs found. Most likely purchased at Guncraft Arms, a local store where he legally purchased the AK. He passed the background check."

Mike frowned. "A Muslim foreigner can waltz in and buy an AK?"

"He purchased two, actually."

"What do we know about him?" the chief asked, looking interested.

"Egyptian national, twenty four years old. Came to the U.S. on a student visa. He was on the watch list as a teenager until they scrubbed all the Muslim Brotherhood names. Did a year at Oregon State, where he married a girl in one of his classes. A local named Sandy Thomas. Basam legally changed his name to Billy Thomas and was granted citizenship. That's the name he bought under."

Mike cleared his throat, then spoke distinctly. "Whisky Tango Foxtrot?"

They all looked him. *What the Fuck?*

"Excuse me?" Sommers said.

"Isn't this just a tad bit sloppy?"

Sommers shrugged. "It's all relative. Remember the Boston Marathon bombers? They drove around in a borrowed BMW with "Terrorista #1" on the front plate. No one noticed. It wasn't their car, and the plate wasn't issued by the State. That's nothing. Do you recall the older brother's name?"

Mike shook his head.

The chief said, "Something that started with a 'T.' Timmerlan, maybe."

"Close. The eldest son's name was *Tamerlan* Tsarnaev – the name of the vicious Islamic conqueror of the 14th century who destroyed ancient cities and slaughtered millions."

"You're kidding me, right? No one noticed these red flags?"

"Nope. Not even the media afterwards. Describing himself as the "Sword of Islam" and a descendant of Genghis Khan, the ancient warrior Tamerlan defeated the Christian Knights at Smyrna, captured Turkey and Egypt, and viciously razed the cities of Damascus, Khiva, and Baghdad in an attempt to make his capital at Samarkand the first city of the Islamic world. *The History of the Mongol Conquests* claims that Tamerlan's campaigns ended with the slaughter of over 17 million people. He built pyramids with the skulls of the infidels he slaughtered."

Mike blinked.

Sommers had a smug look his face and was grinning.

"What?"

"Want to put on your tin hat, General? How about a good conspiracy theory, maybe one you've never heard of?"

"Go ahead."

"Remember when President Obama went on TV after the Boston terrorist attack and pondered, 'We still do not know how young men who grew up here and studied here can turn to such senseless violence.' Get the point? Nobody knew. It was 'senseless violence,' not *jihad*."

"I remember. That's not a conspiracy."

Sommers grin broadened. "Maybe not, but some *did* know, hell the Russians warned us at least twice, and suppressing such evidence, history, and knowledge to soften critical views of radical Islam could be, especially if it was an official Executive Branch policy."

Mike said, "Do you know where you are going with this?"

"Ever hear of Anne Hendershott?"

"No."

"Back then, Americans were being bullied by Federal bureaucracies to silence them about Islamic threats. Anne Hendershott, a professor of Sociology, was called to an IRS audit in 2010, apparently because of articles she had written for Christian magazines. She and her husband had filed jointly for 39 years and never had been audited, and the IRS specifically excluded her husband, the major source of their joint income, from the audit. The auditor **specifically** asked who had paid her for each article, and how much, and what were their politics. One of her articles was 'The Sword of Islam.' Tamerlan and the genocide of Christians was her exact topic.

"Dr. Hendershott was highly critical of Islam and it got her in trouble. She was writing a book on Islamic terrorism, but our own bureaucrats intimidated her and shut her down."

"How do you know all this stuff?"

"It's my job, General. Radical Islam is a major threat and we have sleeper cells. The one you are after is new to us. It's lethal and apparently well organized."

"Okay, so you're good," Mike said. "Maybe we're finally catching up, and it's about time. Where is he now? Not Tamerlan, not Obama, but the

Basam boy who bought the AKs and dropped that round at your crime scene."

"We don't know yet," Sommers said. "They got divorced two years ago. Sandy finished school and works as a medical tech in Portland. Billy slash Basam dropped out of school, and out of sight."

Sommers glanced at his watch. "Sandy gets off work at four. We're going to question her then, but we don't think she's seen him for some time. She lives in a two-bedroom apartment with a female coworker. None of her neighbors recognized the photos."

"Police can pick the Basam boy up for questioning." Chief Ward was smiling beatifically. "Prints found at a crime scene, and he's just a citizen. Suspicion of and no alien problems. Politicians and lawyers can't bitch about that."

"That's right. I'm having Basam's photo distributed," Sommers agreed.

Just a citizen. They have some crazy laws out here. "Who's the other one?" Mike tapped the second photo. It was an older man, perhaps mid-30s, with a beard.

"This one's more interesting," Sommers said. "We've been talking about how well organized this operation was, so I wondered if high-level management talent was brought in. I assumed *jihad* and had a scan run on Mideastern foreign nationals coming into Oregon in the past two weeks."

"This subject came in on a Saudi passport, from Canada, Sunday night a week ago. His passport image is on the next page."

Mike flipped the page and looked at it. "Nassar Fuad?"

"That's right," Sommers said. "Age 36. He's a Saudi banker connected to the royal family. He's the son of a minor Sheik, and he visits Oregon every month or two on business."

"Is he clean?" Mike asked.

"Far as we know," Sommers said. "However, this wasn't him."

"What?"

"The CIA reports the real Mr. Faud is in Zurich right now, and the Saudis verify it. He's been there for two weeks as a member of the Saudi delegation to a financial summit meeting. Their Embassy is rather upset someone is using a forged copy of his passport, and their intelligence people want to get involved."

Mike was studying the photo and comparing it to the one on the passport. "It looks like the same person," he said.

"The photo was taken by a security camera in the Portland airport. Yes, it does seem to match the image on the passport. We're trying to sort it out. The Saudis are cooperating."

"Is this Nassar Faud still in Oregon?" the chief asked.

"There's no record of his leaving." Sommers shrugged. "He came in on a round trip ticket, but the return segment was never used."

"So where is he?" Mike asked. *And who is he, if he's not Faud?*

"We don't know," Sommers admitted. "He took a cab from the airport to downtown. The cabbie dropped him off near the Marriott hotel, but he never checked in. No one with that name checked into any hotel or rented any vehicle in the Portland area. He's vanished."

"Vanished?" Mike asked.

"He's dropped off the radar." Sommers nodded. "This subject made some very professional moves. He kept his face averted from the security cameras. The shot I showed you is the only clear one we've got. I think he's a serious player. We've put a team on trying to break his cover."

"The Saudis are helping?"

Sommers nodded. "They seem real interested."

This is a nightmare, Mike thought. *People keep disappearing or turning up dead, and we're not getting anywhere.*

Mike was increasingly glad he didn't work in law enforcement. The tangle of local laws and political sensitivities was beyond his comprehension and tolerance level.

"Look," Mike said. "I have to go back to Washington tonight. I'm sure to be asked how this investigation is going. What do I say?"

"I don't know about you, General Mickelson, but I'm going to report to Special Agent Simpson we're starting to get a handle on it out here," Sommers said confidently.

"We are?" Mike asked, astonished.

"Damn right," the chief said. "Tell 'em it's going good. We've 'bout got this puppy by the balls."

"We do?" Mike blinked and shook his head. "Tell me how."

"We've got us a probable crime and four suspects," the chief said.

"It's better than that." Sommers grinned. "Simpson tells me the Bureau is posting a half million-dollar reward to find the people who abducted John Giles. You told me the Giles family would probably post a reward to get him back unharmed. We're going to splash it all over the news, starting tonight."

"Going to be better than winning the lottery." The chief grinned too. "Half that money and we'd have good ole boys roaming all over the hills with their hunting rifles. Might take some time off and look around myself."

"What about the lockdown?" Mike asked, remembering the President's concerns. "That's been turned into a local political brouhaha."

"Not any more. That was because of Oregon's laws protecting illegal aliens, plus the 'harassing minorities' political issue," Sommers said. "That's past. We now have a crime, with suspects and photos. We're looking for specific suspects using our evidence photos, and it's hardly our fault they all look to be Arab."

"Doesn't get better than that," the chief agreed, munching a doughnut. "Except for having the reward, of course."

"Do you think you can find the people who did this?" Mike asked.

Both men nodded confidently.

"Bet your ass," the chief said. "Where are they going to go? The perps were probably planning to lie low till the heat was off, and then slink away. But you've had the state locked down tighter than a tick on a dog, so that's not going to happen. Now we flush 'em out and hunt 'em down."

"I'll have an APB out in an hour," Sommers agreed. "Armed and dangerous, plus a reward. I'm optimistic. It's one thing to be hassling illegal farm workers, but this is about a local girl who wants her father back. I'll get our PR people on it. We'll ask the governor to have the Oregon Guard help."

"When will warrants be issued?" the chief asked.

"Depends how soon I get out of this meeting. Today, I hope."

The chief looked at Mike. "We can legally help as soon as the warrants are out, General. You tell Ms. Gerry we're going to nail these people and find her dad."

"Tell you what," Mike said, looking at Sommers. "Why don't you make a written report about this to Agent Simpson and send me a copy. Say something nice about the chief and all the help he's provided."

You can have all the credit, Mike thought. *You deserve it.*

"I'll be happy to do that," Sommers said, smiling. "Thank you. What are you going to do?"

"Get back to work and let you do the same," Mike said. "I've got a meeting at Cybertech, and then we need to get back to Washington. I really appreciate your help and want to thank you both. I was getting worried about this. If you need any support, just ask."

Mike looked at his watch, thinking. *With luck, we can leave early and be in Washington at a decent hour. It's going to be a big day tomorrow. Something's happened. The President must have a reason for insisting I come right back to meet with him.*

They wrapped up the meeting, with the chief agreeing to take him to Cybertech and Sommers agreeing to have the FBI data link everything to Mike's aircraft, with copies to his office in Washington. Chief Ward seemed happy to have an excuse to use his siren, and they were at the company within minutes.

CHAPTER NINE
SANCTUARY

Jackson's Knoll, Rural Virginia

Senator Harriet Stiles sipped her white wine, thinking, outwardly relaxed, inwardly anxious. The article about Tibbs' death in the *Post* had been followed shortly by Burt's call.

Their phone conversation had lasted under twenty seconds. "We should get together. It's a nice night for a chat," he said. She'd agreed. He set a time and hung up.

Tradecraft: *Nice night.* Euphonious and easy to remember, it was the prearranged signal to demand an urgent meeting. They'd never used the signal before, but the meeting place was prearranged and the location fit their normal patterns of behavior. It paid to be cautious.

The dimly lit room was empty except for a young couple by the door. Harriet watched them for a few minutes. It was a different couple than last time, but they were about the same age, perhaps late twenties or early thirties. No matter. They were much too far away to eavesdrop. She glanced out at the stream, dividing her attention between the view and the room. Everything looked normal.

She finished her wine and poured another glass. *He's late,* she thought. *Damn it. He has me rush out here, and the bastard doesn't even show up on time.* Then she saw him. Burt walked directly over to the table and sat down.

"Senator," he said, looking around. "Good evening. Nice to see you again."

She studied him carefully. Burt's impeccable image was just a shade off. His eyes were bloodshot. His tie was just a bit crooked.

"Have you been snorting?" she asked. "You're late."

"Jesus, Harriet." He shook his head. "No, on both counts. I'm straight, and I was on time. Please keep your voice down."

"Don't bullshit me, Burt." She tapped her vintage Cartier *Tank-francaise* significantly. "No one is close enough to hear us."

"I know what time it is," he said. "I've been here for a half hour, waiting outside. I watched you drive in and checked to make sure you weren't followed."

He waved his arm to attract the waitress. He waited for her to leave with his order, and then looked back at the Senator.

"We're clear," he said. "No one followed you."

"I don't like being dragged out here on short notice. It's most inconvenient."

"Not as inconvenient as a prison cell, Harriet."

The Senator started to speak, but waited, seeing the waitress coming with Burt's drink. She forced herself to smile until the girl had finished and left. Her smile vanished as quickly as it had appeared.

"Fuck you," she said, enunciating the words carefully. "You're getting paranoid. Of *course* no one is following me. Who would want to? The media loves me, and Hale wouldn't dare."

"If you say so." Burt shrugged. "Tibbs won't be giving us any more help. He's dead. He was falling apart and would have sold me out to save himself."

"I saw the news, of course." Harriett's look was caustic. "Quite tragic. Too bad for him, but hopefully not a problem for us. He won't be talking to anyone now. What happened?"

"Tibbs panicked because he'd been pulled off the project. Replaced by some Marine General. They jerked his clearances and wouldn't even let him back in his office. He said the director did it personally."

"Of course the director did it," she said. "That's normal procedure. Jack Mitchell was his boss. Who the hell else do you expect would fire him?"

Burt looked at her sharply. "What else do you know?"

"I know many things," the Senator said dryly. "There's nothing to worry about. It wasn't even Jack's decision to replace Tibbs."

"I'm listening." Burt took a deep swallow of his drink, not bothering to savor the expensive whisky.

"I think the White House got pissed so little progress was being made and decided to shake things up. It's no big deal. Programs get screwed up, and people get reassigned. Happens all the time."

"Who's the Marine?"

"No one to worry about. His name's Mickelson. He's a washed up hero, a macho-type who got shot up and was given a desk job in Washington as a sop. I met him when he was a lackey for President Hale, a pathetic cripple in a wheelchair. Don't wet your pants, Burt. He's not a threat."

"He could be." Burt scowled. "The Patton woman is still running the program."

"I'm glad you brought that up," the Senator said. "What happened?"

Burt looked around uncomfortably. "They missed her, that's what happened."

"They bungled," the Senator said.

"It was just bad luck." Burt shrugged. "Shit happens. There's no connection to us."

"Your friends don't see it as a problem?"

"Of course not," he said. "It's a minor matter. They expect losses. The problem is she's still there, and now we don't have anyone inside to control her."

"We don't *need* anyone inside. Not any more. GIRL TALK is a troubled program. The rumor is it's being shut down. NSA has the perfect out. If it fails, the agency can blame it on the Patton woman, the Marine, or both of them."

"Are they planning to do that?"

"I can nudge it that way, if needed." The Senator shrugged indifferently. "Jack Mitchell's not a total fool, the program's been an embarrassment to him, and the Marine's encroaching on his turf. You don't need to worry about Mickelson."

"That helps." Burt's glass was almost empty. He picked it up and drained it.

"Why did you insist on this meeting?" the Senator asked. "Is it about Oregon? Or were you just panicked over Tibbs?"

"Tibbs was expendable," Burt said. "I wasn't panicked, only concerned, and you've convinced me we don't need more damage control." He smiled for the first time. "Oregon went well, and there's other good news. I wanted to deliver it in person."

She nodded, watching him carefully.

"It works," he said. "Our friends have perfected the vaccine. We're almost ready."

Harriett was so excited she didn't speak for a time, considering her words. She sipped her wine till the glass was empty, savoring the moment, and then held it out for Burt to refill. He did so with a flourish.

The thrill was almost sexual. *I've waited so long*, she thought. *The balance of the world just tilted.*

"That's excellent," the Senator said carefully. "It makes GIRL TALK and NSA increasingly irrelevant, even if you have lost your source. Stop worrying."

"You're getting what you want, but how do I know you can deliver for my friends?"

"I'll be in charge, Burt. Of course I can deliver."

"You'll be opposed. Congress and the public may not let you keep our agreements."

"It's a little late for getting cold feet," she said. "In fact, it's way too late."

"I've been asked for assurances," he said.

"You've got all the assurances you need."

"I'll be shot if anything goes wrong...."

"Nobody will notice you, and nobody shoots Santa Claus. I'll promise our citizens peace in the Mideast, cheap oil, jobs, and a shift from defense spending to public programs. They won't pass that up. I'll be unstoppable, and the higher I go, the more I can protect my friends."

Burt looked thoughtful. "All right," he finally said, nodding. "I'll pass that along."

"Good." She favored him with a smile. "When can I move?"

Burt finished his drink. "Soon. I don't have a detailed schedule yet. Our friends need to put the vaccine into production, test the production lots, and get them here. I should think a few weeks, plus the time for transportation and distribution."

She thought for a time. "They have adequate supplies of the toxin?"

Burt laughed. "Buckets of the stuff. All we need is vaccine."

"A month will be fine," she said, smiling. "It will take me that long to prepare. Make sure they do their testing well, because you're getting the first vaccination."

"Of course," Burt said. "That's what we agreed to."

"This is going well. I'll get a vaccination program put together."

"Very quietly," Burt said. "Please."

"Not a problem. We have a large number of programs running to safeguard the public health. One more won't draw any attention at all."

This is something I'd better do myself. She smiled at the thought of playing God. *I get to make a list of who lives.* It was going to be fun.

Somewhere over Eastern Oregon

Gerry settled into the comfortable seat. She looked over at Mike and gave him a weary grin. "We got a lot done today. I'm glad you and my brother hit it off so well."

The Gulfstream had leveled at 51,000 feet and was on its way back to Andrews, running light and fast, helped along by a hundred knot tailwind. The plane was empty except for them and the flight crew. Clover and his SEALs stayed behind to make sure Cybertech was safe until its own security was in place.

"Your brother's presentation was impressive," Mike said. "If he can do all he promised, President Hale's going to be pleased."

"Will keeps his commitments. We've had occasional differences, but he's never lied to me." Gerry paused. "If I'm not intruding, what did you and he discuss?"

"Money," Mike said, smiling at the memory. "We talked about money."

Gerry frowned, puzzled. That didn't sound like her brother.

"He's studied history, hasn't he?"

"Some." Gerry shrugged. "Will's not your normal nerd. He's a deep thinker. Sometimes he goes off chasing things that pique his interest. Why do you ask?"

"He asked me which fighting general did the most for America's cause, back during the Revolutionary War. I expected he wanted me to say George Washington, so I told him Gentleman Johnny Burgoyne."

"I don't understand."

"Burgoyne."

"Who's that?" she asked. *And what does this have to do with money?*

"Your brother knew," Mike said. "Burgoyne was the British General who did the most to lose the war. He blundered around in the deep forests at great expense, bringing fine wine, his mistress – the wife of one of his officers, incidentally – and entourage along for entertainment, but accomplishing nothing of military value. Some say Burgoyne's surrender at Saratoga was the turning point of the war."

Gerry nodded, puzzled. "If you say so…"

"I did say so, actually, but Will told me I was wrong."

"Why was my brother discussing military history?" she asked. *We're in the middle of a crisis. Why would he take up Mike's time discussing arcane historic trivia?*

"I didn't have a clue." Mike grinned. "But it was the best conversation I'd had all day. So I asked him who he had in mind."

"Who did he name?" she asked, still feeling embarrassed, even though Mike obviously hadn't taken offense. She was never sure what her brother was going to do.

"Benedict Arnold."

Her jaw dropped. "Was he joking?"

Mike shook his head. "Not at all."

Gerry was appalled. *Mike's worried, we've got a security leak, Dad's missing, and my brother is talking about Benedict Arnold? This is surreal.* "Is that true?" she finally asked.

"In a way." Mike shrugged. "Some might argue the point."

"I'd expect so," she said. "Arnold was a traitor."

"Eventually," Mike said, "but George Washington once said Arnold was the best fighting General he had – up until when he switched sides, of course. Arnold's flag is still kept at West Point. Never displayed, but still there."

Gerry was mystified. "However did my brother get off on *that*?"

"It gets better," Mike said. "He asked me why Arnold had turned traitor."

"What did you say?" Her embarrassment was gone, and her mystification was turning into bafflement. *Even for my brother, this is very weird behavior.*

"I said it was because Arnold's wife was a British loyalist. Which is true, of course, but your brother looked me dead in the eye and said, 'Because Congress never fucking paid him what they'd promised.'"

Gerry suppressed a groan, averting her eyes.

Mike chuckled. "Your brother set me up, but his point was valid. He was talking about money."

"You'd already promised to pay him. He's unfathomable."

"No, he's right." Mike smiled wryly. "He said he has one hundred and eight people depending on him and can't meet payroll this week without the money he's owed. He also needs to buy equipment and add staff quickly. He called it a 'fast ramp' and explained in detail how much money it costs."

"The burn rate to develop new technology goes exponential," Gerry said. "The front end is ugly. It's risky and uncertain, but the early investment in discovery and planning largely determines the outcomes. If you don't get it right early, it costs thousands of times more to fix it later, if you can at all. People forget that Edison developed a thousand light bulbs that didn't work before he found a design that would."

"Will talked about clueless bureaucrats pulling up the flowers to see how they were growing." Mike grinned. "He was passionate. It was like listening to some kind of a wizard for occult science. I only understood about half of what he was saying."

"That's my brother...." Gerry said softly.

"He said if management gets nervous, demands proof, and delays funding, the project falls off the ramp and needs a lot more money to restart. You wind up with nothing to show for what you've spent."

She nodded. "That part's right, and it's what happens most of the time. Innovation is an act of faith. Organizations like the old Lockheed Skunkworks are legendary, but as rare as unicorns. If Edison had been an MBA, he would have invented a large candle."

"Your brother said that too."

"Large organizations and business schools are about process and numbers. They have a hard time with new things." Gerry looked at Mike earnestly. "What did you tell him?"

"I said I'd have five million dollars in Cybertech's bank account by next week."

Gerry blinked. "Can you do that? The agency's procedures take months."

"I'm going to try," Mike said. He glanced at his watch. "I trust your brother. I'm meeting with the President in the morning, and one of my main objectives is to get those funds disbursed. I need you to hustle and get the contract paperwork in place to cover it so it's legal. If I need to sign anything, get it to me tomorrow."

"It's on my list." She frowned. "Are you going somewhere?"

"Maybe. There's something else going on, Gerry. I didn't think much of it when the President wouldn't discuss it on my secure phone, but he refused even the COM gear on the plane, which is as bulletproof as anything we have."

"What do you want me to do?"

"Run the program. Get it done. I'll back you up and stay as involved as I can. I'll be meeting with Agent Simpson right after I see the President. We're going to keep the heat up about finding your father."

"Why do I feel like I'm being abandoned?"

"Maybe because you don't trust me yet?"

"Maybe because I'm wondering who's going to find my dad, with you chasing off somewhere."

"You were there, Gerry. Good people are on it. They'll find your Dad."

"Law enforcement."

"Yes. Talking with Will was easy compared to the meeting I had with Chief Ward and Agent Sommers."

"I'd go mad if I was in law enforcement."

"Me too." Mike shrugged. "The main thing is they're competent, and they're rolling. I'm comfortable leaving matters in their hands. We have our own jobs to do."

Gerry looked at Mike intently.

"We'll find your father. The President is worried about him."

"I know how Dad was. The mission was everything. You strike me the same way."

"Your father didn't leave anyone behind."

"Not if he could help it...."

"Right."

She said, "I want your word on this. That you'll do your best to get Dad back."

"I won't risk the mission, Gerry. Right now, keeping you and your brother safe and getting the job done comes first. We have experts at hostage rescue and detective work, and I promise you the President and I will keep the intensity up as high as we can."

She put her hand on his and looked into his eyes. "Promise me. I need your word on it."

Mike met her gaze squarely. "We'll do everything possible to get your father back. I promise."

"Thank you." She gave his hand a squeeze, let out a deep breath, and seemed to relax.

"I watched the local news while I was waiting," Gerry said. "They've got checkpoints up all over. If the people who took my father are still in Oregon, I think they're stuck there. The reward's going to help."

"It should," Mike said. "Will and your mother were helpful...."

"We got lucky," she said. "Will had already figured out he'd have to run Cybertech. He didn't like it, but he accepted it."

"Because of you."

She shrugged.

"I want you to stay at my place tonight. I don't want you going home until I check the security arrangements personally. I don't want to take any chances on that."

"Okay," she said.

"I'll pick you up at work tomorrow in time for dinner."

"I'd like that," she said. "What if Director Mitchell wants to know what's going on?"

"Have him talk to me," Mike said. "Tell him I gave you a direct order to that effect."

She nodded.

"I want the names of everyone who's had program access."

"I've got a list in my safe at work," she said. "I'll cross check it and get you a copy."

"Do it officially," he said. "Give me two copies. I'll sign for them."

Mike clicked the lights down, and they eased their seats into full recline, lying there in the darkness, listening to the drone of the engines. After awhile he dozed off. She watched him for a time, wondering about the future. When she finally fell asleep, she dreamed of her father.

Remote Farm House, Jasper County, Oregon

Mohammad Habib knocked tentatively on the door of the bedroom Ahmed was using for an office.

"Come in," Ahmed snapped.

"Your picture is on the television. They've posted a reward."

"*What?*" Ahmed rushed into the living room. He was just in time to see a full screen image of his face, and then the cameras cut away to a news commentator.

Yasir said, "The FBI has identified four of us."

Ahmed waved him to silence, wanting to hear the rest, but it was the end of the newscast. He punched the off button. "Do they have photos?"

"Yes, Sir," Mohammad said in a strained voice. "They showed one of me, one of Yasir, and several of Basam. The photos for Yasir and me are the same as on our driver's licenses. They have our names."

Ahmed groaned. "You used your true names, instead of aliases?"

"Yes, on the licenses. That's what we were ordered to do," Mohammad said apologetically. "We always use the Oregon driver's licenses for identification. The ODL lets you get all kinds of other ID, but merchants usually ask to see the license too."

"What identity did they give for me?"

"A Saudi named Nassar Fuad," Mohammad said.

Good, thought Ahmed, feeling relieved. *They don't know who I am. The Fuad identity won't lead them anywhere.*

"What of Basam?" Ahmed asked.

"I got United States citizenship under the name of Billy Thomas," Basam said. "I was ordered to do it, Sir."

"How did you accomplish that?" Ahmed didn't bother to ask why, knowing Basam wouldn't have been told.

"I married an American woman." Basam looked terrified. "She wasn't Muslim. After I got my citizenship, I divorced her, just as I was instructed."

"They had his wife on." Mohammad was holding a pistol. "Their FBI interviewed her."

"I haven't seen her for years. She doesn't know where I am," Basam said desperately, looking at the gun, then at Ahmed. "I was just doing as ordered."

Basam babbled on until Ahmed ordered him to silence. He thought for a long moment. "Did the Oregon officials say anything? Are they cooperating in the search?"

Mohammad looked blank. Ahmed searched the other faces. "Well?" he demanded.

Yasir said, "Portland's Mayor said they were cooperating reluctantly, because there was evidence of a crime, a kidnapping, and that gave her no choice. She didn't look happy about it. Apparently protests are continuing."

"They're only looking for four suspects?" asked Ahmed.

Yasir nodded. "Portland's Mayor said their cooperation was limited. She was with an FBI agent, but he didn't say anything except about the reward."

Ahmed looked at Mohammad, who nodded. "The Americans seem divided about what to do."

That may save us yet. "Anything else?" Ahmed asked.

"John Giles is worth a lot of money," Mohammad said. "His family is offering a reward for his safe return, no questions asked. Two hundred and fifty thousand dollars."

Ahmed didn't care about the money. The FBI wouldn't stop looking for them even if they freed the American. That was out of the question anyway, but he might still be useful as a hostage if they were cornered.

We need to get out of Oregon before this gets worse, Ahmed thought, shivering. *There is still a wide gap between the FBI and Oregon's state officials, and I need to keep it that way. If Ayatollah Fouhad blames me for losing this sanctuary, I'm doomed.*

"What else did they say?" asked Ahmed.

"That's all, Sir," Mohammad said. "Nothing else."

Ahmed looked as his men, seeing their heads nod in agreement. "Yes," Yasir agreed. "Just the rewards and the photos."

"We need more information," Ahmed said.

"You could send someone they're not looking for into town, Sir," Mohammad said. "He could buy newspapers and a portable computer. Then we could check the WorldNet and know what's being reported."

Ahmed thought for a time. It wasn't a bad idea.

"Sir?" Yasir interrupted.

Ahmed looked at him. "Yes?"

"Karim is getting weaker, and they showed my photograph on the news. He's going to die if we don't get him medical help soon, and it would be best if I put some distance between the searchers and myself. I could easily get out of Oregon with Karim."

"How?"

"I know my way around the state. They have checkpoints in Portland and on the interstate highways – I-5, I-205, and I-84 – but that's all. I could take one of the vans and leave Oregon on back roads. They'd never notice."

Ahmed frowned. "How do you know there aren't more checkpoints?"

"It's been on the news. Only the interstates, airports, and mass transportation hubs are covered," Yasir said.

"Is that correct?" Ahmed asked, looking at Mohammad.

"I think so. It's what they said on television."

"How would you get out of Oregon?" Ahmed asked.

"It's easy once you get away from Portland," Yasir said. "You just have to drive a hundred miles or so east. There's a small bridge across the Columbia in Hood River, another in The Dalles, and others further east if those are being watched. You can see the bridges from the hills, so I can make sure it was clear before I crossed. Washington's on the other side."

That has possibilities, Ahmed thought. "Then what?"

"I'd leave Karim at an emergency room near the Canadian border. He's not wanted for anything. American health care would take care of him and get him fit to travel. He could say he shot himself by accident."

"Continue."

"I could escape into Canada. He could follow when he was released from the hospital. The Canadians aren't involved in this, but my being seen up there could help draw off the search.

"Oregon won't keep the checkpoints up if they think we've left. Once they open the roads, you can easily slip away."

Ahmed smiled. "Yasir is loyal, and he has a good idea. He risks himself to help us escape. Praise Allah."

"Praise Allah," his men echoed.

"Get Karim ready to travel," Ahmed ordered. "I have some records I want you to take, and I'll give you money. Don't linger in Canada. I want you to buy plane tickets and keep moving. Go to Cairo and contact the embassy when you get there."

"Thank you, Sir," Yasir said.

"One thing," Ahmed said. They all looked at him.

"You will not allow yourselves to be captured alive. Not under any circumstances. Anyone who leaves will wear Palestine belts until they are well clear of the search area. This is my command. Do you understand?"

Mohammad looked puzzled.

"Palestine belts," Ahmed said, with exaggerated patience. "You trained with them at the camps."

"The explosive belts," Mohammad said, nodding. "They're out in the barn."

"Yasir and Karim are to wear the belts and use them if necessary," Ahmed repeated. "Our sanctuary must be preserved."

"I understand, Sir," Yasir said.

"I don't want anyone captured in Oregon." Ahmed stared into each pair of eyes. "Do you understand me? This order is a *fatwa* from Ayatollah Fouhad himself. Punishment will be harsh for those who fail to obey."

They knew what that meant. All the men nodded, lowering their eyes in submission. "Allah is great," they chorused.

"I will give you more detailed instructions before you leave, but you are to remember the *fatwa* beyond all else. Allah will show you no mercy if you fail to obey."

"Allah is great," the men chorused.

"Should we send someone into town for news first?" asked Mohammad.

"No," Ahmed said, shaking his head. "Everyone is to stay inside, except for one guard watching the road in. The guard is to be changed every two hours and stationed in a sheltered position where he won't be visible from the air."

"Yes, Sir," Mohammad said, nodding.

"Have someone bring me a road map of Oregon," Ahmed ordered. He was smiling as he went back to his temporary office. *It's all going turn out just fine. Allah will provide for us.*

CHAPTER TEN
LOW PROFILE

The White House

The Marine Guards took Mike directly to the bubble.

"The President knows you're here, Sir," the Sergeant said. "He sends his apologies. He's in conference. Can we get you some coffee?"

"Absolutely," Mike said. "That would be greatly appreciated."

Mike was deep in thought when he felt the door open, more a feeling of pressure difference than sound. *"Kumusta ka."*

Mike looked up and smiled. "Greetings to you, my friend," he said, in English rather than Tagalog. "How have you been, Gerardo?"

"Good." The old Filipino grinned at him. He was carrying a silver tray with coffee, bagels and sweet rolls. His bushy black hair was sprinkled with gray. "You look better than the last time I saw you, Sir. Are you all right?"

"The doctors say so."

"I'm glad, Sir. We're serving the Jamaican Blue Mountain coffee now. I think you'll like it."

"Thank you," Mike said.

The porter had been his friend, back when he was stationed in the White House and recovering from Yemen. It was a difficult time for a man who took pride in his fitness, especially since Mike had to sometimes be helped in and out of his wheelchair. Gerardo, a retired Navy Chief, talked the staff into helping. He'd always checked in to see if Mike was well before he went home and more than once had quietly gotten him medical assistance.

Ever since, Mike made it a point to send Gerardo special gifts for Christmas and birthdays. The old man's grandson was now at the Naval Academy and doing well, thanks in part to a letter Mike had written for him.

Mike took a sip and smiled, looking at the presidential seal on the Lennox china. "It's excellent. Hell of a lot better than what we got in the field, for sure."

"Yes, Sir. You watch your ass, General. The scuttlebutt is there's a Senator…."

Just then the President entered and Gerardo stopped abruptly.

"Would you like some coffee, Mr. President?" Gerardo's tone and demeanor was suddenly crisp and formal. He carefully draped a white napkin over his arm as he prepared to pour for the President.

President Hale nodded absently, preoccupied. *He already looks tired, and the day hasn't even started*, thought Mike. Gerardo poured the President a cup, then excused himself and left, securing the door behind him.

"Good Morning, Mr. President."

"Hello, Mike," the President said. "I'd allocated an hour for you, but I have to cut it short. We've got some flaps going, and I'm running late. I was distressed to hear about Colonel Giles. How'd it go in Oregon?"

"They have some odd laws out there, Sir, but I think it went as well as could be expected." Mike proceeded to give the President a quick briefing.

He finished by saying, "The Tangos were Arab *jihad* types, the same as what hit us at Gerry's house. FBI's on top of it, but Iron John's still MIA."

"I want everything possible done to get him back."

"Yes, Sir. That's what I promised Gerry."

The President raised an eyebrow. "Did you now…?"

"Yes, Sir, I did. I gave her my word. We don't have a program without her."

"How is she?"

"Grieving, but functional. She's back at NSA. Her brother, Will, is running Cybertech. We'll have a running program again as soon as we get Cybertech the payment I promised them."

"I'll make sure that's attended to, Mike. Just get the damned paperwork in place to cover it." The President was silent for almost a minute, thinking. "Have you seen the morning news?"

"No, Sir." He'd gotten back home after midnight and had decided sleep was his first priority, even skipping his morning workout.

"I want you to check in with Judy regularly. She'll keep you current on the political situation. There are several major items. The protests in Portland are continuing, and now we have a Senate investigation spooling up. You get to be the target."

Mike frowned, puzzled.

"Do you know who Senator Harriet Stiles is?" the President asked.

"I've heard the name, Sir."

"Powerful lady. Chairs the Senate Committee on Health, Education, Labor, and Public Welfare. She gave a speech on the floor yesterday. Seems to be after your head."

Mike frowned. "Why me?"

"Judy will give you the text. The Senator spoke of entrapment and jack-booted military thugs running around the country harassing minorities and killing people."

"Meaning the Tangos we nailed at Gerry's house?" Mike asked. "Self-defense. It was a kill team, and they damned near succeeded. We took casualties."

"More than that," the President said.

"I don't understand, Sir."

"Politics," the President said, looking disgusted. "There was an anonymous call to a TV station in Portland. It warned of suicides and demonstrations."

"What's their problem?"

"They say it's you."

Mike blinked.

"You ordered the lock down," the President said. "Threats get news and so do the protests in Oregon. That attracts political interest, hence Senator Stiles' speech. She wants you subpoenaed to testify about the checkpoints in Oregon and the shootings in Maryland."

"Wonderful," Mike said dryly. "What should I do, Sir? I don't want to become a political liability for you."

"You are to do nothing," the President said, "and that's an order. Keep a low profile, just like you did in Oregon. No interviews. No public comments, and if you do get subpoenaed, you say nothing. Just keep doing the job I gave you. I need Gerry's system deployed."

"Yes, Sir," Mike said. "Do I allow myself to be subpoenaed?"

"We'll try to avoid it. The last thing we need is another media circus right now.

"I've got other people tasked with the political, PR, and the legal aspects of the problem. FBI and DHS can take the heat for the checkpoints."

"Yes, Sir."

"We'll give Stiles some serious pushback. There's a fuss brewing in the Senate over what committee should have jurisdiction. It probably won't be hers, though she's requested purview."

"Yes, Sir," Mike said. "Is there any good news?"

"There sure is." Somewhat to his amazement, Hale flashed him a brief smile. Grim, but definitely a smile. "The FBI has some news. Agent Simpson will be waiting outside by now and he'll brief you after I leave."

"Yes, Sir," Mike said.

"I also want you to meet with Doctor Moira. Most urgent." The President pulled an envelope out of his folder, jotted a name and number on it, and handed it to Mike. "I've got to go. Give the doctor this note and keep in touch. The main thing is to remember I want the closest possible hold on everything. Above all, keep a low profile."

"I understand, Sir."

"Your picture is in this morning's *Post,* and there are reporters lurking outside."

That's just what I need, Mike thought.

"Don't let it bother you," the President said. "Check with Judy when you leave. She'll get you out of the White House without attracting media attention."

"Yes, Sir." Mike stood up respectfully as the President gathered his papers and left.

Keep a low profile. Mike shook his head, imagining himself sitting before a Senate committee refusing to answer questions he probably didn't know the answers to anyway.

Mike muttered a curse, fingering the envelope. Now the President wanted him to see some damned doctor. *I thought I'd put all the concerns about my physical and mental fitness behind me. They cleared me for active duty.*

Southern Washington State

Yasir heaved a sigh of relief as he swung the van into the rest area. He parked carefully in a corner of the lot, under the trees, where he could see both the entrance and exit. He studied his surroundings carefully while feigning casualness, following his training.

The rest area was almost empty, only three cars, one large truck, and two motor homes. None had Oregon plates, none were close to his vehicle, and no one seemed to be paying his van any attention.

Yasir shut off the engine, rolled his window open a crack and savored the fresh air. He took several deep breaths, willing the tension to pass from his body.

"Can you hear me, nephew?" he called softly to Karim in Arabic.

"Yes." The voice from the back of the van was weak and strained.

"Allah is great," Yasir said. "He's kept us safe. We're out of Oregon."

"Allah is great," his nephew agreed in a labored voice. He was barely able to speak. It was a prayer from a man desperately clinging to life.

"It went as planned," Yasir said softly, still watching his mirrors. He had a good view of the area, but there was a blind spot directly behind the van. He needed to ensure it stayed clear.

Patience, Yasir thought, glancing at the clock on the dashboard. *Wait for at least five minutes to check for surveillance and make sure you've not attracted attention,* he remembered. *It's important to look relaxed and unconcerned.*

Karim gave a grunt. It might have been pain, but Yasir chose to interpret it as a question.

"Stay quiet," Yasir said, continuing to survey the area. "I'll give you some water as soon as I'm sure this area is clear. I was right. There were no checkpoints. We're across the river in Washington State now, outside the search zone. I'll have you to a hospital very soon."

Yasir poured himself a cup of water from the jug, savoring its cool taste, forcing himself to take slow sips. *The important thing now is not to attract any attention.* He held his hands out, pleased they were no longer shaking.

It had been a near thing. He'd felt the nets closing. *Ahmed wanted to kill my nephew, because Karim was slowing us down. Ahmed wouldn't have taken him to safety or left him for the Americans to arrest.*

The allocated time was up, but Yasir forced himself to wait two more minutes before he eased himself into the back of the van. Karim's skin was cold when Yasir touched it, and the bandages on his abdomen were soaked dark red with blood.

His body temperature is dropping, Yasir thought. *That's not good.* He put another blanket on his nephew, then lifted his head and tried to give him some water. Karim took a few sips and opened his eyes.

Karim was pale, and Yasir saw the fear in his eyes. *He's only twenty. This is a stupid way for him to die, gut shot by an old businessman. They trained us for assassinations, bombings, and suicide attacks, not for kidnappings where we're restricted by rules to let infidels live.*

"Try to drink more water," Yasir said, holding the cup and gently cradling his nephew's head.

Karim nodded weakly, taking another sip, then another.

"I dare not give you food," Yasir said, "but I'll get you to a hospital soon."

Karim managed two more sips before an electronic beeping interrupted them. Yasir whipped off the blankets and then froze in horror. He stared at the red light blinking on Karim's belt, knowing he had ten seconds to live.

He grabbed for the door handle, letting Karim fall with a thud. He was twenty feet from the van and running hard when the explosion blew him off his feet. Jagged metal ripped though him, breaking both legs and ripping his intestines open.

Yasir hit the asphalt hard, face down, breaking his nose before he twisted and managed to roll over on his side. A secondary explosion racked the van, spreading sheets of flaming gasoline and a towering column of black smoke.

The parking lot was on fire and his clothes were burning. He tried to work his arms, willing them to pull him to safety, but nothing happened. There were white bones sticking out of his legs.

He screamed in agony, still aware and watching helplessly as his flesh started melting. Pain faded with consciousness. Yasir never felt a thing when his own belt exploded.

The White House

Agent Simpson nodded pleasantly as he entered the bubble. "Good morning, General." He eased himself comfortably into a chair, giving Mike a broad grin.

Mike glanced at his watch, then back at Simpson. *What's so dammed amusing?* "Did you swallow a canary or something, Obie?"

Simpson's grin got even wider. "Pretty day. Interesting stuff on the news."

Mike noticed he had a gap between his front teeth, which glistened pearly white in vivid contrast to his jet-black skin. "Would you like some coffee?"

"Yes, thanks," the agent said, shaking his head in exaggerated wonderment. "Looks like it could be a full time job protecting you."

"It should be quite safe here," Mike said dryly.

Simpson looked dubious. "Depends on your viewpoint, I guess. The Bureau's not real worried about more assassins – figures your SEALs can handle them – but there's a lot of shit being stirred up. Reporters, protesters, Oregon politicians, now maybe Senate hearings."

"I know," Mike said. "The President wants me to keep a low profile."

"Good luck." Simpson chuckled. "You're the best show since the Super Bowl. How'd you get so popular?"

"I'm not sure. How many reporters are there outside?"

"All of them, I think." Simpson took a sip of coffee, still looking amused. "Camera crews, trucks with satellite feeds, all the goodies. They're herd animals, you know. Nobody wants to be left out."

"How'd they know I'm here?"

"Leaks, probably." Simpson shrugged. "Or maybe just alert reporting. Your Humvee stands out, General. My boss said to offer you some Bureau cars, unmarked sedans, at least until things settled down. How about a nice inconspicuous Ford Fairlane? Got an old brown one, dented and everything, you could start with. Looks like a square turd with wheels."

"Marvelous," Mike said. "Will the Bureau help me dodge subpoenas too?"

Simpson shook his head. "We're on the other side."

"Never mind, then. I'd better make my own arrangements for transport."

The two men looked at each other for a long moment. Mike finally broke the silence. "I assume you didn't come all the way over here to loan me a car or do stand up comedy. What's up? The President said you had some news."

"Bukhari," Simpson said. "More and more connections."

"Keep talking," Mike said.

"Were you briefed on the nuke they found here in DC a month or so back?"

Mike nodded.

"We still don't know how they got it in. Russian technology, but we're pretty sure the Tangos were from Bukhari. One was a suspected Bukhari intelligence officer."

"That was an act of war," Mike said.

"If we could prove a connection. Hard to do, now they're dead." Simpson shrugged. "State wanted us to back off, and the Bureau agreed."

"Why?"

"We're more interested in finding their control and who helped them slip the nuke past our detectors. That was quite a trick. We think they had high-level inside help."

Mike nodded.

"We do know the subjects your men shot in Maryland were connected to Bukhari," Simpson added.

"Your agent Sommers said that too. Were they Bukhari nationals?"

"One was." Simpson nodded. "The rest were Saudis, but they were all members of the Lions of Allah. Three of the four subjects identified in Oregon are also known members. The Lions are a group funded by Bukhari intelligence and used for wet work."

"Like the Syrians use Hezbollah?"

"Bloodier and more focused on assassinations. Remember, Iran's behind Hezbollah."

"They're the paymaster," Mike said, "but Syria fronts for Hezbollah operationally, and the whole region pretends 'The Party of God' is an independent political organization. It's a charade. Syria was forced out of Lebanon, but Hezbollah stayed on as their proxy. The ruse is Hezbollah gives to orphanages. They use their militant wing, *Islamic Jihad*, for terrorism."

"Mideast politics make my head hurt," Simpson said. "I'm not going to argue with you."

"Tell me more about the Lions of Allah," Mike said. "What's the FBI's view? We don't run into them much on the military side."

"You wouldn't. They do assassinations mostly, usually in Arab countries, or in Europe, in countries with a large Muslim presence. Mostly they target competing Muslim groups with eliminations, bombings, and violent public acts to spread terror. You didn't see them much in Iraq or Afghanistan, because Al Qaeda is their mortal enemy. They don't get along with the Muslim Brotherhood either, though the two groups are not in open conflict."

"Why not?"

"It's hard to say. The Muslim Brotherhood and the Saudi Government are tight, and the Lions of Allah have pretty much left both of them alone." Simpson shrugged. "The Lions mostly do targeted messy OPs for Bukhari and its allies."

"What kind of OPs?"

"Soft targets, typically. Martyrdom operations and wet work a government doesn't want to be associated with. What's odd is they had a team in Oregon, and the nature of the operation they mounted there."

Mike frowned, shaking his head in puzzlement. "What do you mean?"

"The Lions of Allah are more likely to blow up Cybertech than to mount a covert snatch and grab." Simpson shrugged. "They're normally high profile and violent, but now they're acting covert and gentle. Doesn't fit."

"Kill teams hosing Americans with automatic weapons fire is gentle? I don't think so."

"Maybe careful is a better word," Simpson said with a shrug. "My point is they're not acting normal. They left a tidy crime scene in Oregon. No blood, no bodies, nothing blown up. Even the Maryland operation seemed to have a tight leash."

"Not very," Mike objected. "They caused a firefight."

"That was an accident. They're trying to be inconspicuous."

"Tell me why."

"I don't know why," Simpson said. "It's just a feeling I have."

"You're scaring me."

Simpson grinned. "I thought Marines were fearless."

"It bothers me we have one of the terrorist front organizations involved. Remember back during Reagan when Hezbollah snatched Terry Anderson, the Associated Press reporter?"

"Lebanon, March 1985. It led to Iran Contra," Simpson said. "I seem to remember there was a Marine involved there too....."

"Ollie North, and it ruined his promising career," Mike said. "The operation was a cluster fuck, but President Reagan really wanted those hostages back."

"He must have."

"It took seven years to get Anderson back. I hope you've gotten better at hostage recovery over the years."

"What's your point?"

"I gave Gerry my word we'd get her dad back if at all possible."

Simpson gave him an odd look. "Did you now?"

Mike nodded.

"It could be a tough job...."

"Damned tough if Gerry's father has been passed over to another terrorist group so Bukhari can deny responsibility."

"This shit is way over my pay grade," Simpson said.

"Need I mention the President wants him back too? I think that's an FBI responsibility."

Simpson sighed. "The Director thinks so too. We're doing all we can."

"Do you think Colonel Giles is still alive?"

"The Bureau is divided, but the current view is that he is. He'd have more value as a hostage than dead."

"You said three were members of this Lions of Allah group. Who was the fourth?"

"Good question." Simpson pulled a small computer out of his pocket. "Take a look at this."

Mike watched a video clip of a man coming through security at an airport. The time and date stamp was overlaid, as were location and camera codes. "I assume PDX stands for Portland International Airport?"

Simpson nodded.

"Then I've seen that shot before. Sommers showed me some stills. He told me the Tango's ID said he was a Saudi banker, but was phony."

"Nassar Fuad," Simpson agreed. "Who was definitely in Zurich at the time this was filmed. The Saudis are pissed about that."

"So who is he?" asked Mike, pointing at the screen. There was something about the video nagging at the back of his mind, something familiar.

"We don't know," Simpson said. "We only got one clear shot of his face and can't get a match on any of our databases. We sent the clip to CIA, who is sharing it with Mossad, Saudi Intelligence, and our other friends in the Mideast."

"Intelligence, but not criminal agencies?" Mike asked. "Not Interpol?"

"No." Simpson shook his head. "Not yet, anyway. We think this one's an executive. A pro. We'd like to take him alive, and we also want to rescue Colonel Giles. I'd like your SEALs to help."

"If you are quick, but they have a broader mission."

Simpson nodded. "I was going to get to that. The Director wanted me to ask you something off the record. Are you cleared for direct action against Bukhari?"

Mike looked into his eyes and nodded slowly.

"What are the limits?"

"Three redlines. No regime change. No invasion. Plausible deniability. Low profile and quick. You can have the SEALs for 36 hours, no more. How would you employ them?"

"Independent action under Lt. Clover, if that's okay with you?"

Mike nodded. "I don't need to give him a specific order for that."

Simpson grinned. "Good. That's what he said too."

"There's still a problem. We have to find the bad guys first."

"We may have gotten lucky," Simpson said. "A civilian in Oregon reported a suspicious group who'd rented an old farmhouse. The lead came in an hour or so after the reward was posted."

"Jesus, Obie," Mike frowned, "that's ancient history. How long does it take you to follow up? Colonel Giles could be dead by now. If these people are the Tangos we're looking for, they'll be long gone."

"Like I said, we got lucky." Simpson looked embarrassed. "We did an aerial recon within a few hours of the tip, but didn't see anything. Then the citizen seeking the reward called back and asked why the hell nothing had been done. Luckily, he talked to Chief Ward, who believed him and checked it out."

"Ward's a good man."

"The Chief took some photos with a telephoto lens." Simpson clicked his computer, pulling up a small photo.

"Can you blow it up?" Mike asked, straining to see.

"I can try," Simpson said. He tapped some keys. Mike could barely make out a shadowed figure in dark clothing concealed under the trees. It looked like he was holding a long gun of some type.

"They set out a guard," Mike said, "Putting him where he couldn't be seen from the air. The Islamists worry about drones."

"That's right," Simpson agreed. "The subject is guarding the entrance to the farm. They rotate guards every two hours. The weapon is an AK variant. Could be a drug gang, but these guys seem too disciplined. Mostly the cartels grow their pot on the Federal Lands and brew meth on the Res these days. Federal Lands used to be sanctuaries, especially along the borders."

"Do you think it's them?"

Simpson nodded. "Chief Ward thinks so and so does Clover. Our threat guys think they are dirty, whoever they are."

Mike frowned. "We're not good at arresting people. I've authorized lethal force. Do you have any problems with that old Posse Comitatus law? I don't want to get your ass in a sling."

"No problems," Simpson said. "You're covered. We got an okay from Justice. They say the Navy's probably exempted in times of national emergency."

"Clover's not going to lose more of his men screwing around. Nor will I order him to."

"We know." Simpson nodded.

"You better."

"The big issue is time, General."

Mike's eyes narrowed. "You've already started this, haven't you?"

"Don't worry. We put agents on site to guard Cybertech until Clover's people get back."

"Where is he now?"

"Clover's team is in position at the farm. Everyone else is holding back. He reported four Tangos, but thinks there are probably more inside. They've not seen Colonel Giles, but they did a recon and found two recent graves."

"What's he waiting for?" asked Mike. He didn't like to interfere with his subordinate commanders, but it was embarrassing hearing about a planned action from another agency. *Well it's my own damned fault*, he thought, looking around at the triply shielded walls of the bubble. *I couldn't be more out of communication if I was on the dark side of the moon.*

"Clover says he'll take down anyone who tries to leave, but he wants a sniper team in place to support him before he assaults the farmhouse. The Bureau offered one, but he insisted on using SEALs. A team is being flown in from California. They should be getting there around now."

"It's a good call," Mike agreed, reluctantly. "Clover's teams train constantly for rescue ops, and it's better to have everyone on the same page when people start laying down fire."

"Command is a bitch, isn't it?" Simpson gave him a sympathetic look. "We don't need another Ruby Ridge."

Mike nodded, wishing he were there. "Do you have FBI assets involved?"

"Like I said, Clover convinced Agent Sommers his SEALs are better for this mission. He agreed to let Sommers observe, but won't allow anyone else close. We have twenty agents and a medevac chopper standing by off the property." A glum look crossed Simpson's face. "My boss will not be pleased if this doesn't work out."

"Clover's there, I'm not, and he's making good calls. So what do I do now? Rush back to Oregon?"

"Nope," Simpson said. "Now that you're briefed, you and I get to go visit the spooks. CIA has been chasing down foreign connections, and there's something new about Bukhari they want us to hear. Wouldn't tell me what, even on a secure phone, except to say the orders to brief us come from the DCI."

Mike raised an eyebrow. "When are we supposed to be in Langley?"

"Nine thirty, or 09:30 as you military types like to say. We'll make it easy. In view of your new celebrity status, the President loaned us his helicopter, Marine One." Simpson grinned. "You can wave at the reporters when we take off. The blonde from CNN is a looker."

Mike groaned and pushed his chair back. "I need to leave a 'good luck' message for Lieutenant Clover."

"And make sure he checks in when he completes his mission?"

"Command's a bitch, Obie," Mike said, vowing to check for messages and leave his secure phone turned on.

Rural Jasper County, Oregon

"Heaven to Angel One. God's arrived. ETA your position one zero."

Clover keyed his wrist mike, "Angel One copies. I'll have Angel Four meet God at the intersection off the main road."

"Heaven copies," the voice said. "Please confirm, God."

"Roger, we got it Heaven," came a weaker transmission. "God copies."

Heaven was the command center, a van now swarming with FBI agents two miles away. Clover had sent Angel Two, Lieutenant Junior Grade McClintock, back to make sure there was support rather than interference. No friendlies would be cleared into the area without his approval.

By convention, the bad guys were Tangos. If they detected any hostages, they would be designated Halos, with Colonel Giles preassigned Halo One. The two-man sniper team was God One and Two, and Chief Petty Officer Jensen, the shooter, was one of the best.

He was glad to have CPO Jensen, but it was daylight, and Clover would have preferred a night assault. *You take what you can get*, he thought, looking at his watch impatiently. Finally, he got the message he was waiting for.

"God's in position. Say Tango count, Angel One."

"Tango count is not confirmed. Suspect four, repeat four Tangos, three plus one," Clover said, identifying a total of four men, three inside the farmhouse, plus the sentry. "Wait a minute, there's a new one, just coming out of the farmhouse, toting a long gun with a big clip."

Clover watched the man as he crossed the open space and disappeared into the woods. He looked older than the others, and not especially alert.

Clover keyed his mike again. "Tango count is now five, three plus two. The outside two are confirmed. Stay alert. There may be more Tangos inside. Count is not confirmed."

"Hey, Jensen," a voice said quietly, "the new Tango is headed your way. They might have caught a glint off your scope."

That was Jensen's roommate and friend, Petty Officer Third Class Ditmar, from New York. Clover recognized the accent.

Ditmar was slightly built, only five nine, but a crack shot. The kid was too small for hand-to-hand and didn't have the reach to be a knife fighter, but he was a wizard with a long gun.

The last three times Clover had tested Ditmar's skill on the shooting range had cost him $100 each. *The kid shot better each time. How does someone from New York learn to handle a rifle like that?*

"This is God," Jensen said in his soft mountain drawl. "I see him, Ditty, about ten o'clock." He was defining twelve o'clock as the barrel of his rifle, now sited on the living room window of the farmhouse.

"Yep, just entering the woods. He's definitely heading for you," Ditmar said. "I'll keep an eye on him. Just wanted to give you a heads-up."

"I appreciate it," Jensen said. He rechecked the settings on his scope, making sure he had the distance and wind corrections dialed in to his satisfaction. The shot was an easy range, just a shade over two hundred and forty yards.

"Okay, everybody, this is Angel One. It's rock and roll time," Clover said. "Angel Four, take out the sentry."

There was a short pause. No one heard the shot from the suppressed rifle, and no one but Angel Four saw the rounds punch a hole the size of a half dollar in the Tango's head. The man's head snapped sideways in a spray of blood and bone, and the rest of his body followed, dropping out of sight in the low bushes. He never knew what hit him.

"This is Angel Four, the sentry is down. Repeat, sentry is down. The Tango is a hard kill." CPO Simmons didn't elaborate.

"Angel One to God, we're moving in," Clover said.

"Copy that, Angel One," came the soft twang. "God loves you."

Jensen pulled back on the set trigger until it clicked into place. This step expended most of the energy required to fire the weapon, thus removing even the slight tug induced by a cold trigger pull. Even at this relatively close range, a small twitch of Jensen's rifle could easily cause a miss. If needed, death was now just an ounce of pressure away.

Using hand gestures, Clover put his team in motion. The squad broke up into two fire teams. The first, Clover, Simmons, Gladstone, and Bailey, took the front of the farmhouse. The second, Dillon, Delaney, and Martin, covered the back. CPO Dillon, Angel Five, was the leader.

Missing was Angel Three, Senior Chief Kowalski, now sitting back comfortably behind his M2 50-cal machine gun, which was cocked and had a full nine-yard belt of ammo in place. "Ma Deuce" was Kowalski's preferred weapon.

The M2 was usually vehicle mounted. Most thought "Ma Duece" was too heavy to lug around in the field, but Kowalski wanted firepower. Everyone agreed the M2 hit like a freight train, was accurate, and dead nuts reliable. It got the job done.

Kowalski was situated off to the side where he could cover the farmhouse, barn, and the entry road. He was chomping an unlit cigar and watching carefully.

Kowalski's job was heavy fire support, and he needed to stay very cool. Friendly fire accidents were a major concern, especially when there was resistance and a high volume of direct fire was needed for suppression. Kowalski's heavy rounds could punch clear through the farmhouse and still penetrate body armor like tissue paper, but he was an artist with the weapon.

Jensen watched the front window through his scope. The curtains moved, then were pushed back, and he saw a figure drawing down on the assault force. Jensen gently caressed the hair trigger.

With a satisfying crack, the round erupted from the barrel in a blast of superheated expanding gas. The view from the scope briefly went out of focus as a cloud of hot gas from the barrel floated across his line of sight. In the distance he saw the man's head explode, throwing the Tango back across the room.

"Was that you, God?" asked Clover, into his lip mike. He and his team sprinted for the front door, knowing Jensen was covering them.

"Affirmative." Jensen slid the bolt back and chambered another round. "Tango at the front window with an automatic weapon is down." He announced it with the emotional detachment of a surgeon who'd just removed a malignant tumor.

Clover reached the front door, taking a position on one side while Simmons took the other. Before they could move, a long burst of automatic weapons fire shattered what was left of the glass in the front window.

Gladstone and Bailey were about ten yards behind. They frantically dove for the ground, as green tracers screamed by them. Bailey cursed as a bullet tore into his arm. They rolled away from the fire, struggling to bring their weapons to bear, but there was no cover.

"Son of a bitch," Kowalski muttered, stroking his trigger twice. The fusillade from his machine gun splintered the aging clapboard siding and removed both sashes of the double hung window. The hostile fire ceased.

Protected by Kowalski's punishing cover fire, Clover kicked in the front door with such force the lockset ripped free of the wooden frame. Simmons immediately tossed in a flash-bang grenade.

Flash-bangs worked in training and when surprise was total, but experienced Tangos could shield their eyes and ears to minimize the effect. Still, with luck and surprise, they could buy a rescue team a few seconds of time.

The problem with non-lethal weapons is they're not lethal, Clover thought as he waited for the concussion. To lead a SEAL assault team, he had to be first through the door. Nothing said he had to like it.

Clover counted to three in his head, *one thousand and one, one thousand and two, one thousand and three.* The cabin shuddered from the grenade's sonic assault and Clover instantly leapt through the door, his Browning 9-mm pistol in both hands, sweeping the room right to left.

Clover preferred his pistol for close work. Simmons, right behind him, had traded his assault rifle for a short-barreled 12-guage loaded with double-ought buckshot. They were deadly at twenty feet, worthless at a hundred. It was better than trying to swing a long gun quickly in a confined space.

There was a body lying against the wall. Most of the Tango's head was missing, and there was blood spray all over the wall. Another was slumped over a light machine gun near the window, his body cut almost in half. The room was clear.

Simmons entered behind him, staying to Clover's right. The two men moved forward, each man training the barrel of his weapon, and his attention, on a pie-shaped wedge of space that expanded in front of him. The overlapping wedges were each man's field of fire, and each was responsible for what happened in his kill zone.

"Angel One confirms two more Tangos down. Count is now three down," Clover said.

They were looking down a long hallway with doors on both sides. Gladstone and Bailey entered behind them, the latter with blood on his left sleeve and a field dressing on his arm.

Without looking back, Clover motioned for them to check the rooms on the right. He and Simmons would take the left. Clover saw a blur of motion in the hallway. Someone had run from a room on his side into another on the opposite side.

No one fired because there might have been hostages, and they didn't have a clear target. Then they heard the distinctive crash of window glass shattering. The rolling boom of Jensen's rifle came seconds later.

"Tango just exited the side window," Jensen said. "He's down."

"Four Tangos down," Clover said, calmly. "Keep your eyes open, people. One Tango is still loose outside. Checking status inside."

The two teams moved down the hall, checking the rooms in sequence. The house shuddered repeatedly with the impact of flash-bang grenades as each room was cleared.

All the rooms were empty. "Main floor is clear," Clover said into his lip mike. "No Halos."

Just then there was a roar of a racing engine. Clover saw the doors of the barn burst open as a white van raced for the driveway. It slewed sideways and slid to a stop as a volley from Kowalski's machine gun shattered its engine block. Two Tangos leapt from the doors with their automatic weapons swinging, seeking targets.

An invisible hand smashed one man sideways. He fell limply, a hard kill. Two seconds later, the crack of Jensen's rifle came rolling down from the woods.

"Drop the gun," Clover shouted, hoping to capture the other Tango alive. His hope was in vain, as the man spun, bringing his weapon to bear.

An instant later, he was cut down by a deadly crossfire from Simmons, Clover, and Kowalski.

Clover rushed over to the van. A body was slumped in the driver's seat. The back of the van was empty.

"This is Angel One. Negative Halos. We now have seven Tangos down," he said. "Anyone got a line on the one that's loose?"

"Negative. House is clear," Simmons reported.

"Barn is clear," Dillon reported. "Negative on the loose Tango. We lost track of him when he entered the woods."

There was no report from Ditmar or Jensen.

Mohammad Habib was crouching in the underbrush. He'd thought it unlikely anyone was out here, but one of his men thought he'd seen a glint of light. Reflection from water or a rock could do that, and Mohammad was eager to get out of the cabin and walk around.

He was in charge now, and it made him uneasy. Ahmed had left in the middle of the night, taking the American prisoner with him. He told Mohammad to wait for instructions, but the phone in the farmhouse had never rung.

The sounds of gunfire took Mohammad totally by surprise. He looked back at the cabin, seeing half a dozen men with weapons clearing the area for targets. He realized his men were all dead. It had happened so quickly.

The bullet-riddled wreckage of the van in the side yard was the last vehicle they had. There was nothing left to do but try to escape on foot. If he could get to Portland, a friend would hide him. Oregon was tolerant of strangers, and he should be able to drop out of sight entirely.

Mohammad started moving away from the area, especially away from the cabin and the small hill where he knew a skilled sniper was situated. Fear made him want to run, but his training prevailed. He moved cautiously, pushing branches aside with his gun barrel, being careful to make no sound.

There was a small clearing ahead. He approached it warily, looking and listening. Detecting nothing he started across, moving at a quick jog, still striving for silence.

"Freeze!"

The command came from behind him. The voice was American, but the accent was strange. Mohammad tensed. It would take only a split-second to spin and hose a spray of bullets. His weapon was on full automatic, and he'd practiced that move many times in his training.

"Don't even think about it," the voice cautioned.

Mohammad cringed as a bullet ripped past his ear, just missing his head. It passed so close he could feel the wind of its passage. The supersonic round made a sound like the crack of a whip, coming an instant before the report of the rifle.

"That's the only warning shot you get."

Mohammad didn't move.

"I'm a U.S. Navy SEAL," the voice said. "Put the weapon on the ground in front of you and step away, or I'll kill you. Your choice. Makes no difference to me either way."

Mohammad hesitated.

"Time to decide," the voice said. "You can die for nothing, or you can put your weapon down and live."

Ditmar clicked his carbine to full automatic. The *snick* of the selector seemed loud in the silence of the glade. Mohammad twitched.

"I'll give you to a count of three," Ditmar said. He started counting, slowly.

"Don't shoot."

Mohammad put his weapon on the ground, moving slowly and carefully. He straightened up and took one step back, then another, raising his hands. *I submit to Allah's will*, he thought. *We believe in Allah and what has been revealed to us, and to Him do we submit.*

Mohammad felt strangely relieved. Allah had spared him. It was over, at least for him.

CHAPTER ELEVEN
ANTHRAX LADY

CIA Headquarters, Langley, Virginia

They turned in their badges at the guard station and thanked their escort, an attractive young woman who wanted field OPS but was stuck in administration to gain experience. "I'm ordered to keep you informed," she said. "Who's my contact?"

Mike and Simpson exchanged a look.

Mike shrugged and gestured at the FBI agent. "You're more in the loop on the investigations than I am, especially the law enforcement side."

"I know where to find you, General." Simpson grinned and gave the CIA agent his card. He pulled out a pen, glanced at her badge, and wrote his secure cell phone number on the back. "Call me anytime if you get more information, Ms. Frostick."

"Especially about Bukhari," Mike added. "If you get more info on their bioweapons or *jihad* actions, we need to know right away."

"Yes, Sir." The woman looked at Simpson, smiled, and excused herself.

"What do you think?" Simpson asked. Both men assumed the CIA lobby was monitored, so they'd said nothing until they were well clear. They'd left the building and were approaching their helicopter to return to the White House.

"Tell you in a minute," Mike said. "Gotta make a call."

He pulled out his secure phone and punched in a number. "Judy, this is General Mickelson. I need you to make an appointment for me."

He took the phone from his ear and stared at it.

"Green light. We're scrambled."

He listened for a moment. "The President wants me to see a Dr. Moira, and apparently the doctor is located somewhere in the White House. I'll be there in about 40 minutes. When I'm done I could use some help dodging the reporters outside so I can get back to work."

Mike listened. "Yes, thank you very much, that will do." An uncomfortable look crossed his face. "Can you tell me something? I'm a bit puzzled. Are there concerns about my health and fitness?"

"Oh," he said. "Got it. Thanks." He pushed the off button.

"What's that all about?" Simpson asked.

"Bioweapons," Mike said, obliquely.

"Interesting," Simpson said, entering the copter and strapping his seat belt. "So what did you think of the CIA's briefing?"

"Operation Headstone?" Mike smiled wryly. The CIA was getting on board, coming around to the President's thinking. It was now treating Encapsulated Camel Pox as a serious threat. This had prompted a bit of a pissing contest between them and the Bureau.

"Ouch," Simpson said. He winced at the memory. "Not the beltway politics. I meant the Israeli report about camelpox and ECP they kept talking about."

"It was interesting," Mike said.

Mike fastened his belt and the engines roared as the big chopper lifted off. He waited for the sound to diminish. "I feel sorry for the CIA."

Simpson blinked. "Why?"

"They have an impossible job when it comes to looking for weapons." Mike shrugged. "They got burned bad over Saddam, and it's worse now. They're as nervous as a bunch of whores in church, worrying about appearances. 'Slam Dunk' Tennent is a ghost who still walks the halls at Langley."

"It's their own damned fault. The agency depends too much on technical assets, like satellites that can photograph license plates. License plates seldom attack us. "

Mike grunted noncommittally. It was an old argument.

"CIA's only source is Mossad," Simpson said. "No validation, no vetting. You'd think they haven't learned a damned thing since Chalabi."

Mike shrugged. Few things were provable in intelligence. He damned sure didn't want to revisit the Iraq WMD witch hunt, which had continued unabated even after the "missing" WMDs were "found" and used in Syria, exactly where many thought they were all along.

"Maybe, but it's all we have, and they could be right. What do you think?"

"Could be the blind squirrel found an acorn, but who knows? An agent delivers photos and incredibly detailed records from an advanced facility to develop and produce virus weapons, but Mossad refuses to allow direct access."

"Damn it, Obie, I know the Bureau's party line. Help me with this." *Mossad also reported through CIA about Gerry's program, and they were correct in every detail.*

"The threat is plausible," Mike said. "Right?"

Simpson nodded.

"Langley's convinced. What if they're correct this time?"

"We can't ignore it," Simpson admitted. "Did you see the look on the DCI's face when I told him who the mystery man on the Portland airport videos was? We got us a big fish...."

Mike looked away and took a deep breath. It had been a shock to him too. Ahmed had changed his appearance greatly.

Simpson didn't seem to notice. "Colonel Ahmed Mahmoud Muhammad, Director of Bukhari Intelligence, in charge of security and low intensity warfare. What's he doing here? Directors of intelligence don't do covert field ops."

"Not unless the stakes are so high they're afraid to delegate."

Simpson raised an eyebrow and looked interested.

"I need to talk with the Israelis," Mike said. "Why did the DCI refuse to set that up? All he has to do is ring up Mossad's director and ask him to extract his agent and arrange a visit. This camelpox thing has to scare the hell out of them."

"ECP," Simpson corrected.

"Whatever," Mike said. "A genetically engineered new bioweapon. Mossad should welcome our interest and help. Why aren't they falling all over themselves to cooperate?"

"Personal opinion?"

Mike nodded.

"Maybe the report's valid, and Israel's too nervous."

"You think the DCI already had that discussion with his Mossad counterpart?"

"I do," Simpson said, "and was turned down flat."

"Why?"

"Because Mossad isn't about to risk their source just to help us. They probably want to take out that facility themselves, but don't dare. If the Israelis attack Bukhari, the whole damned Mideast will blow up."

"They're used to that," Mike said. "It's part of their lives, every minute, every day."

"I don't think their source is a Mossad agent," Simpson said. "I'd bet it's an Arab asset."

Mike blinked, shaking his head. He tried to imagine the Arabs and the Israelis working together. *It's possible*, he thought, *unlikely, but possible.*

"Doesn't fit. Why is the control through Mossad rather than intelligence for the Arab country that owns the asset?" Mike was shaking his head. "The Arabs wouldn't let Mossad control one of their agents."

"What if the source is Palestinian?" Simpson said. "Maybe someone from one of the non-governmental Palestinian organizations."

"The same organizations that are dedicated to Israel's destruction?"

"Sure." Simpson nodded. "Why not?"

Mossad has the equipment and infrastructure to run a deep cover agent, but the Palestinians don't. "Are you serious?"

Simpson nodded. "Personal guess and don't tell my boss, but why not? It makes sense."

"The Israelis and Palestinians working together makes sense?"

"Sure. The Israelis and Palestinians working together **publicly** is a political impossibility, but that's irrelevant if the stakes are high enough."

"Maybe...." Mike said, trailing off and leaving the question dangling.

"Mossad's cooperating covertly to share the take from a Palestinian agent would make a lot of sense if it was important enough. Their single-minded goal is the safety and security of Zion, the state of Israel. They have no other reason for existence."

What a crazy theory. It's just crazy enough to have a chance of being true.

"Are you saying Mossad won't produce the source because it would be politically embarrassing to their government?" Mike asked.

"No." Simpson was watching him intently. "They shared with Langley. Wouldn't have done that if they were worried about leaks or blowback."

"Then why?"

"Risk-benefit. They know we won't be able to do what they want. There's no chance in hell that we'd commit an act of war against Bukhari."

"Mossad wants action," Mike said. "They're frustrated because they can't do anything themselves. They're frantic to protect this source because it's the only asset they have in place to watch this ECP, but desperate enough that they shared. Is that what you're saying?"

"You got it," Simpson said, nodding. "Their asset is fragile. There's probably a long list of people in Palestine who'd kill his ass if they knew the information was benefiting Israel, and all it would take is one phone call to Bukhari. That's my read. Unofficially."

"President Hale might move," Mike said musingly. "But not on his own, and not without a debate in Congress. Which would take time."

"And probably be leaked to the media...."

"Yes," Mike said.

Simpson said, "Debate is the last thing Mossad wants. They want a preemptive strike. They need to take the site out before Bukhari's ECP is in full production and distributed to Israel's enemies."

Preemptive, Mike thought. *It's the same word that the President used.* "Would Mossad trade access for an assured covert raid?"

"You're joking, of course. We'd have to make it credible that we could deliver. That wouldn't be easy. After Iraq, they think we're a bunch of bungling pussies."

"If we took out the facility, would they care how we did it?" Mike persisted.

Simpson laughed. "You haven't worked with Mossad much, have you?"

"I've never worked with Mossad at all. My expertise is in the Mideast, but most of my contacts are in Arab military organizations." Mike smiled wryly. "Close working or personal relationships with Mossad would be somewhat counterproductive to my career interests and ability to deliver results."

"Trust me on this one," Simpson said. "Mossad would make a deal with the devil himself if it served their interests. If you took out that facility by strapping a nuke to Prime Minister Tamlon's firstborn son, they'd go for it." He paused for a minute, frowning. "So long as it didn't become public, of course. Because that wouldn't serve their interests."

"So all it takes to get access is convincing Mossad that someone capable would take out that site," Mike said. "If we could assure that, would they take the deal without quibbling or interfering? Would they give me access?"

"In a New York minute," Simpson said. "But you'll never be able to convince them."

Mike was smiling. "Tell you what, Obie, I've changed my mind. When you get to a really secure phone, call Langley and get me a back channel Mossad contact with the authority to make that agreement. Can you do that?"

"Sure," Simpson said. "No problem. I'll get you the contact, but it's up to you to convince him you can deliver. How can you do that?"

"We Marines are 'can do' sorts of guys. I'll think of something." He felt better than he had since this whole thing started.

Whitehouse Basement

There was no sign on the door, just a number. *It looks like a storage closet for office supplies*, Mike thought, puzzled. He rapped gently.

"Come in," a female voice said. It was distinctly American.

That's odd, he thought. He opened the door, frowning. "I'm sorry. I'm looking for Doctor Moira. I must be in the wrong place...."

The woman blinked and looked up over her reading glasses, scowling. "I'm Doctor Sanderson. Doctor *Moira* Sanderson. And I'm somewhat busy. In fact, I'm busy as hell. What do you want?"

"Oh," Mike said. "He said 'Doctor Moira.' I'd expected a medical doctor from India?"

"Show me some ID," she said, ignoring his question, uniform, and photo badge.

Mike passed it over. She scanned it, frowned, and typed for a moment on her computer keyboard. "Just a minute."

She punched a button on her phone. "Judy? It's Moira. I've got some God damned Marine General standing here in my office." She paused. "Yes. Mickelson. I'm holding his ID chip in my hand. My scanner says it's valid."

She listened for a long moment. "He said that? Yes, of course. No, it's not a problem. Thank you." She put the phone down and handed Mike's chip back.

"May I sit down?" Mike asked, closing the door behind him.

"Might as well." She gave him a resigned look. "Why not? You're here anyway."

He looked around the room. There was a combination of machines all over the place, mostly computer workstations. The machines were interspersed with books, journals, and conference papers. Computer disks and conference proceedings were piled high, and every computer he could see had multiple windows open on the displays, even a small laptop.

She clicked something and all the displays simultaneously went blank. *They must be integrated somehow*, he thought. *It's almost surreal.*

Every wall had overflowing bookcases. There was no window, of course. The only chair in front of her desk had a stack of thick books on it. He picked one up and studied the title.

"Observations on the prophylaxis of experimental pulmonary anthrax in the monkey," he said. "I missed this one, somehow. Do you think they'll make it into a movie?"

"Very funny," she said without smiling. "Just set the books on the floor."

He did so and sat down. "The President sent me."

"I know," she said, glancing at her watch. "That's why I didn't throw you out. So why are you here, General Mickelson?"

He studied her for a moment. She had very large eyes, a round face, and dishwater blond hair, somewhat disheveled. She looked very intense, and he wondered idly how she rated an office in the White House, even as a troglodyte.

"I need a briefing," he said.

"Sure," she said. "Germs and viruses can kill people. Some nations spend a lot of effort making them into weapons. We are not one of those nations, because we signed a treaty banning the production and use of biological warfare agents. Therefore we don't know as much as we should about biowar. In fact, we don't know shit. Some of your soldiers will die because of our ignorance."

Mike felt a flash of irritation. "We drill and fight with CBW protection, Doctor."

She looked at him carefully, finally giving a slow nod. "Yes, you do. Among other things, I'm on the technical staff at SBCCOM, the Army's Soldier and Biological Chemical Command. Don't you think the title itself shows a weakness, General?"

He frowned.

"Your Marines use our gear. Fortuitously, the safeguards needed to protect personnel from chemical weapons are indistinguishable from those needed to protect them from bioweapons. So, yes, we can and do give you containment suits, HAZMAT DECON teams and fast medevac to field hospitals. Do you think that's adequate?"

Mike said, "Are you saying it's not?"

"We've been lucky," she admitted with a shrug. "Every recent war has left a legacy of health problems, and it's been getting worse. Agent Orange in Vietnam. Chemical weapons exposure in Desert Storm and afterwards. Aerosolized anthrax in Yemen."

"I was there," Mike said slowly. "In Yemen. Most of our causalities came from conventional weapons."

"Like I said, we've been lucky. The first two cases I cited were accidents of our own making, not enemy attacks. The dioxin in Agent Orange caused cancer. Desert Storm accidentally exposed 20,000 of our own troops to something bad when we destroyed a weapons bunker in Iraq."

"You call that lucky?" The bunker had been in Kuwait, but it wasn't worth arguing about.

"Damn right. Except for Yemen, which was minor, those were all chemical weapons accidents. Chemical weapons are inefficient, unless you can dunk your enemy in the stuff. In those incidents, the damage didn't show up for years or decades."

Mike said. "I lost three personnel to anthrax in Yemen."

"Yes," she agreed. "I know. And none were using their protection. I got endless grief about that woman who died. What added insult to injury, was the military gave her a fucking medal because she died from enemy action."

"Captain Richards was my communications officer. We were being overrun, and she was calling for fire support. She took her mask off so they could hear her better."

"Bad move." The doctor shook her head. "She won't do it again."

"Your bedside manner is a bit lacking, Doctor."

"My point is we've been lucky. A fiasco like the Agent Orange thing with a bioweapon could do some real harm."

I wonder how this woman would define "real harm," he mused, deciding not to ask. "There have always been accidents and friendly fire incidents. It's unavoidable, hard as we try."

"Did you ever play football, General?"

"In college," Mike said. "I played strong side linebacker at the Academy."

"Then you know you can't win with only a defensive team."

"What are you saying?"

"I'm saying we have a fundamental disadvantage. That's dangerous. We do what we can, but we don't really know what's out there. Half the time, we don't even know what's dangerous until it's too late. Our intelligence sucks, and our so-called contingency planning has more holes than a Swiss cheese. There, you got your briefing."

"Excuse me?"

"You got your briefing, General," she repeated. She took off her glasses and gave him a direct look. "Now go away and let me get back to work."

She gestured at the door, dismissing him. He didn't move.

"I can't do that, ma'am."

She was quiet for a long moment. "If I had a dollar for every hour I've wasted trying to brief curious officials about biowar, I'd be a wealthy woman." She gave a long sigh. "There are standard manuals about bio weapons. All the services have them. Go read one."

"I have." He didn't move. "I've read them all, doctor. I need to know more."

"You have, have you?" She looked at him speculatively. "What was the first time bio weapons were used in warfare?"

He blinked. "Is this a test?"

"Think of it as a qualifying exam. We should have a large staff assigned to biological warfare, but we don't because of the treaty. My average workday is fifteen hours, and that counts Saturday. I take Sunday off and use it to catch up on my reading. I don't have time to screw around with dilettantes who collect cute biowar factoids to impress their superiors."

Mike glanced at the books piled all over the office. *This woman needs to get a life*, he thought. She was starting to get on his nerves. He took a deep breath and counted to ten mentally before he responded.

"What else?"

"What do you mean?" She looked surprised. Obviously, she'd expected him to lose his temper and leave.

"Doctor, you have one hell of a big chip on your shoulder. I came to you looking for help so I can do my job. The President sent me, but, instead of help, I get a shitty attitude and a brush off. Since you're obviously a dedicated and responsible professional, I find it a bit puzzling."

"So go somewhere else." She shrugged. "If I wanted to make friends, I'd have picked a different career. Medical doctors shun me because I'm interested in diseases, not healing. Congress, for the most part, is embarrassed that jobs like mine, however few, even exist. They take every opportunity to cut my funding and jerk me around. It sucks."

She doesn't socialize well, Mike thought. *Well, neither did most Marines.*

"What else?" he persisted.

"The military is my main customer." Anger flickered in her eyes. "But it gives me a lot of crap and very little support. Most commanders don't even use the gear we design to help keep them alive. Your captain died because she took her fucking mask off, General."

"Yes," Mike admitted. "She did."

"If she shot herself in the head accidentally, would you blame the firm that made the weapon?"

Mike shook his head. "No."

"It's not my fault, but I got to spend two days in front of a Senate committee getting my ass chewed about it." The doctor heaved a long sigh. "It's technically impossible to keep out microbes without restricting air supply. Isn't that obvious?"

He spread his hands in a placating gesture. "I suppose it might be to an expert."

She didn't reply, but her look seemed just a notch less hostile.

"I came here because your work is highly respected," he said, hoping flattery might soften her. "You're the best we have, and I need your help."

"I admit the CBW masks are uncomfortable. I don't like the damned things either, but they work."

"I know they do."

"We lost two volunteers developing the current model." She gave an exasperated sigh and shook her head. "Some days I wonder why I bother."

"What else?" he asked softly.

She looked at him for a long moment before she spoke. "Why does there have to be something else?"

"I just think there is," he said. "Something personal."

"Fuck you." She enunciated the words precisely, with heavy emphasis on the first.

Mike sighed. "Can I mention a few small points without increasing your irritation? For one thing, I didn't seek you out: the President himself ordered me to see you. For another, I've not asked you for anything that I can't get from your records."

She drummed her fingers on the desk for a time, staring into his eyes, before she finally nodded. "I don't have much of a personal life. My ex-husband was a Marine officer. Because of our jobs, we didn't get to spend much time together." She lowered her eyes. "He left me for a girl young enough to be his daughter."

I see, Mike thought. *Hell hath no fury.... This woman is pissed off in about four dimensions, especially at Marines, and I need her help. Marvelous.*

Mike was quiet for a long moment, thinking. There were times when it was best not to say anything. He waited.

The doctor finally looked up. She stared at him intently. "There, I told you," she said. "Now what about my question?"

"All right, I'll play your game, Doctor." He thought for a moment. "The first time bioweapons were used in warfare? Not counting natural plagues?"

"That's the question," she said. "I'm making it easy for you. Weapons, not diseases. The plagues go back as far as human history is recorded. They may have been a significant factor in the fall of Rome."

"You want to know about the deliberate use of biological weapons? Is that your question?"

"What other kind of use is there?" She looked interested, for the first time.

"Inadvertent use and accidents. The Spaniards wiped out most of the native populations in South America with the plagues they brought."

"Correct. The Amerindian population there suffered between a 20:1 and a 25:1 drop from pre-Columbian levels to the bottoming-out point," she said in a didactic tone.

Good God, he thought. "Are you saying there was over a **ninety percent** casualty rate?"

"Not initially." She shook her head. "The first wave of disease was most likely smallpox, but the popular book *1491* claimed viral hepatitis is what did most of the initial damage. Whatever it was, it killed about one third. That was followed by Measles. Something else hit about fifteen years later, probably typhus. Then malaria. Then diphtheria, mumps, and so forth. The die off we're discussing occurred over about three generations."

"That's horrible."

"Correct again. Unimaginably so. Whole civilizations died."

She was looking at him intently. Was there a flicker of respect in her eyes? Mike wasn't sure, but hoped so. *I'm out of my depth here*, he thought. A long moment passed.

"Was that the answer you were looking for?" he finally asked.

"Actually, no. Those epidemics were merely fortuitous accidents. Don't change the subject, General. When was the first planned, overt, use of bioweapons in warfare?"

"The epidemics weren't fortuitous for the Aztecs."

"No, they weren't." She impatiently drummed her fingers on the desk. "Are you going to answer my question or not?"

Mike was thinking furiously. "I'd say the French and Indian Wars, in North America. Back before the Revolutionary War."

"Why?"

"Both sides gave smallpox infected blankets to the Indians. That's the overt use of a bioweapon."

"It is," she admitted. "But it's the wrong answer. The first documented use of a bioweapon was in 1346.

"Bubonic plague was raging in Asia Minor, in the Crimea. The locals, Mongols, may have used it as an excuse to attack an unpopular minority group, Christian merchants. In 1344 they set upon a Genoese trading party in the city of Tana, chased them to their redoubt in Caffa, and besieged them for two years."

"That's not a bioweapon," Mike objected. "It's another plague."

"I'm not finished. By the winter of 1346-7, the plague was taking a heavy toll of the besiegers, and they decided to call it off. Before they left, they spent a few days using their siege catapults to lob the corpses of plague victims over the walls into the city – it's now called Feodosia, incidentally. That's the first recorded deliberate use of a bioweapon, General."

I blew it by about four hundred years. Mike gave a resigned shrug. "So the Genoese got infected and died there."

"No, they became a disease vector. They fled in their galleys and brought the Black Death home to Genoa in January of 1348. They probably didn't know they were bringing the plague because the first cases didn't break out until two days after they docked. Too bad for them."

"Oh," he said. "The President was talking to me about the Black Death. He said a quarter of Europe died."

"That's the figure most often cited, but it's probably conservative. The death rate was more like a third in England. The only really accurate records are for the clergy. Their mortality rate was about forty-five percent, on average."

"And the Black Death was caused by a Mongol bioweapon that got out of control?"

"No, no, no," she said. "You are missing the point. It's true that the later and most horrific Mongol leaders were Muslims, 'Timur the Lame' being the poster child for the genocide of infidels, but the Mongols were barbarians who started off by slaughtering Muslims."

"Timur the Lame?"

"Today we in the West call him Tamerlan. The Muslims called him Tamerlane the Great, 'The Sword of Islam.' He held the world genocide record up until moderns like Hitler or Stalin. He was late 14th century, the last and most powerful of the Nomad Rulers, and many bloody generations down the Genghis Khan Blood Line. He died in 1405."

Mike nodded slowly, recognizing the name. "Tamerlan, the 'Sword of Islam,' the ancient Muslim Hitler who conquered much of the world and slaughtered millions of Christians? The one who spread terror and made pyramids from the skulls of his enemies?"

"That's the one and he was a nightmare, but I think the plague was a crude *Muslim* bioweapon originally used *against* the Mongols. One that went viral a century too late to save its wielders."

"Really?"

"Sure. Think about it. The Mongols were *nomads*. They were about plunder, not about religion or science. Where would they get a bioweapon?"

"No idea."

"They wouldn't. The Mongols didn't have the capability, but in the 13th century, the Muslims had the most advanced medical science in the world. They knew about germs and were using vaccinations to immunize against smallpox."

Mike frowned. "A century is long time. How could a bioweapon possibly take so long to take effect?"

"Easily. Widely dispersed nomads are not a good disease vector. They must have learned that when they banded together, they died. Europe was a different situation, with its dense populations and towns with poor sanitation. I think the Mongols were infected long before they besieged Caffa. Life was nasty, brutish, and short in those days."

Mike thought about it. "That's an interesting idea. The Muslims were trying to defend themselves, used a crude bioweapon, and The Black Death in Europe was collateral damage."

"No one knows, but I think it's possible. The irony is that the Mongols lived and became Muslims themselves, having adopted the religion of the sword. By then they knew enough about the plague to know they'd die if they didn't disperse. I think that's why they gave up the siege of Caffa and fled."

"Tell me when and how that conflict started," Mike said. Her story made sense.

"The Mongols, led by a grandson of Genghis Khan, Hulaga Khan, killed the Muslim Caliph at Baghdad in 1258 and sacked the city, thus ending the Abbasid Caliphate that had been in existence for over 500 years. Kahn said he'd spare those who gave up their arms, but he lied.

"The Grand Library of Baghdad, containing countless precious historical documents and books on subjects ranging from medicine to astronomy, was destroyed. Survivors said that the waters of the Tigris ran black with ink from the enormous quantities of books flung into the river. Baghdad was a depopulated, ruined city for several centuries."

"You're claiming that the Black Plague was caused by a specifically designed bioweapon, not a natural disease used as a weapon?"

She nodded. "Again, that's a personal speculation, and one I don't often share. What is known is that the Battle of Baghdad was pretty much the end of Islam's advanced civilization. Like Churchill, western leaders could learn much from a deep study of scientific history, but few bother.

"For example, some historians have alleged that the Mongols were aided by Shi'a Muslims who bore a grudge against the Sunni Abbasids. And it's generally agreed that the Mongols killed the Caliph by wrapping him in a rug and having their ponies trample him." She laughed, but without any humor. "Think about it: Those tidbits of knowledge alone could have given Bush II an entirely different perspective about the amount of force required to pacify Iraq.

"What if Islamic Fascism originally started as a response to the Mongols? The Muslims may have used the first WMDs, a horrific bioweapon that took too long to work."

"You pose interesting theories," Mike said quietly, "two ancient civilizations destroying each other in a fury of violence, and almost taking the emerging West down with them."

She shrugged. "I'll never publish on that, as there's no documented proof. What is known is that after obliterating advanced Muslim civilization, the Mongol horde dispersed and took the plague with them to Russia, India, and China. It then spread slowly to the West down the Silk Road, along the trade routes.

"The disease vector that decimated Europe came in through Italy. Twelve Genoese galleys brought the plague to Messina, Sicily, in October 1347, three months before it hit the mainland."

"The galleys came from Caffa?"

"That's unknown, but probably not. If so, they would have had to depart months before the ones that went to Genoa. Most speculate they came from elsewhere in the Crimea. The crews were apparently dying when they arrived. 'Sickness clinging to their very bones,' was how one Franciscan friar put it, writing ten years after the event."

"Well, thank you for the history lesson." Mike sighed. "I guess I failed your test."

"No." She smiled for the first time. "You passed. I may have misjudged you. The photo threw me off."

He blinked and shook his head, puzzled.

"Yemen," she said. "I had you down as a glory hound."

"Oh," Mike said.

She was referring to the photograph of Mike being carried out by his grim and bloody troops after his command post was almost overrun. "Your picture made the front page of *Washington Post, Washington Times,* and the *New York Times.*"

"I had nothing to do with it. There was a reporter on the rescue chopper. It won him a prize."

"The Pulitzer," she said. "A bit beyond what I'd call 'a prize.' Within the month I saw you'd gotten your Colonel's eagles. It seemed, ah, shall I say perhaps a bit too theatrical…."

You bitch. Mike took a deep breath. She was accusing him of grandstanding.

"You're entitled to your opinion," he said. "There was discussion at the time about whether to court martial me or give me a medal. The latter view finally prevailed."

She was watching him intently.

"The Corps promoted me while I was still flat on my back in the hospital. I'd gladly have traded my eagles and medals for the people that I lost over there. The plan was to give me a promotion, a medal, and toss me out into retirement on a medical discharge."

"They didn't do that."

"No," he agreed. "Doctor Cohen at Bethesda tried bone grafts and an experimental nerve regeneration procedure on me. I served as his resident guinea pig for almost two years. I can assure you that there were many times when I wished that I hadn't agreed to that."

"Because you expected to be a cripple?"

Mike waved his hand dismissingly. It wasn't something he wanted to discuss. "In any case, after I passed the physical they had to let me stay in."

"I know Bernie Cohen," she said slowly. "His procedures are controversial. They've not been generally successful."

"I was lucky."

"Whatever you may be, you're not a dilettante." An odd look crossed her face.

Mike tried to decipher it. He tentatively decided it was respect. At least that's what he hoped. *Is she going to help me, or not?*

The doctor was quiet for a long time. He wondered what she was thinking, but didn't ask. He waited for her to continue, not wanting to push his luck.

"Well, enough chit chat," she said, finally. "Call me Moira. What do you want to know?"

"Thank you." Mike thought for a moment. "Let's start with the basics. Given modern medical science and procedures, are bioweapons really as serious a strategic threat today as they're made out to be?"

"Of course." She looked astonished. "Now, more than ever. Populations are dense, travel is rapid, borders are porous, and too many insane people have access to such weapons. Why would you ask such a stupid question?"

"Military history interests me. The President told me that the major powers, even during the World Wars, avoided bioweapons."

"He's mistaken. The Germans used anthrax in World War One, though not against humans. They used it to contaminate animal feed and livestock. The first mass use of anthrax spores against humans as a weapon was in the Second World War during the Japanese occupation of China. Manchuria, to be precise."

"That was strongly denied. I've taught that period of military history."

"It's *always* denied." She gave a disgusted look. "Ten thousand prisoners of the Japanese died of something very lethal."

"There was no proof."

"There seldom is." She shrugged. "Still, I expect the President's intended point was that there wasn't any broad scale use of bioweapons in the great World Wars. Do you know why? Do you know what keeps the big nations from using them?"

"He said they're too horrible."

"Politicians like to say such things," she said dryly. "It's bullshit. They prefer to believe it, but it doesn't match reality. Horror has rarely prevented a weapon from being used."

"So what's the real reason?"

"Four things: politics, stupidity, fear of retaliation, and the fear of accidents have limited the use of bioweapons. Even a persistent chemical weapon like mustard gas dissipates in a few days, but bioweapons are forever. Or they can be. The Brits tested anthrax spores on a little island called Gruinard off the Scottish coast. They made it totally uninhabitable."

"Did they ever clean it up?"

"Eventually. They became fearful that if they didn't, the contamination would spread. In the end, they had to dowse the entire island with disinfectant. The cleanup was enormously expensive and took ten years."

"They must have used a hell of a lot of cotton swabs," Mike said wryly.

"Two hundred and eighty tons of formaldehyde and two thousand tons of seawater."

"Tell me more about the 'stupidity' part. What do you mean?"

"Stupidity overlaps politics. The Tuskegee Study in the 1930s, where two hundred poor black men with syphilis were left untreated as a study group, is infamous. The subjects weren't told they had the disease and neither were their wives. That still pisses people off."

"That wasn't the military," Mike said.

"The Navy sprayed San Francisco with bacteria in 1950. They claimed it was harmless, but many became ill and one person died. The CIA released bacteria in the Tampa Bay area in 1955, and there was a subsequent epidemic of whooping cough. In 1965, the Army subjected seventy prisoners at Holmsberg State Prison to dioxin. They developed lesions, which were left untreated for up to seven months. Later many of the subjects got cancer."

"The Army didn't know dioxin was a risk. They used Agent Orange in Vietnam," Mike objected. "And after that...."

"The Army knew. Technically, they didn't use it themselves. They let the Air Force and the Navy deploy it for them. They just never told their sister services about the risk."

"That's not possible." Mike said.

"The hell it's not. Admiral Zumwalt, the local commander of Naval Forces at the time, so testified under oath. As you may know, his son served on riverboats in 'Nam, was exposed to Agent Orange, and died of cancer."

Mike was quiet for a long moment. "I see your point."

"Stupidity. That's my point. There are many other examples, mostly classified, but some very public. Defense had a deputy director named McArtor who went to Congress for money to develop an incurable disease in the late sixties. He didn't get the funding, but immune systems disease, AIDS, came along anyway about ten years later."

"So in the end we banned bioweapons?"

"In 1972." She shrugged. "Over one hundred and forty nations eventually signed the treaty. Naturally the outlaw nations *didn't* sign, and some of those who did kept right on working on bioweapons. Such work is hard to conceal because of the occasional accidents. The Russians had one in 1979 that caused at least sixty-eight deaths from anthrax."

"But we stopped?"

"Yes, we stopped," she agreed. "We actually did."

"Because of the treaty?"

"Partly. That and an unacceptable probability of getting caught with our hand in the cookie jar if we dared violate it. The Russian anthrax accident, especially when followed by Chernobyl, may have helped end the cold war."

"Perhaps." Mike suppressed the urge to point out that economics might have been a greater factor, waiting for her to continue.

"Bioweapons have a life of their own, you know." She smiled darkly at her little joke. "They scare people. I think severe acute respiratory syndrome, better known as SARS, was a Chinese bioweapon that got loose, but no one listens to me."

Mike shrugged, keeping a carefully neutral expression. He needed her help.

"Your reaction is typical," she said. "The military doesn't fucking listen. SARS was a second generation weapon and potentially a good one."

"How do you know?"

"I connected the dots, General, that's how. SARS appeared from nowhere in late 2002. It's far superior to the Avian Flu that showed up in the late 90s. It's better to have people, the primary targets, spread the infection. Another plus is SARS kills off hospital workers very early. Compared to bird flu, it's easy to contain. The SARS epidemic was over by the summer.

The doctor was watching him closely. "The fear and horror of bioweapons are mostly what politicians like to talk about." She paused and ran one hand through her hair. "There's more to it than that, of course."

"More than killing off entire populations? That's hard to imagine."

"The politics are uniquely messy," she said. "To test a gun, you can punch holes in pieces of paper. To test a missile or a bomb, you can blow something up. But to adequately test a bioweapon, you have to kill healthy people, or at least be willing to let them die. That's politically incorrect. It's frowned upon in many circles."

Mike smiled grimly. "I can see how it might tend to limit a weapons development program."

"Damned right it does. That's why the Japanese were testing their anthrax weapons on Chinese prisoners back in the 1930s and 1940s. They also dropped bioweapons on several Chinese towns." She looked disgusted. "The democracies have always been at a disadvantage. I can't even test on heinous criminals who've already been sentenced to death."

"You have a point," he admitted. He looked at her speculatively. "So what's your job? Are you a physician?"

She laughed and shook her head. "MDs heal people, and that bias somewhat limits their thinking. I'm on the other side. I've a PhD in virology. I study diseases from the microbes' point of view. Right now, I've got a roving commission to be paranoid. They pay me to think about the unthinkable."

"What do you know about camelpox?"

She frowned and gave him a sharp look. "It's a common disease in some parts of the world and one quite harmless to humans."

"That's not what I hear."

"What exactly do you hear?"

"Bukhari," he said. "That's what I hear. Do you want to talk about it here?"

"Son-of-a-bitch," she said, enunciating each word carefully. "There goes my afternoon."

He looked at her, waiting for her to continue.

"Engineered pathogens are terrifying," she said. "The fucking Aussies designed a mouse pox with effectively a 100% kill rate. Even after vaccination, the rate was 60%. By comparison, smallpox, for all its virulence, has a kill rate in the low thirtieth percentile."

"What about an engineered camelpox, ECP?"

"CIA has discounted it as a general purpose military weapon or a WMD. They argue it's not effective, even if fully lethal to humans."

"Why?"

"In general, you want weaponized pathogens to spread quickly, infect easily, and kill slowly. You want an exponential growth of the infected population, and you want them to live long enough to help spread the disease."

Mike nodded. "Makes sense...."

"If CIA's information is correct, the parameters of this ECP pathogen are backwards. It's apparently difficult to spread infection. The vector seems to be an exchange of fluids. Conversely, after the incubation period it disables and kills its hosts quickly."

Mike shook his head. "Exchange of fluids...?"

"CIA reports that injection was the preferred infection mechanism for Bukhari's ECP research but they don't say why – presumably because they don't *know* why. They concluded that possibly ECP could be spread by ingestion, but optimally it should be injected or at least spread into an open wound. CIA concluded it's almost like AIDS or rabies for its transmission vector. They assume you need a relatively intimate contact to spread the disease. That would make it a poor bioweapon."

"Why?"

"Inefficiency." Dr. Moria shrugged. "It's quicker and easier to shoot someone than to inject them. And if you can get at an open wound, why not just cut your enemy's throat?"

"Could you use ECP as a weapon?"

"If I had to, yes, of course." She nodded. "Absolutely. But I'd prefer not to."

"Because it's too lethal?"

"Partially," Moira said, "but mostly because we don't know enough. CIA has been wrong before. It would be professionally embarrassing to kill myself, my staff, and perhaps 200 million Americans through a monumental pathogenic blunder."

Mike blinked and shook his head. "You've lost me...."

"A lot more research needs to be done before I'd have any part of spreading an engineered pathogen into the wild. With today's leaky borders and global travel, an out-of-control bioweapon could literally destroy Western civilization. I'm damned sure not going to accept Bukhari's limited research data or CIA's conjectures without an independent scientific validation. Bukhari might be mistaken about the infection vector. They might have chosen injection for their research out of convenience or because of preference."

"Oh...."

Moira said, "Don't get me wrong, General. I don't in the least mind killing off the people who'd unleash a weapon like that. I'd just want to be damned sure I get the right ones."

"Understood," Mike said. "Can you think of ways to counter an ECP attack?"

"Sure," she said. "Nuke the place that's making it. Problem solved."

"I was looking for a somewhat more subtle approach."

"I doubt one exists," she said. "Certainly none that would be politically acceptable."

"Screw the politics. If our nation depended on it, could you negate an attack?"

"You pose interesting questions." She paused for a long moment and then hit a button on her phone. "Let me get us booked into one of the bubbles."

CHAPTER TWELVE
PRIMARY THREAT

NSA Headquarters, Fort Meade, Maryland

Gerry looked up from her computer screen when the phone rang. She picked it up, noting the secure light was lit. "3824," she said, giving just the last four digits. Anyone who called this number would know who was going answer it. If they didn't, they shouldn't be calling.

"Are those your measurements?" Mike's voice had a chuckle in it, but he sounded tired.

"I wish." Gerry laughed. *It's good to hear his voice.* "Hey, wait a minute. I'm supposed to be working for you. We're talking harassment here."

"Worse than kissing?"

She smiled into the phone. "Depends on the kiss, I suppose."

"Good point," he said. "We could do some research."

"We should be so lucky." She felt a tug at her heart as reality came crashing back. "Be careful, Mike. I saw the *Post*. That Oregon political nonsense is turning into a drumbeat. Somebody's trying to set you up."

"Don't worry about it. At least they spelled my name right."

"If you say so."

"I do," he said. "I'm just a dumb Marine. Is 'harass' two words, or one?"

She smiled in spite of herself. "I'll explain it to you over dinner."

"We have a change of plans, I'm afraid. I've got a slight problem."

Are you all right? was her first thought. *Is there news about Dad?* followed immediately. She said neither aloud, of course. Secure light or not, she'd worked for NSA far too long to trust telephones, even if this one was scrambled and on a hard line.

"What do you need?" she asked.

"I got tied up. I'm still at the White House. It's a long story, but I can't take you out for dinner. The coverage was a bit wider than the *Post*. I've got half the reporters on the East Coast chasing me and need to keep a low profile. I'd better avoid public places for a while."

"Have you eaten?"

"Not since breakfast." Mike paused. "I can catch a helicopter and be there in about thirty minutes, if that works for you. Can you meet me in the lobby? I don't have the damned badge your security trolls gave me, much less the time or patience to get screened in again."

"Tell you what," she said. "Our cafeteria is pretty grim after hours, and you'd still need a security check to get in. Why don't I just meet you at the helipad? I'll fix dinner at my house. Your SEALs have it fully secured now, and it's quite private. We can talk there."

"I don't want to impose," Mike said. "Maybe we can grab some take-out on the way."

"Don't worry about it. We'll negotiate the details when you get here." She laughed. "With any luck, we won't get shot at this time."

"The reporters are worse," Mike said. "Believe me."

"Why?"

"You're not allowed to kill them."

"Be thankful. You're in enough trouble already."

Mike laughed. "Gotta go. I'll be there as soon as I can."

River Glen, Maryland

They rolled into the driveway at Gerry's house, and two SEALs immediately materialized out of the darkness with weapons ready, one on each side of the car. Gerry stopped and rolled her window down.

"Evening, ma'am," the one on her side said. "You're cleared, but they want a level two check. I'll need you to get out so we can inspect your car."

He shined a flashlight into the vehicle.

"Good evening, Lieutenant," Mike said.

"Sir," the man said, snapping a salute. "We didn't expect you, General."

"Just got back from Oregon." Mike said, returning the salute. "Clover and his team are still out there kicking ass."

"Roger that, Sir."

"Get out of the car, Gerry." He opened his door. "They know who we are, but we need to let them check the vehicle and verify we're not under duress."

She complied, clicking the trunk and hood open before she got out. They stood well clear of the vehicle while the lieutenant checked it. He looked in the back seat and under the car with his light, and then checked the engine compartment and trunk. He stood up, nodded, and gave a hand signal to his CPO who vanished into the trees silently.

"All clear," he said. "You can get back in now. Good to see you, Sir. Have a nice night."

"Thank you, Lieutenant," Mike said. "Tell your men it's important we keep her safe. Also, I've got reporters hunting me. No access."

"Yes, Sir," the officer said. "We already got the word. No one gets through the perimeter without authorization. Don't worry about a thing. We've got full combat loads this time."

Gerry insisted on fixing dinner. Mike helped by opening the wine, crackers, and slicing the cheese he'd bought. Low profile or not, a quick dash into a supermarket seemed safe.

"That young officer seemed tense," Gerry said.

"Ensign Mallory was badly wounded. I expect he's hoping some Tangos come around so they can get payback." A grim look passed across Mike's face. "And Lieutenant Clover's men got the people who abducted your father. They took one alive and he's talking."

Gerry almost dropped the dish she was holding. "Is Dad safe?" She realized as soon as she spoke how stupid the question was. *He would have told you.*

"We don't know," Mike said, "but at least we know who took him."

He proceeded to brief her about the events in Oregon, holding nothing back.

"They murdered Dad's pilots?"

"And his security man. We found them buried in shallow graves, each with a bullet in the back of his head."

"Ed DeMott was Cybertech's chief pilot." Gerry looked sad. "His wife Cindy was in my sorority at college. She's a child psychologist, and they have two boys now."

Mike had an odd look on his face. He wouldn't meet her eyes.

"You tell me this Ahmed person has my father," she said. "He commanded the raid and ordered the others killed."

"Colonel Ahmed Mahmoud Muhammad of Bukhari intelligence is a dangerous man." Mike's voice had an unfamiliar tone. "But there's hope. Ahmed has some reason for keeping your father alive. He gave orders not to harm him."

"Why?"

"We don't know," Mike said. "There are some peculiar things about this. It's strange Ahmed dares show himself in the United States. Too many people want him dead."

He pulled a paper out of his pocket, unfolded it and tossed a digital print down in front of her. "That's him."

Gerry studied the photo, frowning and shaking her head.

"I didn't recognize him at first."

"You *know* him?"

"We met briefly in Yemen."

"Tell me what happened."

"There's not a lot to tell," Mike said. "I screwed up. Got sucked into meeting with him under a truce flag, and it was a trap. He almost killed me. You know the medical part. The doctors said I'd never walk again, but they were wrong."

"Are you all recovered now?"

He gave her a grim smile. "Your security people weren't entirely wrong about me. I was pretty rocky for a while. Nightmares. That sort of thing."

"I'm so sorry," Gerry said, her words spilling out into the growing silence. They sat lost in their thoughts for several moments, before she returned to the subject. "Where did you get this?" She tapped the print with a finger. "Is it recent?"

"It was taken by a security camera in the Portland airport three days before your father was abducted." He took a deep breath. "Ahmed's had plastic surgery, but if you look closely you'll see a faint scar on his left temple."

She studied the photo carefully. "I see it."

"The scar is from a 9-millimeter round. If my aim were better, all this might never have happened."

"I expect maybe he moved."

"That too." Mike nodded glumly. "Ahmed came to the meeting in mufti. It didn't fit his profile, and I should have figured why. He had body armor under his robes."

He gestured, trying to brush the past away. "Ahmed's had bio sculpting, but it's him for sure. The Tango Clover's men caught confirmed it. In a strange way, the fact it was Ahmed who took your father might be helpful."

"What do you mean?"

"You have no idea how many people are looking for him. Like I said, it's surprising he'd dare show his face outside of Bukhari, bio sculpting or not. If we're lucky, he might decide to keep your father alive as a bargaining chip."

"Is there anything else you want to tell me about Yemen?"

"The Saudis warned me not to trust Ahmed or his truce flag. All those months in the hospital, I kept thinking about how he manipulated me by using my sense of honor. I should have shot him summarily and dared them to court martial me."

She took his hand.

Mike seemed far away, lost in thought.

"Look at me," she said.

He took his gaze from the darkness outside, or perhaps the darkness inside. Somehow, the room seemed smaller and the night more sinister. She was glad there were heavily armed guards outside.

"We can't change the past."

Mike took a deep breath. "You're right. We have a job to do. We need to talk business, but if you don't mind, let's have dinner first."

She nodded, returning to fixing the pasta. He refilled her wine glass.

They'd finished dinner. It wasn't much, just pasta and marinara sauce out of a can, but Mike seemed to like it. She'd added some meat to the sauce, laughing and saying she'd heard Marines were carnivores. The bread he'd bought was wonderful, as was the wine, but she hadn't been able to relax and had limited herself to two glasses.

She was just finishing preparing coffee. "They roast this on Thursdays. I pick it up on my way home and grind it myself. I hope you like it."

"Saw the label," Mike said, nodding. "Excellent choice. I was stationed in Hawaii for a time and developed a taste for Kona. I like the Sumatra as well, but somehow the Kona Coast blends seem more patriotic."

A Marine with gourmet tastes. Gerry smiled to herself. "I'll bet they don't serve it in the Corps."

"You take your pleasure where you can. I'd have good coffee shipped in whenever we had a permanent HQ set up. Couldn't do it when we were moving around, of course."

She poured him a cup. He took a sip and smiled appreciatively. She got one for herself, pulled out a chair, and sat down across from him.

"There are some issues we need to discuss," Mike said.

Just that suddenly, the mood was broken.

Something's happened, she thought. *Something urgent, or he would leave the serious talk until tomorrow.* "Okay, if you insist, let's talk business." She gave him a direct look and tried to suppress her irritation. "What's up that can't wait until tomorrow?"

"We need to show how Congress can be dispersed. How soon can you have a demo system running?"

She blinked her surprise. "Mike, I've only been back for a day. We're just now getting the program restarted."

"This is important. What's your best guess?"

"I talked with my brother this afternoon. I don't know how you did it, but Cybertech has received the long overdue payment. God Bless America."

"Bank transfer," Mike said. "I didn't want money holding this up. We can settle the accounting details later."

"Will's getting offer letters out this week to add engineering staff, and he's taken an emergency leave of absence from the University. But it's going to take time. People have to accept, give their employers notice, relocate, get trained...."

She stopped. Mike was shaking his head.

"We don't have time, Gerry. Just give me a guess."

"I don't know. Six months, maybe more. It's hard to say. Knowledge work isn't like digging ditches. Adding people slows you down at first."

"How's that?" Mike said. "Tell me why."

"They call it 'the mythical man-month.' The phenomenon is well documented."

"I don't have any idea what the hell you're talking about." Mike sighed. "Just give me the *Reader's Digest* version, Gerry. I need you to keep it simple enough that I can explain to the President and Congress."

"New product development is counterintuitive. When you assign more technologists, it actually slows work. Productivity depends on communication and coordination. You have to use the engineers that are in place to get the new ones up to speed. That means they have to stop working on whatever they're doing to train the new ones. Throwing bodies at a project always causes a temporary delay."

"What if I told you the President needed this in sixty days?"

Gerry felt a flash of anger. "I'd say it's impossible. It can't be done. Will hasn't even identified the people he wants to hire yet. The required skills are rare, and he needs people he can trust.

"The task is to develop what is termed 'a trusted, managed network,' a secure end-to-end computer system. It has to be strongly encrypted and resistant to attack. It has to be redundant, reliable, and self-healing. It has to identify and resist attempts at penetration and corruption. In addition...."

"Can it be done?"

"In theory and under constrained conditions. We already have robust systems at the agency, but...."

"NSA should set the bar pretty high. Why isn't that adequate?"

"The system proposed by Cybertech operates in the real world, not in a black environment behind walls and guards. It links over public networks and has to be usable by laymen. In this case, the system will be used by technical morons, members of Congress, some of whom can't even work a word processor."

"Is that all?" Mike smiled to soften his words.

"It's not even the beginning. NSA operations are compartmentalized. If someone hacks into one of our systems, we might compromise an operation or lose a few agents. If someone breaks this one, they could misdirect our entire government, maybe even take it over. The downside risk is enormous."

"I'm not talking about running the government, Gerry. All we need to start with is a small test system."

"Prototypes are fragile. This one will be tested in a spotlight so intense it makes an antimissile laser beam look like a candle."

He looked at her, ignoring his half empty coffee cup.

"It has to work reliably. It has to be both robust and user-friendly." She could hear the strain and frustration creeping into her voice. She stopped, took a deep breath, and met his gaze.

"How soon?"

"What I said. At least six months, maybe more."

"The absolute best you can do?"

She nodded.

"Okay. I just needed to be sure before I told him."

"It's Will's best guess." Gerry spread her hands in exasperation. "This is something we should have been working on long ago. The model the country uses for our representative government dates back to 1776, for God's sake. They didn't have weapons of mass destruction back then."

Mike said, "The model predates Rome, actually. Men would get on their horses and ride to a central location where they could talk in safety and make laws to run their societies. In ancient Greece, they didn't have horses, so they walked. The distances were smaller."

"So how'd Alexander the Great get around?"

"He was Macedonian and a lot more interested in conquest than democracy or ruling. In fact, what got his career started was when he commanded the left wing of the Macedonian army in the defeat of the Greeks at Chaeronea in 338 BC. Alexander destroyed opposition as he saw necessary, but allowed subservient conquered societies to retain their traditions and organizational structures, especially the Greeks, thanks to his being tutored as a boy by Aristotle.

"When he died at 33, Alexander's Empire died with him. He's a poor example of stable government, not that the Middle East has progressed much since then. I expect Alexander and Saddam would have understood each other."

Gerry sighed. "I don't know what to do about the political and social issues, Mike. Society took decades to adapt to new technologies like automobiles and airplanes. Political changes are slow. Christ, they still can't handle hanging chads in Florida, let alone computers. It took the United States a hundred years to let women vote."

"That one was a bitch." Mike grinned. "I'm still trying to get over it."

She made a face and stuck out her tongue. "Don't change the subject."

His grin broadened. "What about Alexander?"

"Fuck him," she said. "I'm sorry I brought it up."

"Yeah." Mike nodded. "So what about the system?"

"I agree with you. A Cyber-Republic is going to be a tough sell. Few trust the technology, and no one trusts the government."

He smiled. "Some don't trust Congress to tie their own shoelaces."

They looked at each other for long moments. She freshened his coffee, then her own, taking a careful sip.

"What do you want me to do?" she finally asked.

"I don't have the technical knowledge to direct you. All I can do is help you get resources and remove blockages. If you need assistance, ask. Your project has the highest priority. It's crucial to our national security and maybe our survival as a free society."

"I'll do my best," she said. "I'll let you know when more money would help, but I don't think it will at this stage. We're still trying to recover from losing Dad. Trying to ratchet up faster would just add to the confusion."

"I believe you, Gerry. It's in your hands. You'll be fully supported."

"That sounds more like abandonment than support. What are you telling me?"

"I have to go away for awhile."

I knew it. She waited, not speaking, knowing there was more.

"Some things are need-to-know."

"Bullshit." Gerry set her cup down carefully. "We're in this together. We need to be partners for this to work. You've seen my clearances. You know what happened to my father, and you know the men who shot at us were probably after me."

He looked into her eyes.

"Are we in it together or not?"

"The truth is you ought to be running this project...."

"No," she said. "*Together.* It's the only way it can work. Trust me on this one. I know more about it than you do."

"You sure do.... Is it safe to talk here?"

"This house has been deep scanned four times in the past twenty four hours. First by NSA. Then by the FBI, then the Secret Service, and finally by your SEALs. We have a secure perimeter. If we can't talk here, we're screwed anyway."

Mike sighed.

"What's going on? Where are you going?"

He was quiet for a long time. "I don't want to burden you with peripheral issues."

"I work for NSA – the blackest spooks in the government, the keepers of the codes – and you're giving me a lecture about the dangers of privileged information?"

He looked uncomfortable. "What I'm going to tell you is only to be discussed with the President and myself. I need a tight hold on this. If your director asks, you say nothing. If you're subpoenaed, you still say nothing, even if you go to jail."

"That's our motto. Never say anything. Remember?"

"This is personal. It's not information you need to do your job."

She met his gaze, staring directly into his eyes. "Every **part** of this is personal. Do you think I'd ever dishonor you or the President?"

"I know you wouldn't...."

"I'm aware of the risks. I'm the one who got you into this, Mike. President Hale and I decided you were our best hope."

"His instincts were right," Mike said slowly. "I've seen a glimpse of the primary threat your project is intended to defend against."

"It comes from Bukhari. That's why they took my father."

"Yes."

She waited, staring at him intently, willing him to say more. "I have to know what's going on."

Mike sighed. "The Bukharis have a new bioweapon."

"Homeland defense is prepared for bioweapons."

"Not this one." Mike looked grim. "There isn't any defense."

"No government would deploy a bioweapon that couldn't be contained. Even Hitler wasn't that crazy."

"Terrorists would, but it doesn't matter. Bukari has an effective vaccine. They can target their weapon selectively."

"Against Washington?"

"It's the most likely scenario," Mike said. "Congress first, to disrupt the government. A variety of follow-up attacks are possible. So is a coup."

"You're needed here. There should be many people working to defend Washington."

"That's part of the problem. The President's advisors don't support his threat assessment. He has political constraints that severely limit what he can do."

Gerry was watching him carefully. "And if it blows up politically, you'll take the fall?"

"It's part of my job. I'm also here to give you cover."

He's as isolated as I've been. How does our country survive?

"I'm becoming a lightning rod. We're getting pushback from Hale's political enemies. That's why the press is after me for harassing ostensible aliens. That's why a Senator is giving press conferences about rogue military actions and preparing to subpoena me. You don't need to get dragged though an investigation as well."

"Senator Stiles." Gerry frowned. "Is she a part of this?"

"It's hard to tell. Political dissent is part of a free society. If the President said the sky was blue, someone in Congress would object."

"Surely all the watchdogs can't be asleep?"

"The National Intelligence Center is clueless, but CIA is starting to wake up. They're getting inputs from the field that disturb them." Mike sighed and spread his hands. "Bureaucracies move slowly. Top officials are cautious. We'll be hit long before there's enough agreement to do what's needed."

"That's a chilling scenario." Gerry shook her head, pushing back visions of horror. Congress abandoned, and a city of the dead and dying. "What are you planning to do?"

"Buy you time and give Bukari a few problems, if I can. But the main thing is to get your program running. The President needs it in place."

Gerry nodded.

"I'm leaving for the Mideast tomorrow. President Hale is letting me use the Gulfstream for awhile longer."

"You're not planning to invade Bukhari in an unarmed civilian aircraft with a handful of SEALs?"

"No, of course not," Mike said. "The region's a tinderbox. Military action by the United States is out of the question. We don't need more entanglements like Iraq."

"You're scaring me."

"It's perfectly safe. I'm just going to brief some old friends in the region."

"That's all?"

"I'm a diplomat, a messenger. I won't be gone long."

Gerry waited, watching Mike carefully, but it soon became apparent he wasn't going to say anything more. They sat in silence for a time. Then she reached out and took his hand.

"Are we done with the business part?"

He met her gaze, searching her eyes. He nodded slowly.

"I want to get to know you better. You know, a man and a woman, like real people...."

"Real men and women?" Mike gestured vaguely at the world outside.

"With normal lives...."

"I've wanted that since the day you walked into my office," he said softly.

"Will you stay here tonight? With me?"

"Yes." But his brow was furrowed.

"What's wrong? We're adults, I'm not in the military, and neither one of us is married…." She left her words dangling in the air.

"I don't want you to do anything you'll regret."

I like this man, she realized. She shifted slightly to emphasize her curves. "I'm a big girl."

"I've noticed."

He slowly ran his eyes over her body. Somehow it made her feel good, a caress without physical touch. Later, she would wonder if it was lust or affection, but for now she didn't care.

"Do you want to stay with me tonight?"

"You know I do…."

"Good." Gerry smiled seductively and started slowly unbuttoning her blouse. "Help me with this, please." *Before I lose my nerve.*

Mike stood, took her hand, and led her into the bedroom. At least for tonight, their private perimeter was secure. For a time, they could both feel less alone.

CHAPTER THIRTEEN
HEADSTONE

State Department Gulfstream, 53,000 feet over the Mediterranean, the next day...

"Excuse me, General. There will be a secure call coming for you in a few minutes."

Mike opened his eyes and looked up at the crewman. "Who is it, and where are we?"

"FBI headquarters, but they wouldn't tell me the caller or topic. We're over the Med and will be passing Malta soon. I don't have an ETA for Tel Aviv yet, Sir."

"Can I take it here?" Mike asked. He elevated his seat from the fully reclined position, blinked, and opened the shades. Outside it was full sunlight, and he could see the blue water far below.

"Certainly, Sir. I'll bring you a phone and patch it in. Is there anything else?" asked the airman. Well, actually, it was an airwoman, he supposed. A perky brunette, with corporal's stripes on her sleeves, except he knew the Air Force didn't have corporals, they'd call her an Airman First Class or E-3.

"I'd love a cup of coffee and a bagel," Mike said. "I'm going to clean up and splash some water on my face to wake up, so give me at least five minutes."

"Yes, Sir," she said. "I'll make some fresh coffee."

"Hello," Mike said, into the phone.

"Where the hell are you?" said the voice. "I've been trying to reach you for hours. Your cell phone was out of service, and your office said you were unavailable. They finally gave me this number, but it took a call from my director to get it."

"Hi, Obie." Mike chuckled. "Something came up. It's a long story."

"I need to see you," Simpson said. "Right away."

"No can do. I'm a long way away."

"When will you be back?"

"I'm not sure." Mike frowned, gazing out the window and thinking. "Several days at least. How's the flap with the reporters?"

"You weren't in the newspapers today, if that's what you're asking," Simpson said. "No Senate hearings, either, despite the interviews Senator Stiles is giving."

Simpson's voice sounded hollow because of the redundant encryption, but it was recognizable. Still, there was a time lag of over ten seconds from the satellite link and scrambling, which was distracting. Each time Mike said something, he had to wait at least twice that long before he heard the reply.

No hearings, hence no subpoena, Mike thought. *Good.* He glanced at his watch, and realized it was after nine in the evening in Washington.

"You're working late, Obie."

"That's right, and it doesn't help my disposition a bit. You sound like you're on the moon, what with all this delay time on the channel. How secure are your communications there, General?"

"Supposedly, very. I'm in a U.S. facility," Mike said, stretching the truth just a bit. "This is a State Department COM link they use for international diplomacy. I have no idea how they have it routed, but they claim it's more secure than our military command channels."

"Is anyone logging this call?" Simpson persisted.

He's not worried about foreign intrusion, thought Mike. *He's worried about our own government.*

"Not at this end." *Surely the FBI has secure lines*, Mike thought to himself. "I've got a green light on the unit."

Almost a minute passed before Mike heard Simpson's reply. "Tommy's been helpful. You must remember the **subject**." Simpson's inflection gave emphasis to the last word. "Do you recall what Cousin Charlie said? He's a sensible fellow. "

Mike blinked and shook his head. He took the phone from his ear and stared at it for a moment. *He doesn't trust the link.*

It took him a moment to decode what the agent had said. The FBI had been interrogating the Tango Clover's men had captured. Bureau called Tangos "subjects." That was what Simpson was referring to.

Tommy's been helpful. 'Tommy' would be the Tango, of course, the subject. *He's talking, apparently,* Mike thought. *Good.*

The Bureau and the Agency strongly disagreed about if and how Bukhari could effectively exploit a biological attack on Congress. Their viewpoints were poles apart.

CIA argued that any attack by Bukhari using ECP would be designed to ensure a transition of political power, and, therefore, government insiders had to be involved. Its viewpoint was paranoid and classically Machiavellian. Its summary had concluded, "To prevent effective retaliation, deployment of ECP would optimally be coupled with a prearranged insurrection. The strategic objective would likely be targeted kills, not societal genocide."

Conversely, the Bureau hadn't identified a U.S. connection and doubted one existed. It thought terrorists were just doing business as usual.

FBI said the purpose of the nuke found in Washington and the development of ECP was simply to ratchet up fear. The Bureau thought the purpose was terror, nothing more. It said a small bioweapons attack, or the mere threat of one, would be sufficient to accomplish that.

Something's changed. The winds have shifted back in Washington. "I thought Cousin Charlie was a pain in the ass," Mike said. "Isn't that so?"

Simpson came right back. "Not any more. God loves pains in the ass too." The acerbic dryness in his tone was clear, even over the scrambled channel.

"That's very interesting," Mike said, choosing his words carefully. "Are you telling me Charlie and Fred have stopped banging heads?" *Do the CIA and FBI now agree?*

There was a long delay, much longer than the communications link could account for. Forty-nine seconds passed – Mike was timing – before Simpson's words came back.

"One big happy family," Simpson said. "Cousin Charlie might be a bit peculiar, but he occasionally gets one or **two** good ideas."

CIA was right: Bukhari plans to use ECP. Simpson also is telling me he really doesn't trust this link. He thinks someone may be monitoring us.

He specifically said two ideas, Mike realized. He felt a chill. *There will be a bioweapon attack, followed by a coup. The vaccine makes this imminent.*

"What about the second part of Charlie's theory?" Mike asked. "I was fuzzy about the details." *Who are the traitors?*

This time the response was even longer. Mike waited patiently.

"I've got kids," Simpson said, finally. "The wife and I worry about their **health**. It's a good thing the government has programs for healthcare. You should thank your friend."

Thank my friend? Mike frowned, puzzled. *What is he trying to tell me?*

"Say that again," Mike said. "There's some noise on the channel."

"I'm going to get the kids checked," Simpson said. "It's good the government supports so many **health** programs."

Senator Stiles chairs the committee on Health and Welfare. Dear God, Mike thought, *Bukhari's going to use one of our own public health programs to administer ECP?*

"You're a good parent," Mike said, testing his understanding. "You look out for their **health** and **welfare**." He was careful to emphasize both key words. Inflection usually doesn't show up on transcripts.

"Some people think so," Simpson said. "It's hard to **prove**, but I try."

There's no legal proof, but the counterintelligence people are investigating a connection, thought Mike. *That's what he's telling me.*

"I understand, my friend," Mike said. "You take good care of the kids. I'm going to be out of town for a week or so. Is there anything I can do for you before I get back?"

"No," Simpson said. "I just wanted to chat with you. Let's get our **heads** together as soon as you're back."

"Get it in your **head** that I'm just a rolling **stone**. I'll check in when I roll back your way. Meanwhile, call me anytime."

"You bet I will," Simpson said. "See you soon, I hope."

HEADSTONE rules and something's going down in Washington, Mike thought. *That's what he wanted to tell me. President Hale was on that page weeks ago, and now his advisors are finally catching up. Whatever it is, I can't help him from here. Gerry should be safe, and the FBI is just going to have to pull their thumb out and do some serious counterterrorism.*

He clicked the phone off, wondering if he dared communicate with the President when Simpson was so suspicious of communications security. He decided it wasn't worth bothering him in the middle of the night. Plausible denial or not, Hale knew what Mike was doing. He wouldn't be shy about intervening if he deemed it necessary.

NSA Headquarters, Fort Meade, Maryland

An analyst knocked gently on the entry to her superior's cubicle. "I've been monitoring that FBI guy's secure phone. He just made an odd call. Do you want to see the transcript?"

The more senior analyst glanced at the paper, snorted, and shoved it aside. "The dumb asshole is talking about his family problems on a black channel. Why are you taking the time for this shit?"

"You told me to. Project Tin Can."

"When did I tell you that?"

The analyst shrugged. "A few weeks ago. I can check the logs."

"The training exercise for Deputy Director Tibbs?"

"Uh-huh," the analyst said. "Tin Can."

"Bullshit project. Waste of time," the superior said. "Tibbs has been replaced, and we don't need to waste resource on this. Shut it down. Make sure the file notes that we did this surveillance only because Tibbs ordered it."

The senior analyst shoved her intercept into his shredder. He didn't need trouble. Everyone knew Director Mitchell had been quite explicit about Tibbs being out of line and was asking questions about his projects.

"Shut it down?" The younger analyst watched the machine grind her work into small bits of indecipherable paper.

"That's what I said," confirmed the superior. "Total shut down. No more intercepts, shred the ones you have, delete the audio files, and send the logs over to archives. Tell them to mark them as closed. Do we have any more programs running for Tibbs?"

"I don't think so."

"Check. If we do, shut them down too, the same way and right away."

"Okay, okay. No problem."

The analyst shrugged and returned to her workstation. She'd only been with the agency for three years, but had already learned not to try making sense out of conflicting or changing orders. She liked working with expensive, cool technology, but had no aspirations whatsoever of moving into management. *It made people too weird.*

Tel Aviv, Israel

The Gulfstream swept in off the Mediterranean and put its wheels down gently on Israeli soil. The old Lod airport was now called Ben-Gurion, and the Arrivals Hall had been modernized for the flood of international travelers.

Mike was not destined to see it on this trip. The tower directed them to a remote part of the tarmac, a small private terminal building. A set of portable stairs was rolled up to the plane as soon as the engines shut down.

A spry Israeli of middle age came bounding up the stairs. He looked fit and had a spring in his step. He was short and wiry, perhaps five foot eight, and was wearing an impressive Italian-made charcoal gray suit, a pastel shirt, but no tie. He had thin, gold, wire-rimmed glasses.

The man rapped on the door, and the crew opened it. "I'm to meet General Mickelson."

"Need to see some ID first," the crew chief said suspiciously, with his hand casually on his sidearm. "We expected to be met by someone from the U.S. embassy."

"They were supposed to call you," the man said. "Check it out." He produced papers and waited politely while they were checked.

Mike, watching out the window, noticed two burly guards wearing dark glasses, blue jeans, and cotton shirts who accompanied the man. They had Uzi submachine guns slung casually over their shoulders, barrel down. They stood with their backs to the aircraft, watching the ramp attentively. He could see the radio plugs in their ears.

They look like our Secret Service, Mike thought, *but without the blazers and making an obvious show of their weapons. Less class, but more assertive.*

The checks and validation took some time, and the crew popped the door closed to make it easier on the air conditioning. When the man was finally admitted, he introduced himself as Benjamin Pearl. That's what his ID claimed too. It might even have been his name. He had a British accent and intense blue eyes that gave nothing away.

Pearl handed Mike a folder that contained two letters and stood while they were examined. The first was from the U.S. Ambassador. Mike recognized the name, though he'd only met the woman once. It mentioned a change of plan and apologized for being unable to meet with him. It said the Israelis would host his visit.

The letter said Mike was to "check with his direct superiors" if he had any questions. *Yeah, right.*

It was typical State Department bullshit, polite and proper, but not helpful. It was obvious the Embassy was being distanced from Mike. *Damn right I have questions. I have so many freaking questions I don't know where to start.*

Mike opened the second letter. He noted the letterhead and signature, raising an eyebrow. *Prime Minister Tamlon,* he thought, *President Hale's been on the phone.*

The letter welcomed him to Israel and pledged "full cooperation and support for his advisory mission." Mike read it twice, seeking to get some guidance, or at least an insight into what was going on. He didn't find what he was looking for. It wasn't at all specific.

To hell with it, Mike thought, *I'll just act like I know what I'm doing until it's morning in Washington and I can get in touch with the President. If I can't use the embassy, I'll use the communications on this aircraft.*

Mike looked up at the man. "Are you with Mossad, Mr. Pearl?"

The man shook his head. "Shin Bet."

Shin Bet was Israeli counterintelligence, roughly the equivalent of the FBI, but without the law enforcement responsibility, which no doubt made life much simpler for their agents.

"I'd expected to go the embassy and meet with Mossad," Mike said, frowning. "I'd planned a brief visit."

"Plans do change," Pearl said dryly. "Matters have progressed substantially while you were in transit. We're very interested in the recent *jihad* actions in the United States. My personal mission in life for the last five years has centered on Colonel Ahmed Mahmoud Muhammad."

Mike blinked. "I see," he said. He didn't, but perhaps things would become clearer if he could keep Pearl talking.

"I understand you and Ahmed met in Yemen?" Pearl continued in a conversational tone. "He has a rather nasty scar, thanks to you. They reconstructed his skull, but there's still a slight indentation. Rather helpful, that...."

"We've met," Mike said. "It damned near ended my career."

"My job is to end *his* career." Pearl smiled thinly. "Governments don't like to execute heads of state, so Supreme President Nassid is safe for the time being. But I have a hunting license for Ahmed, and I can save you Americans a lot of trouble."

So much for diplomatic chitchat, Mike thought. *This guy doesn't beat around the bush.*

"You almost had him in Oregon, I dare say. Your lads missed, but that's fine by me."

Mike looked at him.

"I plan to take Ahmed alive if at all possible," Pearl said. "We have things to discuss."

"I've been in the air for sixteen hours. I wasn't in Oregon when Ahmed's cell was taken down, and I'm a little behind on the specifics."

"Your government has been kind enough to share information with us. I've seen the preliminary interrogations of Ahmed's subordinate, the man you captured in Oregon. His name is Mohammad Habib. As it happens, he was in charge of the *jihad* cell there."

Pearl smiled again, grimly. "We've requested the opportunity to interview Mr. Habib. I'm looking forward to it."

"Do you know where Ahmed is?"

"He's running. Do you know how he got out of Oregon?"

Mike shook his head.

"He just hopped on a Canadian airliner and left." Pearl's smile had turned into something uglier. "He slipped through your fingers like smoke, using an Israeli passport and the identity of an Aaron Goldstick. An excellent forgery, incidentally. Much superior to their usual work."

"We'd like to get his hostage back, Colonel John Giles," Mike said. "Do you have any information?"

"We're apprised of that need. Colonel Giles is at the top of my list of discussion topics when I get my hands on Ahmed."

"Do you think Giles is still alive?"

"I think it's possible. We do know Ahmed wasn't traveling with anyone. We just missed him in Toronto and again at Heathrow in London. We lost the trail in Paris. I think he's changed identities again and is on his way back to Bukhari." Pearl shrugged. "Ahmed apparently went to some trouble to take your Colonel alive."

"Is there anything else you want to tell me?"

"We know about ECP," Pearl said bluntly. "It concerns us. My organization thought a small nuclear weapon was the best solution, but other views seem to have prevailed, at least for the time being. I'm instructed to cooperate with you."

"Israel's never officially admitted to having nukes."

"Quite right, old chap. We haven't declared, have we?" Pearl shrugged dismissingly and showed a flash of teeth. It wasn't a smile.

Mike frowned, thinking. "Is there anything you want to ask me?"

"We've been trying to get your government to take the ECP threat seriously for some time." Pearl gave him a penetrating look. There were cold blue eyes behind those glasses. This was not a man you'd want hunting you. "We've not had much success, and we're running out of time."

"Yes," Mike said, "so I understand."

"We need a solution. Bukhari would use such a weapon without hesitation. Not just against you. Against us and perhaps its other neighbors, especially the Saudis, one would expect."

"Yes...."

Pearl stared at him without blinking. His eyes gave nothing away.

Mike said, "I agree with you." *And I'm not going to discuss President Hale's views with anyone.*

"So do the Saudis." Pearl gave a thin smile, and looked smug. "They seem to have rather a lot of respect for you, General. We're impressed."

"You knew my next stop was Riyadh?"

"Actually, I know it is not. I'm to take you to meet with Prince Fahad. He's in Jerusalem. We're always happy to work with our Arab friends." Pearl choked only slightly on the last word.

"Crown Prince Fahad is here?"

"No," Pearl said, shaking his head. "The Crown Prince and our Prime Minister have conferred about this matter, but you are to meet with his brother, Prince Fahad, their Defense Minister."

That makes more sense. It will be good to see Rafi again, Mike thought. "What are your orders?"

"To assist you. We've reserved a suite for you at the King David, in Jerusalem. I think you'll find it comfortable. I highly recommend the Regency Grill. The food is excellent."

Mike nodded.

"Prince Fahad has a suite adjacent to yours, and Mossad will brief you both. My organization is responsible for the security arrangements, which I trust you'll find adequate. You may park your aircraft here, or we can arrange the use of one of our military bases, if you'd prefer."

"Here would be fine," Mike said. "We'll keep crew on board. We'll need ground power, fuel, and cabin service."

"Of course," Pearl said. "The hotel is only thirty-five kilometers. This is the closest airport, and my men will make sure your aircraft isn't bothered."

"Thank you."

"Secure phones will work reliably from the King David. Your rooms have been swept for bugs, of course. Presidents, Kings, and Prime Ministers frequently stay there, so the staff is used to dealing with such issues. Or, if you wish, we can shuttle you back here if you'd prefer your own communications."

"I'd expect most of the staff works for you," Mike said, softening his remark with a smile.

"Assume what you wish." Pearl shrugged. He seemed to take Mike's comment as a compliment. "The Prince brought along his own staff and technicians."

I'm sure he did, Mike thought. *No matter what assurances he had, Prince Fahad would never trust an Israeli phone line or COM channel. Still, Pearl's superiors are probably nervous as cats about being tasked with the local security for what's shaping up to be an Arab covert op.*

The rooms might actually be clean. Mike found the thought amusing. *A security breach would embarrass their government. Nothing brings people together like a common enemy.*

"One has to be careful," Mike said obliquely.

"Our security is the best in the world, General, but your time here is short. If you're ready, I have a helicopter standing by."

"Let's go," Mike said.

CHAPTER FOURTEEN
REUNION

Forward Base Alpha, Saudi Arabia

The Gulfstream dropped out of the sky, shepherded by a pair of Saudi F-35s in desert camouflage with air-to-air missiles and long-range tanks hanging from their wings. Mike caught a glimpse of the airport as the plane banked on its base leg. It was out in the middle of nowhere. He couldn't see anything but desert stretching endlessly into the distance in every direction.

The runway looked short, but Mike's concerns were needless. The pilot made the landing look easy. There were minor problems sorting things out on the ground, which were resolved when they simply shut down their engines and let the Saudis tug the big plane into a safe parking place with a tractor.

The graceful, silver Gulfstream looked out of place amongst the drab fighting vehicles and helicopters. *An elegant lady at a mud-wrestling contest,* Mike thought, as he watched it being carefully pushed backwards into a revetment between a tanker truck and an armored personnel carrier.

He looked around as the Saudi fighters made a low pass down the runway, wagging their wings. *It's hard to believe I was in a posh five-star hotel only a few hours ago.* The fighters punched their afterburners and climbed vertically into the dazzlingly blue sky, vanishing from sight before the rolling thunder of their passage had faded.

There were no buildings, just tents, and several squads of men wearing commando garb, most of them moving at double-time. He counted a dozen military helicopters and several large four-engine transports, C-130s in Saudi markings. Defensive positions had been dug around the airport, and he could see most of a heavy tank company deployed on the dunes surrounding the airport. A lonely strip of concrete two-lane road stretched off to the west.

This must be an auxiliary field used for maneuvers near the border, he thought. The runway was concrete as were the ramps and revetments. Everyone had weapons, and the pungent smell of cordite and diesel fuel was in the air.

In the distance he could hear the constant rattle of weapons. Mostly the *kak-kak* of small arms, interspersed with throatier bursts of machine gun fire, and the *thunk, thunk, thunk* of bushmaster cannons firing their distinctive three-round bursts.

Mostly, he noticed the sand. Everyone could taste it in the wind. Every desert seemed to have its own unique shade and texture of sand, and it always got everywhere. Every morning, no matter how tightly they sealed their tents, soldiers woke up with sand in their mouths.

It was warm, but not yet scorching, perhaps eighty-five or ninety degrees. He'd dressed down into desert camo and combat boots. His old 9-millimeter was slung in a shoulder holster, the first he'd worn it since Yemen.

"Good to see you again, Sir," a familiar voice said. "We expected you sooner."

He turned to see Lieutenant Clover, who snapped him a salute, which Mike returned. "Tel Aviv took longer than planned. How long have you been here?"

"We got in last night. Nice drill," he jerked a thumb at one of the transports. "We landed with no lights at all. Practice combat assault. They're not bad," he added, meaning the Saudis, of course.

"My compliments, Lieutenant," Mike said. "You did well in Oregon."

"I hope so, Sir. We only got one Tango alive, and we didn't find Ms. Patton's father."

"That's one more than we had before, and you can't find what isn't there. The FBI is happy, and the Israelis almost wet their pants. Have you met our host commander?"

"Hell yes." Clover was enthusiastic. "Colonel Mustafa. He seems like a hard charger. Runs a tight operation. No beer or women, but we've got ice, Coca-Cola, and plenty of ammo and demolition charges. What more could a man want?"

"He's a good man," Mike said. "I suggest you listen to him. You'll learn things."

"I am, Sir."

"Where is he?"

Clover pointed into the distance, toward the sounds of firing. "They're capping off a few rounds and getting ready. Word is we go tonight."

Mike nodded. "I brought our targeting information, courtesy of the Israelis if you can believe that. Some of the best intelligence I've ever seen, right down to architect's drawings, security system plans and codes, inventory lists, and guard schedules. We've got everything but the keys to the buildings."

"It is hard to believe, Sir," Clover said, shaking his head. "I never imagined the Arabs and Israelis would be able to cooperate on anything, except maybe killing each other."

"Until you consider what has everyone so puckered."

"Yes, Sir," Clover said. "Nasty new bioweapon. We were briefed in the States and updated when we got here. We've got good COM. I brought a trio of command satellite radios."

"Three of them?"

"A pair and a spare," Clover said. "Plenty of batteries too. We also brought some lady doctor with all kinds of HAZMAT gear and a couple of geeky technicians. She said she's coming with us."

Mike nodded. "Doctor Moira Sanderson is one of the foremost bioweapons experts in the world. She's an integral part of our mission. She's not expendable, Lieutenant."

"We know," Clover said. "It was in the briefing we got before we left. We'll cover her."

"Part of your mission is to make sure she and her samples get back to the States."

"Yes, Sir," Clover said. "We know that." He looked uncomfortable. "I still have a question, General. I was waiting for you to get here to ask it."

"Go ahead."

"We're going to be over 400 clicks into bad guy territory. That's a long way to walk home. If it turns to shit, what are my priorities, Sir?"

"The samples come first. They'll be in a sealed case, perfectly safe to handle."

"That's not my question, Sir," Clover said. "You said she's not expendable. Do we let them take the doctor alive?"

"Did you ask her?"

"She said, 'No.' She was emphatic about it. She's requested a weapon."

"Do what the lady wants," Mike said. "That's a legal order, Lieutenant. There are precedents."

"I understand, Sir."

"If you have to kill her, make it painless. Give her a pistol too, something simple, a revolver, maybe. Check her out with it."

"Yes, Sir." Clover looked somber. "I already gave her a .38, and she's a fair shot. I'll pass the word."

"I'll be going along with you. It's a Saudi raid, but we're responsible for penetrating the bioweapons facility and getting Doctor Sanderson and her samples back."

Clover didn't look surprised. "Don't you worry, Sir. Nobody's going to bother her unless they get through us first."

"Thank you," Mike said. "There will be a commander's briefing at 1800."

"That's what they told me, Sir. Here he comes now," Clover said, nodding to his left.

A command car came racing over the top of a hill leaving a trail of dust, then slowed as it approached the perimeter. Mike could see one of the sentries pointing in his direction. The car changed direction, approached them, slowed, and rolled to a stop.

A slim man with Colonel's insignia, dark eyes, and a pencil-thin mustache jumped out from behind the wheel. He looked Mike up and down carefully. "You look better than the last time I saw you."

Mike was grinning broadly. "It wouldn't take much."

The two men embraced each other without speaking. Some gestures are universal, crossing the barriers of rank and culture. Clover took it as an opportunity to exit, and did, leaving his commanders to talk in private.

It started on-plan. That's what Mike would always remember afterwards.

Colonel Ali Fahad Mustafa's two helicopters with the scout force swept off into the desert just before midnight. With no running lights and muffled blades, they vanished into the night like ghosts.

The Saudis were as good as Clover had claimed. These were crack troops, and it showed.

Mustafa glanced at Mike, sipping his coffee. The two men were alone. "It's been a long time," he said softly in Arabic. "I tried to visit you in the hospital."

They were sitting in Mustafa's command copter, the interior lit softly by dim red battle lights. Glancing outside he could see shadowy forms. Clover's team and Mustafa's assault force were checking their weapons and talking in hushed tones. The night was still, and the myriad stars were bright beacons in the clear desert air.

"I know you did," Mike replied in the same language. "Thank you. At first they wouldn't let me have visitors, and then there was a time I didn't want to see anyone. I wanted to meet with you when I was in Riyadh with the President, but never got the chance."

"You looked dreadful."

"Didn't like the wheelchair much. It was hard keeping up with the President, and I was always afraid I'd miss something important and cause an international incident."

The two men studied each other. *He's matured*, thought Mike, remembering a brilliant but arrogant young Major.

"I learned a lot from you." Mustafa switched to English. "My troops have improved greatly since Yemen."

"So have you. I've followed your career. You've done well."

"I mean you can depend on us tonight."

Mike said. "Of course I can depend on you. You did your job in Yemen. You held our flank like a rock. You certainly have nothing to apologize for."

"I almost pulled back. I was going to leave you. I thought all was lost when I saw your command post was being overrun. At the end, your men were calling down fire on their own positions."

"Almost doesn't count," Mike said. "It's what you did that matters."

"I was terrified." Mustafa's eyes were troubled. "I've never been so scared. I wanted to run. If you hadn't shifted your reserves to support me, I would have lost my entire force."

"There's nothing wrong with being afraid. It's how you handle the fear."

"I wasn't afraid for myself. I was afraid I'd make a mistake and get everyone killed for nothing," Mustafa said.

"You were afraid I wouldn't send the reserves."

"You kept your word, even when your own command was being overrun."

"And you kept yours." Mike took his friend's hand firmly. "It was a near thing. Your counterattack made them panic, and when my men rallied it turned into a rout. Our countries call it a victory and give us medals, but we both know the real heroes."

Mustafa nodded solemnly, returning the grip. "I was almost too late, my friend."

"All we can do is our best. You did, and I'm grateful," Mike said. "Thank you."

The two men sat for a long moment, remembering. Both were glad the bond between them was still there.

"We compete at your National Training Center now," Mustafa said proudly. "My men almost beat your Army team last year."

"I know," Mike said. "I reviewed the exercise when I learned I was coming over here."

"What were your conclusions?"

"I think you were nervous." Mike shrugged. "Your adversary underestimated you. He made two mistakes, one of which you forced. Your tactics were good. You were slow to take initiative, or you would have won. Overall, you did damned well."

"The monitors told me pretty much the same in the After Action Review. We still play the action and AAR on video before we train. Next time, I'm going to win."

"I think you might. You almost did win. The senior observer-controllers split two to one on the ruling."

"It was a good learning experience." Mustafa smiled. "NTC teaches war is about information. Ever since, I've put a stronger emphasis on reconnaissance. That's why my scouts are going in first tonight. We'll be an hour behind them at the target."

"It's a good plan," Mike agreed. "My only concern is you shouldn't be risking yourself, Prince Mustafa."

Colonel Mustafa chuckled softly. "I notice you're here, even though your lieutenant seems quite competent to lead a small force. Why should it be different for me?"

"I'm not a member of the royal family, Ali," Mike said mildly. "This is a simple operation, but accidents happen. You're not expendable."

"Neither is your Doctor Sanderson. She reports directly to your President, is a national asset of your nation, and under strict travel restrictions. Yet you are taking her into danger."

Mike looked at the Colonel, surprised.

"Our intelligence is perhaps not as intrusive as the Zionists', but we do pay attention."

"Keep talking." Mike was watching his friend intently.

"This was a difficult decision for us. The leader of Bukhari is not to be trusted, but the long hatred in Palestine defines our regional politics. Your closeness to Israel causes Americans to be distrusted."

Mike waved a hand dismissingly. "The conflict will end when the Palestinians decide they love their children more than they hate Israel...."

"Golda Meir. She also said, 'We intend to remain alive. Our neighbors want to see us dead. This is not a question that leaves much room for compromise,' did she not?"

"She did." Mike sighed. "But America often gets blamed for what happens in the Mideast, and, invariably, for what Israel does or doesn't do."

"Sometimes you deserve blame. It's hard to trust you. Carter pledged to fully support the Shaw, but he lied and Iran reverted to fundamentalism. The region has never been the same. Obama was worse. His Arab Spring, that turned into Islamic Winter, with the radicals ascendant and the region in flames. How can you be so stupid?"

"Don't blame me. The Presidents you mention were controversial. Both were associated with foreign policy debacles, but still awarded Nobel Peace Prizes. The Arab League approved Obama's foreign policy actions, which our own Congress and most Americans did not. His 'apology tour' of the Arab World was widely ridiculed."

"I'm not blaming you personally, my friend."

"So why blame America? Do you prefer the UN?"

Mustafa laughed. "No."

"No one trusts anyone in the Mideast," Mike said. "And no one has a solution to the Palestine problem. Those who think they do, on either side, are dangerous. The militants on both sides are part of the problem."

"Don't Americans think every problem has a solution?"

"Far fewer than before Iraq, and I'm not one of them. Neither is President Hale. You will note we're not trying to solve the problem of Bukhari, just to contain it."

Mustafa nodded. "That's understood. Abdul Nassid is dangerous, and my government doesn't want a new bioweapon in his hands."

"He plans to use it on us first."

"I know, and then Israel." Mustafa smiled, his teeth a flash of lighter color in the dim red lighting. "The thought has some appeal in this part of the world."

Mike grimaced.

"Don't worry; we're not fools. We know Bukhari would get around to us eventually. Nassid's lackey, Ahmed Muhammad, is using a Saudi identity for cover. The Zionists may find it amusing, but we do not."

"Mossad has better intelligence on Bukhari than we do," Mike said. "It's embarrassing."

"It's worse than embarrassing," Mustafa said. "Have you vetted it?"

"We've tried. I'm convinced they have good INTEL, but others are not."

"That's why a General is going on a small raid? To show commitment?"

"Partly," Mike admitted. "When I was young, military leadership was about standing up and yelling 'follow me.' Today we have lawyers and diplomats to negotiate agreements and set limits. We have rules of engagement, reporters, and politics. If America raided Bukhari, there would be repercussions. So I'm here with you at my own initiative, as your guest."

"Political fiction. But you're still here."

"True." Mike looked into his friend's eyes. "I just hope we don't get each other killed, Ali. We're going in unsupported, and we haven't trained together."

"Just as you Americans did when you were trying to rescue your hostages in Iran." Mustafa shrugged. "That was a time of disaster. A patchwork mission with poor planning, the wrong equipment, and unrealistic objectives. You looked like inept fools."

"So let's not screw up this time. It'd piss your Uncle off for one thing."

We sent the best we had, and they never even made it to their target. Leadership failures and the fog of war. Little mistakes that add up to get you and your men killed.

"We've done what we can to avoid a repetition. I can assure you our men are out there discussing that and refining their orders. At least we know our equipment works in the desert."

"You have operational command," Mike said. "It's your show."

The two men were silent for a moment, lost in thought, considering contingencies.

"Is it true Israel wanted to go nuclear?" Mustafa finally asked.

"They suggested a small tactical nuke. We thought it unwise."

"I should hope so. They're mad. We worry this mission depends on Mossad information."

"The Israelis want us to succeed. I checked their INTEL."

"As much as was possible," Mustafa said dryly.

"Yes."

Mustafa sighed deeply. "I'm here, in part, because I trust you, Mike. When we send troops into a foreign nation and kill people, it's an act of war. In this case, the fact that Bukhari is a Muslim nation makes it awkward for us."

"I know. But if America or Israel sponsored a raid on Bukhari…"

"The Mideast would go up in flames," Mustafa finished for him, "and just when the news and the UN have assured us things are settling down."

"That's my government's fear. It could be a set up."

"It's a valid concern," Mustafa said. "A Holy War is exactly what Nassid wants. This could be a trap."

"It's possible," Mike said. He remembered Yemen.

"So now we know why we have a General and a Colonel going along on a small raid. You're right about one thing. If this goes to shit, it's going to be hard to explain to my uncle."

"If that happens, I expect you'll have other things to worry about. We're taking a force of ninety-six men into a hostile country run by a psychotic despot."

Mustafa nodded grimly. The two men had been increasingly looking at their watches. Finally Mike touched his, significantly. "Shouldn't your scouts have reported in by now?"

"Correct," Mustafa said, frowning. "They're late. The upper time limit just passed. Something is wrong." He keyed his command radio, demanding an update.

Al-Razi Research Center, Republic of Bukhari, four hours later...

They flared over the courtyard, troops sliding down fast ropes and running to secure a perimeter. There was no resistance. Less than five minutes later the secure signal was given, and Mustafa keyed his microphone again. "Stage two," he said.

The chopper with the heavy weapons landed by the front gate, while the gunships orbited protectively and the advance scouts scanned the barren region around the complex with weapons ready. Mike, watching his friend, saw the flash of a smile in the dim red battle lights.

A ramp opened at the back and two squads fanned out to cover the road. As soon as the main gate was open, a SAM vehicle rolled down the ramp towing a support trailer. It headed for a small hill behind the complex where its radar would have the best view of incoming aircraft.

Mike watched approvingly, feeling surprised. The vehicle was a Mongoose and the missiles were Hawk IVs. The Marines were just getting their first units, and this was the first one he'd seen except for prototypes.

"Splendid weapon," Mike said. "I've seen the demonstration. Holographic radar and AI based target selection and tracking. For a small raid, you're well equipped."

"Over equipped. I brought it along to help morale. If we have to light up its radar and start launching SAMs, we're blown and in deep trouble. This is a raid, not an invasion. We can't fight the whole Bukhari air force."

"It's still a good move. The best weapons are often those you don't have to use."

"I'll let you explain to my superiors if we have to abandon it. It's the only one we have. Not counting the missiles, it costs more than six tanks," Mustafa said wryly. "Still, so far so good. No resistance." He clicked his radio. "This is Red leader. Report."

Having the Crown Prince for an uncle does have advantages, Mike thought.

The voices came back, crisply. "Red one, all secure." "Red two, all secure." "Red three, we're on the ground and deploying. Nothing on the sensors."

"We don't detect any movement. The main building seems clear," Mustafa said.

Mike said, "I'll take luck anytime. Let's do it."

The big chopper settled gently in front of the main building, and Lieutenant Clover and his men hit the ground running. There was a brief flash as the main door was blown, and men ran inside. Others were deploying to form an inner perimeter.

"Main thing is we don't shoot at each other, Colonel," Mike said. "This was put together pretty fast, and we don't want any friendly fire accidents."

Mustafa nodded and started to answer, but stopped when Mike held up his hand. The tactical radio was loud and clear, even with the background hollowness of a digitized spread-spectrum channel. "Twenty-Mike, this is Mikey-2," Clover said.

Mike was using his old call sign from Yemen. Mustafa had wanted that, and Lieutenant Clover agreed. "The interior is secure. Send in CINDERELLA."

There was no one at the facility, except for the four guards who'd been secured by Mustafa's scouts. The satellite scans showed the workers lived in a small village about twenty miles away. They normally started showing up about 08:30 local time, and the raiders expected to be long gone by then.

"Roger that, CINDERELLA's coming with the PUMPKIN," Mike said. The PUMPKIN, Dr. Sanderson's special environmental container, would be used to take the bioweapons samples back to where her team of scientists was waiting.

Dr. Sanderson relished the thought of being able to develop countermeasures and turning ECP back against its makers. "We must have samples. I want to see the people who turn weapons like this loose on the world experience their own pathogens," she said. "It would make a great clinical study."

Mike shivered at the thought but hadn't made any comment. He did agree simply destroying the weapons was inadequate. Bukhari would just make more.

Dr. Sanderson was already moving, carrying her big silver case for biological samples. Her computer expert was with her toting a duplicate case and a portable computer, followed by her medical technician. A seaman, one of Clover's SEALs, brought up the rear, scanning the area with his weapon ready.

Mike watched them go into the building, checking his watch. They weren't moving very fast. Full speed for CINDERELLA was a moderate waddle.

It's pretty gutsy of her to come along, Mike thought. *Even the President had to back down and let her go.*

"CINDERELLA's in," Mike said into his radio. "I still wish we could monitor each other's COM channels," he added vocally for Mustafa.

Mustafa nodded while relaying the information to his own troops. "They're in," he said. "Main building is secure." That prompted acknowledgments from his squad leaders.

"Communications is one of our weak links," Mustafa said.

He gave an order, and his helicopters repositioned into sheltered positions. The inner courtyard was large. Mustafa's command ship was parked in the center. The assault copters spread themselves with maximum separation, guided by men on the ground with red wands. A collision would be disastrous.

Slowly their rotors spun down and silence descended. They needed to conserve fuel for the flight back. This target was at the limit of their range, and they had no mid-air refueling capacity.

Mike was timing. Five minutes had elapsed. "We're getting further behind schedule," he said. There was nothing to be done about it.

They wanted secure communications links to both Riyadh and Washington, but only the latter was available. It would have to do. OLYMPUS could relay to MOTHER and KING.

I hope it holds together, Mike thought.

Mustafa punched his friend on the shoulder. "I think you Americans call this 'sweating it out?' Our jobs would be so much easier, except for the political constraints."

Mike kept thinking of Yemen. *This isn't the time to lose your nerve*, he reminded himself.

The night air was still. There were no lights, and their heat sensors detected nothing. The seconds dragged endlessly.

Ten more minutes had passed when Clover checked in. "We're into the mainframe, and downloading. I'm taking CINDERELLA to the lab now."

"How long will the download take?" Mike asked.

There was a long pause before Clover's voice came back. "CINDERELLA says the mainframe is crap. Only access is a slow Ethernet port. Ten Megabits per second, she says. Figure twenty, she says."

Mike suppressed a curse. "Repeat that Mikey-2. Confirm two zero minutes?"

"That is affirmative," Clover's voice came back. "Two zero, I say again, two zero, minutes."

"Understand, two zero minutes. Do your best. Twenty-Mike out."

Mike looked at Mustafa. "Our timing is falling apart. It's going to take twenty minutes more to get the data downloaded. They're just moving into the sample lab. Then we still have to get our people out of the building and uplink to OLYMPUS."

"How soon can we leave?"

Not soon enough. Mike was calculating frantically in his head. "Twenty five minutes, maybe thirty, worst case, and we can start the upload. That will add another ten."

"Forty minutes?" Mustafa asked. "We've used up our margin."

"I know," Mike said. "Forty for the upload. I have no idea how long it will take for them to find what they're looking for and plant the Thermite charges in the labs."

One couldn't just blow up a bioweapons laboratory. Dr. Sanderson said it would only spread the contamination into the environment, and there were easier ways to commit suicide. Mike suggested burning the buildings. Sanderson just laughed.

"Total energy release is proportional to the fourth power of the absolute temperature," she said. She insisted on using Thermite grenades as igniters for Napalm canisters. The white-hot inferno would melt steel, crumple concrete, and kill any known organism.

"Just to make sure," she said. "Six thousand degrees ought to do it. A nuke would be better, but this will do."

"The manuals say two thousand degrees is plenty to kill biologicals," Mike said.

"Fuck the manuals," Sanderson replied.

Mike watched Clover's SEALs stagger into the building lugging the bulky canisters. They weren't moving fast enough either.

The friction and fog of war, he thought. *Little things go wrong, and it can kill you.*

Mustafa muttered a curse in Arabic. He glanced to the East, seeing the dim glow of predawn. "We're going to be sitting here exposed."

"Yes," Mike said.

"Forget the data link," Mustafa suggested. "Torch the place, and let's go."

"Wouldn't help," Mike said. "The pacing item is probably how long they spend in the labs getting samples."

"We could go back in daylight…"

"You know better, my friend. It's over three hundred miles to the border. The schedule started slipping because your scouts and main force had to dodge patrols. It would be worse in daylight."

"I'm not going to leave you here. Don't even suggest it."

"One Bukhari fighter plane and your copters are dead meat. After sunup, they'd stand out against the desert no matter how low you flew. It would be like shooting fish in a barrel."

"What do you suggest?"

Mike started to answer, but held up his hand when his radio link came to life.

"Twenty Mike from Mikey-2," Clover said. "We've got a hold at this end. CINDERELLA says she needs you in here right away."

CHAPTER FIFTEEN
MONGOOSE

Operations Center, White House Basement

G erry was trying her best to remain inconspicuous, but the duty commander, an Air Force Colonel named Hampton, was both curious and nervous. He kept pressing her.

Hampton pinned her with a look. "I don't quite understand how NSA is involved in this operation, Ms. Patton?"

Gerry shifted uncomfortably, looking the man over. The Colonel was thin, tall, with close cropped gray hair and a command pilot's wings pinned on his blue uniform over several rows of ribbons. The only one she recognized was the Air Force Cross, an award often given posthumously for valor.

An aging warrior stuck in a Washington staff job where everyone can second guess him, she thought. *Just what Dad always tried to avoid. It's probably the Colonel's last duty assignment before retirement. Mostly, he's going to be worried about not screwing up.*

"I can't say, Sir," Gerry admitted.

"This isn't a public show. Why are you here?

"My assignment doesn't involve this operation, though I do work for General Mickelson. I'm just observing."

"Observing...." The Colonel's tone dripped skepticism. "What's your chain of command?"

"I report to General Michelson."

"Michelson's a Marine. Who's his superior officer, and where can I reach him?"

"I'm sorry." Gerry shrugged helplessly. "General Michelson told me to refer such questions to him."

Colonel Hampton frowned. "This is a military operation. Could you tell me what exactly your assignment does involve?"

"I'm sorry, Colonel. It's classified and irrelevant."

"I want to know why the hell you're in my OPS center."

"I'm an observer," Gerry said. "You've seen my authorization."

Hampton scowled, clearly wondering if he should exclude her, authorization or not. He looked around the room, letting his gaze focus on the older officer in the corner, Toby Myers, the USMC Commandant. "Can you shed any light on this, General?"

Myers made a sound somewhere between a grunt and a growl. He sounded like a bear coming out of hibernation that didn't want to be bothered. He shook his head. "Negative. General Michelson's not subordinate to me at the present time."

"I need to know what's going on here. A general officer and a SEAL team are in harm's way deep inside a hostile nation, and I can't cover them."

Myers raised an eyebrow.

"I have no forces at my disposal to cover or extract. None. I have no support forces whatsoever. That bothers me."

"Understandable," Myers said. "What's your point?"

"You might want to reconsider this OP, Sir."

"Nothing to reconsider," Myers said. "It's not my OP. Wish it was."

"I checked the org charts. General Mickelson is your Director of Intelligence."

Myers shook his head. "Not anymore. Mike's on a detached assignment. He borrowed a few SEALs for personal security."

"Detached where?" the Colonel said. "To do what?"

"I can't say," Myers said. "He's outside DoD purview."

"I see." The Colonel looked at Gerry. "Is this a NSA OP?"

Gerry shook her head. "Not to my knowledge, Sir."

"Is that a denial?"

"It's a statement, Sir. I'm trying to be helpful. I don't think it's a NSA OP."

"You don't know?"

"No, Sir."

"They don't tell you much, do they?"

"No, Sir." Gerry shrugged. "The Agency has a reputation for that, Colonel."

"What the hell is your boss doing hundreds of clicks inside Bukhari?"

"I don't know," Gerry said. "My instructions are to relay such questions to him."

The Colonel turned back to General Myers. "I'm ordered to support BLUE BANDIT with communications relay and coordination.' They gave me frequencies, scrambler codes, and call signs. But I didn't get a full briefing about the mission I'm supporting, and no one told me a damned thing about any need for any observers being present in my OPS center."

"Check her pass again," Myers growled softly. "It's signed by President Hale."

The Colonel scrutinized Gerry's authorization again and passed it back to her without comment. He didn't look happy.

"I have no support forces, General Myers," the Colonel said. "Can you help?"

"No," Myers said, shaking his head. "That would be an act of war."

"I was going to mention that myself. This is way outside the limits. I want to know who's responsible."

Myers shrugged. "What do your orders say?"

"Nothing," the Colonel said. "I assumed you were in charge."

"You assumed wrong," Myers said. "I think it's a Saudi OP with Israeli support."

The Colonel blinked. "I'm not accustomed to thinking of those nations as allies."

"Neither am I, but it's not a Marine operation. That's all I can tell you."

"May I ask why you're here?"

"To observe. A friend and former subordinate is in harm's way."

Political fiction, Gerry thought. *Two squads of armed-to-the-teeth SEALs don't exist because they've been moved into some twilight zone off the org charts.*

We're all here to watch, including the President, because there's nothing better on CNN. Yeah, right.

The downside is if something goes wrong, Mike's left out there twisting in the wind. He has no official support. His friends are his only lifelines.

The Colonel thought for a time. He opened his mouth, but closed it without speaking.

Myers relented a little. "There's a very close hold on BLUE BANDIT. I don't know much about it. Perhaps the President can fill us in more when he gets here."

The front of the room had a large map of Bukhari, with a red star near a town called Al-Razi. Next to the map were some high-resolution satellite photos of the town, and, separately, a constellation of photos of a complex of buildings. The town didn't look like much.

The map showed the distance from the town to the complex was about thirty kilometers. The largest building was labeled "Bioresearch Facility." Oddly, the complex was on a two-lane paved highway, though the town had only dirt roads.

The building complex was inside a security-fenced perimeter – Gerry could tell, because it was labeled "chain link and barbed wire, 3 ½ meters high" – not because it showed up well on the photos, even the ones taken from low angles. There was a guard shack at the only entrance from the main road.

Someone had supplemented the photos with detailed design plans of the building complex. The buildings were all one-story, but some had basements and tunnels.

Pretty good HUMINT, Gerry thought, looking at the plans with professional approval. *There's nothing like a spy on the ground to give you the details.*

On the wall were two old-style analog clocks. One showed Washington time, the other was labeled "Al-Razi." Under the clocks was a large, red, digital counter. It currently said 00:00:17:23, and was counting down to zero.

"Has there been any unusual military activity from Bukhari?" Myers asked.

The Colonel shrugged. "Their patrols have escalated. They've been running fighter sweeps along the borders all night, about thirty minutes apart. That's unusual, but I'm not sure if it's significant."

Myers frowned. "How do we know?"

"The Saudis put up an AWACs aircraft to track them, and we've got a data feed." The Colonel pointed at one of the large monitors.

The technician at that station looked up. "They've got four Mig-43s on Return to Base. Another four are about at their RTB limit and should be turning back in a minute or two. The next patrol should be coming up in about 15 if they stay on schedule."

"Is the Saudi AWACs provoking patrol activity?" Myers asked.

"Unlikely," the Colonel said. "It's been staying about 80 miles back in Saudi territory. We haven't seen Bukhari activities near the target, just unusually intense patrolling of the border."

"Has it caused mission problems?" Myers asked.

"I'm not sure. BLUE BANDIT called in a two-hour delay, but they didn't say why, and there's been no further communication. They're under radio silence and won't check in until zero hour." The Colonel pointed at the counter.

"That's going to be pushing daylight for the return."

"Yes."

"I'd call that a mission problem," Myers said.

"Technically it's not," the Colonel said. "At maximum speed BLUE BANDIT can still get back to Saudi territory before sunrise."

"Are they on the ground at the target?" Myers asked.

"I think so," the Colonel said.

Myers just looked at him. His expression conveyed volumes.

"We'll have satellite coverage a little before sunrise, but they'll have blown the place and be gone by then," the Colonel said.

Just as the timer reached five minutes, the President entered. He looked around and nodded. "Good evening," he said.

The Colonel responded and gave him a quick status report.

President Hale frowned when he heard about the delay. "When's sunrise?"

"Put up a timer," ordered the Colonel. One popped up immediately, in blue on their monitors. "Sunrise over Al-Razi in one hour and twenty-three minutes."

"We're monitoring and relaying, but I don't have operational control, Mr. President." The Colonel sounded uncomfortable.

Gerry had a sick feeling. *Mike's going to be caught there on the ground in daylight, and the Colonel's trying to cover his own ass.*

The President nodded absently. The mission counter said three minutes.

"We've got IR coverage only," a technician said. "I don't see a thing. It's dark."

"Watch for the flare," the Colonel said.

"I was told it's a simple plan, Mr. President," he explained. "Quick in and out, blow the buildings and leave. We're expecting a call at zero, to check in and start an upload. The only thing we have to do is relay."

"The only thing we *can* do is relay," the President corrected. "It's a Saudi OP."

"Yes, Sir," the Colonel said.

He waited. They all waited. The seconds counted down slowly to zero.

Nothing happened. When the mission timer was minus eighteen minutes, the Colonel looked at the President. "We'd better inform KING and MOTHER, Sir."

The President nodded. He was drumming his fingers on the console in front of him.

"This is OLYMPUS. Negative BLUE BANDIT contact at plus nineteen," the Colonel said.

"Confirm negative contact," KING said.

"Understand negative contact," MOTHER said. The speaker had a heavy British accent. "It's almost bloody sunrise. Can you confirm MELTDOWN, please?"

"That's a negative, MOTHER," OLYMPUS said. "Negative contact. Negative MELTDOWN. We'll let you know."

"The Israelis are impatient," the Colonel said.

The Israelis are right, Gerry thought. *We would have seen the IR flare if Mike took out the buildings. Something's wrong.* She kept her mouth shut.

More time passed. The room was quiet. No one spoke, and even breathing was hushed. Gerry watched the timer, hoping against hope Mike would report in.

"Visible images are coming in now," another technician called.

A highly pixilated digital image formed on their monitors. It slowly cleared, and a sigh went up all over the room. The buildings were still there, and they could see helicopters parked in the courtyard at the center of the complex.

Oh my God, Gerry thought.

"They're still on the ground," Myers said. His gruff voice was harsh in the stillness.

Al-Razi Research Center, Republic Of Bukhari

Mustafa came trotting into the main building, looking grim. "It went pretty smoothly."

"Define 'pretty smoothly,' my friend." Mike had heard gunfire.

"We took thirty-four prisoners without incident," Mustafa said. "Five tried to escape. The ones who tried to escape were apparently with Bukhari Intelligence."

"Ahmed's men," Mike said. "I'd like to interrogate them."

"That will be difficult. We shot them all. Two had radios, but I don't think they managed to communicate. One of my men was wounded."

"Is he going to be all right?" Mike asked.

"It's not life threatening. How's your end of the operation going?"

"Not well. We have some decisions to make."

Mustafa sighed. He slowly sat down, took out his canteen, and sipped some water. "We're in a tight spot. What was the delay?"

"Technical problems." Mike sat down next to him, pulled out two ration bars, and handed one to his friend. "Unavoidable, I'm sorry to say."

"My helicopters are at bingo fuel," Mustafa said. "We have enough to get back, but just barely and only if we fly slowly. The people we shot would have pre-assigned check-in times. When they fail to report, someone will come to investigate."

"Yes," Mike agreed. "They'll send a force. If not immediately, for sure when several reports are missed. This facility is important to them."

"The Bukhari Fifth Armored is based in Al Haskah. They could have tanks here in two or three hours. We can't stand up to a tank column, much less an armored division."

"Can you delay them?"

"Not for long," said Mustafa, shaking his head. "We can't fight deep. My attack copters have antitank missiles, but it would be a one-way mission. They wouldn't have enough fuel to get home if they fought, and the rest of my force needs them for support."

"As soon as we torch the facility or break radio silence, we're blown. They'll know we're here, and they'll be coming," Mike said. "They're not stupid."

"Not that stupid. But they'll be reluctant to destroy the facility."

"They don't need to," Mike said. "They'll just roll tanks through the fence, through the buildings, and right over us. When they arrive, we have to go to MELTDOWN."

"True," Mustafa said glumly. "They're not likely to take prisoners, and we can't defend from inside burning buildings."

"I can suggest an alternative."

"Let's hear it," Mustafa said.

"You and your men can go back with CINDERELLA and PUMPKIN. I'll stay here with my SEALs. When we're detected, we'll commence MELTDOWN. We made duplicate disks and you can carry them back. We'll escape and evade. Marines and SEALs are trained for such actions."

"It's an excellent plan," Mustafa agreed, "but there are two small problems."

Mike looked at him.

"The first is you are not a very good liar, my friend, and you're my guest. We both know you have no chance of escaping across three hundred miles of desert with half the Bukhari military chasing you. Even if your leg is better, and even if Marines are 'tough mothers,' as you like to say."

"What's the second problem?"

"The rest of the Bukhari military would be chasing me."

"You might make it."

"I might," Mustafa agreed. "But if I didn't, I'd get your scientist killed. After having abandoned my guests to the tender mercies of Bukhari."

"She'll be killed anyway. She's not to be taken alive."

"I know," Mustafa said. "But your President would be unhappy, and my uncle would be left with a political embarrassment. We need a better plan."

"You're right. That we do."

"Do you have one?"

"They'll probably send recon aircraft first," Mike said.

"Armed recon. I'd send strike fighters to take out the transport and anti-air defenses."

"When we're discovered, we have nothing to lose by breaking radio silence."

"Nothing whatsoever," Mustafa said. "What happens then?"

"You blow the shit out of their air assets with your missiles, while I get on the radio, call OLYMPUS for help, and do the upload."

"Then we die heroically a few hours later when Bukhari's armor arrives?"

"Maybe," Mike said, "but you get Paradise and the seventy-two virgins, we'll have completed most of our mission, and my President and your uncle will remember us fondly."

"I've never had much use for virgins," Mustafa said doubtfully. "Even my youngest wife could use some training."

"Do you have a better plan?"

"No."

"Well," Mike said, "there you are. You'll even get a few hours to think of one."

Operations Center, White House Basement

"We've got activity near Al-Razi, Sir," the technician said. "A flight of Bukhari fighters just changed course and increased speed. They're heading direct. Very purposeful move. Four hundred and fifty knots over the ground."

Gerry had been dozing. She looked at the mission timer. Incredibly, it stood at minus seven hours and nineteen minutes. There had been no contact with BLUE BANDIT, and the President had left hours ago to get some sleep.

For a while MOTHER had been calling every half hour, demanding information. They'd stopped when the Colonel, badly worried, said, "We'll tell you as soon as we know something. Keep the frequency clear. If you want to do something useful, pray."

That had been hours ago. Outside the room, Gerry knew it was morning in Washington. A new day was starting, and people were on their way to work. She'd been in there all night. Her eyes felt gritty, her hair was stringy and she needed a bath.

Most of all, she was damned worried. Her father was lost, and she could feel Mike slipping away from her. Despite the fact the satellite photos showed peaceful stillness at Al-Razi, she knew every second brought Mike and his small force closer to disaster.

"What's their ETA?" the Colonel snapped. He'd not slept in forty-eight hours, but was cleanly shaved and looked fresh. Gerry wondered how he managed that.

"Twenty minutes, Sir," the technician said.

"Put it on my monitor. See if you can overlay the AWACs data on a map."

"Yes, Sir."

It came up on Gerry's monitor as well. She watched the changing vectors. There were track symbols indicating two fighters, and the readouts showed four hundred and seventy knots. ETA was now less than ten minutes.

"Someone get the President," the Colonel ordered. "Now."

"Yes, Sir," a Major said.

"They're going supersonic," the technician said. "I think they're on an attack run."

"That's wrong," said Gerry quietly.

"What do you know about fighter tactics?" the Colonel demanded.

"Nothing," Gerry admitted. "But I do know Bukhari isn't going to drop bombs on that facility, not without looking it over first."

The Colonel looked skeptical. The ground speed was now 825 knots and increasing and the ETA was counting down to zero. The people in the room shifted their attention to the satellite feed, waiting for the explosions and smoke. Nothing happened.

"It wasn't a strike. They did a low pass, Sir," the tech said. "So low the Saudi AWACs lost them in the ground clutter." The screens with tracking data were flashing "Target Lost" in red letters.

"Get 'em back," the Colonel ordered.

"Working," the tech said. "Ask the Saudis to boost power, if they can."

A blonde captain was now handling communications; they'd had a shift change. Before she could make the transmission a technician called out, "Missile launches. We have multiple missile launches." His voice was very high pitched. He was almost screaming.

Gerry's display came back to life. "AWACs data feed is back." That voice was calmer.

The Bukhari fighters were turning hard. The read out digits under their track symbols indicating direction and speed were changing so fast she had trouble reading them.

"They're running," the Colonel said.

"Tough shot, Sir," the technician said. "Rapidly receding small targets."

The displays blinked, then cleared, as they shifted to a larger scale.

"They're going like hell, but what's tracking them is hypersonic. I'm showing Mach six." The technician paused. "That can't be right."

"The Saudis took along a Mongoose with the new Hawks," a calmer voice said. No one had noticed when the President entered.

The Bukhari pilots saw they couldn't outrun the missiles. They broke hard in opposite directions. They were putting all their thrust energy into speed. The ground speeds were over 1200 knots and still increasing, but more slowly.

"That's flat out for a Mig-43 in full burner. They must have punched off their externals," the technician said. "I wonder which one the Hawks will track."

Gerry watched as the blips suddenly disappeared.

"It's a double kill," the technician said. He sounded impressed.

Gerry's heart stopped when the secure channel came to life. "OLYMPUS, this is Twenty Mike." He sounded very far away. "Are you ready for upload?"

"Roger that," the blonde captain said. "Commence your upload, Twenty Mike."

"Relay the feed to MOTHER and KING. And make sure we're getting triply redundant parity checks on the data blocks," the Colonel said.

"Yes, Sir," the blonde said crisply.

She seems quite competent, Gerry thought, listening to the radio chatter. MOTHER sounded like they were about to wet their pants. KING sounded relieved. It took eight minutes and twenty-one seconds for the upload to complete, with full parity checks on each block of data.

"Twenty-Mike, this is OLYMPUS." The Colonel had taken over the channel himself. "Upload is complete. Say your status. Are you ready for MELTDOWN?"

"We're ready for MELTDOWN, but holding," Mike said. "We're okay. Some delays, one casualty, but the mission is still running." There was a pause. "Is EAGLE there?"

"Affirmative, Twenty Mike. He's right here. Do you want me to put him on?"

"Sir," Mike said, obviously talking to the President, "CINDERELLA requests a mission modification, and I concur. We need to discuss it with you in private."

The President took the microphone. He chuckled in relief. "Twenty Mike, this is EAGLE on the most secure COM channel we have. Tell me what you need."

There was a long pause, much longer than the communications lag, before Mike's voice came back from the other side of the world. "Sir, this is a bit tricky. Can you get everyone else out of the OPS Center and off this link? CINDERELLA has a request."

The President looked at the Colonel. "Do it," he ordered.

"Yes, Sir," Colonel Hampton said. "We'll be right outside. Just press the button when you want to talk and open the door when you want us back." There was a scramble as everyone rushed for the door.

Gerry and the President exchanged a look. She mouthed a silent, "Thank you," on her way out.

CHAPTER SIXTEEN
DAYLIGHT

Bukhari Intelligence Headquarters, Nassid City, Bukhari

Ahmed pulled up the video clip and let it play, nodding confidently at his Supreme President. "Our sanctuary in Oregon is more secure than ever, Your Eminence. This was taken from one of the Portland television stations, broadcast the day after federal forces murdered my men. The tone of the broadcast is highly critical of the U.S. government."

President Nassid watched until the clip ended, then looked at Ahmed appraisingly. "The demonstrations and riots are continuing in Oregon?"

"Yes," Ahmed said. "Not every day, of course, but at key times. The bridges in Portland are still being blocked during rush hours on Fridays and Mondays. That causes maximum inconvenience for people trying to get to and from work."

"Is there a backlash?"

"It makes the locals angry," Ahmed said, "but not at us. If the government dares to suppress these demonstrations, it further serves our cause. It's turned out as Ayatollah Fouhad wished. The operation was successful, and Oregon won't change its laws."

"I'll inform him." Nassid waved his hands, brushing the issue aside as minor. "I want to move quickly. Once our friends topple their government, the Great Satan won't be a threat."

"Our plans are proceeding, and they're not at all alarmed," Ahmed said. "The Oregon newspapers briefly reported the Cybertech event, but it's now faded from notice. Nothing is as boring in the U.S. as yesterday's news."

Nassid nodded.

"President Hale is being strongly criticized in their Congress. Would you like to see the speeches?"

"I've seen them," Nassid said. "I'm concerned the Americans may start looking for enemies within their government."

"They're used to dissent, Your Eminence, and there's no proof. The only direct lead back to us from anyone in their government was Tibbs. That problem's solved."

"Perhaps too dramatically."

Ahmed forced a confident smile. "It's being reported as a suicide, and our friends tell us the investigation has been closed."

"There's another problem. If the Americans disperse their Government, we can't take it out in a single strike," Nassid said. "That would be a major setback."

It would be a disaster, not a setback, Ahmed thought. He remembered Colonel Qumar. *I need to change the subject.*

"They can't disperse their government," Ahmed said. "It's impossible. They lack the technology, even if their political leaders agreed to such a change.

"They have no back up plan for the loss of Cybertech. Time is on our side."

Nassid scowled darkly, causing Ahmed to experience a tinge of fear. "We have to use our new weapon now. Why are you so confident you don't worry about time?"

"We have a soft target and many options."

"I want this over." Nassid slammed his fist on the table. "I will **not** allow the Americans to do the same thing to me they did to Saddam."

Ahmed cringed.

Nassid scowled at him, visibly forcing his rage back.

"Their President can't change Washington. Congress and their lobbyists won't allow it."

"They can change if they think their National Security is at risk," Nassid said. "They're dangerous when aroused."

"Even if they want to disperse their government, they lack the technology to do so, Your Eminence."

"Americans are good with computers."

"Not all of them. Tibb's replacement is unqualified. He's a military cripple named Mickelson, a washed-up has-been. Even when he was sound, he was a Marine thug, not a scientist or project manager."

Nassid looked skeptical.

"I'll show you, Sir." Ahmed tapped a key, bringing up a photograph of a thin, haggard-looking officer in a wheelchair. "Does this man look like a threat?"

"You tell me," Nassid said, staring at Ahmed's scar. "He almost killed you."

Ahmed quoted the Koran beatifically. "Those who responded to the call of Allah and the Apostle after the wound had befallen them and guard against evil shall have a great reward."

He touched his scar gently. "I wanted the surgeons to leave the damage to my face, but it would have interfered with my job. So I had them leave traces."

Nassid blinked. "Why?"

"As a reminder. I ended Mickelson's life as a warrior. It was better than killing him outright."

"He's still causing us problems."

"Mickelson's new career as a lackey to President Hale has no future. He's going to be spending most of his time under investigation, testifying to Congress.

"I crippled his body. Somehow he survived. It will hurt him more to destroy his credibility and his honor."

"That would be amusing to watch," Nassid said, "except I will not allow the Americans time. Are you aware our vaccine has been perfected?"

"Excellent news, Sir." He didn't bother to look surprised. The Supreme President would know Ahmed had his own sources.

"Our friends in Washington need one hundred and ninety doses immediately," Ahmed said. "They'll attend to administering the vaccine and dispensing the weapon.

"Those immunized will form the core of the new government. Our friends don't need the weapon yet, but they do need the vaccine."

"They won't accept the weapon until they've been given the vaccine?"

"No, Sir. They're traitors, not fools."

It was the first time Ahmed had seen Nassid smile. "You've done well."

"Thank you, Sir," Ahmed said.

"You've been loyal to the regime. I reward loyalty. There will be a promotion for you when this operation is successfully completed."

"Thank you, Your Eminence."

After the Supreme President left, Ahmed heaved a sigh of relief. *I not only live, but I prosper. My reward is only with Allah, and He is a witness of all things. Allah will reward the grateful. Praise Allah.*

Operations Center, White House Basement

The President opened the door and signaled them to come back. The technicians slid back into their chairs and checked their displays. The satellite photos of the Al-Razi facility still looked peaceful. Parked helicopters. Nothing was moving.

The Colonel keyed his microphone. "OLYMPUS is back on-line. Can you give us a SITREP, Twenty Mike?"

"We've had some unplanned mission delays. Our copters are bingo, but all equipment and weapons are operational. We're just now finishing up some minor details. We'll be ready for MELTDOWN in about 30 minutes. CINDERELLA and the PUMPKIN will be ready to go by then. We're worried about the Bukhari fighter patrols though."

"Describe the nature of your delays," the Colonel said.

"Negative."

"That's off limits," the President interrupted. "I don't want them discussed. General Mickelson's delays were unavoidable."

"Yes, Sir," the Colonel said, his face expressionless. He keyed his channel. "Twenty Mike, the Bukharis are continuing to run fighter sweeps along the boarder at about one five minute intervals. Mig-43s. They'll have look-down, shoot-down radars."

"We ran into them coming in," Mike said. "Had to put down and wait until they got out of range. Give us a time check until dark, please."

The Colonel stroked a key. "We're showing five hours, seventeen minutes, Twenty Mike. Can you wait until then to depart? We're not showing any activity in your area."

There was a long pause. Finally another voice came back. "OLYMPUS, this is BLUE BANDIT."

Colonel Hampton frowned. He shot a questioning look at the President.

"That's Colonel Mustafa," the President said. "He's a Saudi Prince, and the local commander."

"We copy, BLUE BANDIT," the Colonel said. "What do you need?"

"We need to get out of here," the voice said, with a chuckle. "For right now, I'll settle for information. Can you monitor air activity in Bukhari and give us a warning when anything heads our way?"

"Affirmative," the Colonel said. "We're doing that. So far, you're clear."

"Can you re-task a satellite to cover Al Haskah? That's the closest armor we know of. We're worried about tanks."

"Working," the Colonel said, giving a signal to his satellite technician. "We've got an image. Nothing is moving at Al Haskah yet."

"Roger that," Mustafa's voice came over the radio, "please keep us advised and let KING know we're stuck here. Make sure KING knows my copters are bingo on fuel. We've got barely enough to get back."

"We've got activity, Sir," the AWACs technician said. "The border patrols are diverting toward BLUE BANDIT."

"We just got a warning call from KING as well," a second technician said.

"Tell 'em we're on it and give them a feed from my channel," the Colonel said. "BLUE BANDIT, you've got fighter patrols inbound. A total of eight aircraft, in two flights of four. The bearings are 330 and 070 degrees. The first raid, the one at 330, is closer. We're showing ETA in two eight minutes. Can you handle them?"

"We'll try, OLYMPUS." Mustafa laughed over the channel. "We've got our fire control radar on standby. Please give us a warning when they're 100 nautical out."

The Colonel frowned. General Myers was shaking his head.

"Bad plan," the Colonel said. "Think about it, BLUE BANDIT. That gives you only five minutes, even at six hundred knots."

There was a long pause, and this time Mike's voice came back. "This is Twenty Mike. BLUE BANDIT has a limited number of arrows, OLYMPUS.

Tell you what. Give us a call at 100 nautical miles and another one at 50. We'll light up and shoot then."

"Roger, we copy," the Colonel said. "What are your intentions?"

"They're not going to hit the buildings, but our copters are sitting ducks on the ground. We'll volley everything we have at the first raid. If we're lucky, we'll have time to reload. Colonel Mustafa is taking reinforcements over to expedite the reload."

"Understood," the Colonel said. "Distance to the first raid is just over two zero zero; ground speed is four hundred and twenty knots. Bearing now three three five."

"Copy that," Mike said.

"Mongoose has four shots on the rails," Myers said. "The new Hawks weigh three hundred and seventy nine pounds each, and it takes several minutes to reload the launcher."

The President cleared his throat. They all looked at him. He looked at General Myers.

"Toby," the President said, "this has escalated. My senior bioweapons advisor is over there, and she's not expendable. The PUMPKIN, her special equipment, is not expendable either. General Mickelson will make sure we get MELTDOWN, but the other mission objectives are now at risk."

"Yes, Sir," Myers said. "What do you want me to do?"

"I'm going up to my office now. I'll call Crown Prince Fahad and Prime Minister Tamlon, apprise them of the situation, and ask for suggestions and assistance. I need a plan to get BLUE BANDIT back without starting a full scale war."

"Yes, Sir," Myers said. "How much force can I use?"

"That's a good question," the President said. "I won't be trapped into long term troop commitments. We don't want another Iraq. I need some soft options, Toby."

"Sir...." Myers sounded hesitant. The Ops Commander's eyes flicked back and forth between the President and the tough old Marine. He didn't speak.

"Come with me, Toby," the President said. "We can talk while they're putting my calls through."

The President and the Marine left together. Gerry pressed her lips together and waited. It wouldn't help her status if she got emotional.

Oval Office

"What's on your mind, Toby?" The President looked across his desk. "I didn't want to discuss it in there, but I think you were about to tell me you don't have any soft options."

General Myers nodded. "There's a carrier group off the coast. A strike force with air cover might be able to extract our key people. It's right at the end of our range for Ospreys and we'd have to shoot our way in and out. Can you authorize that?"

"What are the odds?"

"Not good. Maybe one in five, and dropping every minute. It would help if I could put an airstrike on Nassid City as a diversion."

"That's not a soft option, Toby."

"No, Sir, it isn't."

"You know I can't authorize an act of war." The President said. "Mike knows it too. He and Clover's team are off the books. They volunteered for this mission."

"Yes, Sir."

"Mike's resourceful. We might get lucky. Soft options only."

"Sir!" Myers said, acknowledging the order. "I'll put my staff on it. We'll do our best to come up with something, Mr. President."

"Thank you." The President's voice was soft.

Operations Center, White House Basement

The room was silent for several minutes. Finally the OPS Commander keyed his radio. "OLYMPUS to Twenty Mike. Raid One is at one hundred miles."

"Copy that," Mike said. They could hear him calling to Mustafa on his other radio.

"Seventy five miles," the Colonel said. "Inbound. Speed is now five two zero knots. ETA is six minutes."

"Copy." Mike sounded preoccupied.

"Radars are hot. We show them at just over fifty miles," Mustafa said in the background. "They're closing fast. Computers are still coming up. We do not have a lock."

More time passed. Mike said, "What's happening, Ali? Talk to me."

If there was an answer, it was on the tactical channel. They couldn't hear it in the Center.

"Twenty Mike to OLYMPUS, I have them visual." Before the Colonel could acknowledge Mike was screaming, "SHOOT, SHOOT, SHOOT," into his other radio, followed shortly by, "Jesus Christ, Ali, I've got eyeball contact. I'm telling you, I'm looking at two aircraft, right up their gun barrels.

"They're on an attack run. They'll walk their fire right over me and into your copters. The flight leader is wearing a red helmet. NOW would be a very good time to SHOOT."

"We have a lock." They clearly heard Mustafa's laugh coming back over Mike's tactical radio, as from a great distance. "Allah would be better, but I'll take all the help I can get...."

"We've got a missile launch." It was the young airman watching the AWACs feed. "Make that multiple launches."

"Put it up on our screens," the Colonel ordered.

Gerry's screen flashed and the track symbols came up immediately. Raid One was inbound at 625 knots, diving, accelerating, shown in flashing red symbols. It had separated into two elements. The display was on the finest scale, very close in, and the track symbols were blurred with motion. Blue arrows were racing toward the red symbols from the edge of the screen.

The airman said, "The leader and his wingman are too close for missiles...." He paused. "Their symbols just disappeared. AWACs lost them again...."

"Big flash on the satellite cameras," the satellite technician said. "We're blind. The IR sensors overloaded. Too much smoke and dust for visible images."

"Twenty Mike, what's happening?"

There was no answer.

"OLYMPUS to Twenty Mike, are you okay?"

No reply. Gerry watched the seconds pass on the counters.

"OLYMPUS this is BLUE BANDIT." It was Mustafa.

"Read you," said OLYMPUS.

"Twenty Mike is down."

"We're screwed," the blonde captain said softly. It was then Gerry realized all the screens were blank. The entire data link was down.

There was a long silence in the room. Finally Colonel Hampton spoke. "Have the Secret Service tell the President we've had a development. Request his presence."

CHAPTER SEVENTEEN
DOWN AND BLIND

Operations Center, White House Basement

The door burst open, and General Myers and the President entered, moving fast. The President glanced at Gerry.

"Mike is down, Mr. President," she said.

"What's the status, Colonel?" Myers demanded.

"Unclear. Like she said, General Mickelson is down and our sensors are blind. We lost the AWACs feed right after Mongoose took out the lead group of Raid One."

"Query them," Myers ordered.

The Colonel keyed his mike. "OLYMPUS here. Give us a SITREP."

"Stand by." It was Mustafa. "We're a bit busy here."

More time passed.

"I'm okay." It was Mike. He was hacking and coughing, but Gerry recognized his voice.

"Are you hit?" Mustafa asked.

"Negative. It just knocked the breath out of me."

"SITREP, please, Twenty Mike." The Colonel was visibly relieved.

"Hell of a shock wave, OLYMPUS. Big fireball. BLUE BANDIT got 'em both. Damned near a ninety-degree deflection shot, at contact range. My SATCOM radio took a hit. I'm on the backup. Lots of dust and debris, but the buildings I can see are undamaged."

Gerry started breathing again.

"We've got the AWACs data link back," the blonde captain said as the screens came alive.

"Twenty Mike, two missiles are still tracking. The rest of Raid One is attempting to evade. One broke left, and the other one right," the Colonel said.

Mike didn't acknowledge. They heard him calling Mustafa. "You're still on target, Ali. Mongoose is tracking."

"Forty-five degree break angles. Showing 1300 knots over the ground." The airman paused. "Make that 1350 knots. Smart move. Their vectors maximize separation and the rate of bearing change."

Gerry watched her screen. The blue arrows were turning. One went left, and the other right. They were moving so fast the track symbols seemed to skip, blinking across her screen between radar hits.

"Bandits three and four are now doing 1400 knots." The airman's voice indicated surprise. "Can't get a good read on the missiles. They're hypersonic and still accelerating."

"We have an image back." It was the satellite technician. "Got debris and multiple craters just north of the complex, but everything else looks okay. No visible damage to the buildings or copters."

Gerry's display was settling down. The missiles had cut the corner and were still tracking, but their targets were now almost off the edges of her screen.

"Never saw Mig-43s move so fast," the airman with the AWACs feed said absently, watching his screen. "Must be an engine upgrade. We should update the database."

"Noted," the Colonel said. The displays blinked and shifted to a longer range.

"There's a kill." The airman's voice went up an octave. "Three's down."

Go, go, go, thought Gerry. She didn't realize she'd spoken aloud until she saw everyone look at her. Surprisingly, Colonel Hampton flashed a sympathetic smile.

The last Mig was frantically juking back and forth. "This one's a Top Gun," the airman said. "He knows about horizontal scissors."

But the missile matched every move, making small corrections, anticipating the target's vectors and closing inexorably. Then the symbols vanished.

A cheer went up all over the room.

"That's four for four," the airman said unnecessarily, but with finality.

"Where's Raid Two?" the Colonel asked.

"Looking, Sir," the airman said. "They broke off. Raid Two is orbiting about three hundred miles out."

"Keep an eye on them, and thank KING for the data feed."

"Yes, Sir."

"OLYMPUS, this is MOTHER. I say, old chap, would someone mind telling us what's going on? We rather expected this mission would end last night."

The President waved on his way out, leaving the Colonel to explain.

General Myers waited until the radio chatter had died down, and then looked at the Colonel. "I have a question."

"Sir?" the Colonel said.

"What anti-armor support do you have?" Myers said.

"None, Sir, but the Navy might be able put in some cruise missiles...." The Colonel stopped when Myers shook his head.

"We can't start a war," Myers said. "Advise KING and MOTHER the President has spoken with their leaders. I have to go, but I'll send my aide. He'll know where to find me."

"Yes, Sir."

"Remind the other stations BLUE BANDIT is not equipped to stand and fight."

"Yes, Sir," the Colonel said.

Gerry watched General Myers leave the room at almost a jog. *If they can't get Mike out before the Bukhari armor arrives, they won't get him out at all.*

Bukhari Intelligence Headquarters, Nassid City, Bukhari

Ahmed looked up as one of his assistants entered. "Is my transport ready?" he asked.

"Sir, there seems to be a problem. Our agents at the Al-Razi facility didn't report in."

"Call the facility," Ahmed ordered. *Why do fools surround me?*

"They don't answer, Sir."

Ahmed looked at the time. "Have the military do a fly over. Do I have to do everything myself?"

"We tried, Sir. The planes never reported. The military is about to dispatch a ground force to investigate."

"Send more aircraft, have the ground force held until I get there, and get me a helicopter immediately," Ahmed ordered. "The last thing I want is to have stupid, untrained soldiers blundering around a biological weapons plant or firing on it. Inform the local commander I'm coming to take charge. Who is that officer?"

"General Abda Aziz," the man said. "He commands the Fifth Armored Division. They are based in Al Haskah."

"Tell General Aziz I'm on my way and this is a matter of the utmost concern to state security. If he bungles this, I'll have him and his family shot. Instruct him to check with the Supreme President's office if he doubts my authority."

"Yes, Sir."

"I'm not finished." Ahmed was getting angry. "Have him find out from the Air Force how they can manage to lose touch with their aircraft without declaring an alert. Get me the names of the officers responsible."

"Yes, Sir." The man was shaking in fear.

"Why are you standing there?" Ahmed screamed, slamming his fist on the desk. "Move! And get me that helicopter immediately. If it's not here in ten minutes, someone will pay!"

"Yes, Sir." The man saluted and rushed from Ahmed's office.

Al-Razi Research Center, Republic Of Bukhari

Mike watched as Mustafa's force left, heading northwest at low altitude. Two heavily laden transport choppers struggled into the air like whales. They'd given the prisoners water and turned them loose to walk into town. Two scientists had chosen to defect, but the rest stayed, fearing reprisals to their families.

Mustafa waved from the window of his command chopper. Mike snapped a salute and held it as the big machine turned away to follow its consorts. *In the end, I still had to stay here for MELTDOWN and to cover you. We do what we must.*

Two smaller attack helicopters covered Mustafa's flanks and two more had gone in advance, but the real security was the Mongoose on the hill. Its radar beams scanned the skies for hundreds of miles in every direction.

It was down to its last two loads of missiles, but had bagged three more kills. There had been no probes for over an hour, but Mike knew the armored column would be there by dark.

One last transport copter was sitting forlornly in the courtyard. Mike would send the Saudis' Mongoose back before the tanks arrived. It was useless against ground forces.

Mustafa's copters disappeared over the low hills, and the desert got quiet. *Less than two hours to sunset,* Mike thought.

Time seemed to be hanging. It was like that in the danger zone. After intense engagements, Mike was always astonished so little time had passed. Ahmed's attack in Yemen had seemed to take hours, but the official logs showed it was over in less than ten minutes.

The second hand on his watch seemed frozen. It had only moved a few ticks since the copters disappeared. Mike smiled to himself, remembering Robbins, a young Lieutenant who'd snapped during Mike's first combat command while waiting for the enemy to arrive.

"I just put my damned watch on a rock and blasted it with my 9-MM. It felt wonderful. You ought to try it, Sir," the young man said with a grin. *"It's good for the soul."*

Mike's smile faded. Robbins had died in Yemen, a good officer who'd left a wife and two daughters.

Mike checked the wiring to the detonators for the third time. Time passed slowly.

"Twenty Mike, this is OLYMPUS."

"Read you," Mike said.

"We think BLUE BANDIT has been spotted. KING says we've got Bukhari fighters heading for them, and their fire control radars just went hot."

"Copy," Mike said. "Give me a bearing and range to the fighters."

"Two niner five and two hundred and fifty miles. Their closest approach to you will be about three three zero and just over one hundred ten miles."

"Stand by," Mike said. "Mikey-2, did you copy?" he said into his tactical radio.

"Affirmative. No targets. They're out of range." Lieutenant Clover had stayed behind to command Mustafa's missile crew and serve as Mike's back up.

Point HOLDOFF was a compromise the Saudis had selected, a point in a desolate canyon marked only by GPS coordinates. The Saudis were flying in support to refuel Mustafa's copters. The Israelis had provided a second Mongoose battery, the only other one in the Mideast, and the Saudis would set it up to cover the retreat.

"There's an emergency override. Go to narrow beam, goose the computer and take your best shot on a bearing of three three zero," Mike said. "Ali's toast if you can't get those strike fighters off his ass."

"WILCO." Clover wasn't much for words.

More time passed. Even though he knew it was coming, Mike jumped when two missiles roared off their rails, heading northwest, trailing supersonic booms and leaving white contrails as they raced to cover Mustafa's retreat. The launcher spun and another shot roared off, heading east toward the opposite horizon.

"What are you shooting at, Mikey-2?" Mike asked.

"Got some low speed targets to the east," said Clover. "I think it's support for the armor. Figured I'd tweak 'em a little, just to keep them honest."

"Good plan," Mike said. He checked in with OLYMPUS and reported the action.

"Roger, Twenty Mike," OLYMPUS said. "We saw your launches. The targets to your east are the lead group of a column from Al Haskah. At least twelve tanks and several other armored vehicles. They'll be there in about two zero. Say status and intentions."

Mike looked through his binoculars. Clover and his crew were struggling to get the heavy missiles on the launcher.

"OLYMPUS from Twenty Mike," he said into the radio. "We're doing our last reload. We're WINCHESTER minus four."

"Confirm WINCHESTER minus four. BLUE BANDIT is now letting down at point HOLDOFF. KING has support on the ground and will have their Mongoose active in five."

"Copy," Mike said. "Give KING a well done from us."

He was getting worried. "Mikey-2, KING has anti-air support almost in place at HOLDOFF. Bukhari Armor will be here in about fifteen minutes. You need to be gone in ten."

"Roger that," Clover said.

"Do you have any targets?"

"Not in the direction of HOLDOFF. I don't think we got any hits, but the bad guys ran. We still have intermittent low speed contacts to the east. Probably helicopter support for the Bukhari armor."

"Copy," Mike said. "I need to get you out of here with the Mongoose. I'm sending the last transport now. Wait for it to set down, salvo what you have left, and get the hell out of here."

"Roger that," Clover said. He sounded out of breath.

"This isn't working," Mike said. "OLYMPUS, those tanks are going to be in range soon. Do you have any way to slow them down?"

"Negative," Colonel Hampton said. "We're working on it."

"Actually, old chap, we have four Tomahawks on the rails," MOTHER said slowly. "They're for anti-aircraft fire suppression, but I can request...."

"Request, hell," Mike broke in. "Put half of them on the Bukhari tank column."

"We're a non-combatant. COM support only," MOTHER said. "I'm not authorized...."

"This is OLYMPUS. Do what he says."

"Sir, we're here under tight rules of engagement. I can't...."

"I don't have time to argue with you," Colonel Hampton snapped. "OLYMPUS is giving you a direct order to release your goddamned weapons immediately. Please acknowledge."

There was a long pause. Gerry watched the seconds tick off. Mike's life, slipping through the hourglass.

She looked at President Hale. He met her eyes and gave a quick shake of his head. *Why are we waiting?*

One minute passed, then another. The room was very still.

"Sorry about the delay," MOTHER said. "Coordinates are locked in. We're firing now."

"Copy that," Mike said. "Thanks, MOTHER. Fire the rest when appropriate and then get your ass out of here too."

General Aziz's command car was just coming over a ridge when someone yelled, "Incoming." The driver nailed his brakes and the car slid to a stop. All the vehicles were stopping, and the crews were diving for cover.

Ahmed found himself face down on the ground about five meters from the vehicle. Behind him, an antiaircraft battery opened up, a steady *chug chug chug.* Lighter weapons were firing too. Sheets of green tracers sliced into the sky. Ahmed couldn't see what they were shooting at.

General Aziz and his driver were crouched behind some rocks, looking around. Ahmed spit sand from his mouth and was preparing to speak when something screamed by heading the other way, moving too fast to see.

Behind him a helicopter disappeared in a fireball, raining down debris. He could hear the general talking into a radio, asking for reports.

"Cease fire," the general ordered. Slowly the firing ceased.

"What was that?" Ahmed finally asked.

"Missiles," the general said. "They came from over the horizon, but we must be under observation. I've ordered a recon. We're bringing up more air support to search the area."

One of the tanks had crashed into a smaller armored vehicle. Troops were working to get them separated. Someone was screaming.

We don't have time for this. "Be quick about it," Ahmed ordered.

The general nodded, looking to the east. Ahmed could hear the sound of rotors faintly in the distance.

Soon four more helicopters swooped protectively over the column. Ahmed could see their guns searching for targets and the air to ground missiles in racks under their pods. They looked formidable.

The copters split off to both sides, climbing and separating so they could cover more search area. "Do they see anything?" Ahmed demanded.

"Not yet," the general said. "We'll give them a few minutes, just to make sure."

"Make it quick."

The general tried his best. The column had just started moving again when Tomahawks hit. Then a wave of Hawks, followed less than two minutes later by the last of the Tomahawks.

Fifteen miles away Mike saw the towering plumes of black smoke in the distance. He took a deep breath, and watched as the Mongoose rolled up the ramp into the last transport copter. "Well done, Mikey-2. OLYMPUS reports the tanks have stopped."

"Copy," Clover said. "Come with us, General, we've got room."

"Negative Mikey-2," Mike said. "That's not the plan, and you've got no escorts. Just get your ass out of here before the bad guys arrive."

"Roger that," Clover said. "Good luck, Sir."

Mike watched as the rotors spun up. The big copter lurched into the air and lumbered northwest, following Mustafa's vector. He watched it until it was out of sight and the sounds of the rotors had faded away.

The desert was very still. Off to the west, the sun was a deep red ball, approaching the horizon. Sunsets in the desert were beautiful. *It shouldn't be much longer,* Mike thought.

CHAPTER EIGHTEEN
MELTDOWN

Al-Razi Research Center, Republic Of Bukhari

Ahmed's head slammed into the steel roof as General Aziz's command car lurched over a slight rise. He grabbed the armrest and tried to brace himself. Blood was dripping down into his eyes, and he wiped at it with his sleeve whenever they hit a patch of level ground.

The first tanks reached the perimeter fence and punched through without slowing. The attack force fanned out, covering the building complex. Men leaped from the armored personnel carriers, weapons in their hands. There was no resistance.

The command car slowed to a crawl, moving through one of the gaps torn in the perimeter fence. It rolled to a stop behind two APCs, and the men dismounted carefully.

"My scouts saw a man running into the main building," Aziz said. "Do you want us to take him alive?"

Ahmed started to answer when the building erupted in flame. There was no explosion, just a gigantic rippling *wooosssshhhh* sound and a blast of heat. The flames were actinic white, almost colorless. It was impossible to look at them directly.

The heat was unbelievably intense. Ahmed could see paint blistering on the tank closest to the building. The men were cringing back, shielding their faces. The building seemed to be collapsing into itself, getting smaller. Another building blazed brightly, then another.

"Pull back to the fence," Aziz ordered. His men started to fall back, the big tanks reversing and backing carefully.

"We need to get into those buildings," Ahmed screamed.

The general looked at Ahmed, then back at the inferno. He shook his head.

"President Nassid will not tolerate the loss of the materials in those buildings, General. I order you to take action."

"What would you have me do, Colonel?" Aziz asked sardonically. "Piss on it?"

He gestured at the main building. It was now fully involved, and the conflagration was growing in intensity. There was little smoke, but the air above it shimmered in the flames.

Ahmed could hear crashes and soft explosions inside the building over the sound of the tanks' engines. He turned to the general, putting a hand on his sidearm.

Ahmed drew his pistol. "You're responsible for this mission."

Ahmed didn't quite point the weapon, but the threat was clear. General Aziz stared at him, his eyes wild in the reflected light.

"Enemy aircraft," screamed one of the men. Others picked up the cry. Troops dove for the ground or ran to shelter behind the tanks.

Ahmed looked back at the main building. Something was rising behind it, but at first his mind couldn't sort out what was happening. The image was surreal. It was distorted and seemed to waver strangely, viewed through the intense heat of the fires.

It was a small helicopter, turning, facing them. Pod mounted chain guns flashed as it raked the formation from right to left. Sparks flew as a shower of 7.62 rounds ricocheted harmlessly from the tanks' armor.

Not so harmlessly. Men were screaming. A gunner slumped, most of his head blown away, and a tank commander fell back into his vehicle's open hatch.

The antiaircraft track had been caught facing the wrong way, facing outward, its radars seeking inbound threats. Its engine roared and treads churned as it slewed around frantically, its guns swiveling toward the new target.

A missile leapt from the copter like a flung knife. It flashed past and something exploded behind Ahmed with the muffled ***crummmppph*** of an armor-piercing warhead.

That was followed an instant later by a larger secondary explosion. The blast wave hit and Ahmed was falling. His head slammed into something hard, then everything went black and the sounds faded away.

Operations Center, White House Basement

Gerry had been dozing again. She came to full alertness when she heard Mike's voice coming over the radio.

"OLYMPUS, this is Twenty Mike. The bad guys are here, and we have MELTDOWN. Please confirm."

"Read you loud and clear Twenty Mike. MELTDOWN is confirmed. That completes the mission. Now get the hell out of there, Sir," the operator said.

"Roger, shutting down now. Twenty Mike out."

Gerry looked up. Colonel Hampton was standing over her. "Why don't you get some rest, ma'am?" he said kindly. "This operation is winding down, and extraction is underway. Leave your phone number, and I'll make sure you're called when we get them all back."

"Thank you, Colonel," she said. "What happens now?"

"I don't expect we'll hear anything more for several hours. The rest of the BLUE BANDIT force is airborne and on their way back to Alpha Base. They've suppressed most of the Bukhari fighter activity. Mother-1 is already out of Bukhari airspace and the rest of BLUE BANDIT is maybe thirty minutes behind. The Saudi AWACs says it's all clear."

Gerry blinked trying to clear her head. "I'm too tired to think straight, Sir, and the military jargon is confusing. I'm a scientist, a cryptologist. My dad was a soldier, but most of what I know about military operations comes from Hollywood. Can you help me understand what's been going on?"

"Just ask. I'll try to translate and fill in for you."

"I don't understand why some of the men left without taking the rest. What was all that about point HOLDOFF? Someone said it was just an empty spot in the desert."

"Exactly," the Colonel said. "A safe place in the middle of nowhere. It was clever strategy and a good solution. As the old adage says, 'amateur warriors study tactics, but the professionals study logistics.'"

Gerry frowned and shook her head. "I'm sorry. I don't have a clue what you mean. I'm afraid I need a bit more translation."

"The most difficult military operation is a retreat from superior forces. That's when the majority of casualties are incurred. Using point HOLDOFF for staging was like pulling yourself up by your own shoelaces, and the plan was executed brilliantly. It's a textbook case of using logistics to shift tactical advantage."

"How so?"

"I'll explain," he said. He took a piece of paper and marked "Point A" in one corner, and "Point B" in the opposite. "You have forces at Point A, and you need to get them to Point B."

"That sounds simple enough."

"It does on paper," he said. "But in practice you have two big problems that make it impossible, or at least impractical. For starters, you're trapped in an exposed forward position by logistics."

"You mean because they didn't have enough fuel to get back?"

"Right," he agreed. "They burned more fuel than planned because they were delayed evading Bukhari patrols. To solve that problem they brought in heavy lift copters with fuel bladders for resupply." He marked an X in the middle of the paper and labeled it 'point HOLDOFF.'

"They refueled the raiders there."

"That's right."

"That doesn't sound so complicated."

"It's not," the Colonel agreed. "But there was another problem, one that was harder to solve. BLUE BANDIT was highly vulnerable to interdiction. The Bukhari Air Force is quite capable, and it was still daylight. That one worried me."

"They were sitting ducks."

"Yes. I was afraid the Saudis or Israelis might take action that could trigger a major war."

"Would they have risked war?"

"I think so. Colonel Mustafa is the Crown Prince's nephew, and the Israelis are trigger happy. Still, something needed to be done, because the copters had no chance at all against Bukhari fighters." He smiled. "General Mickelson teaches innovative tactics, and I'll bet he came up with the solution. I love it."

"What did they do?"

"They brought in a second Mongoose system. Apparently borrowed it from the Israelis. That was a stroke of genius. The Mongoose at Al-Razi covered both BLUE BANDIT's retreat and the relief forces inbound to point HOLDOFF." He looked at her. "Do you understand now?"

"I'm not sure."

"The rescue forces at HOLDOFF had their Mongoose system up and operational by the time the one at Al-Razi went Winchester, ran out of missiles. Then Mikey-2 packed up the Al-Razi Mongoose and flew it out, covered by the second Mongoose."

"And they reloaded the Al-Razi Mongoose when it got to HOLDOFF?"

"Exactly right," the Colonel said. "For a time they had both Mongooses on-line. Bukhari was never able to utilize its air assets effectively.

"It was a gamble, but one that worked." The Colonel shook his head in appreciation. "Innovative strategy, well executed. BLUE BANDIT bootstrapped its forces out of harm's way."

"Why did General Mickelson stay behind at Al-Razi?"

"I don't quite understand that one myself. It's frowned upon to leave general officers exposed, but by then Mickelson was in local command. Maybe he wanted to handle MELTDOWN himself. I'm not sure. I do know Mikey-2, Lieutenant Clover, tried to get him to leave."

"Yes," she said. "He sure did."

"Nor do I understand why CINDERELLA, a scientist, was along on the raid," the Colonel continued, scowling. "It sounded like she screwed up their timing and almost got them killed. The President was tense because she was at risk. Why was she there? I don't know."

Mike and the President must have discussed it when we were out of the room, Gerry thought. "I appreciate your explanation," she said. "It helps a lot."

"It was a tricky OP," the Colonel said. "Mickelson and his Arab friends hung it out a lot further than I'm comfortable with, but it turned out okay in the end."

"Thank you." Her eyes felt like sandpaper. "What about General Mickelson? What happens now?"

"The son-of-a-bitch pulled it off." The Colonel grinned.

"He's safe?"

"He's running for the border like he's got a rocket up his tail. Mustafa left Mickelson his best pilot and stealthiest scout copter. They're flying so low we can't track them ourselves. It's full dark now, less than five percent illumination. He should be just fine."

Gerry thought for a long moment. *I'm not doing any good here. I should get back to work. Mike's counting on me to keep the program running.*

She looked up at Colonel Hampton. "I'm going home to sleep for at least twelve hours. After that, I'll be at NSA."

"I'll make sure you have a driver, ma'am. Do you need any security?"

"Thank you, but no." She smiled faintly. "I'm the only NSA program manager who has a SEAL combat team watching her house."

White House, Oval Office

The President looked up at the soft rap on the door. "Come in."

"We have a secure call coming in," Judy said. "CINDERELLA wants to talk to you."

"I'll take it. Hold my other calls and visits."

The call came in immediately. "How are things, Moira?" he asked.

She gave him a brief report, finishing by saying, "We've got it all, Sir. Everything is in place. I understand we got a confirmed MELTDOWN as well?"

"Yes," he said. "MELTDOWN was confirmed. You've attended to the other details we discussed?"

"I did, Sir. Absolutely."

The President thought for a moment. *You need to be right about that one, Doctor.* "I need you back here ASAP, Moira. We need to talk."

There was a pause. "We're waiting for General Mickelson. He's en route. They expect him in about four or five hours." •

"Sorry, but I've got to override that," the President said. "I want you and the PUMPKIN in Washington as soon as possible."

"You're the boss," she said. "I'm ready to go."

"I'll have you met at Andrews," the President said. "Come directly here."

"Yes, Sir," Moira said. "See you soon."

The President hung up, and then picked up the direct line to the OPS center. VIRGIN was airborne seven minutes later.

Al-Razi Research Center

When Ahmed woke up, a medic was holding him, waving something under his nose. The smell was pungent, especially on top of the cordite and diesel fuel. He coughed, blinked and looked around. His uniform was torn, blood soaked, and grimy. His head was throbbing and bandaged.

"How long have I been out?" His voice didn't sound right.

"Not long, Colonel," the medic said. He examined Ahmed carefully, looking at his eyes. "You took a nasty blow to the head. You have a concussion."

Ahmed moved his arms and legs carefully. Everything seemed to work. "Help me up," he ordered. The medic lifted him to a sitting position. He felt disoriented, nauseous. He took several deep breaths trying to clear his head.

"Water," Ahmed croaked.

The medic passed him a canteen. Ahmed took a sip, then another. He reached into his pocket, pulled out a handkerchief, wet it and dabbed his face.

The main building had collapsed into rubble. It was still burning, as were those adjacent to it. The concrete itself was starting to crumble into powder.

General Aziz came over. He had blood on his uniform. "We lost more men," he said, pointing at the gutted antiaircraft vehicle. Small tongues of orange flame flickered and black smoke was oozing out its view ports.

"Where's that helicopter?" Ahmed demanded.

"Gone." Aziz waved his hand vaguely toward the horizon.

Ahmed looked at him incredulously.

"It flew off to the northwest," the general said. "It was a small American scout helicopter. We had nothing to pursue it."

"Why didn't you shoot it out of the sky?"

"I followed your orders, Colonel."

Ahmed blinked and gave his head a rapid shake. That was a mistake. It hurt badly and he felt another wave of dizziness. His vision went double.

The medic caught him before he fell. "Be careful, Colonel," he said. "We need to get you to a hospital."

Ahmed took a careful breath and glared at the general. *"What did you say?"*

"You ordered me not to fire without your express approval," the general said. "I had no such approval. Therefore we did not fire, even when fired upon."

Ahmed glared at him.

"I have witnesses to your order, Colonel," Aziz said. "Whoever it was in the helicopter, they got away."

This is a disaster, and I'll be blamed. When he finds out, President Nassid will have me executed, Ahmed thought, feeling the first stirrings of panic. Then he looked around and started laughing. There was one building still standing.

Ahmed couldn't stop laughing, even though it made his head hurt. Tears of relief were running down his cheeks. He pointed at the solitary structure. *I've just seen a miracle. The vaccine is safe. Allah is merciful.*

General Aziz was staring at him as if he'd lost his mind.

"Have your men guard that building," Ahmed ordered. "Our mission was successful. President Nassid will be pleased. I'll see you get a medal."

General Aziz blinked.

"Allah is great."

"Allah is great," Aziz agreed, looking puzzled. "Could you please explain to me exactly how we've succeeded?"

Ahmed smiled and pointed at the only untouched building. It was in the far rear of the complex, a hundred meters or more from the rest, and it wasn't even scorched.

"That's the test building," Ahmed said. "It contains all we need. The rest is unimportant."

Aziz was looking at him oddly and another wave of dizziness hit, but it didn't matter. Ahmed slowly relaxed and let the medic ease him onto a stretcher. He was smiling.

CHAPTER NINETEEN
VACCINATION

Jackson's Knoll, Rural Virginia, Three Days Later.

Burt was sipping his scotch when Senator Stiles arrived. Their eyes met across the room, and he nodded, indicating all was clear.

She walked over to the table, sat down, and looked around. No one was close, and the few people in the room seemed to be watching some sports event on the TV over the bar.

Burt smiled his welcome. He was dressed impeccably as always, a charcoal gray suit, pastel shirt, and power tie. His gold cufflinks and watch reflected the dim lights. He looked better than the last time she'd seen him.

She studied him carefully but couldn't tell much except he seemed sober. Burt was the type Hollywood would cast to lead a revolution, the picture of confidence and control. *The problem is he's a bit short on performance, except with his dick.*

"So what's the holdup?" she asked bluntly. "My people are ready."

"So are mine." His smile faded a notch. "There were a few unavoidable delays, but we have what you need."

"You have the vaccine?"

"It came in today."

"It's here in Washington?"

She saw a flicker of discomfort in his intense green eyes. *Shit.* "You don't have it, do you?"

"Not here," he admitted, "but it's safely in the United States. New York. The rest is easy. I'll have it tomorrow. You can start scheduling the inoculations."

"How much?"

He blinked, looking confused.

"How much fucking vaccine do we have, Burt?"

"Enough. One hundred and ten doses."

There was a pause as the waitress came and took her order. The Senator looked at Burt appraisingly, but didn't speak until her wine arrived. She took a sip, nodded, waved the waitress away and waited for the girl to be out of earshot.

"Why is it you can't seem to do anything right?" the Senator asked in a caustic tone. "Are you totally incompetent, or is it just that you don't give a shit?"

"What the hell are you talking about? You wanted to deploy ECP, but insisted on having a vaccine first. We've got it. It took my friends years and quite a bit of money to develop it, but we did just as you wanted. We're ready to go."

"I told you I needed a minimum of one hundred and ninety doses. You're short."

"I got you vaccine."

"Not enough. Not what you promised. I need one hundred and ninety doses."

"You wanted it right away," Burt said. "This is all I could get quickly. Do you want it, or not?"

"What went wrong?" She took a deep swallow of her wine, then another. "I seem to be asking you that a lot lately, don't I?"

"We've got the vaccine. You wouldn't move forward without it, and now we have it." There were beads of sweat on his face. "You shouldn't focus on the negative, Harriet. We're going to change the world together. I've done what you wanted."

"We're going to go to prison if you don't stop screwing up." She was glaring at him. "What went wrong in Maryland? What went wrong in Oregon? And what the fuck went wrong with getting me what I need? I've been waiting for months."

"Please keep your voice down." He looked around nervously, but no one seemed to be paying any attention.

She took several deep breaths, refilled her wine glass, and then downed it. *I've got to control my temper*, she thought.

He refilled her glass before she could reach for the bottle. He looked like a whipped dog. *Fear is useful*, she thought, *but not if it paralyzes him. I should explain what he's done wrong.*

She took another breath and sip of wine, forcing calm. "Everything is set to go, my colleagues are getting nervous, and your damn Arabs can't seem to do the simplest things." She lowered her voice and stared directly into Burt's eyes. "I think you're losing it, and I can't take a chance on that."

"Please calm down," he said in a placating tone. "Yes, we've had a few problems. That's to be expected. None were my fault, and no lasting harm was done."

"Problems caused solely by bad luck and misfortune...."

"Yes," he said nodding. "Exactly. We missed the Patton woman, but the operation in Oregon was successful, despite that loose-cannon Marine General who locked down the state without justification. In the end, you benefited."

"It helped my party," she admitted. "But there was a small war in Oregon, we lost Tibbs and the military captured one of your Arabs."

"Minor losses. We neutralized Cybertech, and you gained politically. Kendrick Tibbs took his secrets to the grave, and the Arab knows nothing."

"He can tie the Oregon operation to Bukhari."

"Perhaps," Burt agreed. "If he talks, which isn't likely. In a few weeks, it won't matter. What are you so worried about?"

She thought for a long moment, taking another sip of her wine. *Maybe he's right. It won't matter much longer.* "The Marine is still a problem."

"He's merely an inconvenience. Unfortunately, one surrounded by heavily armed men. I was counting on you for a political solution."

"That takes time," the Senator said.

"The papers said there were going to be hearings into his misconduct. Can't you influence them?"

"I can influence anything in Washington." She shrugged. "The problem is the general is on assignment to NSA. Protocol gives the Senate Intelligence Committee purview, and they're moving slowly. I don't expect anything to happen for some time. They're not in any rush."

"Without Cybertech, I doubt they can do much to revive his program anyway," Burt said thoughtfully. "Have you heard anything?"

"The rumors are it's been canceled. It's hard to tell for sure. NSA won't say, and the General's dropped out of sight. He's been keeping a low profile since Oregon." The Senator smiled coldly. "The press can't even find the son-of-a-bitch."

"Tibbs said the program was a year or more from delivering anything useful."

"Yes," she agreed. "That's probably right."

"Our plans could be implemented inside a month. Then you can do anything you want. Anything."

He's right, she thought. "Why don't we have more vaccine?"

"There was some kind of an accident at the plant. These materials are, ah, somewhat hazardous. The main thing is the vaccine works."

Bukhari must have diverted some of my vaccine for its own people, she thought. *Well, I would too. That just shows they're not total fools.*

"I have one hundred and sixty nine people in the legislative branch that are certain allies. There are a few more that could be influenced when they see the inevitable," she said musingly.

"Prioritize your list. Wars have casualties. If you're going to rule in the time that's coming, you'll have to make choices like that frequently."

"I could wait for more vaccine," she said slowly. *But he does have a good point. She who risks little, gains little.*

"You could," Burt admitted. "I don't know how quickly we could get it, but I can ask. Right now, I can get you a hundred and ten doses. Tomorrow, if you wish."

"Is there enough ECP for an attack?" she asked, knowing the answer, but wanting to hear it voiced. She felt herself getting excited. *It's coming together*, she thought. *All that power, and it's almost in my hands.*

He smiled. "As much as you want. I've not pressed my friends for delivery, because you wanted the vaccine to take effect before we bring the ECP into the country. I'm advised three weeks should be sufficient for immunity. We'll have the ECP long before we need it."

She thought for a time, and then nodded. "All right. We'll move. I'll get my clinic set up to dispense the vaccine Monday. Try to get more."

Burt nodded.

She calculated in her head. *Three doctors I can trust fully, times four doses per hour, times an eight-hour workday. That equals ninety-six doses per day. I'll allow two days, for screw-ups and missed appointments. Members of Congress tend to be over committed.*

"Let's do it," she said firmly. "I'll tell you where to deliver the vaccine, and I'll expect it there by the weekend. We'll have the vaccinations completed by next Wednesday."

He smiled. "May I pour you some more wine?"

White House, Oval Office

"I want to listen to the recordings of the last meeting Senator Stiles had in the restaurant," the President said.

"I thought you might, Sir," Director Johnson said. "We burned a copy on a disk, with the low light video synched to an audio track. A few segments drop out, but our lab thinks they can eventually get it all."

He pulled a disk out of his inside coat pocket and handed it to the President. "It runs nineteen minutes, Sir."

The President popped it into his computer and watched intently but without comment as it played to the end. He sighed deeply. "It's pretty much as you said, Roger."

"Treason," Johnson said.

The President didn't reply. He ejected the disk and handed it back. He looked sad. "What happened next?"

"They finished their drinks, went to a room, did some coke, and screwed their brains out."

"Illegal drugs...."

"It's not worth pressing drug charges," Johnson said.

"Why not?"

"For one thing it would only enhance her power. The press loves the Senator. She'd claim harassment and politics. Remember the Clinton impeachment? When the dust settled, Clinton was still there, and his accusers were gone or discredited."

"They broke the law."

"That's up to a jury, and we're not optimistic about getting a conviction." Johnson shrugged. "Our lawyers recommend against pressing drug charges. We'd do better to keep her contact running and see where he leads us."

"Did they talk shop in the room?"

"No," Johnson said glumly. "Would you like to see the video?"

"I would not," the President said. "Tell me more about the man."

"His name is Burton Cassidy. Used to be a running back for University of Georgia. He was a good athlete. Might have made the pros, but got involved in a gambling scandal. Nothing was ever proved, but it tarnished his image. The rest of his life has been somewhat less exemplary."

"He's a Bukhari agent?"

"Almost certainly, but not in the conventional sense. The notion of foreign agents is fuzzy in a global economy, and it got worse after Osama and his Venture Capital form of global *jihad*."

"Tell me why."

"Proof is elusive, and the legal and jurisdictional issues are extreme. There was a UN guy named Maurice Strong who was caught red-handed with a check made out to him *personally* for a million dollars as part of the Iraq "oil for food" deal. He skipped to China, and was never prosecuted.

"No one ever proved a major funding connection between Al Qaeda and Iraq, but for a time both political parties were chasing that rabbit. A huge amount of effort went into it."

"There was evidence. There were reports."

"Evidence is not proof, Sir. That takes a court ruling. They might have proved the 'funding' part, but probably not the 'major.' Remember the discussions about Obama's illegal foreign campaign donations that went nowhere? And that was over *Presidential elections*."

The President shook his head. "That was political. The media gave him a pass. Foreign political donations are strictly illegal, but there is no specific law that requires they be tracked."

"If it wasn't worth prosecuting Maurice Strong for a million dollar crime when you have hard evidence, what about cashing a swarm of nameless, small cash donations? And who was to investigate it? Obama's own DOJ? Not likely."

"We don't have that problem. My DOJ would be happy....."

"Actually, if you ask the litigators, I doubt they would. Perhaps I didn't use the best example, but the problem goes far beyond that, Sir. Even if DOJ wanted to prosecute, the courts would have given Obama a pass, because it's just too messy to investigate, prove, and prosecute murky cases like that in civil courts."

"They don't want to spend their time on it."

"Correct, and we would have the same problem. You can drown in a sea of trivial details. It's not easy to track money if it comes in small amounts from many sources."

"Yes, right, but what about Cassidy's income? There you have a single narrow issue, and a specific target, one who is a normal United States citizen. He has to file tax returns."

Director Johnson shrugged. "We put in a week's work on one transaction and tracked it back to its roots: $9,500, just under the limit of $10,000 that triggers special procedures. It took a lot of guesswork at first, but we did it. We tracked the banks, and the banks behind the banks."

"What did you learn?"

"Not much, Mr. President. The money came into New York from Guernsey. From Guernsey, we tracked it to Paris. From Paris to Athens. From Athens to Beirut and from Beirut to Riyadh and from Riyadh to Cairo. The end station was Cairo, and that's where the trail ended. It started with a cash deposit there. The pattern is not atypical."

"What about Cassidy? What can you say about him?"

"His main allegiance seems to be to money and power. He made $763,347 last year. Altruistic guy, lobbies for several charities and non-profits. Institute for Mideast Peace, among others. Along with one oil company, but not Bukhari, or any other nation for that matter. Most of his money seems to flow in from the Mideast along the lines I just described."

"What does his bank say about the convoluted money trail?"

"The normal things," Johnson said. "Muslims are shy. One can hardly blame them when so many think they're all terrorists. And that they're complying with the law, of course."

"Does Cassidy control the Senator?"

"He bundles and donates generously, but it's more likely a symbiotic relationship. If anything, she seems to control him."

The President nodded and gestured for the director to continue.

"The subject has had some brushes with the law, but no convictions. Recreational drugs, driving while intoxicated, bounced some checks. Nothing recent. DEA suspected he was a small time drug dealer, but never built a prosecutable case. If so, he's shifted his focus. It seems influence is more valuable."

"It always has been," the President said. He was silent for a time, shaking his head, and then he looked at the director. "How'd they get their vaccine into the country?"

"We're still sorting it out. We know it came in through New York, we think through diplomatic pouches at the UN. Not Bukhari, other countries. We've got bugs and taps in place, but we probably won't find out until we can pick up the mules and interrogate them."

"How are they going to vaccinate Stiles' allies in Congress?" the President asked.

"In plain sight. As you know, the Senator Chairs the Senate Committee on Health, Education, Labor, and Public Welfare. She's also endowed a private clinic here in Washington. She's on the board. The Feminist Poverty Medical Center."

"She'll use a public health clinic to pave the way for a coup?"

"It's a popular cause and a terrific political asset for the Senator. They help children, unwed mothers, that sort of thing. It was written up in *People* last year. Several big name movie stars help them with fund raising. It's legitimate."

"Assisting a terrorist attack is legitimate?"

"They'd spin it differently, Mr. President. Not assisting, possibly helping to prevent an attack. Her handlers and lawyers would say Stiles was only doing what President Bush tried. I expect the media would buy her story, hook, line, and sinker."

"What the hell are you talking about?"

"George W. Bush planned a vaccine program for mass inoculations against bioweapons."

"I've never heard of such a program."

"In the early days of the terrorist wars, the Bush II administration was going to vaccinate officials and health workers against smallpox. It didn't work out. Forcing people to be vaccinated was a political misstep, and the program never went anywhere."

"Senator Stiles is reviving the Bush program, making it voluntary, and portraying herself as an anti-terror heroine?"

"No, Sir, what she's doing is fully covert. But if we charged her with anything, such a claim would be the most likely response. It would be plausible to many. She's the perceived guardian of public health, and her colleagues are loyal volunteers. They see her as a rising star."

"Does their loyalty include high treason?"

The director shrugged.

The President slammed his fist on the desk. "Don't evade me, Roger. I want to know. How many Members of Congress are in on this?"

"They're setting up for over a hundred vaccinations."

"We have a hundred traitors in Congress?"

"Of course not, Mr. President. That many people can't keep a secret. Not in this town. No way. There would have been leaks."

"I don't find that comforting."

"It's more about ambition than treason, Mr. President. Most involved are power-seeking dupes, but there has to be a core group of traitors. When I get you the short list, will you consider impeachment proceedings?"

The President shook his head. "I'm not going to put our country through that."

"We can find the traitors. We're close. Just let us bug Congressional conversations."

"No. Public surveillance only."

The director sighed. "That's what we're doing, Mr. President."

"The vaccine is here now?"

"It's at the clinic. They plan to start immunization Monday."

"Can you get people inside without attracting notice?"

"We're already inside, plus electronic surveillance. I don't need court orders, since it's linked to terrorism."

"Walk softly, but I want a record of who gets vaccinated," the President ordered. "Be very discrete. Next to pissing off Congress, the last thing my administration needs is to be accused with interfering with citizens' health care providers."

"That's about all we can do right now," the director said.

"Exactly right," the President said. "I need your personal assurance. Nothing but surveillance, and very soft."

"You have my word. I've got my best Counter Terrorism agents on it, and they've been ordered to stay fully covert. They'll disengage if there's any risk of detection."

"Good," the President said. "Keep me informed."

"May I speak frankly, Mr. President?"

"Go ahead."

"Before 9-11, there had been many reports of a planned attack and many years of predecessor events. But the attack happened anyway."

"Your point?"

"We're running out of time. Our enemies can mount a precision attack on Congress any time after Stiles and her allies are vaccinated and the vaccine takes effect. When can we take action, Mr. President?"

"Can you think of any legal way to preempt an attack without taking on Senator Stiles politically?"

"No, Sir."

"As you pointed out yourself, an impeachment is difficult. Senator Stiles is very popular. Charging her with drugs is one thing, but to charge her and other members of Congress with high treason would effectively paralyze all three branches of government. It would also directly involve this office. There's a huge downside. Not just for me and my party, but for the nation."

"We have to do something, Mr. President."

"When do you expect the vaccinations will be completed?"

"Wednesday," Johnson said without hesitation. "That's their plan."

"Then we can discuss legal action a week from Thursday. Is that acceptable?

"Yes, Sir. It has to be." Johnson nodded slowly. "I'll prepare an action plan for your approval. I'd like to ask the AG to attend the meeting."

"Thursday next week, Roger," the President said. "Not before. Bring the Attorney General along, and we'll brief her then."

"Yes, Sir."

The President hesitated. He was watching the director's eyes closely. "Was there anything else, Roger?"

Director Johnson frowned. He looked uncomfortable.

"Go ahead," the President said.

"We're close to the edge on this one. It makes me nervous."

"Sometimes we have to make difficult choices. I've found prayer often helps."

"Yes, Sir," Johnson said. "I'll pray hard."

Fort Meade, Maryland

Gerry looked up when her secure phone rang. *My first incoming call this week. One nice thing about tight security is at least people are letting me get some work done.*

"3824," she said.

"There you go again. Don't get me excited." Mike's chuckle was only slightly distorted by the redundant encryption.

Her heart skipped. "Why not?"

"Might get you in trouble. Have you been behaving?"

"Up until now," she said. "Would you like me to talk dirty?"

"Not yet. Right now, I couldn't handle that."

"I can help."

He laughed. "What are you doing for dinner?"

"Spending time with you," she said firmly. *So much for being coy. Well, I need to talk business with him anyway.* "Not only have I been 'behaving,' as you crudely put it, but we've been making progress."

"That's outstanding. Is it my good leadership, or just that I haven't been bothering you?"

"Mostly, it's my brother. He's doing some clever things. I'll tell you when we meet. Where are you?"

"Sitting in a noisy aluminum tube with propellers, back with the cargo pallets. I've been on this damned thing for about forty hours, not counting ground stops. They claim we're landing at Andrews in about a half hour."

"I'll pick you up. We can have dinner at my place. It's secure, your SEALs are still there, and we can talk."

"That's not necessary."

"I'm a good cook. Besides, I've been surviving on cafeteria food and coffee. It'll be fun to fix something. What would you like?"

"Oh, I'll take you up on the dinner, with thanks. Surprise me. Anything but an MRE or chicken and rice would be greatly appreciated. I just meant you don't have to pick me up. Believe me, you don't want to get anywhere near me until I bathe."

Gerry laughed.

"I'll get a vehicle, shower and change, and pick up some wine if that's okay?"

"It's perfect," she said. "I'll be there waiting."

"White or red?"

"You pick. I'll do pasta again, and I'll get some of that bread you liked."

"I'll get us some good Chianti. Right now I'd kill for a glass of wine or a beer. See you in about two hours."

"Perfect. See you then." She put down the phone slowly. *Tomorrow's Sunday*, she thought. *I deserve a day off.*

River Glen, MD

Mike finished his third bowl of pasta. He wiped the dish with a piece of bread, and sighed. "You have no idea how good this tastes."

"You're easy to please," Gerry said, "at least about cooking."

"Work too. You've done a remarkable job. I'm to meet with the President tomorrow. I'll tell him we can have a demo for Congress in thirty days."

"Thank you."

"I'm not needed on this project, Gerry. You're doing all the work. You've got it under control, and you know a hell of a lot more about this sort of thing than I do."

"You underestimate yourself. It's your presence that makes people leave me alone so I can get work done." She frowned and shook her head. "Just getting Tibbs out of my hair was like a breath of fresh air."

He took a sip of wine. "I didn't have much to do with it."

"You had everything to do with it."

"I ran off and left you holding the bag, as it were."

"Visiting old friends in the Mideast," she said, looking at him appraisingly. "Relaxing and having a good time."

"Pretty much," he said. "Relationships are important."

"I suppose you feel guilty about abandoning our project to go off and have fun with the boys while I was here working my tail off?"

"I do, a little…."

"Bullshit."

He raised an eyebrow, but didn't speak.

"I was in the Command Center. OLYMPUS."

Mike blinked. "Oh."

"They had Al-Razi up on a map. Hundreds of miles inside of Bukhari. Not a good vacation spot." She gently touched the bruise on his forehead with her fingertips. "I saw the craters. You must have been right under that fighter when it blew."

"How long were you there?"

"The whole time." *Almost two days, but who's counting.* "I have friends who let me in. I was worried about you. So were they."

"President Hale."

"I care for you," she said. "There's something special here."

"Yes." He didn't look at her.

"I'm a big girl. If you don't want to be personally involved with me, just say so."

"It's not that."

"It's because we've slept together?" she said.

"We have rules in the service about such things. It's unprofessional. Technically, I'm your superior."

"I'm not in the service. We're not married. This is nothing like Petraeus."

He sighed deeply. "I'm not very good at this."

"I've got no complaints."

Mike blushed.

"It could be worse." She smiled softly. "Did you hear the one about the doctor who was upset because he was having sex with his patient?"

He shook his head.

"It bothered him. He was troubled, and kept thinking he'd done something wrong."

"I can understand that...."

"But he heard a soft voice in his left ear. 'Dave,' it said, 'You're human. Things like this happen. You're single. It's okay to have sex with a patient.'"

Mike was watching her intently. She had his full attention.

"Did that make Dave feel better?"

"For a time it did," she said slowly.

Mike looked pensive. "And...?"

"Then he heard a louder voice in his right ear. 'Dave, Dave,' it said, 'get a grip. You're a *veterinarian*.'"

She watched the emotions flow across Mike's face. Thoughtful concern turned to surprise, followed by incredulity. He guffawed and almost dropped his wine glass. His eyes were watering, and he wiped them with a napkin.

She feigned concern, pleased with herself. "Are you okay?"

"I wasn't expecting that...."

"We can't be serious all the time. Life happens."

He looked at her.

She met his eyes. "Seriously, are you all right?"

"I'm not sure. Where does my duty and honor lie? Should I be sleeping with you? Did I abandon you and our project?"

"I can answer the last two. 'Yes,' and 'No.' Why on earth would you wonder?"

"I ran into a colleague, an old friend, at Andrews. Used to be my mentor. He chewed my ass. Said general officers shouldn't risk themselves needlessly. Dereliction of duty, he said."

"Mentor or not, he's wrong," Gerry said. "You *were* doing your job. You got the Saudis and the Israelis to work together. General Myers and the President were both in your corner. They were prepared to do drastic things to get you out."

"I'm glad it wasn't necessary."

"Do you trust me?"

"Of course I do."

"Then listen to me. Ignore the bullshit, Mike. I'm proud of you. You did what was needed, then and now. Against all odds, you made it out of Bukhari on your own, and without creating an international incident.

No one left behind: A suicide mission where everyone made it back. The people in the OPS center were in awe."

He was watching her carefully.

A lone tear ran down her cheek. She brushed it away. "I was afraid for you, but I never for a moment thought you were abandoning me or the project. You ran toward the guns. It's what Dad would do."

He took her hand. "What do we do now?"

"What we must. Women are used to that."

Gerry took a sip of wine. "I think we know a part of each other that no one else shares, you and I. We're blessed. No matter what happens, we have that."

"Yes."

"We've been put into a situation beyond our control. We're doing something necessary, perhaps vital. We've been given a job neither one of us requested, one that's both urgent and crucial." She gave him a serious look. "Do you want to let the President down?"

He looked somber. "Of course not."

"Neither do I. Do you think he'd let you quit?"

"Not without an explanation, anyway."

"And rightfully so," she said. "Under some circumstances – probably under most circumstances – you'd have a valid concern about our becoming personally involved. But you're a boss I almost never see, one who gives me no directions or constraints except to get the job done for my country. Which is what I'm trying to do anyway."

"I'm dependent on your knowledge. I don't know enough to micromanage you, even if it were my style."

"I know," she said. "But you need to realize I'm just as dependent on your support. If you hadn't been there, Jack Mitchell would have put an agency *apparatchik* in to replace Tibbs."

"To cover his ass?"

"For damage control," she said. "It would make my job harder."

He looked at her somberly. "Maybe so."

"I've got conflicts all over the place, Mike. One more hardly matters. You're my lifeline.

"NSA doesn't *want* to do the program. They *can't* do it without Cybertech. My father wouldn't agree to work with the agency unless they let *me* run the program, and, now that he's gone, my brother feels even more strongly about that. He won't do it without me, and I can't do it without you to protect me from my own management. The main thing we have going for us is our personal relationships, and you know it."

Mike was looking at her carefully. "What do you suggest?"

"Would it change things if we didn't sleep together?"

"I don't think so."

"Me neither. Maybe you should stop worrying, and we'll just do the best we can. Would that work?"

Mike said, "I'm not sure."

"Do you have a better solution?" *He looks worried. This is a man who was single-handedly standing off an armored column a few days ago, and now he's apprehensive because we're starting to care for each other.*

"No."

"Well, there you are," she said brightly. "If it helps, I'll promise not to compromise the RSA algorithms, virtual tunneling, biometric verification, or automatically seeded pseudo random 4096 bit keys because of my sexual fantasies."

"I wouldn't know even if you did." Mike laughed, shaking his head.

"I promise not to do anything to embarrass us."

"Relationships don't always work."

"You're telling me. I'm divorced, remember?"

"It's not easy being married to someone in the service."

"My mother married an officer."

"Who is now missing...."

"Let's not go there. Not now. Please."

"I'd rather not, but...."

"Then don't. Mom and Dad have been together for almost 40 years. Good years, Mike. How many people can say that?"

"Far too few." He looked at her for a long moment. Finally he nodded. "And now, Ms. Patton, we....?"

"Forget the world. Just for one night. Please. Can you do that?"

"Okay."

"Hmmmm," she purred sensuously, moistening her lips, thrusting her breasts, and giving him her most shameless look. "You could open another bottle of wine."

He smiled. "Good idea."

Feminist Poverty Medical Center, Washington DC, Monday

Senator Stiles took off her vest and rolled up her sleeve. "I'll go first," she said. Besides the doctor, there were three others present. Senator Richard Bradley from the other party, and two members of the House of Representatives, one from each party.

A partisan but bipartisan effort, she thought. *Long live the revolution.*

"Do you want to give a speech first?" Bradley said.

"I'll save the speeches for later. There will be plenty of time."

Bradley nodded.

The doctor dipped a cotton swab in alcohol, deftly gave her the injection, and slapped a small bandage over it. "Keep that on for a few hours. You don't want it to bleed."

Stiles turned to Bradley. "It's your turn, Senator." *Put up, or shut up. If you want to be a leader, you have to get your ass out in front. I've got two others who could replace you, if you don't want the role.*

The older Senator looked at her for a moment, and then nodded. "So it is."

He rolled up his sleeve.

Across the street, Obie Simpson peered through large binoculars. He was standing well back from the open window, careful to stay out of sight. He slowly set them down and then turned to his assistant. "Looks like we're going to have a busy day, George."

"Looks like it. There's already a stream of limos lining up. Nothing subtle about this, is there?"

Next to them, a third agent was looking through the viewfinder of a tripod-mounted large frame digital camera with a telephoto lens. He was concentrating intently, and his shutter clicked every few seconds.

"They don't need to be subtle," Simpson said after a time. "It's a free country. There's nothing illegal about going to the doctor and getting a shot."

"Yes, Sir," the younger agent said.

"We've got bugs and cameras inside, but you never know. Don't miss the photos. I want clear shots of faces and license plates."

"We've got two cameras on it. Plus a tap into the clinic's security cameras and those in the parking garage."

Simpson picked up the binoculars and scanned the area again. Another limo was pulling up, but no agents were in sight. *So far, so good.*

"Here comes Stiles," the younger agent said.

The agents watched as the Senator strode briskly out of the clinic. Her driver rushed to open the door of the limo, and the agent with the camera took three quick shots. "Got her face, real clear," he muttered to himself.

The younger agent looked at his watch. "She was in there for twenty one minutes. Here comes Bradley. He was only there for twelve. Maybe they'll get this done today."

"Doesn't matter how long they take," Simpson said. "We've practiced, everyone's been briefed, and these are the best surveillance teams and CT agents we have. I'm still going to stand right here till it's over and make sure we don't have any screw-ups."

"Yes, Sir," the younger agent said.

CHAPTER TWENTY
A SHORT UGLY WOMAN

Georgetown, Maryland

Senator Stiles hadn't slept well. She tossed and turned all night with bad dreams. When she woke up, the vaccination on her arm was itching intensely, and her muscles ached.

To hell with it. I don't have any important hearings until this afternoon. She popped two aspirins, drank the glass of water on her end table, and turned off the alarm.

When she woke up two hours later, she felt much better. The itching had stopped, though the skin around her vaccination was now red and slightly swollen.

I've always had sensitive skin. I'm having a reaction to that damned shot. Stiles dressed, went into the kitchen and rummaged around looking for breakfast fare.

She finally decided on orange juice and a breakfast bar, followed by two cups of black coffee. When she finished, she'd almost forgotten the incident. It's getting better. *I'll stick some aspirin in my purse and get an appointment with Marge if it still bothers me tomorrow.*

By the next morning everything was fine. She didn't need the aspirin. The redness had faded, the swelling had gone down, and she could hardly tell she'd ever had the vaccination. She pushed it from her mind. This was a busy time. Plans needed to be made.

Fort Detrick, Maryland

Doctor Moira Sanderson disliked management and wasn't comfortable working with a large team. She preferred private meetings, the quiet of her office, and sterile interactions with her computers. It was easier to model microorganisms than work with them in the lab.

It was also safer. Unfortunately, there was no choice this time.

The lab area was doubly sealed, both biologically and environmentally. All the external doors were airlocks. The environment was kept at a lower pressure than the outside to ensure nothing could escape. The interior was well lit and maintained at a constant sixty-eight degrees.

Safety procedures were rigorous, and bio-suits were mandatory. When the staff left the inner containment area at the end of their shifts, they stripped off the suits to be soaked in strong disinfectant and left in a room flooded with ozone and ultraviolet radiation. Inner garments were sanitized and everyone scrubbed down thoroughly.

No one left the outer containment area, nor would they anytime soon. Not until the secrets of ECP were fully understood, and everyone who could have been exposed was well past the incubation period.

Moira had the Bukhari scientists who'd defected train her staff on the safety procedures they'd used successfully at Al-Razi. Fortunately, both spoke English.

Being in the same boat, as it were, the defectors were highly motivated to ensure the Americans didn't make any mistakes. There had been a number of casualties in the early days at Al-Razi, and the deaths were memorably gruesome.

Moira's staff consisted of volunteers who now lived in the facility. They were there until any possible threat of ECP infection was past. Those with families had been given a cover story. They were out of the country on assignment, and unavailable. The staff accepted the constraints because bonuses were lavish.

The Bukhari defectors had been promised citizenship along with placement in witness protection in exchange for the risks they were taking. They seemed delighted to be in America.

Outside, the guards were Army Rangers. Deadly force was authorized, and they took their orders seriously. No one was to enter without proper authorization, and no one was to leave, period. The soldiers knew they were the first line of defense against an epidemic in the nation's center of government.

One delivery truck had failed to stop at a checkpoint and had its engine and tires riddled with automatic weapons fire. The driver survived unscathed, but his company paid a stiff fine for ignoring the clearly posted warnings and fired the driver on the spot.

This was arguably the best facility in the country to study dangerous new microbes. Moira certainly couldn't complain about her equipment or staff. She had a team of fifty workers, ten of them medical doctors, and three of them virologists.

It was a diverse group. Not counting the Bukhari refugees, there were twenty-seven Christians of various faiths, two Muslims, five Hindu's, and eight Jews. There were two avowed atheists, five agnostics, one declared vegetarian, several who were indifferent, and one who said her religious preference was her own damn business. Forty-one had advanced degrees and at least two were contenders for Nobel prizes if their research panned out.

The wing adjacent to the lab was a two hundred-bed hospital. If anyone was inadvertently exposed to microorganisms, the best medical care was available. Moira thought that part was nonsense.

"ECP is a bioweapon, not a natural disease. It's been scientifically designed to kill its hosts. If someone screws up, it will be cheaper and safer to give them a lethal injection and burn the body," she'd told the President. *"They're dead anyway."*

He'd ordered the hospital unit be made ready anyway.

She'd given her staff the same warning, of course. They paid it more heed.

Even with all the precautions, Moira was exceedingly careful with the ECP. The PUMPKIN was carefully opened in a closed room by technicians using robotic handling arms. Toxins were sorted by batch and distributed to separate teams for experiments.

Moira wasn't allowed human subjects, of course. She had to depend on the Bukhari test data and computer simulations, as dissatisfying and limiting as that was.

The staff passed time by studying medical texts and the Bukhari files and records. After hours, they mostly watched videos. Some worked out in the health club. There were weights and fitness machines, and even a basketball court. There was a cafeteria with decent food. Occasionally, treats like pizza and beer would arrive with the supplies.

Moira looked up when the phone rang, frowning. The green light was on: a secure call. She picked it up. "Yes?"

It was Judy. "Dr. Sanderson, the President wants to talk to you."

Moira wrinkled her brow. *Is it starting already?*

Judy said, "I'll put him through."

"Yes, Mr. President?" Moira said. "So far, so good here. We've detected nothing that would contradict the Bukhari data. Their intent was despicable, but their science was solid."

"I need you to ready the hospital wing."

"Sir?" she said, feigning puzzlement, though she knew where this was going.

"Some members of Congress seem to have taken it upon themselves to get vaccinations for ECP," the President said. "There have been adverse reactions."

"How unfortunate for them. I hope they get good medical care."

"The scope of the problem goes beyond these patients, Doctor. It has both medical and political aspects. CDC wants these patients isolated immediately. They're afraid of contagion in Washington. They fear if the media gets involved, there might be mass panic."

"I'm sure the Communicable Disease Center can handle this, Mr. President. It is, after all, their job."

"Dr. Damadian just left my office. He's quite upset, Moira. He says CDC's safeguards are inadequate for a totally unknown and highly virulent disease. He doesn't want these patients sent to general hospitals and says the local hospitals don't want to accept them either."

Raymond Damadian has turned into a stereotypical bureaucrat. He was never very competent. Now he's just an asshole.

"I cannot believe the CDC wants these patients sent to me," she lied. *Little Raymond can damned well call his mother if he wants sympathy. He won't get it from me.*

"That's exactly what they want," the President said. "You have a staffed, biosecure facility in the immediate area. You can ensure this infection doesn't get loose, can't you?"

"We do have good containment, but…."

"More reason to get them there quickly."

"We're not set up to play 'General Hospital' here, Mr. President. We're researchers, not healers."

"That's understood and documented."

"I cannot accept any liability for matters that are beyond my control."

"Of course not," the President said.

"My objections to accepting these patients are a matter of record?"

"Yes."

"What about the waiver?"

"He signed one. I'll have it faxed over. You're neither responsible nor liable."

"No reporters?"

"CDC will handle any needed media communications. You won't be bothered."

"That's good, Mr. President." She paused for a long moment.

"We need to move on this, Moira."

"Yes, Sir. Is there anything else?"

"You know what we need. Just get it done. Do what you think is best."

"I understand, Mr. President."

"Thank you."

Moira was smiling when she put the phone down. *I've finally got some test subjects and a release. How fortuitous.*

White House, Oval Office, Monday

"So that's how it would work, Mr. President," Gerry said, keying the last slide on her laptop computer. "Our alpha test system is now running. My brother has done some really great things to get this all put together. It's not secure, but it does demonstrate basic functionality."

"When can we have a secure system?"

"That's the beta test I mentioned. Tentatively six months, depending in part on what reactions we get from the alpha test."

"What do you need to continue? And what's a beta test, incidentally?"

Gerry took a deep breath. *Mostly, we need time. Everyone is running on overload.* She paused for a moment to collect her thoughts.

Mike smiled at her confidently. The smile said, "You go, girl."

"Two of the traditional development milestones in high tech are the alpha and beta tests for new systems. Alpha is the concept demonstration to the team itself and its management. We've done that. I can show you the alpha prototype system if you want to stop by NSA."

The President nodded.

"It's for show only, not operational use. The screens are simulated."

"I understand."

"The beta test is for actual paying customers. Real users, versus techno geeks."

"How does this beta thing work?"

"We get sample customers who typify those who'll be using the system. We train them, and they try to do their jobs using the new products. Our engineers watch. They fix problems and make design changes as necessary."

"You want members of Congress to start using it?"

"The short answer is, 'Yes,' but the problem is that beta testing is work. I'm afraid the process can be rather tedious. It would be best to have volunteers," Gerry frowned, "or perhaps their staffers."

The President nodded.

"Have you ever seen the old movies of automobile races from the early twentieth century?"

"If I did, I don't remember much about them."

"The main thing relevant to the point I'm trying to make is there were two people in the car during the race," Gerry said. "The driver, plus a second person."

"If you say so…."

"The second person was a mechanic, an engineer if you will. He tuned the car and kept it operational while the driver ran the race. That's pretty much what a beta test is about. You're building, changing, and repairing the machine while the customer is using it."

"It sounds like a lot of trouble."

"It can be a messy process, Sir. That's why enthusiastic volunteers are best. I'll need a few Members of Congress to get involved and start trying to use the system."

"Bipartisan?"

"That's a political decision, Sir, but my guess is that eventually it has to be. What I need for this to succeed is involvement and support from people who would actually use this as part of the legislative process. It has to be a win for them too."

"What do the people who help you develop this get in return for their time and frustration?"

"They get to be the lead customers. That's a prestige thing, but it also means they can be the most productive users when the system is fielded," Gerry said. "The lead customers get to help design the system to meet their exact requirements."

"That could be done in six months?"

Gerry shrugged. "The beta test program will take between four months and a year. That's a guess. We won't have a schedule until we begin that phase of the program and start interacting with actual users."

"Why not?"

"We don't know enough." She looked at him earnestly. "We're not exactly sure how Congress works, Mr. President."

The President chortled. "None of us know, Gerry. It's a mystery and great source of bafflement. The main thing is you're ready to move forward?"

"Our funding is sufficient, and my brother is rebuilding Cybertech. The current shortage is wetware. We need people, wetware – real living, breathing test subjects – to exercise and stress test the system. We also need some heavy duty experts to try and break it."

"Go on, Gerry," the President ordered. "I need to understand the implications."

"Well, Sir, the easiest thing to explain is that we need actual users. That's what we've been discussing so far. But we need testers too, to try and break the system."

"Don't you have testers? Quality assurance people?"

"Yes and we're adding more, but they tend to be highly expert geeks. We also need to get some technically naive Congressional people using the system – people who are clueless about electronics, crypto gear, and cyber security, people who are representative of those who'll actually be using the system to do their daily work."

"Those can be made available," the President said dryly. "A sufficient supply exists."

"We also need some highly motivated outside experts working to break the system while it's in use. That's going to be essential, Sir. The system must be fully secure. It has to be bulletproof. We don't want enemies listening in on the private deliberations of Congress."

"Lord no," the President said. "We don't even want the press or our friends listening in."

"Security, verification, and validation are the toughest design constraints. It's why we'll need to publish how the system works and get people to attempt to break it."

The President blinked and shook his head.

Gerry looked at Mike. He was frowning.

This is the difficult part of the discussion. It's not easy to explain to laymen.

"Tell me why we have to break the system," the President said finally.

"Do you know why the West won World War II?"

"Superior leadership. People like Churchill, Bull Halsey, and your own great granddad, 'Blood and Guts' Patton. Even Roosevelt hung tough. He stuck with the plan to focus on Hitler first even after the Japanese hit Pearl Harbor."

"It's kind of you to include Granddad, Sir." *But it wasn't the answer I was looking for.* Gerry turned to Mike. "What's your answer? You've taught military history."

"More and better weapons," he said without hesitation. "Better aircraft, like the P-51, P-38 and the B-17, and a much better Navy. The Japanese did us a favor when they forced us to shift from battleships to carriers. Our early ground equipment wasn't the best, but it was reliable. By the end of the war that was superior as well, even the tanks. The atom bomb ended the war."

Gerry nodded slowly. "Those are good answers, but they're not what I was hoping for. I'd argue we won because we broke their codes, and they failed to break ours. We knew the enemy plans, and that let us win even though we were badly overmatched. After we'd won for a few years and the enemy war machine was in tatters, we eventually had the best weapons."

The President smiled. "That's a typical NSA viewpoint. The argument has merit, of course."

"Initially, our enemies had superior technology," Gerry said, "including excellent codes and more advanced cipher machines, like Enigma. It was very difficult to break."

"I know that history," the President said, with an undertone of impatience. He wanted her to get to the point, but she needed to walk through this carefully if she was to be understood.

"We eventually captured an Enigma, analyzed its mechanisms, and figured out how their cipher machines worked. That gave us the structure of their best codes."

"That's what let us break their codes?" the President said.

"Not quite, but close. The most secure codes are seeded with pseudo-random numbers. Once we learned how the Axis generated the seeds for their keys, then we broke their codes. Eventually, all their codes. And yes, it took several years of work and helped create places like Bletchley Park in Britain and agencies like NSA."

"Your point, Gerry?"

"Even the best secrecy no longer works for electronic security, Mr. President. As long as their cipher machines' workings were unknown to us, the Axis' codes were unbreakable. As soon as they were known, it was inevitable they would be broken."

"Keep talking."

"In today's world, any decent system must be resistant to machine cryptanalysis. In addition to getting it to work, we have to do our best to break the system. If expert hackers with inside knowledge can't break it, we're pretty safe."

The President was staring at her. "Unlike most NSA briefings, I can actually understand most of what you've said. In a nutshell, you contend malicious code breaking has to be included in this project?"

"Exactly right, Sir. With modern computers, those old systems are no better than a child's decoder ring. Today any serious security system has to be published. You tell your adversaries how the system works and challenge them to break it. That has to be part of our beta test."

"Like one of those hacker contests."

"Exactly," Gerry said. "No secure system can be trusted until it has been published and experts have a go at breaking it."

"How long will it take?" the President asked.

"We don't know, Sir," Mike interjected. "That's one of the main reasons why Gerry and Cybertech can't set a schedule for completion of the beta test right now. It involves more than technology and engineering implementation."

The President looked at him, then back at Gerry. "If not technology, then what's the problem?"

"Oh, it's about technology and engineering," she said. "It's also about hacking and reverse engineering. But the most crucial questions are about policy."

"I was assuming that NSA would just deliver a working system with a seal of approval."

"I'm not sure that's possible, Sir," Mike said.

The President looked at Gerry.

"Assuming our system worked perfectly and was easy to use, what would it take to convince Congress that virtual, electronic meetings could be held in a secure manner?"

The President looked surprised. "I'm not sure I can answer that."

Mike said, "I suspect there are multiple answers, depending on the topics being discussed in the meetings. A committee tasked with naming bridges shouldn't take much security, but the Senate Intelligence Committee might take more than we could provide for years, or perhaps ever. Sometimes people will still need to go into a bubble."

"There can be multiple levels of attempts to break the system too," Gerry said. "We can start with the universities and the hackers' conferences. They're good. They typically break the best commercial codes and encryption schemes in days, maybe weeks. We'd hold contests and offer prizes to anyone who breaks the security."

The President was scowling. "The ability to disperse our government depends on hackers, thieves, and outlaws. Why don't I feel good about this?"

Mike said, "Think about Sun Tzu, Sir. The chaos of freedom is our friend, and so can be our culture of clever hackers. If you know your enemy and yourself, you can win every time."

"That's how it works, Sir," Gerry said. "It's reality."

"How long does this go on?"

"There's no end. It's a journey, not a destination. How good is 'good enough'? Different users or experts would have different answers. When to deploy is a judgment call."

"We should have our own intelligence services try to break the system," the President said. "Congress won't trust it until they are convinced it had survived serious penetration attempts. Nor should they."

"I agree," Gerry said. "There are multiple levels of testing needed. Friendly intelligence services can help."

"Hostile ones too," Mike said. "They'll work to break it for sure. We can set traps, and task our own spies and moles to report back. I think we are moving to a new level of cyber war."

Gerry felt discouraged. She looked at Mike. "This is going to take a long time...."

"It's the nature of the beast," Mike said. "We've had secure phones and scramblers in the military for over half a century. They get better every year, but we still don't trust them fully There have been a few suspect cases, but we've never had a verified breach."

"We've had leaks," the President said.

"Far too many, Sir. But our military COMSEC has been good. Most known breaches have been attributed to human error and treachery. The weak link is always people."

"Both NASA and CIA have had their computers hacked."

"Bad architectures." Gerry said drily, "I sometimes wish Al Gore hadn't invented the Internet."

The President said, "Or invented Global Warming. No one is ever going to believe we can make the Internet secure. Do we have a problem?"

"No Sir. What she's working on is a different breed of cat. What we are deploying will never touch the Internet. Restricted access, non-public systems can be made very secure," Mike said. "Right?"

Gerry nodded.

"How?"

"With a lot of work," Gerry said. "Developing and testing a limited-access, highly-secure, trusted, managed system is tedious, but that doesn't prevent us from getting started and making progress. We can start educating and concept testing in a month.

"Cyber security is an ongoing process. The big question is how soon we could have a system sufficiently robust that Congress would trust it. It also has to be easy enough to use that they would be willing to make the effort."

"Years, not months," the President said glumly. "They'd want to hold hearings, hear expert testimony, that sort of thing."

Mike said, "Congress will have to be actively involved in setting the acceptance standards. I don't see a way around that."

"Shit," the President said. "We have domestic enemies. Some of them will do all they can to sabotage or compromise this."

"I'm sorry, Sir. The technology intersects with politics."

After a pregnant silence, the President looked at Gerry. "Of course it does. Excuse my vulgarity. It's no reflection on your work. You've done a great job."

"Thank you." She still felt depressed. *This is difficult enough without getting tangled up in politics and turf issues between the branches of government.*

The President frowned, deep in concentration. He thought for a long time, several minutes. Gerry started to say something, but stopped and pressed her lips firmly together when Mike shook his head.

"We'll need to develop a network of advocates in Congress," the President finally said. "When we announce the system, the media will pick it up, and discussions will quickly become political and public. What we are doing changes our current form of representative government. It keeps power in Congress, but shifts it away from the beltway and the lobbyists."

"Exactly right, Sir." Gerry said. "Congress would have to be more than a participant. It would have to be an actual partner for this to work."

The President looked at Mike, who shrugged. "The public will like it. The Party elites may not, at least not at first."

"Say more. You're the one who just got a Doctorate from Georgetown."

"Mideast studies, Sir. Not political philosophy...."

"I still want your opinion."

"The United States Constitution is silent on the issue of political parties; at the time it was signed in 1787, there were no parties in the nation. Indeed, no nation in the world had voter-based political parties. The need to win popular support in a republic led to the American invention of political parties in the 1790s. Americans have always been especially innovative in devising new campaign techniques that linked public opinion with public policy through the party.

"I think they'll handle this just fine. We'll probably come out the other side better for the experience, but it's going to take some intense public debate."

"I hope you're right." The President nodded, and spoke firmly. "For now, I want you to back off, to slow down."

Gerry looked at him blankly. *We've been working sixteen-hour days, and now he wants us to slow down?*

The President smiled gently. "Hurry up and wait, right?"

"Yes, Sir."

"We'll lose momentum," Mike said. "We could roll VINEYARD out on a small scale…." He stopped. The President was shaking his head.

"No," the President said. "That's an order, Mike. Slow down. Trust me on this one. Congress is not going to be ready for a concept demo next month."

"Yes, Mr. President." Mike had an odd look on his face.

What's going on here? Gerry wondered.

"Can you do the security testing without involving Congress?" the President asked.

Gerry nodded. "We can start it…."

"Good," the President said.

"We'll need to re-plan," Gerry said. "That's a change of scope."

"Whatever," the President said. "I'm going to give you a direct order."

They looked at him, waiting. To Gerry's surprise, he smiled.

"Get out of Washington. Go somewhere remote. Take some vacation. Stay away least a month. I don't want to see you before then."

Gerry shot Mike a perplexed look. *You handle this one. I have no idea what's going on.*

"Thank you, Mr. President," Mike said slowly. "A vacation would be good."

"Use the Gulfstream and take some security with you," the President said. "Can you be gone by tonight?"

Mike looked at Gerry. She nodded.

"Yes, Mr. President," Mike said. "Thank you, Sir."

"You've done well," the President said.

Gerry was baffled. *Something else is going on. Something the President won't discuss.*

She realized she didn't care. *Washington's strange, but this is the best vacation offer I've ever had. I'd be crazy to pass it up. If I work this right, I'll get some time alone with Mike. We can be like real people.*

They excused themselves and took their leave. Gerry smiled all the way to the car. So did Mike.

Georgetown, Maryland

Senator Stiles was shivering, but felt burning hot. Her back and muscles ached and she felt dizzy. She was reaching for the phone when the first vomiting hit her. Violent retching was followed by wave after wave of convulsions.

Some time later, the Senator raised her head from the befouled bed. Her eyes wouldn't focus. She squinted, trying to see the clock on her end table. It was late afternoon. The dizziness had passed, but she was very weak.

She reached out for the phone again, it took enormous effort, and then she stopped, looking at her hands. Her palms were red and inflamed.

I've got to get help. She punched the emergency button by her bed. It would dial 911. Then she passed out again.

When Stiles woke up, she was in a hospital room. Everything was white and there was daylight spilling in though the window. A figure was standing over her in a moon suit.

It's a woman, the Senator realized. *A short woman. A short ugly woman.*

She could see the woman's round face. She had owlish brown eyes and small rimless glasses.

"How do you feel?" the moon suit asked.

"Terrible," the Senator said. "I'm not shivering anymore. I was weak and dizzy, but it seems to have passed."

The moon suit said. "That's actually quite interesting. You had a raging fever when we checked you in, 104.2, but your temperature is almost back to normal. The fever stage has passed temporarily."

"What's wrong with my face? It feels hot."

The moon suit held up a mirror. The Senator saw her face had the same rash she'd seen on her hands. It was scarlet. She looked down. Her palms were still red, though not as vivid. They seemed blotchy somehow.

"Why is my face red?" the Senator asked. "Will it go away?"

"I think so. The rash on your face should fade in a day or two."

Senator Stiles felt a wave of relief sweep over her. "I was worried..." She stopped and let her words trail off. The moon-suited woman was shaking her head slowly.

"I believe the next stage is the rash develops into pustular pimples. That's the reported pathology." Moon suit shrugged, her motion obvious even in the clumsy protective garment.

"I've only observed the symptomatic progression once personally, but it is what seems to be happening on your hands." Moon suit's tone was interested but aloof.

"Pustular?" the Senator asked. She looked closer and noticed her hands were covered with small red bumps. They were starting to itch, she realized, resisting the urge to scratch them.

"The word means 'pus filled.' In the next stage, the pimples will either fade, leaving scars, or progress and grow together. Most likely the latter, although one reported case exhibited an atypical pathology."

"The rash should appear on other parts of your body within one to two days," she added helpfully. "The pustular pimples, as I said, follow the rash by a day or two, but you don't need to worry about the fever. It doesn't come back until the final stages."

The Senator said, "You said you've observed this once. Was it recent?"

"Very." Moon suit nodded. "The subject was a lobbyist named Burton Cassidy. Perhaps you knew him?"

"*What's happening to me?*"

"You're in a hospital. You may have been exposed to some type of bioweapon. I need for you to describe how that might have happened and the symptoms you've been experiencing in your own words. May I have permission to record your responses, please?"

Senator Stiles started screaming.

EPILOG

Green Turtle Cay, Bahamas

"How did you pick this place?" Gerry rolled over on the white sand and looked up at Mike. They'd been there for three days. Except while watching the news last night, she was becoming relaxed. Colors seemed brighter, sounds clearer.

The sun was a buttery ball in an electric blue sky. The day was pleasantly warm, not searing, with a steady breeze. She could taste salt spray on her lips. In the background there was the ripple of waves and occasional cries of seabirds.

Mike grinned. "We needed the basics. Cold beer, good weather, privacy, and to be able to understand the language."

"You speak several languages and brought your own beer, plus a good wine selection, which I appreciate."

"True. Unfortunately, my working languages are indigenous to places where significant numbers of people tend to shoot at you. I thought that might prove distracting and thus impede our getting to know each other more intimately on a non-professional level."

Gerry smiled. Getting to know each other would be good. "I like it when you're off duty and relaxed, even with the erudite bullshit. Seriously, how did you find this place?"

"Simple deductive logic, my dear, plus superior male intellect."

"*Au contraire*," Gerry murmured. "I rather suspect monkey hormones played a large part."

"There you go again. Leave my body parts out of it...."

She stuck out her tongue.

He ignored her. "We needed to be able to land the Gulfstream. The Treasure Cay airport was adequate. Also, the locals didn't mind an invasion by heavily armed SEALs. Some places are picky about such things."

"I can imagine."

His grin broadened. "We have a plethora of amenities and few people to bother us."

"And a separate island for Clover and his men to drink beer, clean their weapons, fish, and do whatever it is SEALs do in their time off." Gerry pursed her lips and nodded thoughtfully. "What exactly do they do?"

"Unspeakable things. That's why we're here, and they're there. It's easier for women who skinny-dip. You have nice tits, by the way…."

Gerry felt herself blushing. She averted her eyes.

"I love our little cabin," she said, after a minute or two. "I appreciate having electricity, but didn't you think the news last night was a bit disturbing?"

"Um," he said. "Must we go there now?"

She nodded. "I think so."

"I think maybe I'd rather be shot at…."

"Please," she said. "I need to think it through."

"We shouldn't have turned the damned thing on. News is *supposed* to be disturbing. If nothing happens, they invent something. They exaggerate events to boost ratings."

Just like you minimize them so I won't worry. She was coming to know him well. He was kind. "Senator Stiles is dead, Mike."

"So they said."

"Half of Congress was injected with a lethal virus."

"Not half, I think, but many. Thirty-nine reported dead so far."

"So far…."

"Yes."

"The commentator said there might have been a suicide pact or something."

"Like drinking the Jonestown Kool-Aid." Mike wouldn't meet her eyes.

"They're saying Senator Stiles was behind it. The same Senator who was after you. The one whose office checked my dad's flight schedule on the day he disappeared."

Mike didn't respond. He was watching the waves rolling in on the white beach.

"Hello!" Gerry raised her voice to get his attention. *"Talk to me, Goose."*

Mike smiled in spite of himself, recalling the famous words from *Top Gun,* the movie. Tom Cruise's character Maverick calling for his copilot to tell him where the threats were.

Gerry said, "A large number of members of Congress willingly received potentially lethal injections."

She was watching him closely, waiting to see if he was going to lie to her. The explanations being postulated on the news were suicide or gross error. Both were implausible.

Working in intelligence could make you cynical, and counter intelligence was worse. Nothing was ever as it seemed. What was it Churchill had called it? *The bodyguard of lies.*

"Yeah," Mike said. "Seems pretty crazy, doesn't it?"

This wasn't going anywhere. She wanted to ask him directly, but dared not. There were too many coincidences. There had to be a reason Mike was reluctant to discuss what happened.

President Hale told us to take a vacation. He practically ordered us out of Washington. Mike wasn't surprised by the news on the television.

What was it President Hale had said? *"Stay away at least a month."*

Hale knew, she thought. *He must have known.*

The President had obviously chosen to distance them from the events unfolding in Washington. It wouldn't end with Senator Stiles' death. The events now being reported were certain to be the focus of prolonged investigations and intense media attention. There would be years of speculation and conspiracy theories.

She pictured Mike and herself giving testimony under oath, wired to lie detectors. *"We learned about the deaths on the news. We were on vacation. No, we never talked about it, other than to speculate about the reports. I wasn't in Washington at the time and have no direct knowledge of what transpired."*

It would be best if they could each give that answer truthfully. Even so, Gerry needed to know. She had to know what was going on. "I don't know what happened in Bukhari."

"Officially, nothing."

Yeah, right. Which is why the POTUS was unofficially there in the OPS Center, Gerry thought. *CINDERELLA is one scary lady and the presence of her team on your raid at Al-Razi was odd. Why was she there? Obviously her mission was so crucial you considered yourself and your men expendable. Whatever it was, she almost got you all killed.*

Gerry said, "That Doctor woman. I don't know what a civilian was doing over there."

"Technical support," Mike said. "That's as far as I can go."

"I need to ask you something."

"Sure."

"If we speak of evil, do we become tainted? If we touch evil and turn it back on those who inflict it, do we become evil ourselves?"

Gerry could feel her words rippling out across the beautiful beach, disturbing its tranquility, the verbal equivalent of pouring thick black crude oil on the gorgeous white sands. Ugly or not, she needed to ask.

Mike turned his head and looked at her, raising an eyebrow. "People have been asking that question since ancient Greece."

"It affects their lives. If we survive, but our spirit is wounded, how do we heal?"

"I'm not sure we do," he said slowly. "Many veterans were psychologically wounded by Vietnam and the Gulf Wars."

"More than in past wars?"

"As a percentage, yes," Mike said. "We've gotten better at healing bodies. Not so much at healing minds."

"Why?"

"Maybe it's because we've forgotten our history, lost our roots. Our troops endured horrors in Vietnam, but came home to be vilified and spat upon."

"Because of people like Jane Fonda and John Kerry. My dad hated them."

"It's more than that. Society once had Priests and Shamans to hold healing ceremonies. They were respected and honored. Spiritual healing was considered to be extremely important. There are well-reasoned arguments that medicine men were better at psychological wellness than today's shrinks and therapists.

"The Shamans would cleanse and purify the warriors and wizards who protected their tribes, both before and after battles. To heal their souls and wash the blood off their hands." Mike's look was somber.

"But we don't do that anymore."

"No."

"Now we have lawyers instead of spiritual cleansing." Gerry's voice sounded bitter, even to her. "The legalistic, moralistic second-guessing never ends."

"Right. We get flensing instead of cleansing. Having our bones picked clean by legions of lawyers who second-guess combat decisions."

"Flensing for the wizards too," Gerry said. "Einstein, a pacifist, wrote President Roosevelt urging an atomic bomb to safeguard freedom from the Nazis. The bomb worked, and the world survived, but now physics is blamed and powerful science is distrusted."

"We've gotten pretty screwed up, and it's worse for the warriors. Most of the time we fight as a nation bitterly divided, counting bodies and pretending we are at peace. The best military force in the world hasn't won a war for over 60 years."

Gerry nodded, even though she didn't want to admit what he was saying. "The old hands at the agency say they miss the Cold War. Threats changed. The world got more complex. We got more legalistic, more bureaucratic, and more politically correct."

"Fourth Generation warfare," Mike said. "I gave that lecture at West Point."

"We don't value our heroes enough, Mike. Most people don't have a clue. I saw a bumper sticker that said, "War isn't the answer.'"

"Yeah. Except for ending slavery, Nazism, Fascism, the Cold War, and a fair number of genocides, it's never solved anything."

Mike's eyes looked haunted. *The hundred-yard stare.* "Fail to prevent an attack, and you're in deep trouble. But you might be in more trouble if you watch the bad guys too closely or treat them too harshly. We drown in our own political correctness."

"Are you okay?"

"I have ghosts."

"Yemen."

He looked out across the sea and was quiet for a time. "I let Ahmed and his party through our defense perimeter. I knew his history, but I did it anyway."

"He was under a flag of truce."

"Too many of my people died. People I loved. People who trusted me."

"A long time ago. You'll destroy yourself if you can't get past it." She took his hand. "Let me be your Shaman."

Mike sighed.

"You saved your command. And Bukhari was a total success: everyone came back."

He shrugged, still watching the far horizon.

"Talk to me. What brought your ghosts back?"

"I let Ahmed escape, Gerry. The same man who took your father."

"Look at me."

He turned slowly.

"Could you have prevented Dad's abduction?"

"I honestly don't see how."

She could see the pain in his eyes. "It wasn't your fault."

"It was my error. I had Ahmed under my gun in Yemen, and I let him live."

"That's nothing between us. Do you think I'll blame you for what happened to Dad?"

"If not now, someday…."

"No." *That would destroy him.* "I'll never blame you."

He looked at her.

"Not now, not ever." Her voice broke. "You saved my life. I'll thank you to my dying day for helping me, for helping my family."

"I've got my ghosts and demons. Do you want to be around them?"

"I want to be around you," she said, wiping tears away. *For the rest of my life, I think.*

"I've touched evil. I might be infected."

"You're not evil."

"Are you sure?"

"Positive. You resist evil."

"Be careful," Mike said softly. "Hatred is infectious too."

"You're not evil; you're wounded. You're not poisoned with hatred either."

"It's what-ifs that tear you apart. If I'd shot Ahmed out of hand in Yemen, I'd have broken the rules and been tried by a court-martial. But I might have saved some lives."

"Why do you still torment yourself over Yemen?"

"It's a part of me. The Israelis brought it up to test my resolve."

"Inevitably," she said dryly. "Their tactics make them widely hated."

"Not just them. Even the Saudis made sure I wouldn't hesitate over legalistic niceties. We were under their rules of engagement."

Gerry said, "Do you hate Ahmed?"

"The main thing is I'll kill him if I get the chance. Sometimes all the choices are bad. I'm afraid it's the way of the world."

"Fuck the world," Gerry said. "We need more heroes and less ambiguity."

Mike blinked. He looked at her. "Are you all right?"

"Working with intelligence people makes me paranoid, but am I paranoid enough? Sometimes I ask myself, 'Where does insanity start?' What scares me is I don't know."

"You're one of the sanest people I know."

"I wonder," she said. "Why *did* Senator Stiles and her colleagues kill themselves?"

"I can't say, Gerry."

"Speculate."

"What if the Senator and her allies staged a coup?"

"Americans wouldn't tolerate that."

"What if we were assured of cheap oil? Maybe at half OPEC's prices?"

"Why would Bukhari give us oil?"

"In exchange for armaments and abandoning Israel and Bukhari's Arab enemies."

"What kind of armaments? Nukes?"

"Sure, why not? Along with delivery systems and missile defenses."

"We'd never abandon Israel," Gerry said.

"Abandonment need not be an explicit policy."

True, Gerry thought. "So how would we pull it off subtly while appearing supportive?"

"Along with the occasional accident, simply becoming inept in our support would be sufficient. Israel's Six-Day War reshaped the Mideast. We helped by making sure the world debated and argued until after its objectives were accomplished. The same could happen in reverse."

"In the process we put politics over the lives of Americans," Gerry said. "NSA won't ever forget that war. The USS Liberty's flag is displayed in our National Cryptologic Museum. Thirty-four Americans died and 172 were wounded. They called it an accident."

"Liberty took two hundred and six casualties out of a complement of 280," Mike said grimly. "Her Captain got a Congressional Medal. They don't usually give medals for accidents, do they?"

Gerry said, "And to avoid embarrassing the Israelis, Captain McGonagle's Medal of Honor was presented in a quiet ceremony in the Washington Navy Yard."

"Yeah. Instead of in the White House by the President as is customary. I wrote a paper on the incident back when I was getting my doctorate."

"Yemen is termed an accident. They gave you a medal too."

"It's nuts, isn't it?"

"Is this the same kind of accident?"

"Perhaps."

"Senator Stiles couldn't get away with a coup. The American public wouldn't allow it."

"Some might if they saw enough benefit."

"What kind of benefit?"

"Peace in the Mideast, major cuts in defense spending, and expanded social programs."

She looked at him, unwilling to accept what he was saying.

"Wouldn't you like peace? Better schools? Maybe free health care?"

"The notion is absurd. No one can guarantee peace in the Mideast."

"We could withdraw from the region," he said. "We'd be at peace. If we had assured access to oil, and American lives and interests weren't at risk, would voters care if Muslims killed each other?"

"Some would. And few would tolerate another holocaust. What about Israel?"

"Israel would probably strike first and go down fighting. Then the factions and nations of Islam would go to war against each other as the various states and sects were assimilated. But we'd not be involved, it wouldn't be on television, and the carnage would end eventually. Then there could be peace in our time."

"Millions dead and a Bukhari empire? That's awful."

"But not unthinkable. The dream of an Islamic Caliphate has been around for centuries. The Arab Spring revived it."

"Israel might win."

Mike shrugged. "It's possible."

"It's still awful, and in any case we couldn't trust Bukhari to keep its commitments."

"I agree with you. Can I stop *speculating* now? Please."

She nodded.

"Whatever happened, Stiles' group made a huge mistake. People make mistakes. Accidents happen, and people die. Just like the Liberty incident."

"Yes," she said slowly. "Accidents happen...."

You can't talk about it, but you manage to speak truth anyway. You're a good man.

"President Hale promised an inquiry," Mike said. "It might all come out eventually."

"Perhaps." *In a hundred years maybe, when we're all dead and the records are unsealed. The main thing is Mike didn't lie to me. He's never lied to me.*

There wasn't any accident. It was murder. CINDERELLA switched the vaccine for toxin.

Mike knows. I know he knows, and he knows I know that he knows. And we both know we must never speak of it.

"How do you think the history will be written?" Gerry asked.

"After the Senator's tragic death, they'll probably name the Health and Welfare building after her."

"It ends as a mystery? Our nation bumbles through yet another crisis because of its good luck and fortune?"

"Why not?" Mike took his gaze from the far horizon and looked at her. "That's how history is usually written. Partly truth and partly fiction...."

"Like the old song? 'A walking contradiction, taking every wrong direction on the lonely road back home....'"

"Pretty much. In the end, it doesn't matter. What matters is we survive as a free people."

"I suppose." Gerry felt a little better. Not much, but a little.

They sat quietly for several minutes, watching the sea, listening to the wind in the palms and the gentle lap of the surf. There were gulls running along the beach, scavenging and occasionally squabbling with each other. Offshore a pair of brown pelicans dove for fish.

The sun was lower with a more reddish tinge, and the sky had lost its disturbing electric intensity, shifting to a beautiful azure. Large flocks of red flamingos, a type she'd not seen before, were working the tidal pools, straining the water with their bills, feeding on the algae.

The flamingos dipped their heads under the water almost in unison, tucked their bills in, and scooped backward with their heads upside down. It was fascinating to watch.

I need to tell him, she decided. *He needs to know.*

She nudged Mike's arm. "There's one more thing...."

"I hope you're not still thinking about the news."

She blurted it out. "Ahmed was at Al-Razi. You almost got him."

Mike's jaw dropped, and his eyes flashed disbelief. "How do you know?"

"I've seen the intercepts. He's in a Nassid City hospital with a fractured skull. You blew him halfway across the courtyard and into a tank."

Mike was shaking his head.

"Langley's on it. So are the Israelis. Do you know a man named Pearl?"

"Benjamin Pearl. Yes, I met him. Nice guy. He was very helpful."

Gerry raised an eyebrow. "You have some interesting friends. Pearl is a senior Israeli counter terrorism operative in the Shin Bet Arab Affairs Department. He's been given the lead on Ahmed. Pearl is not a nice guy. He's an assassin, a hunter of men."

Mike shrugged.

"If Pearl gets to Ahmed, he'll kill him."

"So?"

"We'll never know what happened to Dad. I'll never have closure."

Mike was shaking his head. "I think you should be more hopeful."

"Tell me why."

"The Israelis don't suffer from our legalistic constraints and political correctness. Pearl isn't about to kill Ahmed until he wrings him dry. If

Pearl can get his hands on him, maybe we can find out what happened to your father. He's our best chance."

"Maybe...."

"I think there's a good chance your father is still alive."

Gerry blinked. "Why?"

"Call it an act of faith. I just do. It your father is alive, we'll find him. This isn't over for me either, not until we get closure."

She was quiet for a time, then said, "Thank you."

"The main thing for now is we're alive and well. We defeated evil, saved lives, and found each other. We're fortunate."

She raised an eyebrow questioningly. "At a cost...."

"Yes. There is that." Mike looked away again, reflecting on his own ghosts.

Gerry watched him and thought about what he said. *He's right. We survived, and we're together. Amongst the bloodshed and hatred, there is still beauty. We're here, alive in the middle of all this beauty. We have each other, and we have the moment. Thank you for reminding me. The world may be crazy, but a few good things remain....*

They sat in silence watching the ocean together. The warm breeze felt good, and it was comfortable sitting there next to Mike. She moved over to lean against him. That felt good too.

"I'm glad to be here with you," Gerry finally said, shaking off the horrific events back in Washington. *It's someone else's problem, at least for now.*

"It's good," he said. "I'm glad too. Now may I ask you a question?"

She nodded.

"Can we get past that damned newscast?"

And the rest of it, she thought. *Good question.*

Mike was frowning. "Are you okay?"

She sighed and made a vaguely dismissive gesture.

"I need you to be okay," he said. "It matters to me."

"I'm working on it." She took a deep breath and let it out slowly, choosing her words. "I don't care about Senator Stiles and her cronies. The bitch is dead."

"It doesn't need to screw up our lives, Gerry."

John D. Trudel

"I just needed to talk it out with you. It's a part of healing for me."

"We do that in the military too. After an action we talk to our buddies. It helps, but sometimes it takes time, maybe a long time. Veterans have reunions years later to share memories, remember friends, honor the fallen, and get closure."

"Does it work with lovers too?"

"I think we're going to find out," he said softly.

"Good," she said, relaxing a little. "Oh, yes. I think that would be very good."

Gerry turned her head up, inviting his kiss. It lasted a long time, and her thoughts of Washington faded.

Maybe we have a chance, she thought. *Maybe together we can make it.* She kept thinking of the old Eagles song, *Desperado*, where the lead vocalist, Don Henley, begs the subject of the song, a "hard one" who'd spent his life "riding fences," to return home, and tells him that the things he enjoys doing will hurt him eventually.

Maybe my desperado can come down from his fences before it's too late. Maybe we can lead normal lives. Maybe he will let me love him.

She wanted to believe that. With all her heart and soul, she wanted to.

The End

FACTOIDS OR FANTASIES?

I hope you enjoyed my novel and thank you for sharing the journey with me. My non-fiction book *Engines of Prosperity* included a quote from Dr. Alvin Toffler, the futurist. He said, "The sophistication for deception is increasing at a greater rate than the technology for verification. This means the end of truth."

My novels are fiction, but in today's world there can be a lot of truth in fiction, and a lot of fiction in publicly perceived truth.

Special OPs: This community of heroes has been at the point of the spear defending America for a long time, but now they suffer intense political attention. This is a time where successful operations (e.g. killing Osama) are exploited for partisan advantage, and, conversely, debacles (e.g. Benghazi, 9-11-2012) are the subject of cover-ups and stonewall at the highest levels.

Benghazi is still sorting out, as is the little-known tale of Extortion 17, an aging, unescorted, cargo helicopter shot down on Aug. 6, 2011, causing the **greatest single loss in SEAL history**, and the worst losses (31 KIA) of the Afghanistan War in a single event.

Extortion 17 is spine-chilling. On August 6, 2013 (the 2nd anniversary of the event) a book titled ***Betrayed: Exposing the High Cost of the War on Terror*** is scheduled for release. It is authored by Billy Vaughn (father of fallen Navy SEAL Aaron Vaughn) and Major General Paul Vallely.

These are unhappy topics best left to non-fiction writers and investigative reporters. I'll pass along quickly, just noting that we are at an odd time where favored Hollywood producers get un-vetted access to classified information, whistleblowers are threatened with 20-year jail terms if they dare testify to Congress, and high-level officers are removed for attempting to send help.

I've done my best to craft my fiction to entertain, but hopefully also be realistic and honor the warriors who wreak violence on our enemies that we may sleep safely in our beds. I will let them and my other readers be the judges of how well I've succeeded.

Captain Larry Bailey, USN, retired, commanded the SEALs and was kind enough to endorse my book. He co-founded a PAC called "Special Operations Speaks" to learn truth about Benghazi. This is the first time in history where the entire SPEC OPs community (a nonpartisan, non-political group by nature, and one that never says much, if anything, publicly) has come together to demand truth and accountability from our elected officials.

You can reach them at www.specialoperationsspeaks.com, read their messages, and donate if you choose. I have. It is a worthy cause.

Historical Events

The background events in my novel are documented, not that people have ever agreed about history, and perhaps less now than ever. So much past history is being erased or twisted so as to be "politically correct" in current settings, suit biases, or fit ideological agendas.

Islamic Genocides and the Black Plague

The horrors and devastation wreaked upon the Muslims by the Mongols is historically accurate, as is the irony that eventually the Mongol leaders became themselves Muslim. The legendary Islamic warrior Timur iLeng, Timur the Lame, laid waste from Asia almost to Egypt.

Known to the West as Tamerlan (or Tamerlane), the "Sword of Islam" was a descendant of Genghis Khan who killed over 17 million people. This was quite an accomplishment with the weapons and infrastructure of the day, a tally beyond comprehension until Hitler or Stalin.

As a percentage of the world's population, Tamerlan's record may be unsurpassed, but mass death was so common in the 14th century that knowing who or what to blame is cloudy. As the liberal philosopher Thomas Hobbes famously said in 1651, "Life was solitary, poor, nasty, brutish, and short...." Hobbes described the natural state of mankind as a "war of every man against every man." His view was that only rule by a strong central government could change that, and that totalitarian autocrats were better than freedom.

There was a time when people understood such ruthlessness. In 1587, Elizabethan era playwright Christopher Marlowe presented *Tamburlaine the Great* to London audiences. It was the hit of the century. It even inspired Edgar Allan Poe to write softer interpretations in the 1800s. Poe's poem contrasts Tamerlan's ruthless bids for power with his inability to find true love. *He was just lonely and misunderstood....*

Good grief. Some things don't change.

The "American experiment" has been an historical anomaly. Freedom and responsibility is a wondrous thing, but it is something that those on the left distrust. The various socialist tyrants of the 1930s were once well-loved by the masses, the media, and academic elites.

Were bioweapons wittingly used in ancient times, or was the plague just exploited? The Black Plague was raging at the same time conquering Muslims were at their peak of slaughter and pillaging. It is likely impossible to discern if this war and pestilence was strategically connected. My characters discuss that. One speculates they were, but she doesn't know for sure.

What about Tamerlan Tsarnaev, the 2013 Boston Marathon bomber? Was his Muslim name an obvious threat, a symbol, or merely a coincidence?

Obviously, the FBI didn't deem the name Tamerlan (or the *jihadist* himself, for that matter) as threatening. Still, a Catholic sociology professor who was intimidated by an intense 2010 IRS audit into **not** publishing a book critical of Islam, Anne Hendershott, might disagree.

http://www.catholicworldreport.com/Blog/2207/the_sword_of_islam.
aspx#.UbuhX_vn_IU

Bioweapons

These are real, and incredibly scary. The background in the book is accurate. My personal view is that of all the glimpses that science has given us into the hell of WMDs, possibly the notion of bioweapons is the most frightening.

Why? As one of my characters says, *"They have a life of their own."*

A Virtual Congress

> *"I date the end of the old republic and the birth of the empire to the invention, in the late thirties, of air conditioning. Before air conditioning, Washington was deserted from mid-June to September.... But after air conditioning and the Second World War arrived, more or less at the same time, Congress sits and sits while the presidents--or at least their staffs-- never stop making mischief."*
>
> Gore Videl

This old quote got me to speculating. What if advanced technology – biometric IDs, geo-referencing, trusted managed networks, and all that – could allow America to return to our roots and to the Founders' model for our Constitutional Republic?

Consider. In early America, elected officials spent most of their lives at home with those who'd elected them, those whom they served. Occasionally they would go to a central location, meet, vote, but soon return to real life in actual America. That was the time of "by and for the People." Today, our officials are distant from their constituents. They live in **the echo chamber,** out of touch, inside the Beltway, in the land of lobbyists, foreign influence, propaganda and spin.

Which construct worked best? Are there better Constitutional options than what we are doing?

Power corrupts. Checks and balances erode or are worn down. It's not been working out well of late and the trends are not encouraging. So I thought, *What if* ....

The concept behind my story is of patriots and a President with the science and technology to build a distributed government with a Virtual Congress. Unfortunately for my characters, their heroic attempt at the near-impossible coincides with a bioweapons-based attempt at a coup.

ABOUT THE AUTHOR

John Trudel has authored two nonfiction books and three Thriller novels, *God's House, Privacy Wars, and Soft Target*. His next, *Raven's Run*, will be out in 2014. He graduated from Georgia Tech and Kansas State, had a long career in high-technology, wrote columns for several national magazines, and lives in Oregon and Arizona.

Thank you

Thank you for choosing my book and investing your time in reading my novel. I hope you found it enjoyable and thought provoking. I welcome comments and questions. There is a contact form on my website and I answer all email. Visit http://www.johntrudel.com/.

The best way to thank an author is to write a review.

I am an "Indy Author" with essentially zero marketing clout. While my books are technically available everywhere, the unfortunate truth is that most bookstores will not stock or promote Indy published books. If you like my novels, posting a reader review on the online retailer sites is especially helpful. Please consider returning to the site where you bought this book and leaving a review.

A short email via my website will ensure you are notified when my next book is available, and if I am in your area doing signings. Thank you again.

Made in the USA
San Bernardino, CA
17 December 2013